the broken line

Books by Linda Hartley

Fiction
the broken line
angel wing

Non-fiction

Wisdom of the Body Moving
Servants of the Sacred Dream
Somatic Psychology: Body, Mind and Meaning
Embodied Spirit, Conscious Earth

Edited collections

Contemporary Body Psychotherapy: The Chiron Approach
The Fluid Nature of Being: Embodied practices for healing and wholeness

the broken line

Linda Hartley

ELMDON
BOOKS

For Jill Gerrish –

friend, inspiration and courageous spirit

November 3rd 1947

The heart gathers burdens as it journeys through a life,
some from deep in the past, secrets of the ancestors,
their untended wounds.
A lineage of grief rolls on into the future,
pulling lives apart and scattering dreams.
We are helpless in the grip of our wounding past.

Eliza O'Neal

Part I

The Art of Survival

The iron gate closed behind her with a hollow thud. She held her breath and listened — for a door opening, a shout, an alarm being raised. There was no sound but the wind whipping through the tall spruce trees that lined the wall. For now, at least, she was safe.

Outside the gate she paused, breathing in the crisp, clear air. A full moon cast its silvery light over the field that stretched down to the bank of the stream. So many times she had looked out on this field, through the misted windows, between the iron bars, longing to run across it. Right down to the stream, and up over the wide hills beyond, lying in silent folds all along the ancient skyline. But tonight it would not be safe to run in the moonlight. She would be easily seen.

Turning to her right, she headed down towards the edge of the wood. The shadow of the trees would hide her well enough. She clutched her small bundle of possessions — tied up in a thin grey blanket — to her chest as she ran. The thick woollen coat she had picked up by the back door was much too big, and flapped about her ankles.

Along the path that ran along the edge of the wood, across the stream, down a farm-track, then — finally sure that she was out of view of the house — she struck out over the open moor — running, running, clutching her bundle of possessions. The moon shone, the clean wind blew, her red hair streamed out behind her like a flame. She ran and ran until at last the clouds covered the moon, and the faintest hint of dawn began to show.

By the time the morning bell rang and they realised she had gone, she would be far away.

One

The north-east – 1969

I grew up knowing it in my bones, in my blood. Sometimes it came with the scent of jasmine and warm milk, drifting like a spirit through the night air. Or in the fleeting image of a girl with red hair, just like mine, running, fast, like a gazelle through woods and over moon lit fields. Another time, a place unknown. Not a memory or a dream, just a shadow passing by. A spirit piercing through the veil.

But after Richard came into my life, I knew it in my heart. Love is grief, and grief is love. They are the same. Like water turning into ice, ice melting back to water.

It all began one afternoon in June – I had just turned sixteen. The sky was deep blue and the air hot for this time of year on the wind-swept Northumbrian coast. The beach was not yet crowded. Before the storm of holidaymakers arrived, there was calm and just a gentle breeze blowing in off the sea.

I was sitting on the seawall dangling my bare legs against the rough stone. Warmth against my skin. Cupped in my hands lay a small bird, not long hatched – an ordinary little fellow, a sparrow, with greyish brown feathers still damp with saliva from the mouth I had just rescued him from. I called my baby chick Tom. The cat that had almost finished him off was a sleek grey tabby. His amber eyes had narrowed to thin slits and his whole body was poised, still and alert, low to the ground with tail flicking side to side. I knew the cat was about to pounce.

Tom was still breathing. His heart beat quickly, just a flutter of life in there, his round little chest pumping in and out. A naked soft heart throbbing through thin skin. Specks of white and cream threaded through the grey-brown of his mangled feathery breast. His eyes were closed. He was still recovering from the shock of being very nearly swallowed alive.

I cradled him in my hands to warm him back to life. If he couldn't fly, I would take him back to my aviary – no more than a small chicken coop really, but it had served its purpose for many years.

The midday sun was burning into my bare shoulders. I wore my green halter-neck top, ever hopeful of a sun-bronzed back but knowing that my white skin would only turn pink then red and very sore. I should find some shade but the long stretch of beach and promenade offered none.

Looking up from marvelling at Tom's tiny throbbing chest, my gaze wandered down to the water's edge. And it was then that I saw him. His skin as brown as a chestnut, wet hair black and slicked back. I noticed the way he walked, his stride bold and confident as he pulled his canoe up out of the water. Broad shoulders, slim hips, taut muscular body. He was perfect.

I know he noticed me too. He kept looking my way. I could see myself as if through his eyes – my red hair, ironed out to a sheen, lifted gently by the sea breeze in fluttering waves – my white jeans rolled up to the knees – the skimpy green sun-top and my bare feet bouncing against the wall. I felt shy, but curious too. I wanted to see everything about him. I would paint him later that day, walking up the beach with his blue canoe, denim shorts clinging to his thighs.

By the time he reached the steps up to the promenade, I was sure I had fallen in love.

I climbed off the wall and walked back along the prom and up through Briar Dene. When I reached the bush where I had rescued Tom earlier, I crouched down and opened my hands to see if he was ready to fly away. He wasn't. So I took him home and settled him into the aviary. I had nursed many wounded birds and small animals back to life in this sanctuary, and when they wouldn't return to life, I buried them beneath the beech tree at the bottom of the garden. Many spirits lived there now.

Three days later he came to our house, an album he wanted to lend Martin tucked under his arm. Later he told me that was just a pretence, a way to meet me. I sat on the cream-tiled hearth in the sunlight and listened as they talked music. He asked Martin to play with his band while he was home from university and Martin agreed. So I could be sure of seeing Richard often over the summer holidays.

As he talked, he spread his arms wide, as if opening to embrace, then rested them casually along the back of the sofa. I wanted to melt into them, to be held in those strong arms, sun-browned and taut as springs. I felt my heart reaching towards the invitation of his opening body, longing to be taken in.

He stretched out his legs in a relaxed and confident way, but there was less certainty in the way he tossed his head back to flick an errant curl of dark hair out of his eyes, darting a sly glance towards me. As if by accident. Hidden behind the bold appearance was the hint of a being that felt small and insecure. I loved this part too. I wanted to see it, touch it, help it to feel strong. His eyes were almost black and they pierced right into me.

Martin was oblivious to what was going on, to this little dance of glances, and kept talking music. But Richard turned the conversation and soon Martin was inviting him out to the back garden. I followed them. I showed Richard my bird sanctuary.

'Nice. Who built it?' He tapped a knuckle against the quaint wooden structure and peered in to study its gnarled platforms and doors, nooks and hiding places.

'My dad helped me build it.'

'You mean Dad built it and you just got in the way, dancing about, tripping over tools and planks and wire mesh,' said Martin laughing.

'No, I didn't. We built it together.' I was cross at Martin for embarrassing me in front of Richard. He didn't realise how serious this was.

'Where d'you find the injured birds?' Richard was studying me now.

'I watch. I can see where a fox has been, or when a cat's on the hunt. Or when a storm might have washed up a young seabird, or an old or sick one. I look for the signs …' I gestured with my hands as if to show exactly where the fallen creatures could be found, trying to cover the shyness that was washing over me as I revealed my strange talent.

'How d'you learn to see like that?' I believe Richard was genuinely interested.

'She's always been like that,' replied Martin. 'Always looking into things – small things, growing things, dead things.' Martin, being more practical than me, had always thought this was a bit weird, and he enjoyed teasing me about my animal hospital. That's what big brothers do. But I knew he loved me so I didn't usually mind. 'She'll study a blade of grass for ages, as if it were the most interesting thing in the world, won't you, Nita.'

'No,' I replied in a tone that suggested Martin had just said something really stupid. I didn't want Richard to think I was weird.

'I think it's great you're so observant,' said Richard, coming to my rescue. 'I never notice things like that, but I listen. Any old noise can be music if you listen right. Like that lawn mower – hear how it harmonises with the traffic on the seafront – and the gulls.'

'Oh, that's lovely. I never thought of it that way.' I wanted him to know I was impressed.

I returned to the cat and mouse theme. 'You know when a cat's trailing a mouse or a bird because its tail curls to the side – like a tongue, licking its lips – and it crouches down, like this, watching.' I demonstrated. They laughed. I pounced and Martin fell back, landing on the grass, pretending to be dead. We had always played games like this but suddenly I felt embarrassed that I had let Richard see our childhood game. I wanted him to think I was quite grown up.

The next time he came to our house he brought a small woodcarving of Tom with his wings spreading, as if ready to fly. They reminded me of Richard's arms gesturing as he talked. Maybe it was not an embrace but a flight they were about to make. He gave me the little carving of Tom, which was just as well, as Tom died the very next day. I was glad to have him immortalised in wood and placed the carving underneath the beech tree, over the buried corpse.

The first time he held my hand we were on St Mary's Island looking for crabs. We wouldn't catch them. I just wanted to show Richard how many different kinds you could find amongst the rocks. Our faces were reflected, side-by-side, in the clear water of a pool, against a background of pale brown and barnacled rock and a sky littered with frothy white clouds. My long red hair and translucent skin floated there, next to his dark waves and sun-browned face. He took hold of my hand and pulled me to my feet. We stood looking into each other's eyes for a long while. I thought he might kiss me, but that came later.

'Come on, race you.' Laughing, he pulled me after him as we leapt from rock to rock, over the pools of captured sea water. My feet were light and skimmed over the rocky surface. With the force of his movement carrying me along, I was flying through the air.

'I'm flying, I'm flying,' I called to the back of his tousled dark head. Then of course I tripped and came crashing down on my elbow and knees, right in the middle of a pool. It hurt. I laughed and I cried, but I cried mostly out of joy. I felt happy – happier than I remembered ever feeling.

He took me to see *Love Story*. It was so sad but so utterly romantic – the girl dies and leaves the boy broken-hearted but you can see he's made a better person by it. He's left solitary, serious, and very mysterious in his grieving. I didn't question the romance of the story. I lived in a glow of love that turned everything golden, and even grief was uplifted by it.

This love was different from what I felt with my father and Martin. The love we shared was always merged with grief. We lived in a small triangle of pain. Nobody had been able to pierce this tight knot we three were tied in, not even Nancy. But now Richard had come along and I felt the grip of it loosening each time he looked into my eyes or opened his arms to hold me.

The blue canoe was small, but just big enough for the two of us. I was still quite skinny, though I was filling out into slender curves. I knew Richard liked how I was. I could tell from the way he looked at me – for a long time, taking me in, really seeing me.

He sat behind with his legs wrapped around me. His thighs pressed tightly against my hips in the narrow space. At first I felt nervous of this closeness, but soon began to relax into it. I felt held. A sweet sensation spread out from my squeezed hips. Sea spray and sunlight bathed my face as I tilted my head back. I felt his nose trace down the bones of my spine. His lips touched my shoulder blades.

We glided smoothly through the waves, ribbons of glittering white against the blue. My hands gripped the wooden paddle and his hands were over mine, doing most of the work. A constant dip and rise as the waves rolled gently past us with a continuous swishing sound – I imagined Richard was listening to the music they made. The sky was clear and bright.

Out beyond the breakers there was just a soft swell lifting and lowering the canoe, and the two of us gripped tightly as we leaned together into the tug and release of the paddle. We kept going, further out into the open sea. Further than I had gone before. The sweetness surged through my body each time he came in closer, pressing his chest against my back as we gathered water into the cups of the paddle. Tilting side to side – left to right to left. I dared to lean into him as we churned the water behind us and glided through.

But this heaven was not to last. Without warning the weather changed. A bank of heavy cloud was rolling swiftly down from the north and the wind began to gust and swipe. It happened so abruptly. I began to panic when I saw how far out we had come.

'We've got to get back,' I shouted, but Richard was already turning the canoe around and paddling with all his strength.

The tide was going out so we got no help there, no easy ride back to the shore.

'We won't make it!' I cried, seeing how little progress we were making. The wind was whipping up around us and rocking our tiny boat. Choppy waves splashed over the sides and soaked us. Now it seemed that the dark heaps of cloud surged in from all sides, pummelled by the crushing wind. As the clouds covered the sun, the sea quickly turned from summer blue to steely grey and menacing.

'Course we will. It's okay, Nita. Here, put your hands on top of mine. I can pull better that way.' I could feel the muscles of his body, behind me, all around me, straining against the mass of sea that lay between us and the land.

I was scared. Strength was draining from my arms and legs. But I did as he said and tried to add my drop of strength to his. I tried not to think about how deep the ocean was beneath us.

Just as the rain began to fall in sheets, we reached the beach.

'Are you alright?' he asked as he wrapped his arms around me. I was shaking. He held me so tight I could hardly breathe.

'Yes, I'm okay.' I shivered as I thought about what might have happened. But I felt safe now. I was absorbing his strength, his courage, through my drenched skin. As long as Richard was by my side all would be well.

I didn't tell my father or Nancy. They were not totally accepting of Richard and if they knew what had happened, I was sure they would try to stop me seeing him. My father thought he was a bit rough, not from the right background – not good enough for my daughter – he didn't exactly say this but I knew he was thinking it. But he didn't know how kind and gentle Richard could be. He always asked how I was, what I wanted to do. I felt so cared for. And he told me he loved me. No-one had ever said that to me before, not directly, the way Richard did – I love you, Nita.

It was evening and we were back at my house. I was not allowed to take him into my bedroom – not unless Martin was there too – so we sat on the small landing at the bottom of the stairs, leaning against the wall with our legs entwined. Conversation had slowed down and we were both in a reflective mood.

'Weren't you scared?'

Richard leaned his head on one side and thought for a moment. I wanted him to be honest, not just full of empty bravado like most of the boys I knew.

'Yeah, for a moment. But once I was rowing hard, I guess I didn't think about anything else.'

'You're lucky. I was scared stiff.'

He gripped my hand in that rough and earnest way he had. 'Sorry I got you into that. But I wouldn't have let anything happen to you. We were okay, really.'

'I know.' I believed him. We sat quietly for a while.

'My dad would be mad if he knew. He's so protective of me.'

'Well, I've got some competition then! I guess he won't let you go without a fight.'

'He treats me like a porcelain vase – something fragile that might fall over and break. He tries to hang onto me and stop me doing risky things.' I was holding my breath, remembering the constriction of my father's love. 'But I've never let that stop me, not really,' I added, and my breath flowed out again.

'Why's he so protective, d'you think?'

'My mother, I guess. She died in an accident. I was just two.'

'Oh, I'm sorry Nita. That must've been awful for you.'

'Yes. I can't remember her though. It's hard to miss what you've never known, I suppose. I do miss her but I'm never sure what it is I've lost, what it's like to have a mother.'

'How did you manage without her?'

'Well, Martin I suppose. He always tried to look after me, in his own sweet, clumsy way.'

'Ah, so he's the real competition!' exclaimed Richard. He was joking of course. No-one could compete with him in my eyes.

'What about your parents? You've not said much about them.'

He looked up to the ceiling then down to the floor, exhaled deeply. 'Not much to say.'

'Come on, I want to know. What are they like?' I insisted.

'They're from Ireland – Londonderry. Came here when I was young, my two brothers not yet born. Grandparents and all. My dad worked in the shipyards but he drank – lost his job in the end.' He stopped speaking and I saw the muscles around his jaw clenching. I saw the struggle in him. 'I'm Irish really, but I've grown up here and I feel more English I suppose.'

'You don't sound very Irish.'

'No. My parents do though. They're Irish through and through. They seem to be half-proud, half-embarrassed by it. My mam works to support us 'cos my dad's on the dole half the time.' I saw the jaw muscles tighten again and he clenched his right fist. 'I'm not going to end up like him.'

'Course you're not. I know you're not like that.' I took his hand, leant forward and kissed his fingertips, stroked the smooth pads where his guitar strings had worn down the tiny ridges. 'You'll be something great. You can be whatever you want to be.'

'I want to be a musician – that's what I really want.'

'You *are* a musician, a really good one!'

'I'm applying for music college next year – just in case the band doesn't work out.'

After a moment's thought I asked him, 'Do you love your mother?'

'Suppose so. I never really thought about it. She was just – always there – y'know. She works hard – holds us all together.'

We sat quietly for a while, studying our hands as we twined our fingers together. He was tapping out a rhythm with his foot against mine, then began to hum a tune, a beautiful lament. It soared and wavered and fell in heart-rending crescendos of sorrow, finally coming to rest in an exquisite D minor descent. He told me it was D minor – I didn't know that myself.

'That's beautiful.'

'An Irish love song.'

'A sad one.'

'Yes. Irish love songs always seem full of sadness.'

'D'you believe in God?' I had no idea that question was going to come out, but there it was, glittering like the pearly gates themselves. An invitation for us to enter.

'In a way – sort of. Not the bearded old man in heaven that my mam believes in. But I'm sure there's something – I mean, something more than what we can see and hear. I believe in something...'

'Me too. Not the God I was taught about as a child. But maybe something more like energy...'

'Something universal, everywhere...'

'Yes. In the animals and birds, and the sea, and out in space too...'

'And in music, in that song...'

'Yes, in the song. Or in a painting perhaps. An experience, a feeling, somewhere inside us, not God like a person up there, above us.' I was struggling now. 'My dad's an atheist. That's a kind of religion for him, something to believe in, to hold onto – a certainty.'

'My mam's a Protestant – she's certain they have the only true God.' He frowns. 'We can't really know. We can't really be certain of what's there, can we?'

'I wish we could. I want to know, to feel sure.'

He looked into my eyes, brushing my cheek with the back of his fingers so that my skin tingled and a ripple of pleasure fizzed through me. 'We can be sure of this,' he said.

And I knew he was right. Finally, I had something in my life that was mine, and certain, and beautiful, and not full of old grief like my sad family home had always been.

We were diving in, faster and deeper. His mother said, 'You're living in each other's pockets. You'll regret it one day.' But I didn't care. I wasn't afraid. And I didn't regret a day of it.

My father said I was too young to get this serious about a boy. I should look around a bit, take my time, enjoy myself while I was young. But I was enjoying myself, so very much.

When Richard wrote his first love song for me, I knew I had found my soulmate. I showed him how to paint with oils and where to look for wounded birds. He gave me woodcarvings of each small creature I rescued. I loved Tom, Richard's first gift, the best.

And this is how it all began.

Two

London – 1981

The film was disappointing and I can feel Eddie's irritation growing, like a nasty itch beneath my skin, all along the arm I have hooked through his. We don't speak as we walk home through the dreary rain. It falls silently, a continuous vertical sheet of wetness, not heavy or light, just uniform and without character. It seems it has been falling forever and will continue to do so.

It's twelve years since I met Richard, and yet it all still feels so present. As if he walks beside me, like a shadow, his arm reaching out to wrap tenderly around my shoulder even as I struggle to keep up with Eddie's long stride. I can't help but compare them at moments like this. Richard would always shorten his step to match mine so that we walked in rhyme, our bodies hugging close, swaying together like one.

Two cars speed by in a futile race that it's clear neither can win, as the red lights at the end of the road will stop them regardless. They screech past, one swerving dangerously close to the kerb and soaking my legs with the washed-up grease of London's Friday night streets. Some men walk on the kerb side of the pavement to protect their woman from the road, but not Eddie. If you want to be a feminist, you have to pay the price, he tells me. Fair enough. The price of freedom and equality. Except that I feel neither free nor equal with Eddie. Mostly I feel bullied and helplessly bound.

Why do I keep choosing men who will hurt me? I can't even call this a relationship – it's more like an addiction. I have a suspicion I will spoil anything that feels good and clean and right, so I keep seeking the bad, the seedy side of life. As if I want to destroy myself, seeking oblivion in the arms of an abusive man.

It's not that Eddie beats me – unless you count the way he clips my arm when he's irritated with me – but he will lash out with cruel words that cut right to my core.

We arrive at the grand entrance to his mansion block, its solid walls like castle turrets. Thick stonework surrounding the doorway gleams creamy white in the wet glare of a streetlight. He unlocks the door, banging its heavy weight against the wall as he shoulders it open, and we enter the brightly lit lobby. Even at midnight the elegant carpeted hallway looks ready for business. An enormous vase of white silk lilies sits on a polished table. You would be forgiven for thinking this is a place of respectability and decorum.

Once upstairs in the safe enclosure of his generously insulated apartment, Eddie throws his wet coat against the coat-stand, letting it fall in a heap on the floor, and kicks off his shoes. I hang my coat up and peel off my boots, my favourite pink leather boots, soaked through. My feet leave damp prints on the finely sanded wood as I pad after him into the lounge.

He drapes himself across a chair, one leg over its arm and the other foot resting on the coffee table. If only he wasn't so damned good-looking, with his dark hair quiffed back and mouth set in a brooding pout. He has a strong jawline, olive coloured skin and thick black eyebrows that run straight until they dip at a cute angle, just above the outer edge of his eyes. His dark brown eyes look almost black, as pupil spills out into iris. Not like the darkness of Richard's eyes that invited me in – a strange light emanates from Eddie's that seems to threaten. He is gorgeous though, I can't deny it, and he knows it too.

A boy with a teasing smile, a wicked 'come and get some fun' twinkle in his eyes.

'Well, that was a fucking waste of an evening.'

'It wasn't a great film, but...' I want him to say something nice about spending the evening with me, at least. These days we don't see much of each other.

'Like hell it wasn't. What did you suggest it for?'

'Come on, Eddie, it's not my fault. *Time Out* gave it a good review, so I thought...'

'*Time Out*! You artists think that's the Bible, I suppose.'

'No, but they usually give you a good sense of...'

'Bullshit. They know less about film than you do.'

I wish I could take my eyes off him – his thighs squeezed into tight denim jeans, torn and frayed across the knees, but not from years of hard wear – he bought them like that at a trendy shop on the King's Road. The expensive black leather belt really is worn and faded, as if it were the only one he possessed and had been holding up his jeans for decades. The black linen shirt is ambiguously stylish – it could almost go unnoticed, nothing special, but on closer inspection there's an understated quality to the material and design.

Everything about Eddie pretends to be something it is not. He's a rich boy pretending to be poor. A rough diamond set in the luxury of this Marylebone apartment, at Daddy's expense. I'm between acting jobs he told me when we first met. It seems to be a more-or-less permanent position.

'I know as much about film as you do. We just have different tastes.' It's hard not to engage with his provocation. That is what he wants, of course. He'll start an argument just for the sake of it, taking whichever point of view opposes mine. I know it's a game to him, but still it hurts. I'm ready for some cuddling up and try to diffuse the chill that has settled between us. 'Anyway, we can do something nice over the weekend. D'you want to stay at my place tomorrow night, and on Sunday we can go...?'

He throws his head back against the chair and rolls his eyes, letting out a sigh that says 'I'm bored with this and exasperated with you'. I perch on the arm of the chair and run my fingers through his fine black hair. He shakes my hand away. The movement shoots through my arm like a dart aimed right for my heart, and I shrink back.

The snuggly feeling I had a moment ago has gone. I cross the room and slump into an armchair by the fire, its marble surround white against the soot-blackened chimney, and stare into the empty grate. I can't keep up the effort of trying to mend things between us, the pretence at lightness, at not caring when he slights me like this, just so that passion can flare again. I hug my knees up to my chest and bury my head behind a curtain of damp hair, wanting to cry but not wanting him to see that he has beaten me. My limbs lock into place, my bones rigid, like a strangely knotted sculpture that has been incongruously placed in a cream-coloured armchair. I feel trapped in the chair and in Eddie's apartment. I wish I was at home in my bed but I cannot move.

For a long while we endure an uncomfortable silence, broken only by the restless tapping of his foot against the table and the faint slush of cars passing along the wet street below. The room smells of nothing at all, not even cigarette smoke or furniture polish. Eddie's cleaner comes on Fridays and knows to air the room thoroughly after her work is done. His apartment is the one thing in the world he truly takes care of – apart from his own appearance. Beneath the surface veneer of temporary untidiness lies an immaculate interior design in walnut, ivory and cream. Expensive rugs from somewhere far away are scattered over the original oak floorboards. Woodcarvings from Africa are aesthetically placed on shelves and coffee tables amidst his collection of unread collectors' books and exotica from Asia.

'Jesus, stop sulking, will you!' His voice finally cracks the silence open and I begin to cry. 'Oh, Christ, what now?' he mutters.

I sniff into my sleeve and look at him through dishevelled hair. He kicks his feet off the table and lopes over to me.

'Look, honey, I just don't want to be wasting my time watching boring arty films at the ICA, that's all.' He tries to take hold of my hand but I pull it away. 'Come on, give me a hug.'

My breath tightens in my chest. I try to back away from him, from the stale scent of designer aftershave and a strong dose of washing powder that clings to his shirt, but he's up close now and I have nowhere to go. He is insistent and draws my hand out from the folds of my skirt.

'But you don't have to take it out on me like this.'

'Jesus, you're so damned sensitive. I can express an opinion if I want.' He drops my hand and stands up, cracks his knuckles and twines them over his head as he looks about the room. 'I don't have to like everything you like. And no, I don't want to stay at your place tomorrow.'

'So that's that,' I declare, as if something had actually been decided. My energy is returning and I feel angry – not so much at Eddie as with myself. I am a fool to let myself be toyed with, picked up and dropped, seduced then pushed away again. I lose myself in these games. I forget who I am.

'That's what?'

I stare at him, uncertain, suddenly afraid – of his height towering over me, of his proximity, the raw muscularity of his body, the attraction he has over me. In my confusion I begin to cry again.

Eddie kneels down beside me and takes my hands in his. They feel warm and strong. I long to surrender. His eyes seem kind now as he looks into mine and runs his fingers over my teary cheek.

'Sorry,' he says.

'Okay.' And that might have been the end of it but somehow I get started again. 'Why don't you want to stay at my house? You never come over anymore.' I squeeze his hands and look up at him, hoping that some honest talking will repair the wedge of misunderstanding and reproach that has come between us, yet again. He averts his gaze. He can only look into my eyes if he feels in control of the situation, of me.

He sighs. 'Because your house is a dump. It's cold and damp and it's full of crap paintings that give me the creeps. Now will you stop getting at me?'

I have to defend my beautiful home. 'It is not a dump! And the paintings are from our exhibition – you know that, Eddie. I don't mind if you don't like them, but why are you making a big deal out of it now?' I clench my fists and bring them down hard on the arms of the chair. 'You didn't complain when you were at the opening, drinking all our wine.'

'Ah, so I was drunk, was I?' He pulls himself upright and is now looking at me directly, as if I have offered a challenge worth taking up.

'I didn't say that.' I can see where this is going but feel unable to stop it. Like approaching a high brick wall in a car without brakes. I want to go home. We have been here so many pointless times before.

'But you thought it.'

'Don't tell me what I thought! Don't ever do that!' I shout, angry but dangerously close to tears again. He likes bringing me to the brink of tears so that he can act sweet and kind, seduce me into feeling grateful to him. I don't want to go there again. God, what have I got myself into, thinking I could love this man?

'Listen, honey, you don't know what you're thinking half the time. Maybe someone's got to tell you.' He brings his face close to mine and I think he might kiss me but instead he puckers his lips as if I were the taste of bitter lemons. There's a glint in his eye that scares me.

'Then don't come over. I don't care.' I turn away. I want to leave the room, and clamber out of the armchair, but he catches my wrist as I try to head for the door.

'So – what? You've got someone else lined up? That creep Jake perhaps?' He raises his eyebrows, sucks his cheeks in and pulls a long face. 'He is a creep, isn't he?' Eddie's eyes narrow menacingly.

'He's my friend. Don't call him names.'

'Don't call him names,' he mimics.

'God, I hate you! Let go of my arm. I don't know why I'm here with you anyway. I'm going – for good, Eddie.' I try to tug my arm free.

'You're here because you just can't resist me, because I give you a bloody good fuck.' He is looking directly into my eyes. He feels in control again.

I am furious. CAD. Now I know what that means – charming when he wants to be, but cruel and deceitful – cool, arrogant, dashing – deadly – dangerous. I don't think the Bronte sisters ever spelt it out, but here he is, the perfect CAD. I have no reply to his last statement. I just stare at him. It's true. Sex with Eddie is amazing. But the lack of tender words that go with it is equally stunning. I have to take the punishment if I want the prize.

He is suddenly bored with taunting me. Dropping my arm, he saunters into the kitchen to get a beer.

This is my chance. I have a few seconds to choose to end this, for good. Or to stay quiet, keep out of his range for a while, then lose myself in a night of passion, in the grip of my demon-lover.

I flee the apartment without saying goodbye, grabbing my wet coat and boots and not stopping to put them on until I am in the ground floor lobby. I hope never to see him again.

Sometime early in the morning a knock on my bedroom door half wakes me. He comes straight in, not waiting to be invited. 'Go away,' I groan, pulling the covers over my head, and turning my back to him.

Lying down beside me on the bed, he wraps his arms around me and begins to nibble my ear.

'Morning, sweetie. I missed you all night,' he says. As if nothing had happened. As if he hasn't realised I have left him. For good, this time.

'Go away, Eddie,' I mutter, trying to wriggle free of his grip. It isn't an embrace – it's a desperate clinging on. His arms and legs close around me and lock on like a vice. He's as addicted to this dysfunction as I am.

'Oh baby, don't send me away,' he coos. 'I'd be so sad.' He heaves his weight on top of me, drawing his elbows and knees close to my sides. The blankets stretch tightly over me and between us, pinning me down. He finds my face, buried in the pillows, and begins to kiss me. I can't avoid the fervent lips, the alcohol-laced breath, the hard bulge of him coming between my legs, through the blankets. I gasp. Eddie whips the blankets off me and slides up inside my nightshirt, into me. I am utterly powerless to resist him. There is nothing romantic about our union. Just good, raw sex.

He is still sleeping when I wake again. Late morning light filters through the pale blue curtains and ripples over his face. Like a face beneath the water. He looks beautiful, shrouded in sleep and returned to innocence. For a moment it's Richard's face I see there, submerged, the waves rippling over him. His young face is fresh and clear, free from the scars that the years inevitably bring, his spirit unsullied.

Eddie stirs and mumbles in his sleep. Could my lovely Richard have grown into such an arrogant young man if life had roughed him over? Probably not. Eddie's arrogance is astounding, infinite, radiant. If it were a virtue, then he would surely be a saint. Saint Eddie. No, I don't think so.

He's the only son of a wealthy family, not quite aristocratic, but on the way there. His father is aiming for a peerage by skulking around the higher echelons of parliamentary society. What he actually does, I have no idea, but he seems to have had something to do with getting Margaret Thatcher elected. Eddie went to Eton but was 'moved on' after a couple of years – a rare occurrence, it seems, to throw away such privilege. He behaves rough and dirty – his way of rebelling against his father no doubt. At first I thought I could love him back to his true and charming self, do for him what I have not been able to do for myself – heal the pain inside, banish the cancer that has corrupted him. Fill his empty, broken heart and make him love me. I failed, again and again, yet I feel bound to keep trying.

He half wakes and sleepily rolls into my arms. We make love again. Slowly, gently, deeply this time. For a moment I believe he really loves me. But soon he wakes out of his dream world and it all begins over again.

'You know, Nita, I don't think this is working – between us, I mean.' He picks up the clothes that are strewn around my room and begins to get dressed.

'It's difficult at times, I know. Shall we talk about what happened last night? I'm sure we can work it out.'

'I don't see the point in talking about it. I just don't think it's happening anymore.' Something inside me stops still, freezes like a winter stream halted in its downward course. 'It's you. You're not all there half the time. Just half alive.'

I can't think what to say. I feel cut to the core. Found out. A wave of shame sweeps through me and gouges a hole right beneath my heart. It's all my fault because there is something wrong with me. I know it. He knows it. I hadn't known he could see me like this. I thought I'd hidden my empty self well enough, played the game. I feel truly caught out.

'I think we should end it. There's no point in going on.' He sits on the end of my bed with his head hanging down, the black linen shirt not yet buttoned up, his hair already perfectly in place.

He is finishing with me. He has never done this before, and I know he means it. I feel too shocked and upset to argue. Perhaps I could have persuaded him to stay but, truly, I know he's right – there's no point in going on. But so bluntly, so unexpectedly. And after we have just made love so sweetly. It's not fair. It was always meant to be me who would walk out, one day, when I was ready to, not him who would leave me.

I sit in bed with the blankets pulled up to my chin, staring blankly through the curtained window. Eddie picks up the rest of his belongings and leaves the room. It really is over.

By twelve o'clock I've cried the morning away and still can't find the courage to face the day. It's Emms who eventually knocks on my door.

'Are you okay, Nita? Can I come in?' She takes my lack of audible response as a yes.

'Hey, what's up? You look dreadful. Did you and Eddie have a row or something?'

'He finished with me. Got up, said it was over, and left. Just like that. As if he was talking to himself. No discussion, nothing.'

Emms puts an arm round my shoulder and strokes my hair, like a mother might do. 'I'm sorry. You poor thing, dumped by that...' She stops herself but I know what she was about to say. She makes no secret of what she thinks of Eddie. That just makes me more miserable and another torrent of tears erupts. To be dumped by a bastard like Eddie makes me a complete fool, the worst kind of woman imaginable.

'Jesus, I'm a mess. I couldn't even leave him. Had to wait till he tossed me away, like a used-up rag.'

'Don't blame yourself, Nita. It's not your fault.'

'It's always my fault,' I blurt out angrily.

'Don't start that again. I won't listen to it,' says sensible Emms. 'Get up and have a warm bath, put on your nicest clothes, and we'll go to the Patisserie Valerie for cappuccino and cake.' Coffee and cake at the Patisserie Valerie is our wicked treat, the solution to all our miseries. It has pulled us both through many a heartbreak.

'Thanks Emms, but I don't think I can face going into town today.'

'Okay, then we'll just go to Jo's.' She is stubborn but I am more so. I need to be alone, to wallow in this mire of self-pity for a while longer, sliding dangerously close to depression. Strange how that pull is stronger than the sweet comforts of the Patisserie, like a familiar friend whose company I can sink into without effort. And stay there for days. Emms gives up trying. She knows me in these moods, realises there is nothing she can do to coax me back to the world of the living. At least she has initiated the move from bed to bathroom, then into the scruffiest jeans and sweatshirt I possess. But still I can't muster the energy to go downstairs and begin my day.

I sit on the bed staring at the familiar world that has been my haven for the past six years, my attic room painted in shades of pale azure. It reminds me of home on a summer's afternoon when the sky is a hazy blue and the sea a shimmering web of subtle hues. Almost hidden in a corner is the blue embroidered cushion. The lilac envelope tied with its faded red ribbon lies there beside photographs of Richard, my father, and the picture of my mother looking like a film-star – the one my father used to keep on his desk. My dusty altar to the past.

The memory of Richard has become a shrine at the heart of my being. I have to pass through it to find myself, and I do this daily – through the gates of sorrow. And always behind Richard come my mother and father. I have told my new friends little about my old life. I will let them think this current misery is due to Eddie, but I know it isn't really about him.

To survive life in London, at art college, I had to put these relics aside – not forgotten but tucked away in the corner of my room. The emotions that still churn about them – like a restless subterranean sea around a hard and stubborn rock – have been relegated to a distant recess of my mind too. I work hard to keep them there, behind a brittle but thin and fragile veil. But with so much of myself in hiding, held at bay, it's hard to move forward into my life wholeheartedly, sure-footedly, with confidence.

Now Eddie has torn the veil and the old feelings are threatening to erupt again. I struggle to hold myself together, feel the familiar tightening in my chest, the ringing in my ears. A heavy weight drags from my heart down to my belly – a feeling of dread, the anticipation of impending disaster.

Slowly I stir myself and prepare to go outside. My eyes are red and puffy so I put on a pair of sunglasses, turn up the collar of my coat, and step out into the street. The sun glares down at me, highlighting my shame. I walk quickly towards Regent's Park, running over the red light by the entrance to the zoo, not daring to stop in case I unravel right there in the road. In the park, behind the railings of the zoo, a beautiful silvery grey wolf stretches out in the midday sun, safely captured behind the double fence that keeps her wild world separate from mine. She ignores me as I walk past.

Down the wide avenue of chestnut and plane trees, round the Rose Garden, to the lakes and over the rocky hill where the fake waterfall begins its descent. I find a bench beneath the shade of the trees, hidden from the main pathways, and slump down wearily. My right hand clutches Tom's small body – my wooden friend who lives stiffly in my coat pocket.

I begin to breathe more freely as I sit in the cool shade, my fingers tracing over the tiny ridges made by Richard's knife. I can feel the warmth of his strong hands at work, imagine the muscles tensing in his forearm as he chips away to create Tom's perfect form. Finally tears flow – the quiet tears of the heart – as I connect to the real source of my anguish. Eddie has been a distraction, a mistake, a false turn on a road of never-ending false turns. He has been a punishment, a perverse kind of justice. Truly, I am relieved he is gone from my life, but his absence leaves me exposed to the rawness of loss again. I take Tom out of his pocket-home and hold him to my cheek for a moment. A blackbird hops by and cocks his head up at me, as if curious at the sudden appearance of a wooden sparrow. Does the blackbird recognise the life that is still beating in Tom's breast?

My mind begins to unwind, back to when it started – the turning away from innocence, from real love, from men like Richard. The moment when my life was split in two – the life before, and the life after. I was just seventeen and still naïve enough to hope.

Three

The north-east – 1970

I hadn't meant to spoil things. But I did. Richard's band was playing at the Highcliffe and we were euphoric, convinced this gig meant they had made it. I'd been dancing all night with Lucy and Sara. I only meant to sit out for a few moments to catch my breath.

'Hi there. Want a drink?' a voice shouted in my ear over the pound of the music. I turned to see a young man looking at me with a serious expression on his thin and angular face. He wore a black beret and dark polo neck sweater – a little out of place here but I was intrigued. A Beatnik. They were cool. They liked poetry, jazz and were anarchists.

He bought me a drink and we found a quiet corner where we could talk. His name was Mark. He was quite a bit older than me – a photographer with a studio in the city. I hadn't seen him here before.

Mark seemed exciting, grown up, a real artist, and I felt flattered that he was paying attention to me. Richard had seen us together, through the flashing red and green lights that spun around the crowded hall.

A few days later a friend told Richard I had been at the Rendezvous Café with Mark. We had met one morning for a coffee. It wasn't a real date. No further plans had been made and I doubted I would see him again, but Richard was jealous.

'What's his name?' he asked, when we met the next evening.

'Mark.'

'Tim saw you with him at the Rendezous yesterday.'

'We just met for coffee. It doesn't mean anything.' I felt caught out. I hadn't seen Tim there.

'You were talking with him all night at the dance.'

'We were just talking, that's all. I'm telling you, it was nothing special.'

'Nothing special! It didn't look that way. Everyone saw you with him. He just about had his hands all over you.'

'No he didn't! I did nothing wrong Richard. You were playing and he came to talk with me. That's all.'

'So who is he, then?'

'He's a photographer. Has a studio in Newcastle, if you must know.'

'Oh, I see. So he thinks he's better than everyone else, I suppose.'

'Of course he doesn't. Why on earth do you say that?'

'Because he was acting as if he did – swanning around like he thought he was so smart.'

'Richard, why are you being so nasty about it? He just bought me a drink and we talked!' I shouted, angry now. I had never seen Richard like this and I didn't like it.

'A few drinks! Then he took you out yesterday. How do I know what you got up to?'

And so it went on, until Richard got really angry and I felt very guilty. It was the first big row we had had during our whole wonderful, baffling, magical year together.

'I don't think you should come on the holiday. If I can't trust you, Nita... I'm not sharing you with some upstart artist from the city. I mean it.'

I had no defence left. I was in the wrong and I was being excluded from his world. 'Alright. I didn't want to go anyway,'

I retorted, trying to salvage something of my pride. 'And he's not an upstart. He's a professional photographer.'

Lucy and Sara went with Richard and his two friends on the holiday we had planned in Amble. I stayed at home.

When I told Nancy she said, 'Oh, I'm sorry. But you'll get over him in time.' When I told my father he said, 'Never mind, Anita. You'll find someone else.' I knew he meant, 'someone better'.

I closed my brand-new red-leather record player, careful not to jump the needle, and threw myself onto the bed. Four more weeks before school began. I stretched out, tapping my bare feet in time with the music – Marvin Gaye was about to lose his mind. I had just recovered mine after an agonising week without Richard.

A light breeze was blowing from the sea, ruffling the birds' feathers that stood in a vase by the open window. Their shadow rippled across a painting on the wall at the foot of my bed – a barren landscape, a solitary charred tree against a red sunset sky. It was my depiction of the nuclear holocaust. The threat of annihilation – that life could be suddenly and incontrovertibly no more – was both a terror and a fascination to my teenage mind. My painting was an attempt to exorcise the ghost that haunted my youth.

But today the warmth and bright sunlight of early August had dispersed these shadows, for now at least. I felt happy. The scent of roses drifted in through the window with the soft sea breeze and my heart lifted with each beat. In my mind I had resolved the argument and was sure all would be well. I desperately wanted it to be well. I didn't want to lose Richard.

I picked up the book that lay open on the dressing table but couldn't concentrate. Out of the window a crisp blue sky was studded with those fluffy white clouds that shape-shift into old weathered faces, dogs and dragons. The square of sea I could glimpse between the houses on the front sparkled sapphire blue and inviting. I put down Blake's *Songs of Innocence and Experience* – summer reading could wait – and lay back with my hands clasped behind my head, letting my mind flow into the music.

Downstairs the phone rang, then a moment later Nancy's voice called, 'Anita, it's for you. It's Lucy.'

I swung my legs over the side of the bed, tugging my miniskirt back into place, and jumped up, eager to hear from Lucy. As I bound down the stairs, my hair, meticulously straightened through the use of various night-time aids, flew out at all angles. I skimmed the last two steps and took the phone from Nancy.

After years of resistance I had finally surrendered, albeit reluctantly, to the use of her name in place of my rather sarcastic, 'Yes Ma'am'. Accepting Nancy into my life and into our home had not been an easy journey but we had found a place of tentative equilibrium, a fragile truce.

'Hi Lucy. How was the holiday? You're back early,' I chirped. 'Are the others back too?'

'Haven't you heard?' Lucy's voice was faint and small. It sounded strangely hollow, like an echo flying back along a grey metallic tunnel.

A long silence. A stillness seeped into my body and chilled my bones. I wanted the conversation to stop here. I wanted life to stop here, just at this very moment, with Marvin Gaye singing in the background, Blake's *Songs of Innocence*, and a fluffy white dragon sailing through a crystal-blue sky. The air tightened around me like a web of fine metal thread.

I held the receiver a few inches from my ear, as if the space could slow down the movement of information from Lucy's voice to my cascading mind.

'What is it?' Nancy looked at me, lines puckering her forehead into a deep knot. I had crystallised, like the blue sky. I had frozen, like a drop of moisture falling to earth, turning to ice as it descended through the cold layers of space. I landed, a pale, motionless creature, at the foot of the stairs, a telephone receiver held limply in my right hand.

'Richard is dead,' I whispered.

I saw panic in Nancy's eyes. She stepped close and held me. I could feel her heart racing. Mine had stopped.

'You must cry,' she fumbled. 'It's good to cry.' But her gesture of comfort couldn't help me in that terrible moment. I couldn't shed a single tear. Like beads of ice in my blood, they pummelled against the walls of my frozen heart and couldn't escape.

My father was in the lounge, standing by the far wall and staring at me. I longed to feel his strong arms around me but he was retreating into the distance, merging into the wallpaper, disappearing like a ghost, a wisp of smoke.

Richard was dead. My lovely Richard, he had gone. Forever. No. It was not possible. It could not be.

With one long agonised cry, I clasped my arms around my body and sank to the ground.

2

The next four weeks were a void. My mind was a black landscape with no colour, no light. The light hurt my eyes. Thinking was just too painful. I tried to read but Virginia Wolf's once insightful prose now felt trivial to my newly shattered heart.

The green couch that was tucked into the corner of my room became my refuge. I retreated into its hard comfort. During the long days I would lie with my head resting on the old cushion that had been my grandmother's, or curl up around it, its softness pressing against my chest as if it could fill the chasm that had once been my heart. I buried my face into the faded blue cloth with its intricately embroidered design, cried into the web of worn threads. My grief felt eternal, like the silver, green and gold threads that wove, in an unbroken line, across the dusty cover.

I longed for my father's warm chest to rest my head on, as I had done as a child when night dreams woke me and left me afraid of the dark. My father didn't come. He lay in his bed in the room next door. I could hear him coughing, shuffling to the bathroom now and then.

I descended into a deeper yearning. As the scent of jasmine and warm milk drifted through my memory, it was the soft flesh and the gentle embrace of my mother's body that I longed to feel. Though I had no memory of her, there were times when no-one else could take her place. The longing for something that was not there was drawing me out of myself, unravelling my fragile hold. I was dissolving into space.

Richard had gone and he was not coming back. Against this cold fact everything else seemed unreal. I moved like a spectre through the haunted days.

I remembered the day of his funeral – a few disconnected moments of it. The dark polished coffin passing in front of me, just inches away, as it was carried out of the church – I could have reached out to touch it but my fingers gripped the rail of the pew, knuckles turning white. A scream leapt into my throat and stuck there. My knees trembled and threatened to give way.

There was a moment of confusion outside the church as mourners were matched with cars to make the solemn journey from the big church to the little crematorium chapel. The sympathetic look in the eyes of the elderly couple who took Nancy and me as she explained – 'She was a close friend of Richard's'. A hushed silence followed. What was there to say anyway? A leaden weight had settled over every living thing. Life seemed to stop.

I remembered nothing of the service at the crematorium, where Richard's body would be turned to ashes. My next memory was of walking the short distance home from the cemetery ground, the young people up ahead – my friends and

Richard's, Martin, home early from his holiday in Spain – all talking in subdued tones.

The adults walked behind, their voices reaching me as if through water, the submerged vowels reverberating slowly across the distance. 'You can barely imagine…' The voice of one mother trailed off.

'Have you seen his parents?' asked another.

'Yes…completely devastated,' answered a third. 'But their friends and family are there…'

'Terrible, terrible,' muttered a fourth. 'So young, such a waste of a young life. Nice that so many came to the service though.'

'How is Anita coping?' the first woman asked Nancy.

'She's taken it badly – in shock you know – but she's young – she'll get through it, in time.' Nancy was trying to sound positive but it wasn't very convincing. 'Once she's back at school, with things to take her mind off it all, I'm sure it will get easier.'

'Poor girl. Should be thinking about her wedding, not going to funerals,' the woman said. 'It's not right…'

They fell silent again.

I walked alone. A wedding? This was my wedding, a marriage with death. My chest and throat felt painfully tight, the muscles clenched to hold my breath still.

No clouds scudded by that day. The air was a monotonous grey, braced by a faint whiff of sea salt. Although it was still August, autumn would soon be here, then winter. Last autumn Richard had walked beside me, the life pulsing through him. We often walked down the old railway track, talking and laughing. It seemed that every day the sun shone and fresh autumn winds blew, sharp and clean.

Now he was nothing, nothing more than grey ash. Where did he go? The reality of him – his wavy brown hair and eyes that were full of light, the glistening muscles of his forearms, the easy swing of his legs as he ran?

In my mind's eye he still lay on the seabed, gazing up at the sky through the depth of water that had pulled him down.

At night I would dream that I lay beside him, our wide-open eyes reaching up to the light beyond the rippling surface. Waves flickered in the sunlight. In my dream we held hands as we swallowed our last gulp of salty water. My lungs strained beneath the murky green weight that pressed down on my chest. I closed my eyes and let go.

Some part of me had gone with Richard into death.

Nancy and I arrived back at the house in silence. I went straight to my room and closed the door, relieved to collapse into my solitary world again. I stood in the centre of the room, still as stone and barely breathing. My paintings on the wall, the vase of feathers on the windowsill, the grey of the damp afternoon outside – all seemed to taunt me with an existence I resented. A blackbird flew close to the window then out over the garden, disappearing into a hedge. I hardly noticed – just a shadow passing by.

All that protected me from the fragmentation that threatened was a tight wall of muscle that held my beating heart at bay and stilled my breath. To breathe deeply meant to feel deeply. To feel deeply meant feeling the full weight of loss, accepting that Richard had really gone, forever.

Moving slowly, as if my bones might break, I perched on the edge of the couch, clinging to my grandmother's cushion. I looked over the edge of the abyss. Darkness rushed towards me like a swollen river. I gasped, then the gasp broke into a sob as I gulped at the air. I sobbed as the river swept over me, clutching the cushion as if it were a raft that could save me. But my lifeline had broken and I was cut loose, adrift.

I could bear it no longer. Pulling myself out of the nightmare, I went down to the garden, like a person sleepwalking. The neighbour's smoky grey tomcat was on the prowl. I went to the aviary and opened the door.

Down on my knees, I crawled inside and found the white dove I had rescued from the claws of a kestrel. It was just a few days before the row with Richard. Her wing was broken and she couldn't fly. I picked her up, cupped her in my hands – my useless hands, my treacherous hands, my hands that could save nothing worth saving – and carried her out into the garden.

I laid her in the centre of the lawn and stepped back into the shadow of the bushes. The cat prowled around her. He took his time, swishing his tail, twitching his ears and crouching low to the ground. Once sure his prey had surrendered, he crept up and seized her in his mouth. I watched as he tossed and clawed her.

He gripped her head between the sharp spears of his teeth. With a claw dug into her chest, he tore her apart. He ripped her open, ripped out her moist red heart, shook her one more time. Then he left her lying on the green mown grass. A trail of blood-stained feathers lay around her. Her black eye stared at me, accusing. Circling her beautiful white throat was a deep red gash.

She was the last injured bird I would try to save.

Four

London – 1981

Tom is back in my pocket, my cold fingers wrapped tightly around him, as if they might force him back to life. As if that could erase the shame of what I did, erase the death of one by bringing back another. I arrive home but am not ready to face my friends yet. I stop in front of the house and study the brass plate on the wall beside the door. It needs a good clean and polish to remove the wavering line of greenish-brown dirt that is creeping surreptitiously from the edges towards the faded lettering –

> *Jez, Emms, Nita,*
> *Jake & Matt*
> *Artists in Residence*

Matt, the sculptor amongst us, engraved the plaque when we moved in. At the time, all five of us were newly graduated from college, full of hope, burning with ambition. Now the statement seems rather inflated in light of our collective failure to make any significant mark on the London art scene.

This is a high-class squat. It has a bath and running hot water, unlike the dilapidated terraced house in Stepney that we shared as students. There we went for weekly soaks in the Mile End

Road public baths. Jez, Emms and I would occupy neighbouring cubicles so that we could chat while we luxuriated in enormous tubs filled with masses of piping hot water. I imagine that a whole family would once have shared a bath.

I clutch my key in one hand and Tom in the other. Emms will have told them what happened and I'm especially nervous about seeing Jake. Dear Jake, who had been my lover for a while during our college years. We mutually decided we were better off as 'just good friends'. Other relationships have come and gone but my friendship with Jake has deepened over the years – he's like a brother to me. Since Martin married Leticia and moved to Spain, Jake has so perfectly, precisely filled the gap that his absence left. Perhaps this was part of the difficulty. Sleeping with Jake had felt too much like sleeping with a brother.

A feeling of embarrassment, rapidly sliding up the scale towards humiliation and shame, creeps over me as I imagine Jake's reaction to my break-up with Eddie. As I close the front door behind me, I hear the murmur of voices from the kitchen and the smell of coffee percolates through the hallway. I could creep upstairs and hide, but decide against it.

'Hi Nita.' Jez alerts them to my presence, standing in the doorway. The conversation stops, all eight eyes turning towards me as I enter. I have the uncomfortable feeling of having just stepped in on a conversation about myself. A flush of redness grips my throat and threatens to flood my cheeks. I flip Tom over inside my pocket and rub his head between my thumb and forefinger.

'Hi,' I mumble, and sit down behind the empty coffee pot. Silence. An awkward silence.

'So – are you okay, Nita?' Jake finally asks.

'Yes, I'm alright. Thanks.'

'I'll go and get pizzas then.' Matt was never one to be around for a group heart-to-heart. 'The usual?' We all affirm yes, and he signals for Jez to join him. Matt and Jez have been together, a couple, for four whole years now. They bring stability to our group, making it feel something like a family for us all.

I sit there, hands on my lap, twirling my thumbs around each other and not knowing what to say. I examine the squeezed-out grains at the bottom of the coffee pot and notice that the crack in the glass has grown longer. We must buy a new one before it breaks.

'I'm sorry, Nita. You deserve better than that.' There is such kindness in Jake's voice. It nearly sets me sobbing again. I look up at him and see my sadness reflected in his face, in his warm hazel eyes. He is always so gentle and considerate towards me. Why is this not enough? I seem compelled to seek danger instead, as if I don't deserve Jake's kindness. Now, as he reaches a hand towards me, I want to flee. I want him to tell me what a fool I have been, confirm the humiliation I'm feeling. But he doesn't. He simply holds my hand until I can relax enough to feel that he has really touched me.

'I know what you're all thinking. I've been a complete idiot and I'm better off without him.' Again silence.

'Has he still got a key?' Emms asks. 'He could come back, couldn't he?'

'He has. But I don't think he'll come back. When he said it was over, I know he meant it. Guys like Eddie move on quickly. He's probably out looking for someone else right now.' I want to cry again but bite my lip and hold tight to the sliver of dignity I am trying to reclaim.

'We should change the lock, just in case,' Jake announces decisively. For some reason that makes us all laugh and the ice begins to melt between the three of us.

'Just like when we moved in here.' Emms giggles. 'D'you remember the trouble you had removing the original lock? People in the old days certainly knew how to protect their homes.'

'And all of us creeping over the rooftops in the middle of the night. Clambering in through the skylight window,' Jake adds.

I'm glad to escape into happier memories for a moment. I have an image of the five of us silhouetted against the sky, the moon rising behind us as we tiptoe along the ridge of the roof with sleeping bags over our shoulders.

We had entered the empty house from the roof of a neighbouring property where a friend of Matt's lived. It needs renovation but the council, who own it, have no money for that, so our presence is tolerated and we live in style, rent-free and in such a superb location – the grandeur of Regents Park and Primrose Hill on our doorstep, fashionable shops and café-bars springing up, Camden Lock Market selling Afghan coats and exotic crafts. And Oxford Circus is just a good walk or short cycle ride away. Our four-storey, Regency terraced house would once have been a smart white colour, like the ones across the road that shine brightly in the morning sunlight. Ours is a lesser shade of grey, and peeling now, but still it has some majesty about it.

'I never dreamed we'd be able to stay for so long,' Jake says. 'It feels as if it could go on forever.'

'But it won't,' I add. A chill runs through me as I remember the last letter from the council – they are ready to implement their plans for renovation soon, and we should be preparing to move out next year. Of course, we have received these letters every year – a bureaucratic ritual meant to lure them and us into thinking they are in control of the situation – but something about the last one seemed to have a little more substance.

'Let's be positive about it. If we expect the worst it's bound to happen,' Jake counters.

As a friend, I love the lightness and optimism that is Jake's way of being. He is great fun to be with. But as a lover, his lack of seriousness could be quite irritating. I had interpreted it as a lack of depth. Jake, for his part, had an instinctive recognition of the shadows that hovered about me. When we broke up, he told me they frightened him, made him pull back from me, as if my pain might engulf him if he got too close. He felt out of his depth with me, he said, even though he always loved me. I never doubted this.

'I don't believe in positive thinking, imagining we can create something just by wishing it,' I reply. 'None of us are that powerful.' I seem impelled to expect catastrophe. The expectation has grown into my nature like ivy around a tree, sapping life and gaining support from its host until the original tree has been eclipsed.

'Come on, Nita. Life's hard enough without always expecting it to get even worse,' he says.

'But we have to be realistic, and we won't be able to stay here forever. We all know that,' I argue.

'Let's just say you're both right,' Emms chips in equitably. 'That we can't stay here forever but there's no point in making ourselves miserable by worrying about disasters that haven't happened yet.' Emms has a way of riding above conflict, bringing reason and balance to any argument and thus quashing it in its tracks. She's a Libran, after all.

Jake and I look at each other slyly and begin to laugh.

'Yes, Ma'am. The voice of reason has spoken.' He is about to make a joke when the front door opens and in walks Eddie.

Jake leaps up and stands between Eddie and me. 'Hey, you're not welcome here, mate. I think you should hand over your key and leave Nita alone now.' He looks as surprised as I am at this bold flash of assertion.

'Hey, mate,' Eddie mocks. 'I don't think it's up to you. Let's see what the lady has to say.' He turns to me, drunk and unsteady on his feet.

'Go away Eddie and don't ever come back. Ever! We're through!' I declare, stepping up beside Jake. Emms comes to stand on my other side. We are like a battalion, armed and ready. 'Give me the key, and go,' I demand, holding out my open hand. Now it's Eddie's turn to be surprised at *my* assertion. He looks suddenly weak and deflated, like a pricked balloon. He is not used to being confronted like this, and I am not used to the feeling of boldness that has crept in, unfamiliar but welcome. I detect a flicker of fire in my belly, a strength in my legs that makes me stand tall. In a blur of drunken confusion, he drops the key on the table and leaves.

'Wow!' Emms declares. 'You two were good!'

'This calls for celebration. How about a smoke?' Jake is already jumping up to retrieve tobacco, Rizla and a plastic bag of grass from the dresser.

'I think I'll leave it – I've got some stuff to do,' I say vaguely, and make a swift exit before they can object. I need time to re-shape myself around this empty feeling that the loss of interminable conflict with Eddie has left. It's a cold and bleak feeling, yet there is something strangely comforting about it too. An intimation of a new way of being. The possibility of standing alone.

I retreat to the solitude of my room and pick up Richard's photograph from the dusty corner where it lies, next to the lilac envelope that still smells of old roses. As I gaze into his smiling eyes and they look back into mine, a deep longing surges through me. It splits a crack in my heart and begins to fill into the empty space inside. Longing and pain lie side by side, raw pain. I am touching into the very core of it.

Five

The north-east – 1970

It was two days after Richard's funeral. My narrow bed felt hard, the covers too thin, and I couldn't sleep. Out in the night a distant church clock struck three.

A full moon cast fingers of light across my bed and up along the wall, illuminating a poster of a Matisse exhibition, dimly outlining shelves stacked with books, records and magazines, corners scattered with clothes and furry childhood toys – all the accessories of seventeen years of growing up. All useless to me now. A faint smell of white spirit lingered, even though I hadn't painted since Richard had gone. The mess of paper, brushes and paints that littered my desk lay idle.

That night the moon's radiance kept the demons at bay. They had terrified me since his death, their red eyes staring at me from the dark. I felt accused. It should have been me, not Richard. I was at fault. Or had we both been punished for some sin we didn't even know we had committed?

We had loved each other – that was not a sin. It was a delicate meeting, a flight, a place of shared joy. It was a walk along the beach in the moonlight. It was the senses so alive that every scent, every sight was imprinted vividly and indelibly in my memory. Being in love was being awakened – to my own beauty, to myself as a young woman. I had begun to know myself through Richard's loving gaze. He had brought to life something in me I had never imagined before. I had allowed him to witness my shyness and its soft melting, as I grew to trust his passionate impulses.

My body ached with the memory of those strong and urgent embraces, the salty earth scent of him, the exquisite touch of his fingers tracing the curves of my breasts, my belly, my thighs – sculpting my form, giving shape to pleasure. My lips parted, as if I could drink him in one more time. My mouth felt parched, my throat cold and dry. My body was trembling.

The memory became unbearable. I flung the covers off and stumbled out of bed.

Bleary-eyed and dizzy with tiredness, I pulled on my soft shoes and pale blue dressing gown. Careful to avoid the two steps that creaked, I tiptoed down the stairs and slipped out of the back door.

Cold, clear moonlight flooded the garden, highlighting each shrub and tree. I walked onto the damp grass and began to circle slowly around the lawn. My fingers lightly touched each tree and shrub as I passed. The ritual helped to anchor me momentarily into the earth. After making a complete circle, I found myself walking towards the garden gate, turning into the street and heading for the sea front. My footsteps were silent. I cast hardly a shadow in the pale light.

On the cliff path I stopped to sit on the solitary bench. Its weathered wooden seat and frame of curled ironwork, rusted from years of rain and sea spray, were just as they had always been. I had sat here with Richard on a night just like this, gazing out along the path of moonlight that rippled from the beach, out over the sea to the horizon. We sat hand in hand, shoulder leaning into shoulder, absorbing the beauty that stretched out like a pathway into our future – a moment to treasure, to hold in memory for just such a lonely night as this.

The murmur of the waves drew me down the stone steps towards the beach.

This was the place, halfway down, where we had first kissed. It was the day after we had gone crab hunting on the island. Richard had stopped and turned to face me, standing just a step below so I was looking straight into his dark brown eyes. He looked into my eyes, softly touched my cheek, and kissed me. It was a gentle kiss, soft lips touching mine, breath shared, a moment of suspense as we touched the edge of each other's soul, tasted the promise of a whole unknown world to be discovered. Our first kiss told me all I wanted to know – that this was more than a friendship – that we could dare to tie ourselves together in love.

Every place held the memory of a time we had walked there, words that had been spoken, laughter we had shared. Each rock and step and pathway was imprinted with Richard's voice, his presence, the feel of him. The sandy beach was littered with our footprints, side by side along the shore.

I continued down the steps. The iron handrail was icy cold in the damp night air, the cliff wall hard. The sand looked eerily white in the moonlight, streaked with shadows where piles of seaweed had been swept up and left stranded at high tide. The pungent smell of decaying seaweed laced the salty air. Down here on the beach the murmur of the waves had grown into a rushing, crashing, sucking waltz.

I walked down the beach towards the water's edge, my feet sinking into the sand then squelching through mounds of slippery seaweed. The popping of bladderwort pods, as I slithered over them, punctuated the mournful, repetitive melody of the sea.

How could God do this to us? I thought – or did I cry it out loud? If there was a God, surely he would not punish us like this. I could not believe in such a God.

Then came the guilt – just a hint at first, reaching from a murky corner of my mind, then growing into a river that coursed deep and strong. There was the nagging question again. Had it been my fault? Had Richard been so upset by what I'd done that he had not taken care, or even worse, had intentionally swum too far out, knowing there could be dangerous rip tides sweeping along the coast? If I had driven him to it then I had killed him, as surely as if I had plunged a knife into his heart.

I delved into my memory as I began to walk along the shoreline towards the lighthouse. Waves washed up over my ankles, soaking my shoes and the hem of my dressing gown. In the moonlight I could have been mistaken for a ghost come from the sea.

The dance at the Highcliffe – Mark – too many drinks – flashing lights and Richard on the stage, his shirt open and chest glistening with sweat as he pounded out the rhythm on his guitar. Mark at the Rendezvous – then our angry words.

It must be my fault.

As I walked along the shore my mind, drugged with sleeplessness, wandered and raced. My feet brought me to the rocky headland that led to the lighthouse. Its beam lurched round in predictable repetition, scanning the night for wayward ships lost out at sea.

Did all this make me guilty? The rushing waves beckoned to me, called that they still held Richard in their chill embrace. I could follow him if I wished. I felt the pull of the ocean, its hypnotic, mesmerising song seeming to taunt me. The waves rushed towards me, opened up, invited me in, then came crashing down at my feet. Ssshhh – hhaaaa. Like a clammy umbilical cord, the power of the sea sucked and pummelled at my belly. Cold air rushed into my lungs as I opened my mouth, and out came a long howl, the cry of an injured animal, wild and desolate. The sound startled me, filled me with fear.

I shivered and pulled my robe tightly around me. I was cold. Taking a deep breath I tried to steady myself, stepping back from the reach of the waves.

Maybe Richard had not really died. I had heard Harvey's mother telling of how blue and bloated he had looked when they finally dragged his body up, and that the young people shouldn't see him like that. I hadn't seen him and so I couldn't know for sure that he had died. Perhaps Harvey's mother made it up and Richard had in fact been washed out to sea. Perhaps one day he would return home after finding his way to some distant point along the coast, or even across the sea to Norway. I imagined walking along the beach one day and there he would be, striding along the water's edge to meet me, smiling in the sunlight. As if nothing had happened – an ordinary summer's day, just like any other.

My body was aching and tired. I climbed back up the beach and lay down on a flat rock at the bottom of the cliff, my belly to the hard stone. Moonlight and the flashing beam of the lighthouse vied for dominance over the night sky.

It was Martin who found me early next morning, curled up asleep on the sand with my back to the rock. There was a sea fret and the beach was deserted in the grey dawn. He helped me up and held me close as my stiffened limbs began to thaw out. We walked home in silence, Martin's arm around my shoulder, my hands dug deep into my dressing gown pockets and my head hung down. Perhaps I ought to feel embarrassed, or even ashamed at the worry I had caused, but for now I just felt cold and numb.

A worried Nancy greeted us at the door and soon had me bundled up in bed with a mug of sweet tea and a bowl of porridge. The doctor was visiting my father that morning and left something to help me sleep.

When I woke it must have been late afternoon, as the sun had circled round the house and left my room in the shade. The sound of Martin's acoustic guitar greeted me. My head spun as I sat up. It felt thick, heavy as a ball of lead. I wrapped my dressing gown around me and walked unsteadily down the hallway to Martin's room, my hand sliding along the wall for support. A thin waif of a figure stared out at me from the long mirror at the end of the hall. My eyes were dark hollows against the pale skin. My hair, allowed to return to its wayward curls now, shot out from my head in tremulous strands. I felt shocked to see this fragile form, all the life gouged out of me.

'Come on in,' Martin nodded, seeing me in the doorway. As I sat down on the bed beside him, he continued playing the Spanish love song with its beautiful melody and intricate finger-picking. Since meeting Leticia, he had developed an enthusiasm for classical Spanish guitar and had been learning this piece over the summer. When he finished, he turned to me and winked.

'You've got to look after yourself better than this, Nita. You're the only sister I've got, you know.' His capacity to make light of the worst catastrophe was one of his endearing features. He nudged me, ever so gently. I elbowed back. These jibes would have signalled a fun-fight when we were children – nearly four years older and so much bigger and stronger than me, he had always been careful not to hurt me. I smiled and was almost tempted into the game, but didn't have the strength.

'But seriously, you're – almost – all the family I've got. You must take care of yourself.' His voice had dropped to almost a whisper. 'You'll get over this – in time. Please give yourself a chance.'

'I'm sure you're right. I'm sorry I've caused you so much trouble.' My voice sounded small and thin.

'It's okay, don't be sorry. Just promise me, Nita – if you ever – if you ever think of, of doing something – you know, if you can't cope – I mean, please call me first to talk.' Martin was now holding my hand tightly, looking directly into my eyes and speaking with an urgency I hadn't felt from him before. I dropped my gaze and studied his strong hand wrapped around my slender fingers.

'I will. I promise. Thanks, Martin, thank you for being here. You're the only brother I've got too.' I squeezed his hand then added shyly, as if as an afterthought, 'I do love you.'

'Love you too,' said Martin. The words skipped out in a rush, not because they were not heart-felt, but because it was unfamiliar, almost embarrassing, to name such feelings in our family. Richard had been different. He would say 'I love you' with such conviction that I had heard 'forever' hidden within the words.

Martin and I sat quietly for a moment, shy in the face of this brush with intimacy. 'Do you ever think about our mother? Do you miss her?' I asked after a while.

'What makes you ask that now? It's ages since you've mentioned her.'

'I've just been thinking about her, that's all. D'you miss her?'

Martin looked ruffled. 'Sure, of course I do. But it's so long ago now, I guess you just learn to adapt.'

'Yes, I guess so.' I fell silent.

He picked up his guitar again and began strumming some simple chords. I leant back and closed my eyes, feeling soothed by the music and the warm, solid feeling of Martin right beside me. He had always been there when I needed someone by my side – a safe and dependable presence in my life, doing his best to fill the space our mother's absence had created, for both of us. An absence that had begun to feel palpable, like a presence in its own right. The presence of absence – something tangible and substantial taking shape inside of me.

Six

London 1981

I'm sitting on a high stool, surrounded by heaps of canvasses and facing one that's still blank. The exhibition has been dismantled and the remnants of our work – all that has not been sold, which amounts to most of it – have been crammed into every available space. Our basement studio is a long room running the length of the house. Although each of us has our own area to work in, right now the homeless paintings and sculptures have forced us into whatever corner we can find. Just enough light filters through from a large window at the front and French doors at the back.

My gaze wanders out to the small backyard which houses our bicycles, plant pots – mostly the cracked, upturned or weed-filled type – and a pile of wood off-cuts, bits of metal, rope and other junk left over from Matt's sculpting. My mind is rummaging through the past, trying to understand how I could be drawn to someone like Eddie. Now I see how afraid he is of intimacy, how he would lash out if I came too close to him. And am I not the same, choosing a man who can't surrender so I would never have to surrender myself? I long for and I fear it.

The memories are flooding back with a sense of clarity that this led to that, and eventually to Eddie.

The French doors are wide open and the soft June evening drifts in. The meaty smell of a neighbour's barbecue fills the air, and the strains of No woman, No cry come from somewhere inside their house. I take heed of the reggae prophet's words. It's time to stop moping and start painting again. Inspiration is beginning to gather. After a period of the blues, a surge of energy always takes me back into the studio and a new direction for my work begins to emerge.

I feel compelled to create something big in order to give my life meaning. Once a painting is finished, the sense of meaning quickly begins to evaporate. So I keep painting – creating ever larger, more daring, more colourful pictures. With my hold on life so tenuous, this is how I have learnt to survive.

When I first arrived at St. Martin's college I found the large high-ceilinged studios, with their whitewashed walls and minimalist design, cold and soulless. I missed the cosy clutter of Kip's studio, felt intimidated by the scale of it all. The city, anonymous and loud, overwhelmed me. I longed to retreat into a smaller world but gradually I grew into the space that was there for me. My paintings increased in size as my confidence grew, until I was painting canvasses taller than myself. 'Her style is abstract, in the fashion of the day, yet the paintings are so full of energy and colour that they are charged with emotional intensity,' read a review in the local paper after one of our exhibitions. It was a nice review. I pinned it on the wall by my bedroom window.

My attention goes back to the blank canvas in front of me, to the invitation of its white and empty space. I begin with a background of pale blue and mauve. My brush weaves threads of dark violet through it, catching hints and traces of form that are caught up and dissolved back into the misty wash, like clouds into the pervading blue of the sky. My memory is alighting on particular moments – Jake and I watching the morning mist lift over Lake Windermere – Richard's blue canoe dipping through the waves – his fingers deftly strumming his guitar – a dream of my grandmother appearing then dissolving back into the mist. I let my mind empty and my hand take over. From heart to hand to eyes – a triangle of connections moves me to paint. Forms begin to emerge and for a while I feel content.

'Nita, there you are!' Emms' voice rises above the clump of her wooden clogs on the croaking stairs. She startles me out of my reverie, but I see by the quality of light that trickles along the wall that it's getting late and time to stop painting for now.

'Hi Emms.'

'Ooh, I like that...' She tilts her head sideways to study my work.

'Thanks. I'm quite pleased with it so far.'

'I want to ask you about your birthday – what you'd like to do. Shall we have a party?' Emms is clearly full of enthusiasm for the idea.

I've been trying to forget that it will soon be my twenty-eighth birthday. I don't feel like celebrating. What exactly in my life there is to celebrate, I really don't know. But it's expected that each year there will be some extravaganza when each of us achieves the threshold of another year. The art of survival is marked in this way, the passing of time ritualised by getting mindless in the company of cheap wine, good hash, loud music and a houseful of inebriated friends. To become oblivious for a brief while to the fact of ageing seems a necessary antidote to the passing of years.

'I don't feel much like a party at the moment, but I suppose I have to,' I acquiesce.

'Yes, you do. It'll cheer you up. We can ask everyone to bring some spare men along – you never know – Mister Special might just turn up, get you to stop thinking about creepy-eddie.'

I have to laugh. She's right about the cheering up but not about the man. I want to stay well away from relationships for a while. They just aren't working for me.

'Okay. You win, as usual. But you must help to plan it.'

'Course I will. I love all that shopping and stuff.' Emms is positively glowing with anticipation. 'Are you coming up to join us? Supper's nearly ready and guess what – Matt's cooking! Now that's an occasion not to be missed.'

'Oh no! Do I have to?' I groan and clutch my stomach. 'Last time he cooked I thought my intestines had been scoured out with a brillo pad.'

'Don't worry. Jez has been supervising him.'

'Alright then. I'll just tidy up and be with you all in a sec.'

I turn back to survey my painting as Emms clatters up the stairs, long skirt and silk scarves flowing after her. There is a quality of light coming through that intrigues me, right at the bottom of the picture. You have to go down through all the layers to find it. Illumination – emerging into the light after a long downward journey. I am puzzled. It evokes a feeling I don't recognise, a point on the path I haven't yet reached. My hand has run ahead of me and I sway between hope and disbelief. I'm reluctant to open to this new feeling. It's bound to desert me in the end, like everything I have ever treasured.

I feel the tug of memory pulling me back from this edge, this new feeling, this intimation of light. At least the memories are known. I feel some reassurance in their familiarity. They won't desert me, they will always be with me.

Seven

The north-east – 1970

I was sitting on a chair with hard wooden slats across the seat, the paint peeled off and metal legs rusting, idly stirring my soda with a pink and white striped paper straw. My bare feet made little circles in the dusting of sand that covered the stone floor.

The windows all around the café opened out onto the promenade where a few holidaymakers had ventured. Most of them stayed at the other end of the bay, near the Spanish City with its whitewashed dome and cornucopia of entertainment and vice. It must have been the Paisley fortnight. Scottish holidays were staggered so that the English seaside towns would not be overrun by warring factions – Glasgow, Edinburgh, then Paisley – as the inhabitants descended on the nearest resorts over the border. Whitley Bay was a favourite destination.

I watched as a family, burnt lobster-red and squabbling, struggled under windscreens, blankets, lilos and other beach paraphernalia, to migrate to a still sunny spot on the beach. As my friends sat in the Rendezvous chatting about their summer holidays, about boys and clothes and the films they had seen, I found myself on the edge of the circle – not an outsider but not quite part of it either. I found it hard to join in the conversation. Words came too slowly, if they came at all, and I missed the moment to speak.

No-one mentioned what had happened, at least not while I was there. It's better not to dwell on it, Nancy had said – better to focus your mind on other things – you'll get over it more quickly. She didn't talk about it. Nobody did. For Lucy and Sara, sharing the horror of that day perhaps made it a little more bearable – it had drawn them closer. They sat together on a bench by the window.

Amy was talking about her family holiday in Cornwall, an exotic destination for us. Most people from the north didn't travel so far, but Amy's father ran his own car sales business and had become quite rich from it.

'There's these fantastic sandy coves. You have to climb over rocks to get there, so there's no one else around. Me and me sister had just taken our clothes off…'

'All yer clothes? Cheeky things,' piped in Jo.

'We were about to go skinny-dipping when this gang of boys popped up from behind the rocks – out of nowhere, like. A grabbed me dress but Judy was already running down to the sea,' Amy recounted, trying to impress us with her story.

'If they're anything like the lads round here, they'd have no idea what to do with a naked girl on a beach,' quipped Mags, the more worldly-wise amongst us. People said she'd had sex with loads of blokes.

I dragged my attention from the promenade to the soda, then back to the conversation. What were they saying? A naked girl on the beach. Did the girl know the tides could be dangerous?

'So what happened then?' asked Jo.

'Well, Judy wouldn't come out of the water when she saw the boys there. So A started throwing stones at them. They were just kids, y'know, 'bout twelve or so, and when A came hurtling at them with a handful of rocks they scarpered,' she declared triumphantly.

There were gasps of appreciation from some of the girls. Mags looked sceptical but kept her doubts to herself.

'Is anyone going to the Highcliffe this weekend?' Sally asked.

A chorus of affirmations followed and arrangements were made to meet outside the club before the dance began. I wouldn't go with them. I couldn't bear to see someone else on stage, singing and playing guitar as Richard had done that night. This was where I had met the photographer who had precipitated our argument. If I had never met Mark, I would have gone on the holiday and maybe I would have drowned with Richard. Or he might not have gone in the sea that morning if I had been there. Or perhaps I could have saved him. I wasn't sure whether to feel angry towards the unsuspecting Mark for coming between Richard and me, or grateful to him for saving my life. I couldn't face engaging with such a tangled confusion of feelings, were I to meet him again.

The following week school would begin and I dreaded returning to a life without Richard by my side. Last year he had walked me home each evening, with his arm around my waist and my hand tucked into his back trouser pocket. We had cuddled up together in an armchair in our living room and talked, or sat on his mother's kitchen floor and sung songs while he strummed his guitar. Now and then we had sneaked into my room, when Nancy wasn't around, and listened to records.

This autumn I would walk home by myself. I would listen to my music alone.

'It is with deep sadness that I have to announce the death of one of our sixth-form pupils, Richard Kerr. He died tragically in a swimming accident during the summer holidays,' said the headmaster at assembly on the first morning, leaving a respectful pause before continuing. 'On behalf of all the staff, I offer my deepest sympathy to his family and friends.' Another long pause. 'Richard was a bright and very capable young man, much liked by both staff and students. He showed great potential…'

'Where's Anita?' whispered a girl in the row in front of me. She and her friend turned to look for me. Again, the scream that had lodged somewhere deep inside leapt into my throat, but stuck there. My knees trembled then locked rigid. I clenched my teeth and stared straight ahead to steady myself. The wise words the headmaster was offering about life and death and acceptance washed over me.

'I encourage you all to carry on, and do your best this term,' he concluded.

I felt so disconnected. What I felt inside and how I appeared on the outside had come completely adrift. The headmaster's words hovered in the air between us, not quite reaching me.

It was Mrs Sinclair, the small, round Polish woman who had been brought in to teach the German class, who seemed to see my inside self. A rumour had spread round the school that she had lost her husband and son in the war, and escaped by swimming down a river with Nazi bombs dropping behind her. It seemed she had lost her Polish name too. The class treated her with some respect, just in case this terrible story was true.

'Where have you been, Anita?' Mrs Sinclair asked. I'd been staring absently out of the window, lost in my private world. 'A dark place, I think.' She looked at me with tired eyes and a half smile that said – 'I know that place too.' There was an unspoken understanding between us, for I felt more like a seventy-year-old widow than a seventeen-year-old girl on the threshold of life. I knew things only the old should know and Mrs Sinclair was the one person who understood this.

In the art studio I found some solace. The sharp smell of paint and white spirit, mixed with traces of clay dust and the sweet scent of wood shavings, greeted me as I entered the light filled room. The mess of piles of paper, sketches and paintings strewn over walls, tables and easels – paints and brushes everywhere – rows of fired pots on shelves along the walls – odd experimental sculptures propped up in corners – this was my haven.

Here I could I absorb myself in painting and escape from the reality of life for a while. My landscapes and seascapes became more abstract, everything submerged under a blue-green wash, smudged, as if under water. Or expanses of dark and barren land, dead trees – only the rocks seemed to have life, movement, as if they could reach up out of the canvas. My portraits became increasingly unrecognisable as they grew more contorted and complex – Baconesque, the teacher remarked as he studied the figures with shadows for eyes and pale luminous folds of skin enveloping twisted bodies.

'Anita, you have a real talent. Don't ever stop painting. You're really finding your own voice now.' I thought 'voice' was a strange way to describe the art of painting. My voice had been silenced. I couldn't speak of what was inside me and so I painted instead, but I liked Mr Kingsley and was secretly pleased at his words.

Kip, we called him, because he had once been caught napping in the art studio after lunch. Or perhaps it was because his father smoked kippers at Craster. Only the teachers we liked were given nicknames. Kip was one of us, with his long hair, faded jeans and tie-dyed shirts. The sixth formers sometimes met him at the pub, along with the handsome new maths teacher and the geography teacher who was also a folk singer. It was considered cool to be out socialising with the young teachers.

Most of the other teachers were ribbed rotten by the class – taunted, ridiculed and disobeyed. A few had nervous breakdowns sooner or later. Others soldiered wearily on until retirement.

I would find just enough to sustain me, as I too soldiered on.

Best of all, I found a new friend. She arrived late to the first art class of term and came to sit in the empty seat next to me.

'What you painting?' she asked.

'Don't know yet. I'm just painting,' I replied, staring at the streaks of black and brown that I had smeared over the page.

I felt angry and lost. The vivid images that used to come so readily had vanished.

'I like it,' she said, and I do believe she meant it.

'Are you joining this class, then?'

'Yep, I guess so. I'm Terri – short for Teresa, but that sounds too Christian, like a saint or something.'

At that point Kip came over and pointed out that she was late and paper and paints had already been given out. She'd have to help herself.

'That's okay,' Terri said. 'I don't feel like painting today. I'll just watch.'

'You can't just watch,' Kip said. 'You're here to learn to paint, and if you can already paint, to paint better.'

'Why not, if that's what I want to do?' she replied, with the sweetest of smiles on her face. I was soon to learn that Terri was a free spirit. Kip, who she would twist around her purple-varnished little fingernail, was to learn this too. She made a point of not doing what she was asked to do and frequently got into trouble. We became best friends.

I imagined her home to be interesting, Bohemian, and was surprised, on my first visit, to discover that this was far from the truth. We briefly greeted her parents who were watching TV in the lounge. Her father was an accountant and wore a grey cardigan, white shirt, maroon striped tie, and black shoes polished to a shine, even at home. Her mother was something important on the church committee – she wore a neat twin-set in pastel pink and spent much of her time out, attending to 'church business'.

We ignored her younger brother who skulked behind the dining-room door, peering at us as we ran upstairs to Terri's room. Like my bedroom, it was a cosy den cluttered with teenage paraphernalia and decorated with surrealist paintings and pop-star posters. We shared a love of Blake's poems and Milton's *Paradise Lost*. The images of Heaven and Hell depicted by the poets crept into our paintings with increasing garishness.

Terri's work was full of the grotesque and the outlandish – a subterranean world of weirdness and wonder.

In a blocked-up fire-place she had created an altar with candles, a battered copper bowl, three specially chosen tarot cards and some strange metal objects that she had picked up from second-hand market-stalls, all laid out carefully on a purple satin cloth.

We had decided to hold a séance in this unholy shrine. I'm not sure whose idea it had been – it seemed to emerge unbidden during a meandering conversation and ricocheted between us, as if a hidden force were compelling it to grow. For Terri, it would be an adventure into the other world. For me, a desperate attempt to bring Richard back.

In Terri I found a kindred spirit, another troubled soul who was searching – for the elusive, the mysterious, the impossible. There was a restlessness about her that was strangely comforting. With her nearby, I didn't fear falling into the abyss that constantly threatened me. She leapt into every terror her mind could conjure up and came through exhilarated. I followed. We both closed off all thoughts of propriety or risk, and flew. In this way, constantly moving in the wake of her indomitable quest, I could escape the awful sense of falling.

That night our quest would take us to the edge of reason. We would challenge death. Ritual was required.

First Terri cut some white card into small rectangles and placed each one with great care, as if the card itself were infused with magic properties, onto a low table in the centre of the room. I wrote the letters of the alphabet, one on each card, and laid them in a circle near the edge of the table. I pressed hard with the pen to stop my hand from trembling. Working in silence, sitting cross-legged on the floor on opposite sides of the table, we forged a crack between the worlds where the spirits of the dead might enter.

Then we lit twelve candles and placed them around us in a wide circle on the floor. 'The circle creates a protected and sacred space', Terri explained, as she lit the last candle. 'The candles are to ward off evil and invite in the spirits.'

I shuddered. What were we about to invoke? A wave of fear set my spine tingling and my stomach churning, but my longing to speak with Richard was so strong that I pushed these feelings down. I turned off the electric light. Candlelight and shadow leapt and flickered up the walls and across the ceiling. The room had been transformed into a place where magic could happen. Where anything at all might happen.

The scene was set, the circle in place. Terri brought out a wine glass from her bedside cupboard and placed it upside-down in the centre, with the letters radiating around it. The pieces of white card glowed in the semi-darkness. The glass was reflected faintly in the table's polished surface and light from the twelve candles struck its rounded edge, glinting like twelve orbiting moons.

'Have you done this before?' I asked in a hushed voice.

'No, never, but I know how it works.'

We sat quietly for a while, summoning the spirits who might want to speak with us.

'We can't control that. They'll only come if they want to, if they have something to say to us.' She sounded confident, an expert at this game even though it was her first try. 'Then we place the forefinger of our right hand on the base of the glass, our finger-tips touching, like this.' She showed me the correct placing. 'Then we wait.'

'How long will we have to wait?' My voice had lowered to a whisper. It felt rude to ask such mundane questions when the spirits might already be present but I felt nervous. I couldn't tell what frightened me most – that the spirits, Richard's spirit, would come and speak to me, or that he would not come at all.

'Depends. Sooner or later we'll feel the glass being pulled towards a letter. We just let it happen. And that's all. Simple, isn't it.' Terri looked pleased. She was eager to begin.

I felt the tug of fear in my belly again, but the aching

desire to make contact with Richard was growing stronger. I surrendered to the will of the ouija board.

We sat in the soft glow of candlelight, so quiet we could hear each other's breath. Our fingertips touched at the centre of the up-turned glass. The anticipation was so alive it set the air vibrating. We waited, and we waited. For a long time, nothing happened and I began to oscillate between despair and relief.

Eventually, just as Terri had described, we felt the glass begin to pull beneath our fingers. The power was irresistible. Our hands followed the glass as it meandered – left, right, across a little, until it finally settled on the letter A. Then a little more pushing and pulling before it came to rest on B. Then C.

'I think it's just testing us out, checking it's all working alright,' whispered Terri as she caught my disappointed expression. 'We should focus on what we want to know, who we want to hear from.'

I concentrated harder. The glass continued to move through the alphabet. It got all the way to N. Then suddenly it was racing across the board from letter to letter, zipping confidently this way and that. Our fingers glued to the base of the glass, we had no choice but to follow. The glass was spelling out a string of words.

I AM SORRY – HAD TO GO – YOU HAD TO STAY

I was taken aback. My heart began pounding, blood throbbing in my ears, and my eyes opened wide in disbelief. Could it be? Could this really be Richard, reaching out to me as I had dreamt he would? My longing to reach out and touch him had embedded itself as a constant and painful ache in my heart. And now here he was. After a moment's hesitation, just long enough for a flicker of fear to rise up and subside, I regained my equilibrium and entered the dialogue, as if this were the most natural thing in the world to be doing.

'But why, why did you have to go?' I asked silently, so only Richard could hear.

After a long time of shifting a little this way, then that, as if undecided how to reply, the glass finally found direction. Slowly it spelt out the words –

HAD TO BE THIS WAY

'But why, why?'

YOU THERE – ME OVER HERE – WORK TO BE DONE

I was torn between tears of joy and of sorrow. There was something I really needed to know. 'Did I hurt you? Is that why you left?'

I LOVE YOU – NO HARM

Then the glass ripped across the board, dragging our hands with it as it careered from side to side, out of control.

GFHSNIEFKT – YYWRT – OMANBEFHTO – WHGFIV

We both gasped and jerked our hands away after several minutes in the grip of this madness.

'Wow, a bit scary that last bit,' said Terri.

'Yes.' I was shaken but I tried not to show it. I was so happy to have heard from Richard – I would suffer the madness of the ouija board if this was what it took to be with him again, even for just one small moment. 'Yes, the last bit was, but wasn't it amazing.' My heart was beating fast and furious, my palms moist with sweat.

We sat quietly for several moments, staring at the table, the letters, the candlelight dancing across it all. The glass, which now stood motionless off to the side of the board where we had broken contact with it, near to K, was just an ordinary up-turned glass again. The twelve candles still flickered around us as we sat, transfixed.

'Did you understand it?' asked Terri after a while. She knew about Richard but hadn't known him personally, and my relationship with him was not something we had ever talked about. She didn't share this part of my life.

'Yes. I think so. We must do it again sometime – if you want to, that is.' The tremor of fear was still coursing through my body, but it was edged with a feeling of excitement that exactly matched Terri's expression.

'Yep, I'm up for it. I couldn't believe it at first – it was so powerful. Let's do it again next week.' Terri's enthusiasm was as unbounded as mine, though for different reasons. Terri just loved *experience* – the stronger and more weird the better. So the pact was sealed and weekly séances became part of life, for a while at least.

The next time we consulted the ouija board it seemed secretive.

DOCTOR SPOCK, it finally told us.

'What's that about?' I asked.

'My brother's watching *Star Trek* downstairs. It must be picking up the signal. Weird. A kind of interference, I guess,' Terri said. Nothing more intelligible came through from the spirit world that night.

The next time we tried calling up the spirits there were long streams of letters, an occasional word, nothing I could grasp hold of. And the next time.

I didn't hear from Richard again. But I kept going, kept hoping. The promise of one more sweet moment of contact kept me seeking, week after week. Hope kept me going.

Part II

Forbidden truths

Eight

The north-east – 1970

Nancy closed the lounge door, sank into her chair by the fire and dropped her head wearily into her hands. She sighed.

'Are you alright, Nancy?' I glanced up from my book. I didn't really need to ask – I knew how Nancy was. The lifeline that kept her going had worn dangerously thin, just as mine had. I was desperate to hear from Richard again but the ouija board remained silent.

'Oh, I'm okay. Just tired,' she replied, predictably.

It had been eight months since my father had become ill, and she had done her utmost to nurse him back to health. Eight months of worrying about him, praying for him, cleaning him, dressing him, preparing those fussy meals, the endless hospital visits and sleepless nights. And now this. Nothing in the world could have prepared us all for the shock of Richard's death. When Nancy talked about the long nights of her childhood spent huddled in the air-raid shelter, or the news of a distant cousin or the son of a neighbour 'lost in action', I could see that none of it had penetrated her carefully circumscribed world so sharply, so indiscriminately as the tragedy that was now tearing our small family apart.

With her own immanent loss pounding at the membranes of her heart, Nancy had little left inside that might help her be with my own grief. I could feel this, so I expected little. I could feel how thin her resilience had worn, and communication between us could snap at any moment. We existed side by side, each in our own world of silent sorrow.

It had never been easy between us. Nancy put it down to the loss of my mother. She thought my soul had been indelibly scarred, my personality crafted wilful, antagonistic, conflicted. Nancy would tell me this when she was cross and frustrated with me because I would not fit in with how she wanted me to be. To her, I was a ragged mix of exuberance, anger and despair, a wild flower plucked up and thrown to the wind. And she was right – thrown to the wind and of no use to anyone now.

By the time Nancy and my father married, and she moved into our family home, I was ten years old and canny enough to know just how to make her feel like the wicked step-mother of the fairy-tales. I had tried fiercely to preserve the close relationship I had with my father, and deeply resented the woman who was trying to take my mother's place. Of course, mother was little more than a fantasy. I imagined her as ever young and beautiful, as she was in the black and white photograph my father kept on his desk. She wore a summer-dress, gathered in at the waist to emphasise her figure. Her dark hair was brushed back and waved in the style of the day. She was smiling. I thought she looked like a film star. As a young child I had proudly told my school friends that they couldn't meet my mother because she was 'in the movies'.

Nancy could never compete with this and was resigned to her lowly status in my world. In recent years we had made some progress though.

My father stirred upstairs, accompanied by a fit of coughing. In the grate the fire was dying. Nancy threw in more coals and switched on the television. It was all she could do to keep the fire burning and attend to the daily tasks of running a home.

I curled up and returned to my book but I wasn't reading. I had overheard her speaking with Martin the evening before. They hadn't realised I could hear them from the dining room.

'Have you told Dad yet? I've been thinking about it a lot, and I think he should know. We should be able to talk to him about – about what's going to happen. He should be able to talk to us too,' Martin had said.

'The doctor says it's better not to. Best to keep his spirits up, be positive. There's no point upsetting him – the doctor thinks he might get depressed. He says people tend to get depressed and deteriorate very quickly if they're told,' Nancy had replied.

I had felt a dry and brittle sensation in my heart that spread out through my bones, into my muscles. I clenched my fingers into two tight fists. I must hold on.

'But don't you think he knows? Don't you think he's upset, depressed anyway, lying there in his bed day after day, in pain, alone? That's no life. We shouldn't be trying to preserve…just because we can't face…' said Martin, anger in his voice.

'No, he doesn't know. He talks of getting well, of what we'll do when he's strong enough to go out again. He speaks about travelling, seeing all the places in the world he's never seen before – the Pyramids, Machu Picchu, Kilimanjaro, the Himalayas. He wants to travel to all those special places. His eyes light up and he sounds so positive when he talks about them, about being well. He looks happy then. The doctor's right – hope keeps his spirits up.' I could hear the tremor in her voice. Martin would not be able to hang on to his anger if she was about to cry.

'But it's a lie, an illusion. He'll never do those things now. You know that. If we keep up this lie, we just isolate him. He can't talk about what's really important to him.' He was speaking softly now, as if pleading with Nancy. 'Does Anita know?' he asked after a moment's silence.

'No. I was going to tell her soon, but then this…oh Martin, how can I possibly tell her now?' Nancy had gasped for breath.

My heart was lurching in my chest. Panic was rising. What did they mean? What had they not told me? I was sure I did not want to know. I had pulled a big heavy door over their words. I had left the question in the dark.

But now, as we sat in the living room at the end of a long and bleak day, listening to my father coughing in his bed upstairs, I wondered if she was about to tell me.

She wasn't. So I painted a web of denial and tried to believe I had heard nothing.

2

It was early October and autumn was in the air. A crisp wind blew off the sea and the first leaves to turn were glistening, burnished gold in the sun. Here in the north-east winter came more quickly than in other parts and Martin was looking forward to returning south to Bristol. He had put it off for too long already.

Today he had been excited all morning. For his twenty-first birthday Nancy and father were buying him a motor-bike and this was the day he was to collect it from the garage. Father had hesitated on safety grounds, but didn't have the strength to object after Martin had convinced him of all the advantages. He had, after all, been riding around Bristol on an old bike for some time now, until it finally broke down for good. He convinced them that a Harley Davidson would be much safer than that old wreck of a machine.

'That boy could have been a great lawyer. What a waste,' father had said, as he and Nancy discussed the matter. They both sighed, smiled indulgently, and gave in to Martin's persuasion.

It was nearly three in the afternoon when he roared up at the front gate on the shiny black and chrome machine, skidding to a stop on the gravel. I ran out to greet him. Martin was rosy-cheeked from the biting wind and the sheer pleasure of the ride.

'Wow, it's great,' I called over the rough purr of the engine. 'Can I have a ride. Please can I have a ride?'

'Course you can, sis'. Let's get you some gear.' Martin enjoyed trying on his new macho persona.

'Thanks, bro'. I've never been on a bike before. Let's go on a long ride, right out into the country. Can we?' I begged.

'Your wish is my command.' Martin pulled off his helmet and swept it towards the ground in a gesture of gallantry. I guess he was so relieved to see me smiling again, even for just one moment, that today he would grant me anything I wished. Reflected in his broad smile I could feel a hint of my old spirit returning. Always ready for a challenge, I would insist on tagging along when he and his friends, years older than me and twice as tall, would set off for long bike rides up the coast. He didn't mind. I kept up and never complained, though my spindly legs would be exhausted by the end of the day.

We scurried around the house seeking out the warmest, toughest clothes we could find for me to wear, then downed a cup of coffee and a sandwich hastily prepared by Nancy. The ceremonial fitting of helmets complete, we straddled the bike and were out of the driveway with a roar and another spray of gravel across the lawn. I clutched Martin's leather-clad chest, partly out of fear of falling off but mainly from the rush of excitement that caught my breath as we gathered speed.

'Lean into the bends.' He yelled over his shoulder as I struggled to stay upright. Leaning into the bends defied every natural instinct in my body and the road came much too close for comfort, but soon I got the hang of it. We wove through the outskirts of the town then let loose when we reached the A1 heading up north. For long moments the wind whipped my breath away. I gasped for air, seeking a place to tilt my face into, where it would still for long enough to allow me a lungful. I held tighter to Martin's leather jacket. This must be the opposite of drowning – the emptiness tearing at the delicate tissue of my lungs, rather than the pressure of water flooding in and overwhelming the subtle rhythms of blood and breath (I had tried to imagine it many times) – but both would bring a moment of panic as the need for oxygen became intense.

I was terrified and ecstatic at the same time. I laughed each time I found a pocket of air to gulp. Martin was singing a crazy song. He was 'easy rider', hero of the open road.

On our right – through the hedgerows beginning to thin out as they shed their first leaves, and out over the open fields – glimpses of sea, fishing villages and grand ruined castles whipped by. The Northumbrian coast – England's best-kept secret, as it was known to the locals. You could drive through the narrow lanes near the coast, even at the height of summer, and rarely meet another car. The cold north-easterly winds kept the crowds away from the pristine beaches. In my mind the other secret this coast held, besides the sheer beauty of the place, was the bloated face of a young man lying on the seabed. The vision followed me everywhere. It burrowed its way into my paintings and surfaced through my dreams.

On our left the majestic hills began to roll into view. Vistas of heather and bracken-covered moorland, craggy outcrops and wooded valleys – a flood of memories lifted my heart a note. Now it was my turn to sing.

'Well, I've been a wild rover for many a year…'

'And it's no, nay, never – no, nay, never no more…' Martin joined in as I reached the chorus. We both laughed, remembering happy weekends spent with our father, hiking over the hills and bedding down in the evenings at one of the youth hostels that trailed all the way up to the Cheviots. Songs round the fire in the evening, listening to the adventures of other walkers, playing cards – but most of all, the joy of spending precious time with our father who was never happier than on these trips. He loved the hills. His soul was rooted deep in their peat-laced moorlands and broad, bare crests. Cheviot – the very word conjured up a feeling of windswept vistas and unbounded freedom. Martin and I had grown to share his passion for the Northumbrian hills.

Nancy had stayed at home during these excursions, leaving us to enjoy these rare moments together. This was partly out of sensitivity for our need to spend time with our father, who was working much of the time, but mainly because she preferred shopping, lunching with friends, or just relaxing at home, to getting cold, wet, lost and exhausted on a barren, mist shrouded hillside.

We rode all the way up to the market town of Rothbury, nestled into the Coquet valley just beneath the purple ridge of the Simonside crags. By the time we stopped my body was frozen into position. We both laughed as I staggered off the bike and tried to walk, knees bent and legs splayed out wide. In our childhood games of 'Cowboys and Indians' I had always been the Indian. Now my gait marked me as the Cowboy, always the victorious one in our play. I swaggered towards Martin, lunging out with a stiff gloved hand. He caught it mid-sweep and pretended to wrestle me, lifting me off the ground and swinging me around.

'That was wild!' I gasped, once I was safely on the ground again. 'But I'm absolutely frozen.'

'Let's have a drink and thaw out – this is one of my favourite country pubs.' Martin took my helmet and ushered me towards The Queens Head. The light from its windows glowed warm and inviting.

A hint of evening had crept across the sky and an early autumn chill was in the air. Inside, we were glad to find a fire had been lit, and settled ourselves at a table nearby. The pub was empty except for a couple of locals, farming men I guessed, occupying their customary stools by the bar. Martin bought drinks while I warmed my hands over the fire.

He returned with two glasses and two bottles of Newcastle Brown Ale, and immediately set about analysing the performance of the bike. The technical details passed me by but his enthusiasm was infectious and I listened as if enthralled by the workings of a two-stroke engine.

'Sorry you got so cold though. I'll have to get some proper leathers.'

I tried to smile, but I knew he was thinking of Leticia as he said this. It would be Leticia, not me, who would need the leathers, who would be riding with Martin in future. As I dropped my head and lowered my eyes, he noticed my change of mood.

'Hey, what's up? Are you okay?'

It was a struggle to put my feelings into words. I didn't want to end the fun, but more serious concerns were pressing at the borders of my awareness again.

'It's just that you'll be gone again soon, and I'm going to miss you. It's good having you around. I don't know how I'm going to manage on my own.' Tears pricked at the back of my eyes.

'You won't be alone. Nancy's here. And – and Dad. And you can always call me, anytime. I'm still here for you, even if I'm miles away. You know that, don't you?'

'Yes, I do, but it's not the same.' We both fell silent, lost in thought. After a few long moments, I gathered courage.

'What about Dad? Do you think he's going to get better? Nancy keeps saying he's improving, but I don't see it. Tell me honestly – what do you really think?' I was looking at my hands as I spoke. They rested on the table, my fingers lightly holding the half-empty glass as if it could warm them. The fire in the grate shot out a few sparks as the logs settled. The pub was beginning to fill and the broad accents of locals greeting each other could be heard at the other end of the bar. Cigarette smoke thickened the air with its acrid smell.

Martin held his breath. His shoulders tightened. This was a moment we had both been dreading, a moment of truth that we must share before he returned to Bristol.

His silence spoke worlds. I knew, and yet I needed to hear it said.

'I'm so sorry, Anita. He's not going to get better. He's dying.'
We both reached for the other's hand. A tear rolled down my
cheek.

'I thought so,' I whispered. My father, too, would leave me.

Casablanca was just coming to an end when we arrived home.
Father and Nancy were sitting on the settee, holding hands, as
the film moved towards its final scene. I hesitated by the door
while Martin threw himself into an armchair. We waited until
the film credits began.

'How was it?' Nancy asked, peeling her dreamy eyes away
from the small black and white screen.

'Brilliant!' said Martin, grinning and bright eyed. 'Thanks,
both of you. It's really brilliant.'

I was about to speak, but instead went to my father and
wrapped my arms around his neck. 'I love you.' I whispered, so
that only he could hear. Then I turned back to the door. 'I'm
tired. I think I'll go straight to bed. 'Night everyone. Thanks
Martin – you're a hero,' I called over my shoulder as I left the
room.

I caught Nancy looking at Martin with a question in her
eyes. He took a deep breath, nodding his head back slightly.
His gaze gave nothing away, yet the defiant jut of his chin told
everything. In the silent gesture Nancy would read, 'Yes, I have
told her that our father is dying'.

3

The cold winds of autumn were now battering the coast. All
traces of holidaymakers had long since gone, and the beach
and cliff walks were thankfully returned to the locals. The
town seemed deserted after the six-week summer invasion. Big
steel-grey clouds scudded across a dark blue sky and eddies
of brown leaves whipped around my feet as I hurried home

from school. Shrubs in the gardens whipped against walls and fences, as if angry at this change of ambiance. I kicked at the piles of fallen leaves and sent them hurtling back into the air.

'Hello Anita. How was your day?' Nancy greeted me as I flung my satchel onto the kitchen floor and dropped into the wicker chair by the boiler. The smell of baking bread wafted out a welcome but it didn't disperse the chill that had seeped into my bones.

'I'm tired. Think I'm getting a cold or something. Can I take tomorrow off?' I sank more deeply into the chair.

'Anita, it's only two weeks since you went back after your last "cold". You can't keep missing school like this.'

'But I don't feel well.'

'No wonder you don't feel well. You've been out late every night this week. And that coat you're wearing is far too thin for this time of year. What did I tell you?' replied Nancy.

'You never understand, do you,' I retorted. 'You think I'm just making it up. Well, I'm not. I feel awful.'

'Now let's not have another row about it – we'll see how you are in the morning – if you get a good night's sleep you might feel better.' Nancy turned to the pile of books by the window. 'I'll see if I can find something for your cold.' She found her Annie Gilchrist's Home Remedies book and began scouring through for the right herbal concoction.

'Ah, here we are. Why don't you go and rest by the fire and I'll make this up for you – I think I've got all the ingredients.' I did as I was told, for once.

'What's in it?' I asked, wrinkling up my nose as Nancy handed me the foul-smelling potion a few minutes later.

'Honey, ginger – raw onion, mustard and garlic,' Nancy reeled off, as if apologising for the last three ingredients. 'Go on try it. It'll do you good. At least it can't do any harm,' she added hopefully.

'Nancy, you're a witch! Are you trying to poison me?' But I drank the potion, which tasted every bit as bad as it smelt, and settled back into the settee to rest as Nancy prepared tea. I felt too weary to argue with anything at all.

Once again, I had adopted the ritual of taking my father's tea up to him, but it wasn't the pleasant task it had been in the spring and early summer. I knocked gently on his door and entered, balancing the tray precariously on one arm. He beckoned me in with a feeble wave of his hand. How thin he had become. His skin looked like yellowed parchment, old and dry, stretched over bones that were thin and delicate, as if the disease was sculpting them into a new and more ethereal form – preparing him for the next life.

He had always been strong. I remembered those muscular arms being readied for work as he rolled up his sleeves each weekend and prepared to build, or mend, or dig, or paint – whatever needed his capable hand. Now they hung, fleshless and useless, at his side, like the scrawny legs of an injured bird. My father was just fifty years old but he looked like an old man of a hundred or more. How could that be? How did it happen? Having cancer must be like having a black monster inside you, eating your body away, just like the monster that was eating away at my mind. I shuddered and pushed the thought aside.

'How was school today?' he asked, as he had done every day since these evening rituals began.

'It was okay. The art class was good – we're painting a big mural for the hall, the whole class together. It's fun working on something as a group, but some of the boys mess around. One of them really can't paint at all – Colin – he just takes photographs,' I added scornfully. Until the words came out, I hadn't been aware of the contempt I felt towards the unremarkable Colin. Despite the obvious lack of resemblance – Colin was fat and his face potted with acne – he had reminded me of Mark, the photographer who had seduced me away from

Richard and the fateful holiday? Even more than I resented Colin, I resented the unbidden rising of memory from such an unlikely source.

I pushed the feeling away and returned briefly to my enthusiasm for the project, devised by Kip of course. 'It's a city scene, but you see all the elements of nature that went into making it – like taking the city apart and painting all the wood and stone and metal from the earth that went into building it. It's kind of impressionist so you don't see everything in precise detail – the general effect is nice, I think.'

'Sounds interesting.' We both knew he was being polite, but that didn't matter. 'What does the head think of it?'

'Oh, he'll be the last to see it! It'll be a surprise – unveiled at the Christmas dinner. I can imagine his face though!'

We shared a brief, a rare moment of laughter, then fell silent. He began to eat the boiled fish and steamed vegetables, while I sat on the edge of the bed twisting the edge of my navy-blue school cardigan into knots.

I could feel him looking at me as I studied the crumpled hem, a frown creasing my brow. He reached out and touched my cheek with his fingertips – so light, so dry, like smoke, or the brush of a spirit passing by.

'When did my little girl's chubby cheeks fall away to show these lovely cheekbones?' he mused, as if speaking to himself. He touched my chin, the curve of my jaw where it made a soft angle above my neck. He was looking into the hollow at the root of my throat, that place where breastbone touches the tips of collarbones. His gaze looked right through me, as if I were transparent, as if he were looking at something beyond me. 'Ah, Ellen – how I loved this part of you. "We were always meant to be winged creatures," your collarbones seemed to say.' He dropped his hand and closed his eyes.

'Dad, it's me, Anita,' I said quietly.

'I'm sorry, love. Of course it's you. My little girl, who has become a young woman without me even noticing – a beautiful woman, like her mother, graceful, elegant even. What happened to those rosy cheeks and skinny little legs?' I had never heard him speak like this before and I felt shy, awkward.

He brought his fingers up to touch my face again. He held the angle of my chin between his thumb and first finger, the way he used to when I was a small child. 'D'you remember how I would hold you like this, to check you had brushed your teeth before bed? I felt I was holding a heart in my hand, a flower opening up,' he said, his eyes misting over.

'Yes, and I would stick my tongue out at you and laugh, and you would pretend to be shocked.' It was one of those silly games we played. He called me his little red pixie.

'You were always so small, but strong too. Not in the way that Ellen was strong, but still, in your own way…I don't know who you got such a slender body from. Not from me. Not from Ellen, who had the robustness of deep mountain roots and windswept moors. She had courage and daring. Her face was open and full, her auburn hair a cascade of waves that glinted in the subtlest of light. Even at night, with nothing more than starlight to reflect her, Ellen shone.' He was looking through me again. Seeing Ellen, my mother, as if she stood behind me. He was speaking a love poem to her.

'Dad?'

'Sorry, love. The past seems so much more present than the present is these days.' He made an effort to focus on me again. 'I always tried to keep you safe, stop you from falling, keep you out of danger, but I failed. I'm so sorry.'

I could see myself as if reflected in his eyes. I had fallen from his grasp and broken. Now he could only lie here helplessly and marvel at what kept me going. My chest had hollowed, my shoulders rounded over, trying to do what he had failed to do – to protect my heart from further injury. Would I have the resilience to bounce back from it all, or would I crawl deeper into myself and stay there? Since Richard's death I had become like an empty vessel, my substance scoured out.

'It's alright, Dad. You did everything you could for me. It's not your fault.' I took his hand and we sat in silence for a while.

'How have you been today?' I finally broke the spell, secretly dreading the response.

'Oh, pretty much the same.' He shifted in the bed, pulling himself out of his reverie. 'I went down for an hour or so in the morning and we looked through some catalogues – Nancy likes to start her Christmas shopping early, you know.' It was painful for him to have nothing of any account to share, and heart-breaking for me to know this. I felt it would be cruel to say more about my own day, when his had been so sparse. The one thing we really needed to speak about – the forbidden thing – spread like a thick swamp between us, engulfing any further conversation. I sat quietly for a while longer as he ate, then awkwardly excused myself.

As autumn turned to winter, my father became weaker. At night, as I lay awake in bed, I would listen to his long rattling breaths from across the hallway. Then there would be an even longer pause, a silence that deepened with each second. Through the silences I would hold my own breath, counting – wondering if that had been his last. Then the long, rasping breath came, and for a moment I could relax my vigilant watch.

But the whole cycle would begin again. Each breath my father took was like a small death. With each lengthening silence, another drop of my spirit drained away, straining to be with him, to follow his own spirit as it teetered on a fragile thread between here and beyond. I knew the thread would break for him one day soon but, for now, he hung on.

Unlike Richard's passing, and my mother's – swift, brutal, unannounced – my father's was slow and torturous. But whichever way it came, death would be ruthless with each one of us. This I knew.

I was learning that it all comes to the same in the end.

Whatever we have done, however long, or happy, or tragic a life it has been, we all end up here on this threshold, this sliver of a thread that holds us to life or releases us from it. It's a miracle that each breath follows the next for any of us. The miracle, the strange, impossible reality is that we go on living at all, breath after breath, not that we die in the end.

I tried to hold my own breath, to keep in time with his, but I couldn't hold out long enough. I would not follow him. My life would go on, and he would not be here to see me living it, to cheer me on, to pick me up when I stumbled as he had done all through my childhood. I held myself tightly and let the tears roll down my cheeks – silently, so as not to disturb our house of shadows.

Outside a dog barked in the distance. It was answered by another, echoing across the night, then a third, further away and faint. The soft swish of car tyres on a rain-wet road swept round the corner, then disappeared into silence. The sound of my father's breath came rattling down the hallway again.

The faintest hint of jasmine seemed to drift through the night air, as if my mother had just passed by, leaving a trail of scent behind her. Then came again the longing for her warm body, her soft embrace. And with it a vast and empty feeling, as if my very being were dissolving away until there was nothing left of me at all. Nothing but my grief. I was curling myself around it, seeking something I could touch and hold.

I began to recognise that this feeling had always been with me, in the background, but pervasive – long before Richard's death. There was the familiar sensation of falling, with no solid ground beneath me. No place to land. Richard's love had been so compelling. He would be my ground, my anchor. His love would always be there, I had believed. I would be safe with him. His death had brought these old, abandoned feelings pounding into consciousness.

★

I saw that my father's light was still on and the needle had stuck. There must have been a scratch in the vinyl and a staccato sequence of three notes kept repeating endlessly. I crept in to take the record off.

'Who's there?' came his muffled voice.

'It's me, Anita. I thought you were sleeping.'

He sank deeper into the bed, muttering to himself. 'I wish these thoughts would stop. Someone stop these damned thoughts.'

'What is it, Dad? What are you thinking about?'

'There's too much to juggle – it doesn't make sense – I can't see, I can't see. Life is rushing by yet nothing happens, nothing at all changes. There's too much to do. I can't just lie here all day. Help me. Help me.'

I felt desperate. I didn't know how to help him. Each day the net curtains fluttered in the morning breeze as the windows were flung open to air the room. Each evening, as the sun arrived on this side of the house, the curtains seemed to ripple more gently as dusk settled and the pink wash of the sky was gradually replaced by the lamplight in the corner of the room. Besides that, he was right – nothing changed in this dying world.

He welcomed the evening. It was easier to accept than the bustling, rising energy of morning. Autumn, too, had been welcome – the settling down, the drawing in. I know he had found the springtime unbearable, trapped in his room while everything outside was bursting with new life and promise. As he became thinner and strength drained from muscle and bone, I watched as his body was dragged down into the bed, as if it were quicksand sucking him into its airless grip.

'What's troubling you? You can tell me if you want to,' I encouraged him.

He startled, as if he had just noticed me. 'He's not good enough for you,' he said.

My breath faltered. I knew he had watched my relationship with Richard with mixed feelings. Of course, he was glad for my happiness, but underneath lurked a darker impulse that had the nagging, gnarled shape of something like envy. He tried to hide it but I could see how it gnawed away at him. I think he had envied our happiness. Perhaps he was jealous of the young man who was taking his daughter from him. I could imagine he had also been reminded of his own lost love – and life too, now that life had been curtailed. My relationship with Richard had been full of pain for him. Like spring, with its promise of new life, it only emphasised his own slow decline towards death.

'He's gone, Dad. Richard's not here anymore.' I couldn't resent his lack of sensitivity. The morphine had made him confused and he struggled to find a place for these feelings alongside the cacophony of memories that were endlessly bursting up, ripping through his once well-ordered thought processes. The days when he was too tired to read, or in too much pain, when even music or the chatter of the radio only irritated – these days and nights stretched out interminably.

'Isn't this how they describe Hell – suffering without end – no relief, no consolation at the end of it all?' he had asked me one day. I had no answer to that.

'I've never believed in God – I'm an atheist – but I know about Hell. Can there be Hell without a God to redeem it?' he had asked. I didn't know anymore. I had thought there was some kind of God. I had shared him with Richard. But now I only felt anger at a God I didn't even believe in. How could I answer my father's questions now?

'Oh yes, I'm sorry, Anita. He's gone. They've all gone.' His mind seemed to focus for a moment. 'The happy memories, they come bright and clear – my childhood, at least the good parts of it – those golden days with Ellen when we were in love, the babies being born, our few short years as a family.' A dry fit of coughing interrupted his flow. 'But, you see, each bright memory brings a shadow, a dark thought, a sad story that spoils the happiness. All that was good slips away, sooner or later. Then there's just an empty place for this torment to enter. Bad thoughts run after the good in endless cycles, and always banish the good in the end.'

I rested my head gently against his shoulder, careful not to cause pain by leaning my weight into him. I couldn't help him. He was slipping far beyond my reach. I felt his breath deepening and he relaxed a little into my contact.

'Anita, my little saviour. You were my comfort and joy – with your ribbons of curly red hair, your liquid blue eyes, your white translucent skin – you were like an angel to me. I remember you dancing in the sunlight in a green meadow by the Coquet river – how you twirled and twirled in your white pumps and yellow dress, laughing with the sheer pleasure of the movement and the bright summer day,' he reminisced. 'Do you remember that day, Anita?'

'I remember.'

After my mother died, he had poured so much love into me. He worked hard to bring us up, moving from ship's draughtsman to designer in an engineering company. When inspiration struck, and he found himself driven to develop his new idea for a bridge design, I sat on the floor beside him each evening, holding the ruler and set-square steady as he traced lines across the paper. His little helper – 'my design assistant', he called me, and I had felt so proud. I was eight then. He had achieved modest recognition for his innovation, enough to give some satisfaction and a promotion to senior designer in the company.

'Why is it that the joys of life are so short-lived, while the pain and suffering seem so enduring?' James spoke quietly to himself. I wondered if Ellen, from some far-away place, could hear him.

I held his hand. He closed his eyes and accepted the contact – surrendered for a moment to the softness that was buried deep inside. Men like my father don't show their tears but I could sense their presence in some secret place within.

'Would you like another record on?'

'Yes please. You choose something.' I put on Beethoven's *Moonlight Sonata*, one of his favourites.

'Thank you.' A weak smile stretched his pale, dry lips.

I smiled back and slipped silently out of the room, as if trying not to disturb a sleeping child, before my own tears began to fall. I knew he liked to listen to music alone – it was the one real pleasure left to him.

Before I closed the door, I glanced back to see him sink his head into the pillow, letting the melancholic chords of Beethoven's sonata penetrate to the secret place. He must have listened to this piece a thousand times, but it still moved him. I saw a tear fall down his hollow cheek. Crying to music was permissible for men like my father – the mark of a ripe and receptive soul – but he didn't like Nancy or me to see him like this. He still clung to his need to be strong for us.

Nine

London - 1981

I'm searching for something. I don't know what it is, or where to find it. It's not Eddie. Nor Jake. If it were inside me, surely I would know. There would be a flicker, an intimation, a reflection of some sort. But all I feel is the lack of something that seems not to exist at all.

Absentmindedly I squeeze a smudge of dark red paint onto my index finger. Its thick oily fume catches the back of my throat as I bring it to eye level. I study it more closely. Wet, shiny, the colour of blood. I smear it onto the canvas, a deep red arc slicing across the white space. A red gash around a white dove's throat.

A sudden blast of sound from upstairs startles me and sends paint squirting out of the tube and down my thumb. The Sex Pistols, a receptacle for Matt's anti-establishment anger. He loves them. I hate them. I prefer the music of the sixties, when life began, before it ended.

I scrape my oily red thumb over the canvas as the Pistols throb and grate viciously above my head. Matt's boots stomp across the kitchen floor in time to the beat. Surely he's not dancing! I rub the paint in, a swirl of colour in the centre of the empty white space. Then I squeeze more paint, all over my hand. Over both hands. I rub them together and the wetness squelches and my fingers are burning. I slam them onto the canvas, frantically rub and swipe the redness all over. A fire erupts, a volcano. A deep well in the red earth. I am angry and I hurt.

Ten

The north-east – 1970

Christmas was approaching and I wished I could take a strong pill that would send me to sleep for days, to sleep until it was all over. I dreaded the forced jolliness that would be expected – the tinsel and the pretence. Most of all I dreaded the memories that Christmas brought.

Last year I had been with Richard. The visit to his grandparents – walking along the ridge in the snow, hand in hand, then back for tea and his grandmother's mince pies by an open fire. They were so happy to see us together, proud of him, so sweet to me. They made me feel like a part of his family.

'Have another one love, go on.' Grandma, the laden plate in one hand and a large red teapot in the other, beamed at me out of a flushed round face. A smudge of flour streaked across her forehead. 'I know you girls, you think you have to starve yourselves to look pretty, but the boys like you any old way, don't they, love?' She turned towards Granddad and winked, her eyes full of mischief and the memory of delight.

Granddad nodded and smiled, lifting his china teacup in a toast to his plump little wife. 'To pretty girls.' We all laughed and raised our cups.

'So, what are you planning to do with yourself when you leave school, Anita?' Grandma asked in her soft Irish voice.

'I want to be an artist. At least I hope to go to art college, then – well, I'll have to see. It's all about luck, really.'

'And talent too!' Richard added. 'She's really good, you know. We'll have to bring some of your pictures along next time.' He smiled and squeezed my hand. How I had loved him in that moment – so supportive, so keen that his family accept me. And so handsome, with his face still bright from the cold wash of the snow and his hair dishevelled like a dark halo around his head. My angel, my dark-haired angel.

In preparation for the school Christmas dance all the sixth formers had been learning to dance – proper ballroom dances, like the waltz, the foxtrot, the cha-cha-cha. For six weeks leading up to Christmas, PE lessons saw us stumbling and twirling around the gym, girls and boys clutching onto each other with embarrassment or lust or bravado, depending on the nature of their connection. Occasional moments of tenderness and grace could be discerned too, amidst the general clumsiness and teenage acting out. I loved it. I felt so grown up.

When the big night came, I wore a beautiful pale green and silver dress that I had made myself, especially for the occasion, and tied my hair up. Richard had whirled me around the hall, speed and sheer force making up for what he lacked in grace. My feet barely touched the floor as I was spun and lifted on the crest of each waltzing wave. I had felt like a Hollywood star from those romantic wartime movies.

This year, the dress was left in its box at the back of a cupboard in my room.

Last year my father had still been well. We had a Christmas like all the others. For a brief time, Martin and I could imagine we were still children, revel in the excited anticipation, the days of treats and surprises and sheer indulgence. The fresh pine scent of the tree, the house full of lights and colourful paper-chain decorations that we had made when we were children, Nancy excelling with her Christmas dinner and hospitality – an atmosphere of warmth and security prevailed with the precise keeping of these family traditions.

This year, my father's mother would come to stay, as she always did. These days Granny heard little of what was being said but her sharp eye saw most things.

When our mother died, Granny had come to live with us. I remember her greeting us when we arrived home from school with a customary, 'Take your shoes off – don't want my clean floor getting all filthy again. Hey, don't leave your coat lying there Anita – hang it up properly.' Caring for two unruly youngsters at that time of her life was not what she had expected, or really wanted, but she had felt it her duty to help out. She could not abandon her darling son in his time of need, so she had packed up her small house – 'Just for a month or two, mind you' – rented it out, and moved in for the next eight years. That was until Nancy arrived, when she began to feel distinctly in the way, 'quite superfluous' she said.

Along with various bits and pieces of clothes and personal items that she might need, Granny had brought along her three clocks and placed them on the mantelpiece. One told the correct time – the one in the middle. The clock on the left was always ten minutes slow. The one on the right was ten minutes fast. If she wanted to know the 'right' time, she would add up the three times and work out the average.

The three clocks ticked loudly, each competing in its own distinct rhythm to create an oddly syncopated orchestration. This music was the accompaniment to my childhood. All that I had experienced during those years was set against this ticking background.

These days Granny lived in a nice home, cared for by nice people who made sure she was always dressed and clean and well fed – just as she had done for Martin and me all those years. It seemed only fair.

When Christmas Day arrived, I was glad that Aunt Maggie and Uncle Bert would be there too. I had fond memories of my father's only brother and his wife. They arrived promptly at noon. There were Christmas greetings and drinks all round. Gifts were exchanged. Martin played host while Nancy yo-yoed between the guests and the cooking turkey. I scrunched myself into an armchair with my knees tucked up under my chin, wearing a pair of old jeans and the chunky grey sweater Richard had lent me. I wrapped myself up in the salty-sweet smell of him and wished I could hibernate like the animals of the fields. It was the first Christmas I had not dressed up for.

Once the excitement had subsided, Bert went upstairs to see James. They would have lots to talk about – a whole lifetime of memories.

Maggie and Bert had carried the post-war years around with them like a badge of honour. By the late 1950s, when I was old enough to notice things about my aunt and uncle, they still took pride in the task of 're-building our country after the war'. Life was rationed – a little of this, a crumb of that. Pleasure was hard to find, so whenever it was stumbled across they would treasure it. They treasured each other too.

What Uncle Bert enjoyed most of all was his model train set. Behind a green door at the top of the stairs, in the dimly lit spare room of their small terraced house, it covered an enormous table that filled the whole space. He would spend hours there with his precious trains – starting, stopping, shunting, running, polishing, building. There were stations with neatly furnished platforms, shunting sheds, signals and signal boxes, level crossings, roads, bridges and a magnificent tunnel with grass and trees on top. The trains were a dignified maroon and gold, and even whistled.

I looked at my uncle with affection once we were all seated round the table. Metal-rimmed glasses clung snugly to the end of his nose and grey wisps of hair swept back to reveal a receding hairline. I remembered him as he was in my childhood, studying the routes and sidings, the points and stations of his elaborate network. We had to be quiet in the railway room, as if we were in church, all concentration focussed on the chugging trains.

He still wore baggy grey trousers hitched up with braces and, today, a clean white shirt, festively green tie, and new beige cardigan – no doubt a Christmas present from Maggie who knitted all the family's woollies. All this gave him an air of shambling ease and good-natured warmth. The same dusty scent that I remembered from all those years ago still floated about Uncle Bert. My father's brother – his best friend. I was aware of how hard my father's illness was for him too.

'How's your work going?' Martin was asking him.

Poor Bert. I had visited his office once. It was a drab place – the interminable click-click of typewriters, dark wood-panelling everywhere and that ghastly grey paint on the walls – paint left over from the shipyards, a constant reminder of the war splashed all over the offices of the entire city. In fact, it had been splashed all over the schools and hospitals of Britain too – reminders of the sacrifice, the heroes, the hardship. No wonder Uncle Bert still talked about the war years.

'It's fine, son. Someone's got to do it, you know. Like in the war, when we couldn't go to fight because the essential services had to carry on – that's what we were called – essential services.' He laughed, more out of embarrassment I thought. 'We had to stay at home and make sure people's lives carried on as normally as possible. Your dad too, building them more ships all the time. Wouldn't have been a war without the ship-builders, would there?' He waved his knife in the air as if brandishing a tiny sword.

'Did you mind not going? Didn't you feel you were missing out – I mean, some of them talk about the war being the best years of their life – the excitement, the camaraderie, all that?' asked Martin. As children, Martin and I would listen to

Bert's stories as if they were adventures from another world, nothing to do with our own – like the black and white films we watched on TV every Saturday night, of a black and white war where British and American soldiers were always handsome heroes and victors, the Germans the bad guys, and beautiful woman with immaculate hair-dos and milky eyes fell in love with the heroes.

'There was excitement enough when the air-raid sirens went off. We had to get everyone down into the shelters, make sure they were safe – certified Air Raid Wardens, your dad and me – it was a very responsible job, you know. Every night we were out there checking on everyone, dodging the bombs...' Bert paused, looked down at his fingernails. I saw a muscle twitch below his eye, then his gaze seemed to fix on a faint mark, an old red wine stain on the tablecloth.

Martin and I knew that he was not being strictly honest, that the war had been a dull time for Bert and his mates in the civil service, with only the air raids to break the monotony and give them a sense of participating in the damned war. We also knew that what exactly happened during those air raids he would never tell.

'But did you never envy the blokes who went off overseas, while you were stuck here at home?' Martin persisted. He was being provocative, but he was too young to put up with trivial conversation and too old to be fobbed off with half-truths – and it was done with such good nature that nobody seemed to mind.

'Well, yes, I suppose I did envy them a bit, until they came back in boxes or were declared missing in conflict.'

Silence cut through the air like a slither of ice. Young men in boxes – missing – conflict. The words spun inside my head like a merry-go-round.

Where to go now? Would someone make light conversation, change the subject, say something pointless, try to be funny? No, not this time. It was Bert who pulled himself up and stepped in.

'But why am I talking about all this nonsense now? What about James – how is he, Nancy? How do you think he's doing, really?' Bert's face suddenly looked haggard and grey, like the walls of his office, constantly ready for a battle that never came his way. This time it was his brother's turn and the knowledge bore a shaft right through his heart. They had lived their whole lives together. He could not imagine a life without James by his side – just as I could not imagine a life without my father.

Nancy turned a shade paler and tightened her body, just a fraction of an inch. She didn't want to talk about this now. I felt some sympathy for her. All day, and yesterday too, she had been preparing and cooking, creating the most lavish feast of the year, and all she wanted was for everyone to enjoy it. She asked only for a brief reprieve from the reality that was her life. Later we would all have to face it again, but not just now. Her eyes turned towards Bert, silently beseeching him – not now, please not now.

Bert was unrelenting. 'I guess it's not good, then,' he offered.

'No, not good,' admitted Nancy.

'How long?'

'The doctor says a few weeks at best.'

Martin stirred a piece of roast potato around in his gravy until it became so sodden it began to disintegrate. I placed my knife and fork down before I dropped them, and studied my fingers resting on the table edge. They were trembling. Fortunately Granny hadn't heard the conversation well enough to understand.

It was Maggie who came to the rescue. 'Oh dear, how sad. How are you all going to manage without him? I'm sure you will. You'll manage. It'll be alright.' No one believed her, but we were grateful for her optimism. Nancy began to cry. Maggie put an arm around her shoulder and tried to comfort her.

'There, there. It'll be alright, Nancy. We're all here for you. We'll help you get through it. Try not to worry,' crooned Maggie.

Nancy wiped her eyes and blew her nose, tightened herself in again and brushed down her blue Crimpolene dress as she sat up straight. 'I'm sorry. I'm okay, really. Thank you, Maggie – I know you're here for us.' She squeezed Maggie's hand and looked around the table, embarrassed at having revealed so much to everyone. 'Would anyone like more turkey, vegetables …help yourselves, please.'

We struggled through the rest of dinner, conversation faltering like an old car with a cranky engine. Eventually another round of red wine with the Christmas pudding raised spirits a little. I was quiet, my words dammed up like a stagnant river.

It was two weeks after Christmas, and I was back at school. Father's morphine dose had been increased again and he was hallucinating wildly. I could feel the pull on his consciousness, the moments when he was slipping further away. My mind would follow him towards the brink. Perhaps the séances – or the still raw edges of my grief – had opened a channel to the other world, and love for my father was drawing me along its ragged path.

I feared for him, with his atheistic outlook, and longed to be able to talk with him about death. What had he to look forward to? I didn't know, but in my mind I tried to communicate with him, telepathically, because real words were still not allowed. 'Maybe death can be beautiful, full of light, free of pain. Don't be afraid.' And I created pictures for him – of landscapes full of golden sunlight and green sweeping hillsides, purple moors with flowing brooks and bright blue skies. The places he had loved.

At lunchtime I had gone out alone. The sea called. I walked to the promenade and sat on the sea wall, at the very place where I had first seen Richard. The beach was quiet – hardly even a dog-walker out on this frosty January afternoon. I sat and I stared at the empty beach.

Time passed – how much time, I had no idea. I was watching the shoreline. My gaze followed the shifting edge of water as it curved along the length of the bay – a white thread rolling in and out, sending up sprays of foam into the chill air. I pulled my duffel coat tighter around my chest and tucked my hands under my armpits. Cold from the stone wall was seeping into my bones. I shivered.

Above me, three gulls were circling and calling, harsh and plaintive. The sound argued and condemned, and at the same time it carried an anguished cry. My heart was splitting open again.

Along at the farthest end of the bay, towards the lighthouse, a strange movement caught my eye. It was something like a dust storm – a swirling motion just above the waves. A commotion. Something had been disturbed, upturned. A pocket of air had come loose and seemed to stagger and sway – like a drunken man, only there was nothing there, just an uneasy movement of the air.

As I peered into this disturbance, a small cloud began to coalesce out of the shifting air and churned up waves. An uneasy stillness settled over the beach and the gulls fell silent, flew out to sea. The cloud hovered over the very edge of the shore, almost touching the tips of the waves as they rolled in, over the sand, and back out to sea, as if nothing out of the ordinary was happening. It began moving slowly along the water's edge, drifting, the way a cloud might drift through the sky on a calm day. It rolled along the whole length of the bay.

My breath turned to mist in the winter air. I watched the slow procession as the cloud gathered density. As it passed me, I could see figures clustered within it. They stood close together, formed of nothing but vapour yet with the appearance of people, a huddle of people, old people and young people. They wore clothes from earlier times, from centuries before. Our ancestors? Had they come to collect him, to accompany him on his journey? A hollow opened in my throat and a ball of lead landed there.

When the small white cloud reached the other end of the bay, it simply dissolved and disappeared.

I came to, as if out of a dream. I was aware that the presence of the cloud was bizarre and unlikely – yet I had seen it as clearly as the beach and the sea wall where I sat.

Once it had passed, I knew, deep inside I just knew, that he had passed away – my father had finally gone.

I walked down the grey stone steps to the beach. A bitter wind was whipping up from the east. To get some shelter from its sharp bite I squeezed inside one of the concrete bunkers that littered this part of the beach, broken and tipped at an angle. Remnants of lookout posts, they were scattered along the coast, debris from the war. I curled up inside, hugging my knees close to my chest for warmth. Time passed.

No thoughts. No feelings. A numbness crept through my body, into my heart. My mind was adrift in a world of misty shapes, half-formed memories. I huddled, suspended in time, like a drop of water clinging to a tap just before it falls.

A phrase sprang into my mind and began to circle, repeating itself, over and over like a poem with only one line – 'forever frozen in time at the point of collapse'. I tried to remember where I had heard this phrase. Physics class. Mr Greenway. Black holes in space. If you got close to one you would be torn apart by powerful tidal forces, he had told us. Did we need to know this?

Eventually I crawled out of my bunker and walked slowly home, feeling cold and empty.

Nancy greeted me as I entered the living room. Her eyes were red. She looked frail, as if a strong wind might easily blow her over. Her hands were gripping and crumpling up the hem of her sweater.

'He's dead,' she said, as I entered the room.

'I know,' I replied. What more could I say?

★

After a few days his body was brought back to the house. He had been nicely cleaned and dressed. I could visit him, lying in his shiny oak coffin in the bedroom. As I entered the room I was greeted by the sweet-sour smell – like old, dried out musk – that hovers around the dead and dying. He looked peaceful, beautiful even. His skin, soft to my touch, was stretched thin over the high dome of his forehead. His closed eyes were at rest now – no sign of the agonies of the last year, of the pain and isolation and the sheer boredom of it all. No sign of the cancer that had devoured him from within, of the visions that had tormented him during those last few weeks. Had he found paradise after all? Had he found Ellen?

But his life was cut short, only half way through. It was left to me to complete his unfinished life, somehow. I gently kissed his forehead and left the room.

Another funeral. Another visit to the small crematorium chapel by the headland. The ashes of the dead were laid to rest where they would never again be buffeted by the cold north winds, but would be lulled in their sleep by the sound of the sea – the rhythm of the rush and whisper of the tides would be a constant companion to the dead. The smell of roses and lilies would briefly ward off the sharp salt tang of the air, but after all the mourners had left and the pink roses had turned to brown, they would be left alone, for eternity, on this bleak headland.

As before, I remembered little of the service – just a red velvet curtain being drawn as the coffin disappeared behind it. Sombre piped music, clearly meant to soothe, began to play.

I did remember Uncle Bert sitting on a bench outside the chapel after it was all over, sobbing. Maggie sat beside him, her comforting arm around his shoulders. Nancy was too numb to cry, Granny too confused. Martin was angry. He was angry that he had not been allowed to talk with his father openly – angry he had not said goodbye. Most of all, he was angry with himself for going along with the culture of silence that the doctor had prescribed and Nancy had upheld. He said little during those few days and returned to Bristol soon after the funeral.

My own tears had run dry. I sought refuge in my room while the guests ate sandwiches and drank tea downstairs.

That evening, after everyone had left and the house was silent again, I sat on the edge of my bed hugging the cushion that I had clung to, like a fragile lifeline, since Richard's death. Its silver, green and gold threads were even more frayed and faded now. My fingertips traced their continuous, looping path as I stared absently at the floor.

My father – my loving, vexing, brave, capable, dear father – he had always been there. Now, I didn't know how to be a daughter without a father. I was searching for a clue, a whisper of hope, but I heard only wailing, like the voice of a soul lost somewhere out in the cold expanse of space. Was it my own soul, lost and in pain, or my father's? Or was it my mother's?

That night it was not to God that I prayed, nor to my father. It was my mother that I found myself desperately praying to – 'Please help me, Mammy, please help me. Where are you? Come back, please Mammy, please come back.'

Eleven

The north-east – 1971

It was two months after my father died, a Saturday evening. Terri and I had taken the bus up to Newcastle to visit a club she had heard about. We strolled arm in arm from the Haymarket, past Grey's Monument and down Pilgrim Street towards the river. The soot blackened walls of the Quayside warehouses and massive bridge supports loomed around us. The lanes were narrow, dimly lit by a greenish light that came from the old gas lamps. A thick fog hung in the air.

Terri wore a purple feathery scarf over her skimpy black jacket and pink velvet mini skirt, with black leather boots right up to her knees. I burrowed myself into an ancient fur coat I had found at a second-hand clothes shop, and a green silk skirt – a jumble sale bargain – that went right down to my ankles. We had painted black stars around our eyes. My tumble of red curls and Terri's blonde bob glistened in the damp night air.

I felt reckless. I had cast caution to the wintry night, left innocence behind.

There had been a terrible row when I left the house. I know what Nancy really wanted to say was, 'I'm lonely. Please stay home and keep me company tonight.' Instead, out came a furious tirade.

'You are not going out dressed like that! You look like a trollop!'

What I had desperately needed to say was, 'Please help me. I'm hurting so much I can't bear it. I can't cope on my own.' Instead, I shouted back, 'Yes, I am. You can't stop me. I can go if I want to.'

'Don't you dare speak to me like that. I won't have you disgracing yourself, and me, parading around like that. Take those things off, and that ghastly make-up, and put some decent clothes on if you want to go out.'

'No, I won't.'

'Then don't come back here again. If you won't do as I say, you can find somewhere else to live,' Nancy screamed.

'Okay, I will! I've got friends I can stay with.'

'Go and change those clothes, Anita!'

'You can't make me. Why should I do what you want anyway? You're not my mother!' I threw back my most pointed barb. I know I shouldn't have said that, but she was driving me crazy with her nagging and her rules that I just couldn't help it.

Nancy lunged forward and slapped me across the face. I felt a sharp pain, like a knife point stinging my cheek.

We stopped, staring at each other for a brief moment. Then I turned, ran out of the kitchen and fled the house, slamming the front door behind me.

The club was hard to find – up a narrow stairway around the back of a pub, just off the dock road. The entrance was dimly lit but once up the stairs the clubroom was fully illuminated by large, opaque glass globes, the kind you saw in every shop and public building. At the door we were invited to leave our coats on a row of hooks, as if we were joining a gathering of friends at their home. The familiarity of the welcome was soon belied by the surly face and gruff voice of the bouncer, as he nodded towards the bar.

'Mind ya selves. There's some odd folk here the neet.' From Bill the bouncer, this was probably the nearest it got to a gesture of protectiveness towards two probably under-age, middle-class girls, clearly from the sticks. If we wanted a bit of experience of how the rest of the world lived, he clearly thought we were welcome to it.

I looked around the room as we hovered by the door. A bar stretched almost the length of one wall and was being ably managed by two handsome young men with Elvis quiffs and tight, sleeveless black shirts. The grey carpet on the floor was filthy with old beer stains, the wallpaper yellowing with the imprint of endless nights of nicotine absorption. The seediness of the place was reflected in the clientele, though a hint of glamour that some of the motley group displayed was not reflected back to the smoky room.

We had come to the one place in the city where gays, transvestites and transsexuals could meet without risk of abuse or attack. A ripple of excitement, close to the edge of barely discernible fear, ran through me. This was different, new, an adventure. It was so far out from my own world, a world full of pain, the pain I wanted to escape. In this strange universe I could lose myself for a while.

Terri was soon talking to a man who looked so open and fresh he could have been younger than we were. He was a poet. He looked like a poet – tall, thin cheeked, bright eyes that shone out of dark sunken sockets, baggy clothes that hung off angular shoulders and hips.

'Have you read *Dorian Gray* as well?' he was asking Terri. 'I loved it. It's such a shame Wilde only published one novel though.'

'Yes, I've read it. It's brilliant. Is that the kind of thing you write?'

'I couldn't say that – I just write poems, when the inspiration comes,' he said with an air of modesty that seemed to inflate rather than diminish him. 'But you know, I'll write a novel one day. That's something I'm working towards, alongside the poetry. And maybe a play too.' He tossed his head to flick a lank strand of mouse-coloured hair out of his eyes. I remembered Richard, my lovely Richard, tossing his thick wavy hair just like that. But Richard had no place in this alien world. I needed to banish him, the sweet memory of him. I wondered if he could see me from some place high above, feeling embarrassed at the idea that he might be watching me come to a place like this. He would barely recognise the young girl he had fallen in love with. I had become a sullen reflection of myself, with dark thoughts and a dirty life.

I wove my way to the bar to buy drinks. But what should I ask for here? Babycham would not be cool, nor lager and lime. I tried to edge my way towards the front line, squeezing between the bar-proppers wherever an opening presented itself.

'Hi, I'm Suze. What you drinking? I'll get it for you.' A young woman with long lashes and gorgeous auburn hair, tumbling all the way down her back, caught my attention by catching hold of my wrist and fixing me with big brown eyes. She wore a leopard-skin patterned blouse and tight black mini-skirt.

'Er … two … er, vodka and oranges.' That would do. I'd heard Nancy requesting this on occasions – it sounded grown-up.

'Two vodka and oranges for the young ladies, Gary-love,' she shouted above the din of the crowded room, her voice deep and resonant, and immediately one of the young handsomes was at her bidding.

'You're new here, yes?' the woman asked.

'Yes, first time. I'm Anita – that's my friend Terri.' I gestured in Terri's direction.

'Ah yes, with Anton. He's a poet you know, a very good one. Published two collections already.' Suze tapped my wrist with her middle finger as if to emphasise the point. I noticed the strong features of her face, her aquiline nose, the bold jaw-line and high cheekbones. Handsome, I thought, but the downward tilt of her head made her look up out of her big brown eyes in a rather pleading way, suggesting a hidden vulnerability. Was she, or wasn't she? I thought I could detect a soft shadow on her upper lip – so probably she was a boy, not a girl. Did it matter?

I accepted the drinks gratefully and we squeezed our way back to join Terri and Anton.

Conversation and drinks flowed. I felt exhilarated by the vodka, the talk of poets and the risqué edge between reality and fantasy that was ever-present in this world.

When closing time came Terri and I were too intoxicated to refuse an offer of coffee at Suze and Anton's house. I vaguely remembered stumbling, wobbly on my legs and laughing, into an old VW beetle. We were driven a short distance to a row of dilapidated terraced houses.

Inside, we were led into the front room and left to make ourselves comfortable on a sagging settee, while Suze and Anton made coffee. The room was shabby and cold, lit by just one table lamp covered with a red chiffon scarf. I lit the small gas fire and collapsed into the settee again. The walls were spinning, the colours on the posters that decorated them pulsing against my retina. I couldn't string a complete thought together, let alone a sentence. Terri lay back with her eyes closed.

Another young man came in, followed by a woman in a long multi-coloured skirt with a cascade of scarves and beads around her neck. They nodded a greeting in our direction. He put on a record – Pink Floyd's *Ummagumma* – and the two of them stretched out on the floor by the gas fire, propped up on a pile of old cushions.

Suze and Anton returned carrying mugs, a steaming pot of coffee, a plastic bag and a pouch of tobacco. Anton rolled tobacco, and something he prized out of the plastic bag, into a long cigarette. Suze poured coffee. I peered through the dim light of the room and the haze of inebriation. Suze moved in slow motion, her hand unsteady, her outline wavering against the red glow of the lamp.

The music soared and spiralled up a long scale, and my mind spiralled with it. A woman's voice wailed and cried on an impossibly high and breathy note, climaxed, and came rolling down in sensuous, sorrowful waves. The gritty-smelling joint was distorting my senses. My mind was sinking under a heavy cloud. From somewhere in the room short bursts of conversation and laughter erupted but I struggled to understand what they were saying, couldn't catch the jokes, didn't know how to join in. I was sitting on a rusty chair in the Rendezvous again, with my feet brushing the sand on the stone floor, lost at the edge of my circle of friends.

Memories – push the memories away.

The music increased in intensity and the joint went around another time. I began to feel panic stirring inside me but I couldn't move – I felt paralysed. Crazy half-thoughts were beginning to take hold. I felt stupid, hated being so inarticulate, feared that these odd people whose house we had strayed into were going to attack us, rob us, or worse. Visions of violence began flashing into my mind – knives and bare flesh and a white dove lying dead on the lawn with her bloody heart ripped out. I struggled to breathe. My mind totally out of control, all I could do was watch the images come and go, like a horror film I didn't want to see.

Eventually, and with a herculean effort of will, I gathered my fragmented thoughts together into one clear intention – I had to get out of this room, out of the house, get some fresh air, be alone – somewhere, anywhere. I nudged Terri but she appeared to be sleeping. I stood up awkwardly, tripping over cushions and bumping into the arm of the settee as I stumbled towards the door. The journey to the door seemed to take an eternity. I felt acutely self-conscious, unable to utter an excuse for my hasty departure. I imagined them all staring at me, but each was lost within his or her own private world by then and didn't seem to notice me leaving the room.

Outside the house I sat for a few minutes on the low garden wall, my hands gripping the damp brickwork as my mind spun and flailed. I couldn't return to the house so would have to trust that Terri could take care of herself. I began walking.

I sensed the river was to my right. The night river brooded under an unmistakable quality of silence. The broad gap in street lighting, and the sullen swish of the tide against the hulls of fishing boats that lined its edge, revealed its location more precisely as I wove my way towards the quayside. Once by the water, I could orient myself. If I walked with the river on my right, it would lead me home, of that I was sure.

Suddenly I was startled by a car creeping up behind me, so quietly that I hadn't heard it approach until it was there, right beside me.

'Hey there – nice one. How much, luv?' A fat and bald-headed man, reeking of alcohol, leaned over the passenger seat towards me as he rolled down the window. He seemed surprised at his luck. He looked me up and down, from tangled red curls to the damp hemline of my green silk skirt, clinging to my ankles as I walked. 'Ye wanna come with us, luv?'

I walked faster, fear surging through my body. The painful prickling of adrenalin as it swelled my arteries, and the racing of my heart jolted my mind out of its stupor and into alertness.

'Hey, not so fast, hinny. How much d'ye want? Or I'll take it for nowt if ye're gonna make trouble,' the man threatened. Now that he had an eye on his prey, it was clear he was not about to let it go without a fight.

I swerved up a side road and began to run. The road was deserted and lit by only an occasional street lamp. On my left were small factories, workshops, a garage, locked up behind wire fencing and tall wooden gates. On the other side were a row of shops, a pub – all closed for the night – and a few houses, boarded up and awaiting demolition. My mind was sharp and focussed now. I was lost, completely alone and in danger.

The man had left his car and was chasing me along the

wet pavement, his heavy footsteps lumbering after the quick and light click-clack of my heels. He trailed me up an alley, behind a row of backyards with dustbins stacked along the wall. The faster I ran the closer he seemed to get. I could hear him panting. As I ran, I knocked the bins over behind me, hoping they would slow him down.

'Fuckin' hell, ye bitch – I'll give ye one,' he yelled, as he went flying headlong over a bin. In the moments it took him to stagger to his drunken feet and kick the offending bin, I had darted out of sight down another turning and was fleeing towards the main road. I kept running. The man had given up the chase by now but fear had whipped up my blood and was driving me on – across the road and back down to the quayside, then turning to the left, and running, running with the river on my right and the sea some miles ahead.

There was just one thought in my mind now – to follow the river down to the sea, then I could find my way home.

Exhausted, I finally stopped to sit on a bench and catch my breath. I could have been running for hours – I didn't know. The path had taken me uphill a little, through a grassy area in front of an estate of council flats, ugly blocks of grey concrete and glass, six or seven floors high, which stretched along the ridge. This had been the 'promised land' for the families crowded together in terraced slums with privies in the backyards and weekly baths in tin tubs by the fire.

It was still quite dark but a hint of greyness in the air suggested dawn was approaching. Down-river a thin strip of lighter grey clung to the horizon, far out over the sea beyond the mouth of the Tyne. The clouds would lift as the sun rose, as if it were pushing up the sodden bank of moist air from below, levering it across the morning sky.

The pungent smell of decaying fish drifted up from the quayside. A few fishing boats were already beginning to set out for their day's trawl, engines clanking and coloured flags flapping in the damp air. Across the water I could make out the shipyards, as the massive grey hulls of tankers that were being built or repaired loomed into view. My father had worked there when I was young. I remembered him showing Martin and me around the yard – the half-built ships, the giant cranes and dry docks – he had been so proud to show us his work. All I had wanted to do was drive the ferry that had taken us over the river. It was my first childhood dream – to become a ferry-driver, crossing the Tyne day after day, from north to south, and south to north. Breathing in the fresh sea air, salt spray in my face and the screech of gulls ringing in my ears, I had tasted a freedom that felt powerful and bold.

I watched as the drama of dawn unfolded. The dampness of the bench seeped through my thin skirt, but I was already soaked from the inside with sweat and from outside by the persistent night fog. I barely noticed the new discomfort. On higher ground now, away from the dark alleyways and the menace of the quayside at night, I felt safer. At least I knew which way to go – to the mouth of the river, then left and up the coast. From Tynemouth, through Cullercoats and on to Whitley Bay.

I felt tired, hungry and wretched. As I sat, allowing my heart to slow and my breath to calm, I could think through my situation a little more rationally. Perhaps I should call Nancy, once it was properly morning, and ask her to come and pick me up. Then I remembered the row we had had the night before and wasn't sure if I could return home.

Maybe I could catch a bus, to Terri's perhaps, once they began their morning routes. I searched in my handbag to see how much change I had left. My purse had gone. The drug-induced paranoia at Suze and Anton's house flashed back into my mind – but no, I didn't think they would have robbed me. No one in that room had been capable of such an initiative, and they were nice people. We had become friends.

As I watched the sun rise higher in the sky, turning the sea a soft mauve before inviting the whole expanse of water to glitter with light, I began to feel clear, as if washed out and emptied. I had probably dropped it whilst I was running. It didn't matter anyway. Nothing really mattered. I was here, sitting on a damp bench overlooking the river, witnessing the return of day after a night of adventure.

Then, with a rising wave of nausea, the full impact of my night of adventure dawned on me, as clear and sharp as broken glass – how the excitement of the night and meeting new friends had turned into danger, fear and acute aloneness. I began to shake uncontrollably. My body began to convulse with sobs. I surrendered to the energy that was shaking me through and through, as the sun washed over my pale face and signs of morning began to stir around me.

It was nearly seven o'clock when we arrived at the house. The curtains of Nancy's room were closed – she was still sleeping. The young officer rang the doorbell. No reply. I guessed that Nancy had had another sleepless night and would resent being woken at this hour on Sunday morning.

The policeman rang the doorbell again, and waited while its insistent sound reverberated through the house. He called her name. 'Mrs Rose.' After a few more minutes Nancy appeared at the door looking sleepy and dishevelled, her dressing gown wrapped loosely around her.

'Morning, ma'am. Sorry to bother you so early,' said the young policeman, his freshly shaved and polished face smiling politely beneath his helmet – an attempt at reassurance no doubt, but Nancy did not look reassured at all. The sight of the unwelcome caller, with his neat uniform and well-scrubbed face, would alarm Nancy in her current state of 'nerves'. She peered at him through sleep-heavy eyes, looking confused.

'We found her down near the river, North Shields area.

Looked a bit lost. Said she'd dropped her purse somewhere so couldn't get a bus home,' the policeman explained.

The woman police officer stepped forward, an arm around my hunched shoulders.

'Anita! Where on earth have you been? What have you been up to?' Nancy looked concerned, relieved, then angry, all in quick succession.

'I think she's had a bit of a rough time. Not sure exactly what happened – she won't say – but you might want to go a bit easy on her,' said the young woman. She had treated me kindly after they picked me up from the bench, insisting they take me home rather than to the station.

'We were just doing our morning rounds when we came across her sitting there, all cold and wet she was, so we brought her back here,' said the man. He looked awkward. I was sure he would rather be arresting thieves or sorting out drunken brawls than rescuing teenage girls from themselves. I felt so utterly miserable. I wanted to crawl under a stone and die.

They handed me over like a parcel delivery, glad to return responsibility to where it belonged, said goodbye and left.

'Go and put some dry clothes on while I make you some breakfast,' said Nancy in a flat voice. She said no more as we sat opposite each other at the kitchen table, me picking at my scrambled egg on toast, Nancy sipping a mug of coffee as she tried to read the Sunday paper. I kept quiet, so as not to make matters worse.

'Go easy on her', the policewoman had said. I knew Nancy would resent that. She was 'at her wits end' with me. I was too big a problem for her and she probably had wished I had gone back to Terri's and stayed there. Nancy was out of her depth with me, and I was out of my depth with the madness that was growing inside me.

An empty day lay ahead. Life seemed to stop on Sundays and we both dreaded the long haul through to evening. Nancy would make Sunday dinner, as she always did. I would go to bed and by the time I woke dinner would be cold and barely edible, but Nancy would make it anyway, even if she had to eat alone. She would do this just to keep a semblance of normality.

Later we would have to talk about what had happened, all of it, but not now. Neither of us had the energy nor the desire to talk. What good would it do anyway?

It was little more than a week after my father's funeral that our fights had begun in earnest. Now there was such hostility between us that we rarely exchanged more than a few words. I held little hope of any reconciliation after this episode. But for a few more months Nancy was my legal guardian, and she clearly felt she must make an attempt at assembling the rituals of family life and maintaining some discipline.

I finished my breakfast and went up to my room to sleep, leaving Nancy to stare at the newspaper, pretending to read, but I could tell her mind was elsewhere.

Twelve

North Norfolk – 1971

We struggled through the winter months, rattling around the big house like two loose wheels about to spin off. Something had to break, or it would be Nancy or me that would. Help finally came from Nancy's sister, though I didn't see it that way at first.

'I had a letter from Sybil this morning. She wants us both to visit her at Easter. Would you like to go?' asked Nancy as we sat down to tea one evening.

Outside the dining room window the garden was preparing for spring. The first buds had begun to blossom on the cherry tree, and daffodils were bursting out of their pale green winter sheaths, showing tentative signs of the golden stars they would soon become.

'I don't know. I've got lots of work to do for my exams. I have to get a portfolio together and I haven't done nearly enough work for it.'

'Well, I'm not surprised you're behind with your work, Anita. You've wasted so much time this year – out every evening with Lucy and Terri, partying at the weekends with those dubious friends in the city. Late nights, days off school with some mysterious ailment or other – no wonder your school work has suffered.'

I sunk my head into my hands with a groan. I was about to retaliate, though I had run out of excuses by now, but Nancy continued, covering her tracks well – neither of us wanted to go down this worn path again.

'You can take your work with you. And Sybil will let you use her studio to paint. You know she'd love that.'

I liked Sybil. Of course, she was not a true aunt but she had adopted me – 'call me Aunt Sybil if you want', she had offered when we first met – as I had no aunts of my own, apart from Bert's wife, Maggie. Sybil was a real artist, a painter. She had exhibitions and sold pictures, now and then. To make a little regular income she did some part-time teaching at a local college.

'How long would you be going for?' I asked, reluctant to let Nancy see my interest in the plan.

'Well, we could go for all of your two weeks holiday if you like. It could be really nice – walks on the beach, bird-watching on the marshes, time to relax. I've got a box of your father's papers I want to go through. Some personal things – I haven't been able to face them yet but Sybil said she'd help me.' Nancy was clearly longing for the break but she wouldn't leave me alone for so long – not the way things were.

I stirred my bowl of soup – oxtail, my least favourite of the 57 varieties – as I contemplated the offer. Sybil had encouraged my love of painting and inspired me to take it seriously – to take myself seriously – when no one else did. Her lifestyle inspired me too. She had moved to the North Norfolk coast soon after leaving art school, and set up a studio with a group of fellow artists. In time she had been able to buy a small cottage in Salthouse. It was tiny, with stone floors downstairs and no electricity when she first moved in, but over the years she had made it cosy, built an extension with another bedroom, a proper bathroom and a studio, and planted apple trees in the garden. My father had thought she was eccentric – her values, priorities, needs seemed so very different from everyone else's in his view – but he had tolerated Nancy's younger sister, even grown fond of her with time.

The idea of two weeks painting in Sybil's studio was tempting, but two weeks in Norfolk – so bleak when the weather was bad, so primitive, so far from civilisation, from everything – away from my friends and the city for all that time. I wasn't sure I could survive it.

'Maybe. I'll think about it,' I muttered, resting my head in one hand as I continued absentmindedly stirring my soup with the other. I felt so empty of desire for anything at all that I had no idea how to make the decision.

'It would be good for both of us to have a holiday. Do come,' Nancy pleaded. She really needed me to say yes, I could tell. 'Sybil would be so disappointed if you didn't. This is what she said.' Nancy picked up the letter and read – "Please tell dear Anita I'm missing her and would love her to visit too. I'm already clearing a corner of my studio for her so she can paint here. And I'm working on a new series of landscapes I really want her to see – she can tell me if they're any good!" Nancy looked up to assess the impact of her sister's warm invitation on me. I relented.

'Okay. But only if we can come back sooner if two weeks feels too long.' Maybe some time away would be good, as it was all getting quite crazy at the moment. Terri and I had stopped holding séances when they began to get really scary. And anyway, I had found I could talk to Richard in my mind, without the ritual of the ouija board. The parties at Suze and Anton's were weird – they left me feeling disoriented, disturbed – but I felt a compulsion to keep going. It was an escape, another world where I could forget what had happened for a while, and I did like Suze and Anton. I had to admit that Nancy was right though – I hadn't focussed on my schoolwork at all this year. If I wanted to go to art college in September then I had to do some work now. Maybe a holiday in Norfolk would help.

★

And so it was that we arrived at Norwich station in the late afternoon of Easter Friday. We were met by Sybil in her battered old mini, its red paint dulled to a rusty glow by endless lashings of salty rain. There were warm greetings and hugs all round, then we piled into the mini and rattled up to the coast along rickety roads dotted with potholes and lined in places by magnificent ancient trees. I marvelled at the way they formed giant tunnels over the road, scattering the sunlight into golden beams that pierced through the shady woods.

Then woodland would give way to vast expanses of vivid green – the spring wheat, oats and barley at their most vibrant at this time of year, as they pushed up into the light after a winter squeezed into their tight, dark husks. I began to gather inspiration for my painting as Nancy and Sybil talked excitedly in the front seat.

Evening was approaching as we reached the coast road, just in time to see a glorious sunset over the marshes. The hovering globe of the sun cast a golden sheen over the reed-beds, and the creeks that ran through them glistened like silver ribbons. The plaintive call of the Greylag geese, wending their way home for the night, and the circling gulls swooping over the marshlands made a melancholic song. Briefly the sky was aflame with gorgeous shades of pink, orange and gold, whilst the faintest trace of a mist over the low-lying marsh spread an atmosphere of mystery over the land.

The salted air smelt subtly different here. It was the same sea that had taken Richard but the coastline was quite unique. The sea was totally unforgiving during the harsh gales of winter. Jutting boldly out into the North Sea and facing directly up to the icy Arctic wastes, the unprotected Norfolk coast took a battering when the north winds blew and nature showed her ruthless side. This evening it was thankfully mild, with just a hint of a breeze and a clear sky now turning to soft grey and purple as we neared our destination.

Sybil had come here seeking wilderness. Her cottage was just a short distance from the path that led through the marshes down to the shingle beach. To her it was paradise. To Nancy it was bleak but she loved her sister so she liked to spend time here whenever she could. I would swing between despair and elation as the fog and rain and cold winds descended, or cleared to reveal a place of exquisite beauty.

'Here we are,' Sybil announced, as she turned off the coast road at Salthouse and forced the mini to chug the last few yards up a narrow lane to Greycrest Cottage. 'Phew – made it, just! I have to get her seen to soon.' She laughed, patting the dashboard of her beloved car. It had represented freedom to her for the past twelve years, a lifeline, for there were few buses and no trains running past her village.

We bundled out and gathered our bags while she shooed the hens into their coop for the night. The creaking door of the cottage opened into a low-ceilinged kitchen, full of light from two skylight windows during daytime. Coloured rugs on the stone tiled floor and warmth from the Aga welcomed us. The walls were hung with pots and ladles, shelves stacked with handmade pottery – bowls, mugs and plates in deep earthen shades – and the deep recess of the windowsill was home to a small garden of potted herbs.

'Tea first, then I'll heat up supper while you two settle in. I've put you in the new room by the studio, Anita, and you'll be upstairs with me, Nancy.' The cottage was oddly laid out, as was often the case with these old places when they had been built onto over the years. From the kitchen you went down two narrow, stone steps into the sitting room, which was heated by a small open fire. Next to the fireplace was a latch door that led up a narrow, curved stairway to the first bedroom – Nancy's for these two weeks. To get to Sybil's room you had to go through the first bedroom. The bathroom was downstairs in what had once been an outbuilding, but had been attached to the cottage by a corridor at some point in time. My room and the studio went off the other side of the kitchen.

Nancy and I dropped our bags by the back door, which also served as a front door, and sat down at the big oak table. We were thankful to have arrived after the long journey, glad to be able to sink at last into the easy, comfortable charm of Sybil's world.

'I'm *so* glad to be here – I can't tell you. Thanks for having us,' said Nancy, beginning to relax, just a little.

'It's a real pleasure – you're welcome any time. You know that, don't you,' said Sybil, setting down a pot of tea and three mugs. She flicked back her long plait of golden-brown hair as she sat down. The soft folds of a long cardigan in muted shades of blue and purple, layered over an embroidered Indian shirt, layered over a long red skirt with tiny mirrors sewn into its hem (because this was a special occasion – tomorrow she would be back in her old paint-splattered dungarees), settled around her. 'It's going to be fun. I've discovered some new walks – would you believe that – after so many years I'm still finding new places to explore.'

'And can I really use your studio?' I asked.

'Of course you can! We'll paint together – it'll be like the old days when I was part of the artists' collective.'

'Are you not still part of it? I thought you were all friends.' Nancy had always been concerned at what felt to her like the isolation of her sister's life, out here on the edge of civilisation.

'Oh yes, they're still good friends. It's just that, having my own studio now, I paint alone and sometimes that can feel a bit lonely, but I still see everyone. Maybe you can meet some of them, Anita. If you're going to be an artist too, you might like to find out what an artist's life is really like.' Sybil laughed. She loved her life but knew that Nancy and James had always thought she was quite mad to be living the way she did.

'Thanks, I'd love that. And I've got some ideas I want to

work on while I'm here.' I smiled at her as she reached over and squeezed my shoulder.

'We're going to have a great time, I promise you.'

We settled into a rhythm of walking in the mornings – the shingle beaches, the sandy beaches, pathways through the marshes. We walked along Morston creek and over the Stiffkey Freshes, knee-deep in black mud. Another day, through pinewoods and dunes and out onto the magical expanse of Holkham beach. We visited Blakeney harbour and Burnham Overy Staithe, full of clinking boats waiting for the tide to turn, and followed woodland walks and streams.

In the afternoons I would retreat to the studio to paint or go for a ride through the lanes on Sybil's old bicycle. Sometimes she joined me in the studio – sometimes she helped Nancy to sort through the papers and personal belongings that had belonged to my father. They now belonged to Nancy, it seemed.

At the end of each day we cooked dinner on the trusty Aga – Agatha, my father used to call it, because it was full of mysteries, according to him. He had the corniest sense of humour you could imagine, but I would have given anything to hear him tell one of his old jokes again, just one more time.

Occasionally we went for a drink in the Dun Cow after dinner or visited one of Sybil's friends, but mostly we would settle in for an evening by the fire, reading or playing scrabble. Nancy and I mellowed into the gentle pace and began to glimpse why Sybil loved this life so much.

One evening towards the end of our stay, after dinner had been cleared away and coffee made, we were sitting quietly, watching the fire blaze in the hearth.

'I found something in your father's papers today that I think you should see, Anita,' Nancy finally ventured. She looked unsure of how to broach the subject and hesitated, glancing at Sybil for support. I sensed the tension in her voice. It was something I recognised, a tone that made me nervous as it usually predicated something I would rather not hear.

'What is it?' I looked at Nancy, then at Sybil. Both women looked back at me with the same serious expression on their faces. 'Sybil?'

'Why don't you just let her read the letter,' she said, seeing Nancy's uncertainty and feeling for her sister's predicament. She thought it was not really fair that Nancy had been left to deal with all of this.

'Alright, yes.' Nancy picked up an old tin box from the lamp table beside her chair, and prized off the tight lid. It was full of letters in white and pale blue envelopes. A faint scent of rose escaped from the box as she picked up the envelope lying on top. 'I found this amongst these old letters. They're mostly letters between your mother and father when they were courting, after the war when she had gone away to work in Yorkshire. They're personal letters – you can have them all if you want – but this one is, well, it's different.' Nancy handed the letter to me. The lilac envelope was creased and crumpled, and a red ribbon, faded now, had been tied around it.

On the envelope was written the name Eleanor in a round, almost childish hand. Below, in a thin, sloping script was an address in the suburbs of Newcastle – the address of the house where my parents had lived when I was born. I had spent the first year of my life there, though I don't remember that.

I untied the ribbon, breathing in the musty scent of old rose. The fire crackled and sparked in the hearth as the wind, curling around the chimney, licked the flames upwards. Nancy sat on the edge of her seat, her right hand gripping the threadbare arm of the chair. Sybil leaned back into the settee, cradling a mug of coffee in her hands. I felt her artist's eye following my every move, attending to every detail. She would notice the slight tremble of my hand, the way my mouth dropped open slightly and my breathing became stilted. She had taught me to observe like this when I was studying portrait painting at school.

I opened the envelope and took out the single folded sheet of white paper. It looked tired, dog-eared at the corners and slightly torn in places, as if it had been handled many times. A small square at the top right-hand corner had been torn off. Perhaps an address had been written there – maybe a date. I read –

My dear Eleanor, my darling daughter –

I don't know how to write this letter. There is so much I want to say, and yet now that I come to write, to reach out to you at long last, I don't know how to say it.

Yes, you are my daughter – I am your mother. They may have told you that I was dead, but I'm not. I'm here, alive and quite well, considering.

I have thought about you every single day since you came into this harsh world. I can imagine this will be a shock to you. But I can't imagine how it must have been for you, my baby girl, snatched away from your mother at birth and brought up by strangers.

Can you ever forgive me for not being there for you? It wasn't my wish, truly it wasn't, but I had no power to change the cruel course of events that conspired to take you away from me.

I would like you to know what really happened, and then I can only pray that you will be able to understand, and maybe begin to forgive me one day. But I can't tell it to you here, in this letter. I don't know if it will even reach you, or who might read it on the way. There are those who would stop you from knowing about me, and I could be in danger if they knew I had tried to contact you.

*So I will just write this brief message and give it to
someone I trust to send it on its way to you. And hope.
Her name is Sister Mary – if you can find her, she will
help you.*

*Dear Eleanor – did they keep your name? I told them
you were called Eleanor, but they may have had other
ideas for you. Do you mind if I call you this?*

*You were such a sweet girl, so beautiful. Whatever else
I have done in my life, I have always loved you. I want
you to know this, at least.*

*If you receive this letter, I hope there will be a way for
you to find me one day – if you want to that is. I don't
know where to look for you. I have no address of my own
to give you. I must leave it in the hands of fate. What is
meant, will be.*

*Take care, dear daughter. I hope and pray that you are
happy and well.*

May the Sacred Heart be with you, always.

Your loving mother,
Liza (Elizabeth)

Attached to the bottom of the letter by a strip of sellotape
was a tiny silver key.

I read the letter several times, trying to glean every crumb of
meaning I could from the words. The wind was now howling
round the rooftop, rattling a loose tile. The sweet smell of
burning logs filled the room. We sat together, waiting for words
to form again.

'I don't understand. Who is Eleanor? Is she my mother?' I
asked at last.

'I think so. She must be your mother, Ellen,' said Nancy. 'As far as your father told me, your mother never knew her birth mother's name, or where she came from. Her adoptive parents had told her nothing.'

'Yes. The way he told it to me, my mother believed that her own mother had died when she was born. That she was brought up by a couple from Newcastle, then sent away to the country when the war started. She was twelve then. She and Dad met during the war then she died when I was just two. That's all I really know about her.' The story felt threadbare and hollow from so many tellings, empty of any meaning now. It slid through my heart like thick mud after the rain. 'I always thought I didn't have a maternal grandmother. Does this mean I do? Is this letter from my grandmother?' I wanted to be sure.

'It looks like it,' said Nancy cautiously. 'It's hard to be absolutely sure but it does seem that at some time before your mother died, her mother, Liza, wrote this letter to her. If you look, the post-mark on the envelope seems to read 1953. It's hard to see it clearly but I think it's '53. The place looks like 'Belfast', but I'm not sure – the post-mark's faded and not very clear.'

'1953 – the year I was born,' I mused. 'I wonder if that's significant?'

Nancy darted a questioning glance at Sybil, but Sybil had no answers.

'So I could have a grandmother I've never known about.' Feelings of confusion, hope, dismay were bubbling up and jostling for a place. Beneath this turbulence, a sub-current of anger stirred, dark and sullen like an underground stream. Why had I not been told?

'We can't be sure she's still alive, Anita,' cautioned Sybil. 'Be careful of raising your hopes too much. This was obviously written some time ago, and anything could have happened since then.'

'You're right. It sounds as if her life wasn't very safe. She talks about danger. I wonder what was going on?' I felt alarmed as I imagined some of the scenarios that could have been Liza's life.

'We may never know. There's so little to go by here, I can't see a way to find out more about her – if you wanted to, that is,' Nancy added quickly. 'I would hate to see you going down dead-end trails, trying to find out about a grandmother who might already be dead – and who could be anyone. After all, she did abandon your mother, whatever the reason…and the circumstances of her life seem less than savoury…' Nancy's voice trailed off into thought.

Clearly, she didn't relish the idea of me delving into the past, unearthing God knows what. In Nancy's view, it was better to let the past lie, but there was a dark secret in my family history, more than one skeleton in my mother's coffin, and I needed to know the truth.

'Why did Dad not tell me about her? He must have read this letter too.' A sudden surge of anger made me stand up, as if there were something I could actually do about this wretched situation. There were too many unanswered questions and no one who could answer them now that he was gone.

'I don't know why he never told you. On the rare occasions that he mentioned anything about it, I got the sense he felt angry towards Ellen's mother – for abandoning her I suppose – so he must have known something. I imagine he was trying to protect you from a grandmother he thought you wouldn't want to know about – who was no good.' Nancy was also trying to make sense of it and knew that I deserved some sort of explanation. I could see she was doing her best to be diplomatic.

'But she's still my grandmother, no matter what she may have done – nothing changes that. And I know she's alive – I just know it.' I clasped my hands in front of my chest, gazing into the fire as if Liza might miraculously appear from the flames. For the first time in my life I knew I had a maternal grandmother, and that changed everything. I came from somewhere, from someone in particular. I no longer need feel like nobody, at the end of a broken line, insubstantial and weak without connection to my roots. I had an intimation, the flicker of a sense of how it might feel to truly know who I am, and deep inside I felt sure that Liza was still alive, despite Sybil and Nancy's cautious words.

'Then let's celebrate!' It was Sybil who broke the spell. She always knew the right thing to say, and when to say it. Nancy always seemed to get it wrong where I was concerned, but she was trying hard to be tactful tonight. 'I've got a bottle of good red wine hidden away somewhere – shall we?'

'Yes, let's celebrate!' I jumped up to get glasses while she went to find the classy bottle of wine that a friend had brought back from France last summer.

'Ah, here we are. This occasion deserves only the best.' Sybil held up the bottle. 'To grandmothers!'

'To our grandmothers,' echoed Nancy, clearly feeling it best to join in the spirit of celebration.

'To Grandmother Liza,' I added, clutching the stems of three glasses in one hand and Liza's letter in the other. Clutching a tentative thread that felt like hope, or maybe delusion. A hint of fear – fear of the long trail of disappointments that lead towards despair – fell like a shadow, even as I raised the glasses hopefully.

Thirteen

All night long the loose tile had rattled as the north wind gusted straight off the sea and battered the roof of the cottage. I hadn't slept, kept awake by the clattering tile, the howl of the wind and the storm of clamouring thoughts and emotions that had buffeted inside my tired brain. My nerves were wound up, as tight and scratchy as the strings of my father's old violin.

By morning the wind had swept the sky clear of clouds and a bright blue day greeted me as I rose. Nancy and Sybil still slept. That was good, as I needed some time alone. Sunlight streamed into the small bedroom as I pulled on my jeans, Richard's grey sweater, a woolly orange hat and scarf, and laced up my boots.

The air smelt fresh as I walked down the lane, tilting my head back to gulp in the cool sea breeze. It was early and there was little traffic to disturb the peace of the sleeping village.

Crossing the coast road, I found the path that ran through the marshes to the beach, pausing for a moment at the creek that lay just beyond the road. It was teeming with life – teal and pintail ducks, six graceful white swans and various small waders had made their home here for the spring. The birds were darting and diving for food, splashing and squawking as they competed for the best pickings. Life was at its height here.

As I walked down the path, around me the long stems of the bulrushes glowed pale golden in the morning sun, bowing and sweeping in graceful curves as gusts of wind stirred them into motion. I ran my fingers over their silvery brown tips. They felt smooth, then rough at the ends, like a terrier's fur. I remembered the night I had walked round the garden in the moonlight, touching the leaves of the shrubs to anchor myself. The time I had fallen asleep by the rocks, under the circling beam of the lighthouse.

During the night I had a disturbing dream. I was walking towards the sea over the marshes, just as I was doing now, but the marshland kept expanding. In the dream Richard had been buried out there by the beach. I wanted to visit his grave but the beach kept retreating further and further away as the marsh expanded. I couldn't reach it. The air was damp and misty – the place felt utterly bleak and desolate. I was gripped by a feeling of dread and could barely move.

Then a vision had appeared, hovering over the marsh. It began as a swirl of mist, then shapes appeared in the mist. They took on the forms of people, of women, a long row of women, one behind the other stretching back into the distance. I recognised my grandmothers, my maternal line, stretching back into the past. The grandmother at the front of the line seemed to smile and beckon to me, but when I tried to walk towards her the mist and the swampy ground beneath my feet confused and enmeshed me. Now I could not move at all.

As I watched, the line of women began to dissolve into three long threads of green, silver and gold, winding through the mist. The ends of the threads were frayed. They began to separate and drift away, then faded back into the damp grey air.

The dream had left me with an uneasy feeling. The euphoria of the evening before, of finding my grandmother's letter and her name, had been replaced by a deep sorrow that I had lived my whole life without knowing my mother or my grandmother. And the task of finding her, when all I knew was her first name – Liza – felt overwhelming in the stark morning light.

I came to the salt-water lagoon that lay beneath the shingle bank. It was inhabited by a more serene flock of black-headed gulls, terns and avocets, their white and silvery grey feathers glinting in the sun like jewels. I climbed the bank and went down to the water's edge, then began to walk eastwards, over the sea-washed pebbles, turning the fragments of information over in my mind – trying and failing to shape them into meaningful form.

There were several fishermen out on the beach by the time I reached the stretch that bordered Weybourne. With rods pitched and thermos flasks at hand, they sat in a scattered row along the shore, gazing out to sea. Each was hoping for a catch, or perhaps just grateful for this quiet time alone, without the demands and pressures of everyday life to attend to.

Before I reached the first fisherman in the row I stopped and turned, like them, to face the sea. With so much loss in my life, and so unclear the way ahead, the sea was my anchor now – a constant, a familiar voice. It held Richard and it held my memories. I loved it and feared it in equal measure. Standing on the shoreline with my back to the solid structures of the land, facing into the empty space ahead, I could find a kind of equilibrium, a balance between what was known and what was still unknown. The past, present and future seemed to weave and merge in this liminal space.

I stood there, my gaze fixed on the shifting edge of the sea that lapped just a few feet below. The shingle ridge had been worn steep by last night's storm coinciding with a high spring tide, creating a sharp drop down to the water. It must have been an hour or more that I stood there. My heels sunk deeper into the shingle. I barely moved, but for a slow, imperceptible twisting of my body. Weight pressed down my right side, tilting me towards immanent collapse, my whole being balanced precariously at the edge.

My mind was searching – for meaning, for answers, for any sort of guidance. Most insistent was the question of how much my father knew and why he had not told me about my grandmother. A growing sense of betrayal was layering itself over the feelings of grief and confusion. My father, who might have had some answers, was gone. He had left me with no directions and no map. Who had torn the address from the letter? What kind of lock would the silver key open, and where was it now?

I stood motionless, as if I would stay at this spot forever, my heels sinking deep into the shingle. There seemed nowhere else to go from here. My thoughts emptied out with the drag of each retreating wave.

My attention was drawn sharply back to the beach as a man approached along the water's edge. He wore a bright yellow fisherman's jacket and had a kind and ruddy face.

'Are you alright, girl?' he asked. 'It's just that you've been standing there for over an hour, and it's…well, it's a bit strange.'

I unravelled my collapsing spine, dug my heels out of the holes they had made in the shingle, and pressed them firmly against the ground so that I stood up straight again.

'Yes, I'm fine.' I felt embarrassed by this simple intrusion into my private world, but also touched by the man's concern.

'Okay. If you're sure you're alright?' It was a question more than a statement.

'Yes, I'm alright. Thank you,' I replied.

He returned to his fishing line, propped at an angle near the water's edge some distance to my right. He had been standing there for at least the last hour. Maybe I should buy a fishing rod, I thought wryly, then I could stand here for as long as I liked too.

I turned away from the kind fisherman and started to walk back along the beach towards Salthouse. After a short distance I stopped again and looked out to sea. My anchor, my constant – I felt helpless in the face of its mesmerising pull. I needed to stay here while I sifted and sorted through the turbulent thoughts that had ransacked my mind all night. I was searching for a way to find Liza but there were no clues.

An avocet swooped by, its graceful flight and curved beak as distinctive as the flash of black along white wings and tail. I followed it with my gaze. Then suddenly I lost my footing and was tumbling. The thud of a wave breaking against my back, and the icy chill of the arctic waters caught my breath. My heart lurched and shuddered as the cold pierced through it. I was dragged down the bank with the ebb of the wave, tumbling back into the sea with the polished stones, sliding and falling. The white wash of foam stung my eyes. Salty water was in my mouth and stabbing at the back of my nose. I gasped and gulped in a mouthful of sea. I had lost my orientation, couldn't tell which way to reach to find air or land again. The undertow tugged at my thin body and I couldn't get a hold on the ground beneath.

After long moments of floundering, tossed and dragged by the tumbling, pounding waves, a flash of yellow swiped through the foam, right across my face. I felt the painful grip of tight fingers around my arm. My hair was being tugged and the movement made me swallow a mouthful of water and begin to choke. Stones grazed my hands as I was heaved up onto the beach, out of the waves' reach.

I sat coughing and gasping on the ridge as the fisherman held me steady and gently patted my back, hoping this would help expel the water from my lungs. Poor man. He had probably never had to save a person from the sea before, and seemed not quite sure what to do next.

'You gave me a fright there, girl,' he said, in his broad Norfolk accent. 'Are you alright now? Cold, I expect. Here, put this round you.' He put his yellow jacket over my shoulders.

'I'm okay, really. Not sure what happened – I slipped – lost my footing I think,' I gasped between coughs.

By this time another man had come running along the beach. They helped me up and walked me to where they had left their fishing-lines and belongings. The man with the yellow jacket sat me down in his beach chair and poured some tea from a flask, while the second man fetched a blanket. I took off my soaked sweater and wrapped myself in the blanket. Thankfully the sun had brought some warmth by now. With the help of hot tea, my shivering soon ceased and I began to feel calmer.

'I just slipped. I didn't mean to go in.' I tried to reassure them. I knew they were wondering if I had meant to fall in, but I hadn't. I wanted to live – more than at any moment since the news of Richard's death had seared through my world, I wanted to live. And I knew what I must do, however hard and no matter how long it took.

'But I was a bit concerned when you just stood there, like …are you sure you're alright?' the first man asked. He was clearly out of his depth.

'Yes, I'm alright now, really.' For a moment I felt like telling these two kind Norfolk fishermen about everything – about Richard, my father, my mother – and now my grandmother too. But I thought better of it. They stood there just looking at me, puzzled expressions on their wind-beaten faces, not sure what to do with me now. If I were a young seal, washed up onto the beach in a rough tide as sometimes happens, they would know what to do.

Once I had warmed up and my heart had stopped hammering in my chest, all I wanted was to get back to Greycrest Cottage as quickly as possible. I would be able to slip in by the side door, which led straight to my room, and change out of my wet clothes before Nancy and Sybil saw me. It would only cause more trouble if Nancy knew I had fallen into the sea.

'Thank you for saving my life,' I said, picking up Richard's damp sweater as I stood. I meant this in more ways than I could articulate. An intention had been set. I would seek out Liza, no matter what the obstacles may be, and this gave my life a purpose – it gave me the will to go on living my life.

I left the fishermen, climbed up onto the high bank that kept the sea at bay and walked back to Salthouse, safely out of the grasp of the relentless waves.

Part III

Quest

Fourteen

London – 1981

The day begins with a birthday breakfast of chocolate croissants and cappuccino, and the traditional gift giving. Even Matt has gone out of his way, carving a miniature version of his Artemis sculpture – an abstraction of the huntress in full flight, painted in red that exactly matches my hair. It's beautiful. Matt is not the most sensitive of people but he's been kind to me since the Eddie affair, so something good has come out of it after all.

Jez and Emms take me to Covent Garden for lunch, followed by a binge of window-shopping in the West End. Usually we scour the upmarket boutiques for ideas, then buy fabric from the cloth market on Windsor Street to make up our own designs, with an original twist, of course. Today, however, I buy a pair of swanky shoes and a real leather handbag with the birthday money Nancy sent me.

In the evening our friends come around and we party till late. After everyone has gone, Jake and I linger in the kitchen. Not quite empty glasses and wine bottles litter every surface and the sour smell of spilt beer fills the air. With only the soft glow of a table lamp filtering through the still smoky atmosphere, it's easy to ignore the mess. The clearing up can wait till tomorrow but we are not quite ready to sleep yet.

'Great party.' Jake stretches his long legs out beneath the table and yawns. A brush rarely comes the way of his thick brown hair, but tonight it's wilder than ever after some frantic dancing.

'Yes – thanks to you all.' Despite my reluctance to celebrate, it's been a fantastic day. I flop down opposite him, prizing off my new shoes and wiggling my toes. I've danced myself into blissful exhaustion.

'There's something else I want to give you, Nita. I wasn't sure about it, so I didn't give it to you this morning.' Jake feels shy about his gift. 'It caught my attention while I was browsing and I just knew it was meant for you. I'm not sure why.'

He hands me a small parcel, wrapped in the brown paper bag the shop assistant had placed it in. I turn it over in my hands, pretending to guess the contents. I'm enjoying the way he gives me the gift in its original paper bag, enjoying this little moment alone with Jake, my best friend.

'Mmm – let me see – a coffee-grinder? No?' I shake the parcel, feeling mischievous now. 'A box of crayons? An elephant?' We both burst out laughing. Then carefully, ceremoniously, I take the book out of the brown paper bag with 'Compendium Bookshop' printed on it, still smiling at the game.

I hold the book in my hand for a long while, studying the cover as I gather in my scattered thoughts. As I lift my gaze to meet Jake's, I feel a tear spring from the corner of my eye. I'm not sad – it's just that my heart has welled up and overflowed.

The title of the book is *The Myth of Freedom*, and on the cover is a design drawn in red against a deep golden-yellow background. My eye follows the lines as they weave back and forth, a continuous thread that turns and criss-crosses and returns to form a knotted pattern. I recognise the image. It's the very same one that is embroidered onto the cover of my grandmother's cushion.

I hold the book to my chest. 'Thank you, Jake. It's...I think I'm going to enjoy it.' I'm not sure whether I've ever shown Jake the cushion, or explained its meaning to him, but he might have glimpsed it and remembered the distinctive design. Or perhaps it's pure coincidence. Whichever it is, he has unwittingly re-opened a door, and this time I know I have no choice but to go through it.

We say goodnight and I climb the two flights of stairs to my attic room. I bring the cushion out from its dusty corner and lay it on my bed, beside the book. It's unmistakably the same motif – a single line that loops back and forth in a precise pattern, with no beginning and no end – an eternal thread.

I thumb through the book. It's about the Buddhist view of life, written by a Tibetan man with a strange sounding name. The title to one chapter catches my eye – *Aloneness*. I read –

> *The spiritual path is not fun – better not to begin it. If you must begin, then go all the way, because if you begin and quit, the unfinished business you have left behind begins to haunt you all the time …*
>
> *Stepping on the path involves you in continual growth, which may be tremendously painful since you sometimes try to step off the path. You do not really want to get into it fully; it is too close to the heart. And you are not able to trust in the heart. Your experiences become too penetrating, too naked, too obvious. Then you try to escape, but your avoidance creates pain which in turn inspires you to continue on the path.*

As I continue reading, I feel as if the author were sitting right here in the room with me, speaking directly to my own heart. I recognise myself, my pain, my own life in his words. I had not thought of myself as being on a spiritual path – only one of confusion and suffering – but here is someone naming my experience, my deep inner sense of aloneness, and calling it part of a spiritual journey. Could this be possible? He is turning my perception of my life upside down.

Falling in love with Richard opened my heart. Losing him,

then my father, ripped open a chasm in my soul. The path had been opened for me then but I tried to escape – to leave life, to avoid pain, to deny the truth, and to forget what I had to do. But there is unfinished business to attend to, if I am to trust my heart again. First, I must discover the truth about my mother and grandmother, and I can no longer avoid the task.

After Nancy found Liza's letter, I had called Martin, eager to tell him that we had a grandmother. I asked if he would help me to find her.

'It'll be too difficult, Anita. You don't even know her surname. Where would you begin to look?' he asked. The discovery didn't hold the same importance for him as it did for me. He was deeply involved with Leticia and his studies, and couldn't muster enthusiasm for this search into the past.

'I don't know, but I'm sure there's a way. Will you help me, Martin, please?'

'Well, if you tell me exactly what you need, I'll see what I can do. But you must start this thing off – I'll be here to lend a hand if I can.' I heard the reluctance in his voice.

Once I had settled in London, I went to Somerset House and asked to see records. Rows and rows of files held the secrets of generations of families, hidden and lost to the world until someone dared to search for the sometimes-terrible truth of ancestry. About my mother, Ellen Rushton, I learnt nothing more than I already knew. When I asked the librarian, with her impossibly neat bun and dark blue suit, if she could help me find out about a young woman from Belfast called Liza, possibly born Elizabeth, she looked at me over her large dark-rimmed glasses and simply said, 'No.' I felt diminished and dismissed.

Then my life came adrift again, with a string of crises both minor and major. We were evicted from our first squat in Stepney and left homeless for a while. Then it was Martin's wedding – not really a crisis but it felt like another loss, for Leticia and her large Spanish family had taken him far away from me. Finally, a relationship fell dramatically apart and I was left floundering once more.

I had put my quest aside, for the time being, but my desire to find my grandmother has never completely died. Now it is being re-ignited in an unexpected way.

After a restless night I wake early and come downstairs to a house that is still and quiet. Morning light streams in through the high sash window and falls in streaks across the table and the painted wood of the floorboards. I pad about the kitchen in my bare feet, putting on a pot of coffee and piling glasses from the party into a bowl of soapy water. Soon Jake joins me. He's meeting a friend for a cycle ride, and hopes the fresh air will blow away his hangover. They plan to take their bikes to the end of the Northern Line then cycle out into the countryside. As it's Sunday, the others are still in bed.

'Jake, can I ask you to do something for me?'

'Sure.' He sounds cheerful despite the hangover.

'Will you call me Anita. I want to use my full name from now on. I know Nita's easier, but it doesn't feel right anymore. It makes me feel as if I'm – well, not quite whole.' I pause, struggling to find words for a feeling I have just begun to recognise. 'Yes, that's exactly how I feel – not a whole person – as if I'm not all here. I want to grow up, feel like a woman, all of me. Can you understand that?' I see a momentary flicker of incomprehension clouds his eyes, then he grins.

'Does that mean I have to be Jacob, then?' he jokes.

'No, of course not – unless you want to be. But will you do this for me?'

'Okay, if it's important to you. But what's brought this on, Nita – Anita?'

'The book you gave me…'

'Oh no, is this all my doing?' Jake throws his arms up in a gesture of mock despair.

'Yes, but in a good way. I want to explain it to you Jake. I want you to know. Maybe you can help me.'

He pours out a mug of coffee and rests his chin in his hands, looking at me inquisitively. 'Okay. What's it about?'

A strip of sunlight falls across the table between us, as a cloud shifts south-wards. Jake's face looks transparent in its pale reflection, his eyes like bright pools of captured rainwater. He knows about my mother's adoption and her untimely death, but I have never talked about how this affected me. I search for the words that might convey something of my experience to him. Now it feels important that he knows, where in the past it had felt imperative that I try to hide these difficult feelings.

'I've always felt lost, without a sense of roots – as if I had no history, no place of my own in the world. My dad and Martin loved me – but to not know your mother, or your grandmother, where you come from...' My toes slide along a crack between the floorboards, feeling for where the paint has begun to flake. My hands remember precisely the feeling of the rough boards and the paint brush in my hand, swishing back and forth. They know every inch of this floor. It was too stained to leave naked. Years of spills – water, soup, blood (I imagine the many lives and dramas taking place in this kitchen over the decades) – had left it a patchwork of brown shapes, dissected by ragged lines where strips of linoleum had been laid and, years later, unlaid.

'Sometimes I feel as if I'm floating, as if I could fly off at any moment. It takes so much energy just to keep my feet on the earth.' I flap my arms down at my sides in a gesture of despair at ever finding the right words.

'I know. I can see it, how hard it can be for you.' Jake must wonder where this is leading. 'So what does the book have to do with it all?'

'Do you know the cushion that I have in the corner of my room, the blue embroidered one?'

'I've seen it there. I know it's significant to you in some way, but I never really looked at it – it seemed very private.'

'When my mother died, the cushion was given to me. It was from her own mother – a funny thing to have as a family heirloom, but it's all I ever knew of my grandmother. Well, the design that's embroidered on it is exactly the same as the one on the cover of the book you gave me. It's a spiritual symbol called the Knot of Eternity.' I clasp my hands together and bring them up to my chest to contain the surge of excitement that is suddenly pressing against my ribs, forcing me to take a deep breath, as I begin to put the fragments of the puzzle together and into words for the first time. 'There must be a link, a connection of some kind between my grandmother and this ancient symbol. It's just so strange.'

'Well, yes, I guess so.' Jake is struggling to see the significance I've attributed to this coincidence. He rubs the two-day growth on his chin and keeps his eyes focussed intently on me. His brow furrows slightly – a sign that he is trying hard to understand. I try to calm my breath. Maybe this doesn't make any sense at all. Perhaps I'm imagining a connection where there is none, but still, something has awakened in me and it will not be put back to sleep. I continue.

'After my father died, Nancy found a letter amongst his papers. It challenged everything I had been told about my grandmother.' I describe the contents of the letter and the feelings that it stirred in me – the excitement and the anger, the hope and longing it awakened. I pause, long enough to hear the clock above the sink tick one whole minute away, long enough to let Jake absorb the information.

'I just know she's alive, somewhere – I feel it. Reading the book last night, I began to feel her presence again, just as I'd done after reading her letter. I'm sure she's alive and I want to find her.' My feet are planted firmly on the floor now and I am leaning towards Jake, ready to spring up like an animal unexpectedly set free, so strong is the current of energy running through my body.

Jake is following now. He rubs his head, further dishevelling his still un-brushed shock of hair, then reaches across the table, through the stream of sunlight, and takes my hand. Looking directly into my eyes, he smiles – that deep smile which lights up his whole face – the smile that I know and love so well. 'I can see how important this is to you. You should go for it. See if you can find your grandmother.'

I sigh and sink back into the chair. 'Thank you, Jake. That means so much to me – just to know you're on my side.'

'Of course I'm on your side, and if I can help you I will.' He squeezes my hand. 'So where shall we start?'

'I've no idea,' I laugh. It's enough for now to delight in his smile, and feel the relief that his understanding and support bring.

The doorbell rings, startling me with its shrill ding-dong.

'That'll be Steve.' Jake glances at the clock and jumps up. 'Sorry – I have to go. We'll talk about it later – promise.' He gives me a kiss on the cheek as he squeezes between my chair and the dresser, collects his bike from the hallway and leaves the house. I turn my attention to the washing-up, glad to have something to occupy my hands as my mind continues to race.

The last rays of evening light are straying through the high bay window, bathing the room in a warm and golden glow, as the three of us gather. We all lavished our artistry onto this the spacious room, creating a palace of obscure design and chic comfort. Distressed paintwork on the walls gives the impression of an ancient Italian villa whose faded glamour only adds to its charm. A chandelier with half its glass beads missing succeeds in emphasising this effect. It was here when we moved in, along with the grand marble fireplace, still in perfect condition. Old sofas, recovered from skips on the street, had been draped with elegant cloths and piled high with patchwork and embroidered cushions that Jez and I made. The old pine cupboards, bookshelves and coffee table had been bought, over the years, at Camden Lock, and lovingly stripped of their varnish and paint by Matt and Jake.

Emms is sitting cross-legged in the middle of one of the three sofas, amidst a flurry of amber chenille throw and crimson velvet cushions. I feel relieved to have confided in her during a late afternoon walk up Primrose Hill. In the past I feared the shadows inside me might contaminate my friends, or burden them, or turn them away from me, but I don't want to hide myself any longer.

Jake opens a bottle of wine and pours out three glasses. 'Cheers. To questing.' He raises his glass to the room. For a moment I am back in Sybil's cottage, holding three glasses in my hand as I teeter on a knife-edge between joy and despair. I take a sip of the cheap Beaujolais, left over from the party.

'I don't know where to start. I failed once before and the fear of failing again paralyses me before I even begin. Nancy and Martin don't want to get involved,' I confess.

Emms, the more practical and organised one, is feeling pleasantly challenged by this mystery. An avid reader of detective stories, she loves solving problems. She brings out a Miss Marple hat and giggles as she perches it on her head. The jet-black line of her fringe hovers over her eyelids, trembling slightly each time she blinks her big dark eyes. Emms has cheeks that dimple as she smiles, and lips that are wide and full – the mouth of a singer, surely, I had thought when we first met, but Emms' voice is surprisingly soft and wispy. It belies the strength of her character.

'Let's begin by looking at what you know about your mother,' she suggests.

'Her adopted name was Ellen Rushton. Her birth mother named her Eleanor, but I don't know the surname. That's a problem, isn't it.' I look at Emms, who seems to be the one who might know.

'No problem – just a challenge.' She is determined to be positive. Emms refuses to be defeated at any cost, a trait that can lead her to appear frustratingly stubborn at times.

in those days.' Time slows down and my breathing feels tight. Images of ancient horrors are flooding my mind. I hug my arms about my chest, as if I could keep out this nightmare and protect Liza from some inhumane torment.

'Let's not jump to conclusions. We're just gathering information for now,' Emms says, bringing me back to earth. I take a deep breath and look around the room. Familiar colours soothe my eyes – the pale green walls, gold, crimson and purple cascades of cloth covering sofas and framing the wide window, the mellow tones of pinewood and oak. 'First thing is to look for her adoption records. If that doesn't lead anywhere, then you can check the parish records for Belfast,' Emms is saying.

'It sounds quite simple when you put it like that.' Again I am wavering on the knife-edge, wanting to hold onto a glimmer of hope, the hint of a possibility, and yet fearing to trust. Trust seems such a fickle thing. It can lead to the deepest hurts of all.

'Anita, don't expect to find out straight away. You need patience.' I can see that Jake also feels a little overwhelmed by the difficulty of the search, but I know he will be there for me. He always is. His words remind me of a passage in the book. Reading this afternoon, I came across a chapter on patience. The author seems to say that it is a spiritual quality that must be cultivated at the beginning of the journey.

'You're right, Jake – my wise friend. I need patience, and I need you to keep reminding me of that.' I feel a little strength and resolve return as I feel Jake beside me, his unwavering commitment, his good-natured embrace of all that life chooses to throw his way.

He laughs. 'I've not been called wise before. We make a good team – Emms the practical one, Jake the wise one. At your service, Anita.' He sweeps his hand in the air with a grand flourish. It is so reminiscent of the gesture Martin had made that afternoon, all those years ago, that I want to laugh and cry all at once. It was the day I had learnt, for certain, that my father was dying.

I draw myself back to the present. I want to be here, now, not lost in my past. 'Thanks, both of you. Next week I'll see what I can find out about adoption records. I know someone who might be able to help. One thing at a time.'

'Yes, one step at a time. You can do this, Anita,' says Emms. I'm not sure I believe her, but her systematic way creates the illusion that everything is quite clear and straightforward.

'How about another drink?' Jake says, stretching out his long limbs and yawning. 'I think that's enough detective work for one night.' I sigh and lean back into the soft cushions of the sofa. At least I have this, my tribe of friends. I feel a rush of gratitude that momentarily eclipses all fear and uncertainty.

Fifteen

It's time to begin my search in earnest. After the first failed attempt I told myself that one day, when the demands of the moment – and the pleasures too – lessened, and the imperative to seek became irresistible, I would try again, but I've put it off for much too long. Now the path is opening up and I have no choice but to step onto it.

Each Monday morning, I cycle to a local school to lead a group of children with special needs in the arts of painting and clay modelling. It's my most challenging class but also the most rewarding.

The first day is etched vividly into my memory. As I entered the classroom four or five boys were running about the room wildly, throwing pencil spears at each other and screaming at the tops of high-pitched voices. My ears hurt. At a desk two girls, identical twins, sat with their heads close together, almost touching, engrossed in a heated discussion. There was something otherworldly about the scene. As I listened more closely, I realised they were speaking in their own secret language – gibberish to anyone else but completely comprehensible to them. Several children were wandering about the classroom aimlessly, picking things up and dropping them. Others sat at desks or on the floor and looked at me expectantly as I entered, anxious expressions on their faces. I imagined they were the ones needing order to be restored as quickly as possible.

My attention was drawn to a small boy who sat alone in a corner of the classroom. He was huddled under a desk, arms wrapped tightly around his knees, rocking forward and back and staring vacantly into space. This was Johnny.

After two years of diligent effort, I had found ways to connect with some of the most difficult of the children, and draw out of them a magic that no-one had known existed. The art class gave them a way to express feelings they had locked away for years, and channel energy that had often been expressed in destructive ways. It also gave a momentary sense of purpose to my own world of broken dreams. Most of the children threw themselves into the work with passion, producing vibrant pictures and clay figures that surprised, and often moved, their teachers and parents. As for the others, I kept them occupied for a while, giving the staff a break – at least that's how they saw it.

I sit in the staff room after my class, chatting over a mug of coffee with Sue, the fourth-year teacher. We have formed a mutually respectful friendship. Having seen the benefits to the children, she is supportive of my work and wants more art therapy at the school.

'Sue, can I ask your advice about something?'

'Yes, of course.'

'I want to find out about someone who was adopted – my mother actually. She died when I was two and I want to see if I can find out about her birth mother – my grandmother.' I feel shy as I look at Sue to see how she is receiving this. A hint of surprise flickers across her face, then is quickly replaced by an expression of sympathy. 'I wonder if you have contact with adoption agencies, and if you know whom I could ask?'

'We have adopted children in the school from time to time. They often end up in special needs because they've been moved around from home to home, or taken from their parents if they were thought to be at risk. It can leave them quite traumatised, understandably,' Sue explains, raising her voice above the escalating volume of conversation as the staff room begins to fill. 'Like Johnny, for example – he was with several foster families before he was adopted.'

'Ah, yes. He's a really bright boy, no developmental problems – just very hurt and confused.' I had empathised with Johnny from the beginning, and felt protective towards him. I had coaxed him out of his refuge under the desk by sitting on the floor beside him, week after week, with a sketchpad placed between us. I had drawn and Johnny had watched warily as he rocked.

Then one day he picked up a crayon and began to make his own marks on the paper – just black lines and squiggles at first, then monsters, animals and devils, all black with teeth and staring eyes. Over the months his drawings evolved into colourful figures, full of character and humour. He was telling me the story of his inner world and all the parts of himself that peopled it – the sad, angry, lost, frightened, funny and strong parts all found their way into his drawings. I welcomed them all and Johnny loved me for that.

'I can give you the number of the agency that we deal with,' Sue is saying. I struggle to hear her above the din. Sitting in a huddle behind us, a group of women are laughing hysterically. I imagine this is the way they release their tensions after a demanding class, and wonder how they manage to do this job day after day, shuttling from noisy staff-room to the chaos of a classroom where they must convince thirty over-active children that education would be a good thing. Then back to the din of the staff-room, endlessly. 'Each area keeps its own records but the Camden office should be able to point you in the right direction.' She takes a folder from a shelf that runs the length of the staff room, piled high with notebooks, files and reference books. Services and Agencies – she thumbs through to find the page.

'Here we are – Camden Adoption Agency. They should be able to help.'

'If they can at least give me an idea of who to ask, that would be a good start. It all feels a bit daunting at the moment.'

'I can imagine. But it can be really important to find these things out. I didn't know your mother had died when you were so young.' She looks at me quizzically, wondering if I want to tell more of the story, but I've said enough for now. Sue scribbles the number onto a scrap of paper, which I tuck away in my purse. 'Anyway, let me know if I can be of any more help.'

'I will. Thanks a lot, Sue. I'll let you know how it goes.' I scoop up my jacket and bag. 'Must be going now – I've got an idea for a painting I want to get started on. See you next week.'

'See you. And good luck.' Sue returns the folder to its allocated place on the shelf and gathers up her notes for the next class as I leave the clamourous room.

It's a hot and sticky afternoon. I head down towards the Embankment, cycling through the back streets, past Russell Square and Covent Garden, to avoid the crush and stifling fumes of Tottenham Court Road. The aroma of roasting coffee beans, warm beer and lunches being cooked, drifts from the pubs and small restaurants that have sprung up along these lanes. Office workers stand in clusters outside open doors, the men with white shirts unbuttoned at the top, ties loosened and sleeves rolled up. I remember how my father would roll up his sleeves at weekends as he prepared to turn his hand to whatever work was needed in the house or garden. An image of him standing by the back door, a hammer in one hand and cup of coffee in the other, evokes a sharp sensation at the back of my heart.

The young women outside the pubs are slim and pretty in their tightly fitting dark suits that mimic those of the men, but for the short skirts of course. Their hair, uniformly sleek and well cut, advertises the best brands of home colouring with bold shades of blonde, brunette and black. I feel glad to be free this afternoon, as I survey these neatly parcelled creatures.

I don't envy those women who feel the need to dress up like this on such a warm summer's day.

My nostrils are assailed by the hot, dry air, saturated with the smell of burnt dust that seeps up out of the underground stations as I cycle past. By evening this strangely seductive scent will have permeated all the city streets, drawing the young people out to wander in droves. The cool night air will eventually be welcome.

As I pedal my old bike through the city streets, my hair is whipped up into motion, flying out behind me like a flame. The soft fabric of my dress flaps about me like a loose sail. I have a need to be by the water this afternoon.

Arriving at the Embankment, I push my bike along the wide pathway, past a homeless man sitting on a patch of grass beneath a tree, and seat myself on the next empty bench. I feel the old man's gaze follow me, but he turns away as I glance back, pretending he hasn't been watching me. He continues to look in the general direction of the river. I also let my gaze fall on the mass of moving water – we are two lost souls sitting side by side, alone, watching the world pass by. The tide is ebbing and a light breeze ripples the surface of the grey-brown body of water as it slips sluggishly by. Across the river, the smart new buildings of the South Bank seem to mock the dirty water of the Thames.

Despite the background hubbub of traffic, the sultry stillness of afternoon has descended and a sense of calm envelops me on my bench. I am free to dream and reflect here.

I feel the need for space around me, a little time to prepare myself as I begin my search. Though daunted by the seeming impossibility of it, something else is driving me on, like an underground stream that has no choice but to seek the ocean. It's all about timing, waiting for the right moment, I tell myself. On Thursday I have only one class, an evening class – Life Drawing for Beginners. An easy group to teach, they are keen, willing, some of them showing real promise. Thursday will be a good day to begin, a day with little pressure and not much preparation to do.

I take the book out of my bag and begin to read. The contents, as well as the cover, intrigue me. The feeling that this stranger from a far-away land is here, talking directly to me, has lingered. His words both challenge and comfort. He writes about life – the human condition, emotions, familiar problems – in a way I find both strange and very down to earth at the same time. I left home at eighteen feeling rootless and without guidance, unprepared for the world. Like unseasoned wood, I would warp and twist into shape, moulded by circumstances I felt I had no control over. But here at last is somebody giving me clues as to how I might manage my feelings and orient myself in life. I will try to follow some of his advice. For example, breathing – he talks about that.

Returning the book to the bicycle basket, I take out my sketchpad and pencil. As I let the pencil wander across the paper, I'm reminded of the feeling of the glass pulling my hand across the ouija board, weaving a path, connecting letters into words, and words into messages. My mind empties out as my hand begins to trace the familiar design. Then I find I am interlacing the Celtic knot, with its more rounded twists, into the angular turns of the Knot of Eternity.

The similarity to Liza's embroidered pattern had struck me years ago, when my class was studying Celtic designs for a school art project. But now, as I allow myself to be drawn deeper into these flowing pathways, letting my hand follow the complex shapes and inter-weavings, hidden meanings and connections begin to surface. Maybe the Tibetan man is right when he says everything is interconnected – nothing separate. I glimpse a quality of wholeness, a quality I have not truly felt before, as my pencil weaves this new design.

Looking up from the drawing, my eyes rest on the moving water of the Thames again. The constancy of the motion of the rivers and oceans, always ebbing and flowing into each other, is reassuring. It gives me another image for the wholeness and connectedness I long to feel inside myself. I pick up the book again and open it at the end.

My eye catches a few phrases as I flick through the last pages –

> *If a person is able to see the energies of the universe as they are, then shapes and colours and patterns suggest themselves; symbolism happens.*
>
> *The whole world is symbol – not symbol in the sense of a sign representing something other than itself, but symbolism in the sense of the highlights of the vivid qualities of things as they are.*

The words resonate in me. Even though I'm not sure exactly what they mean, they strike a chord in my imagination, a note reverberating through me as a truth intuitively felt rather than logically known. I want to trust this way of knowing, stop being bound by my mind's fierce demand for the rightness or wrongness of things: I was right to love Richard. It was wrong that he died. Esther and Trevor Rushton were my mother's parents – wrong. They lied to her – right. Being bound to this tight way of thinking is so tiring. I'm tired of right and wrong. I want the vivid qualities of the world to fill me.

A softening of the air hints that evening will soon be drawing in. The sun still shines strongly but is dipping into its descending arc up river now. It's time to return home. I put my book, sketchpad and jacket into the basket and begin to wheel my bike back along the Embankment towards the bridge. As I pass the old man, sitting on the next bench now, he beams a big toothless grin. White strands of hair shoot out from under a battered black trilby and his eyes crinkle in delight as I smile back.

'Ah, you shouldn't be going to the end before you've read the whole book, now, or you'll never know the journey,' he says, in a soft but distinctive Irish accent, as I walk past. I stop mid-step. He continues to beam at me through crinkled eyes and a mouth that is half-hidden by a thick white beard. I can't feel embarrassed under such a warm and accepting gaze. Instead I laugh.

'You're right. I'll read the whole book,' I reply, and walk on, smiling to myself.

It's Thursday and I can't procrastinate any longer. The others have left the house, or disappeared into the basement to work. I sit for a few moments, enjoying the stillness that is left in the wake of the early morning activity. A gentle rain is pattering at the window, streaking it with silver rivulets that meander slowly towards the sill. I focus on my breath for a few moments, just as the Tibetan man recommends. It calms me a little, but still I feel anxious about the task ahead.

I'm in the living room, sitting by the phone with the scrap of paper scrunched up in my moist palm. I unfold it and study the number, scrawled in royal blue ink, as if it had to be remembered by heart. Picking up the receiver I dial, and wait, my heart pounding heavily. Eventually a voice pipes out – 'We're sorry, no-one can take your call at the moment. Please leave your name, number and a brief message, and we will call you back as soon as we can.' I slam down the receiver. What am I going to say anyway? During the past few days I have gone over my opening statement many times, but now that I need it, I can't remember the carefully composed message. I gather my thoughts and dial again.

I'm just about to leave the prepared message when a new voice answers.

'Hello, Camden Adoption Agency. Can I help you?' The woman's voice sounds kind but professionally distant.

'Yes, at least I hope so. I, er…I mean, I want to find out… I wonder, if you would be able to give me some information,' I stutter. I haven't felt this awkward since I was five years old and starting school. My father had taken the morning off work and we stood, holding hands, in the doorway to the big entrance hall. From behind us, the sun cast our shadows over the tiled floor, one very large, one small beside it. People stared at us. Every other child had a mother to hold their hand and I felt different, a stranger in this new place. I think this was the first time I really grasped what it meant to have a family that was not shaped like other families. I remember a teacher coming over to us and asking my name. The words stuck in my mouth like cotton wool and all I could do was stare up at her smiling face.

'Well, I'll try – that's what we're here for. Are you one of our clients?' comes the voice through the crackling phone-line.

'No, I'm not.' I hope that doesn't matter. Am I to be rejected because I'm not a client? Do I have to do something, sign up or join something, in order to ask questions? 'My mother was adopted. I want to find out what happened to her, and see if I can trace my grandmother. I think she's still alive somewhere, and I want to find her. Can you help?' The words come tumbling out. My hands are trembling. To steady myself I take a breath and study a single trail of rain that slides slowly down the window-pane. It stops halfway and stays there until it's joined by another drop – then the added momentum sends it on its way again. How I long for another human body by my side, nudging me on, keeping me moving through my life. Richard, always Richard – the one who is missing from my side. He belongs there.

'Oh, I see. I'm afraid I can't help you with that, but I'll give you another number you can call. The records office deals with requests for searches.' She recites a number, which I hastily scratch onto the back of the scrap of paper from Sue's notepad. 'Is there anything else I can help you with?"

'No, that's all, thank you. I'm sorry to have bothered you.' I wonder why I am apologising – it's such a terrible habit, one I must have learnt from Granny who, without saying a single word, was able to fill me with the belief that everything that was wrong in our family had been my fault. She had to look after us because my mother had gone away, and my mother had gone because of me. I never could understand why this was, but it seemed to be so.

'No problem. Goodbye then.' The kind but efficient woman hangs up, and there is silence again.

I feel jarred by the conversation. But at least I could be one small step closer to finding out something that might begin to unravel these mysteries. I take a few deep breaths and prepare to try again.

'Good morning, can I help you?'' replies another voice, this time a man's.

'Good morning. I would like to know if it's possible to trace somebody – if you can help me, or advise me where I could look for her records?' This time I speak slowly, but still feel helplessly inarticulate. I grip the phone tightly and my knuckles turn white.

'I see. And is this person a relative of yours?' asks the man.

'Yes. My mother was adopted, and I want to trace her mother – my grandmother.'

'I see.' I can imagine a slow stroking of the chin as the words are ponderously delivered. 'And is your mother still alive?'

'No.'

'And do you know her original name?' asks the ponderous man.

'Not really.' I notice that the rain has stopped. A pale sun has broken through thinning clouds, and the streams of water that cling to the window-pane have been set alight. Tiny shimmering iridescent shards dart into the room, piercing its stillness with a shower of rain-light.

'I see. And do you know if your mother ever tried to access the records?'

'I'm not sure. Not as far as I know.' I feel as if I am being interrogated for some unknown crime. I want to surrender to the beauty of the prisms of light that are dancing across the room, but I know I must stay focussed. One hand clutches the receiver even tighter, while the other crumples then smooths out the piece of paper with the phone numbers written on it.

'Then it will be more difficult – you might not be given access to her records if this is the case. You should also understand that sometimes people don't want to be identified and contacted. And in some cases, there are no traceable records. You should be aware that this might be the case, especially as this adoption took place many years ago.' The man speaks in a monotone voice, as if reading from a script that he has recited many times before.

Suddenly my energy is draining away, as a sense of helplessness sweeps over me again. My fingers feel numb, my arms turn limp and empty, like a puppet whose strings have been cut. I almost drop the phone and fumble to press it more firmly to my ear.

'Oh, of course. I suppose it might not be easy. But I think she'd want to see me. I have a letter from her,' I offer.

'A letter. Well, that's a start.' The man's voice carries a trace of feigned politeness, as if to cover a lack of genuine interest. 'First you will have to register your details, show proof of your identity – a birth certificate is best.' He pauses and clears his throat. 'Unless you know your mother's full birth name you won't be able to apply for her original birth certificate. In this case, you will need to apply for a copy of your mother's original full adoption certificate. This will tell you which court to apply to for access to adoption files.' Again he pauses. I feel a surge of panic rising through my chest, a thick tube of lead reaching up from my solar plexus to my throat, threatening to choke me. 'As a last resort you can try the General Registrar Office, but they only release information in special circumstances.' He stops speaking and there is silence for a few long moments.

'The court. I see.' My mind is spinning, and I don't see at all. That old feeling of being in the wrong is here again, pressing against the hollow chambers of my heart, as I imagine standing up in court before a judge, admitting the terrible truth – yes, I am guilty, punish me.

'What's your name? I'll make a note, so that if you do want to pursue this, they'll know you have contacted me.'

'Anita Rose.'

'Thank you, Miss Rose.'

'Ms,' I correct him, out of habit, then regret having spoken when he simply ignores me. I forgive myself though, as habits are a useful way to appear to stay present, and I am struggling to do this right now.

'You will need to contact the adoption records office to apply for a full adoption certificate first. If you have them, you should bring along your mother's short birth certificate, which shows only her name and date of birth – no parents' names – and her adoption certificate which will show the adoptive parents' names. This is the address and number. I suggest you call them to make an appointment. They will help you to trace her, if it turns out to be possible.' He gives the impression that he thinks otherwise.

I squeeze the address and phone number onto the now ragged square of paper as he slowly recites them. Next time I'll be prepared with a large notebook.

'Thank you very much.' I manage to stop myself from apologising for taking up the polite man's time.

'Goodbye.' He leaves no space for further questions.

'Goodbye.' I put down the receiver and let out a deep sigh. So this is how it works. A great surge of longing for my father creeps up from my belly, passes right through my heart and escapes from the corners of my eyes in a thin trickle of salty tears. How I wish he could be here at this moment. He would know how to do this.

The sun is now shining brightly and the mesmerising show of rain-light has been transformed into an ordinary morning room. Light reflects brightly from the sparkling houses across the road. I close my eyes, inviting the warmth of the sun to banish the chill that has settled around my bones, before picking up the receiver again.

'Good morning. How can I help you?'

This time I will be brief and concise. 'I'd like to make an appointment please – to apply to see some records.'

'Just a minute. I'll put you through,' says the voice.

'We're very busy and short-staffed at the moment, and with summer holidays coming up, I'm afraid it won't be until September now,' says the second woman. 'I'm very sorry about that, but with the cuts, you know.' I have no choice but to accept, and wait. An appointment is made for the first week in September.

That's enough for today. I feel tired, my head aches, and I need to paint.

'Hi Anita. Come and join us,' Jake calls from the kitchen, as I arrive home. I painted for several hours, digesting the information and ironing out the jagged edges in my mind as I spread colours and refined shapes. Only then could I begin to focus on my evening class. Even so, I was distracted during the class and feel weary now. The solitude of my room calls but I accept Jake's invitation.

'How did it go?' asks Jez. She and Matt now know about my search. Matt considers it a distraction. Jez is intrigued but doesn't quite appreciate the importance of it. Still, we have been friends since our first term at college and she will support me. Emms is out on a date with an old acquaintance who turned up at the party. They hit it off immediately. Like all the other times, she hopes that this one will be 'the one'.

'I don't know. It was frustrating. It feels even more impossible than before. I have so little information, and the man I spoke to seemed to be saying it wasn't worth pursuing. And if I do pursue it, I've got to go to court, and all sorts of things like that. It feels like a nightmare.' I stop to catch my breath.

'Anita, patience, remember. Don't give up yet. What did he say you should do?' asks Jake.

'First of all, apply for a full adoption certificate. I'll need my mother's birth certificate to go ahead with this – I'll ask Nancy if she's found it amongst my dad's things. And I've made an appointment for an interview in September.' At least the next step is beginning to crystallise out of the fragments of information.

'Great. That's something – or it could be,' Jake adds.

'Yes, it's something. If Nancy has the certificate, that is.'

'And what about that book you've been reading all week, Anita – what's that about?' Matt is eager to change the subject.

'The one Jake gave me? Buddhism.'

'Ah – now that sounds like something worth pursuing. Can I borrow it when you've finished?' asks Matt, more engaged with the conversation now. He had been thumbing through the evening paper as we talked.

'Hey – you can buy your own. I thought you were wealthy now, with your own exhibition coming up.' Jake is teasing. Matt doesn't mind – as the only men in the household, it seems obligatory that they indulge in some competitive male banter now and then.

'The exhibition won't make me rich – in fact the mounts for the new sculptures will probably cost more than I could ever hope to earn from any sales they make,' he protests.

'But it's great exposure for you,' Jez interjects, proud of Matt and so keen to see him succeed. 'Lots of people will see your work there – critics too. It's bound to bring you –'

'Fame and fortune!' jokes Jake. We all laugh, knowing it's unlikely, but then you just never do know.

'I hope it will Matt. You deserve it, if anyone does. And yes, you can borrow the book, but it might be a while before I'm finished with it.' I take the mug of tea that Jake has poured for me, and raise it. 'To Matt. To fame and fortune.'

'Yay'. We toast Matt, and our own far-off dreams of imagined futures.

Sixteen

North Norfolk – 1981

I'm about to hang up the phone when Nancy's voice comes over, a little faint.

'Hello.'

'Hi Nancy, it's me.'

'What a surprise to hear from you again, so soon.' Phone calls are usually intermittent, and we had spoken on my birthday just last weekend. 'Is everything alright?'

'Yes, fine. Are you busy?' I ask cheerily.

'No. I was just standing by the kitchen window, trying to muster up energy to do my yoga practice. It's tempting to be out in the garden though.'

'It must be looking nice.'

'Yes. The roses and summer clematis are at their best just now.' An abundance of flowers cover the walls that surround her little corner of paradise, filling the air with their scent at this time of year. Nancy is glad of the privacy the walled garden gives her. Not all the village people had been welcoming when she first arrived. They say it takes three generations for an *incomer* to be accepted in Norfolk, and as a middle-aged woman on her own, she had felt the subject of some gossip and suspicion amongst the locals. I imagine she was being a little paranoid.

Nancy had sold our family home soon after I left for London, and bought a pretty brick and flint cottage, not far from Sybil's. She needed to start her life again, she said. She returned to teaching – more to keep herself occupied and to meet people than because she needed the money.

'Did you have a nice birthday?' she asks.

'I did – really nice. And you know what? I've decided to try to find Liza – the letter, you remember?'

'Oh Anita, are you sure this is wise? It could just lead you into more dead ends and disappointment, like last time. Just when you're doing so well, do you really need to open all of this up again?' I know Nancy longs to put the past behind her, completely, irrevocably, but it has a way of catching up with her when she least wishes or expects it.

'I have to do this, Nancy. I won't ask you to get involved if you don't want to. I just need to know if you have my mother's birth certificate. Do you think it could be amongst some of my dad's papers?'

'Oh dear. I suppose it might be. It's so long since I looked at them, I can't remember exactly what's there. I'll have a look. You and Martin should have any documents like that anyway.' Nancy had kept all the official papers and documents after my father's death – because Martin and I, as students, seemed to live such unsettled lives, she said. Now, at least Martin has a stable life, a family life.

'Thanks, Nancy. If you want, I'll come and help you look. I'll be on holiday from my classes in a few weeks and I could come up for a visit.'

'That would be lovely. I'm sure you'll be ready for a bit of a break.' I can hear the relief in Nancy's voice. I know she won't want to be going through James' papers and finding more relics from his life with Ellen. After his death, unearthing the mementos of my parents' shared past had been painful for Nancy. It was a life she was excluded from, and I can understand why she would prefer not to be confronted with it all again.

Our conversation is brief. I have a friend to meet in town and have to fly. We make a plan for a summer visit, and I put the phone down. I can imagine that Nancy's tentative moment of willpower, the gathering of energy and intention that would have taken her to stretch out on her yoga mat, has vanished. Instead, she will go out into the garden and sit down at the small white patio table. For a moment I am back at Nancy's cottage, remembering a peaceful day I had spent there last summer – just sitting for hours in the garden. I watched chaffinches pecking for insects on the branches of the pear tree and a flock of red admirals fluttering about the buddleia. Apart from that, stillness, and a deep sense of peace. If only every day could be like this, Nancy had said. And I had to agree. There was something about arriving at the end of the road when you reached the Norfolk coast. No one was passing through. Travellers arrived and settled there.

I can still recall the strong scent of lavender that drifted on the soft breeze. The border of lavender, growing around the stone slabs in the centre of the garden, was the first thing Nancy had planted when she moved in. Tending the garden helped give her a sense of belonging there, when everything was so new and unfamiliar, she told me. Over the years it had helped her to grow a sense of roots again.

So I will visit in July and we will go through those final papers together. My room will be waiting, with its pinewood single bed, the matching flowered curtains and duvet cover – pastel blue, pink and lilac on an ecru background. Everything neat and in its place, ready for my next visit. Nancy keeps a room each for Martin and me, so that we will always feel we have a home to come back to if we need.

It had been hard for us when Nancy left the northeast and moved to Norfolk. We both felt displaced and I went to Nancy's new home rarely. My life in London had absorbed all of my attention. But recently I have begun to make more regular trips for long weekend breaks. I find myself looking forward to this visit, hopeful it will yield the information I need.

*

It's rained for three days and the air is much too cold for July. By the time I arrive, Nancy has lit the stove in the living room and stacked logs up against the wall of the inglenook. Neither of us wants to be outside today. It feels like autumn already.

Sybil comes around for supper. We have a lot of catching up to do and stay up till late, talking by the fireside. I agree to wait a day or two before looking for the birth certificate – first, a few days holiday will be good for both of us. School has just broken up and Nancy is sorely in need of a rest, she tells me.

When Monday arrives, the air is still cool, though the rains of the last few days have stopped. The familiar coastal mist has settled in. I have no wish to take any more damp walks on the beach. I am eager to start my search now.

'Nancy, can we look today? If you don't want to do this with me, just show me where everything is and I'll go through it by myself,' I say, as we finish breakfast.

'I'll help you.' Nancy pulls herself heavily out of her chair. She pauses for a moment, her arms propped against the kitchen table and neck sagging between bird-like shoulder blades. She has put on weight since James died, lost her sylph-like figure, but the real weight she carries is that of a burdened heart. I'm dragging her towards the doorway to her past. A door she does not want to go through. I can imagine the feeling of dread rising up behind her serene appearance. Though widowhood and the menopause have left her emotionally ragged, Nancy's softly lined face is always well composed these days. Yoga, she tells me, keeps her calm, but I can see the lines of pain that lie just below the surface. 'Just let me wash up first, while you get dressed. The boxes are in the attic – maybe you can get them down?'

'Sure. It's a squeeze getting in there, isn't it – I'll put my old jeans on.'

'Good idea. It'll be dusty too. I haven't been up there in ages.'

What Nancy kept of James' possessions had been packed

into three boxes. One is particularly heavy. Carefully I pull them out, one by one, and together we carry them down to the living room. I sit on the floor surrounded by the boxes.

'You look, Anita.' Nancy plumps down on the sofa behind me. There's a slight tremor in her voice.

'I'm sorry, Nancy – this is hard for you, isn't it. If you don't want to be here, I really can do it by myself.'

'I'm alright. We do need to sort all of this out anyway. You and Martin should probably have some of these things – if you feel settled enough in your house now, that is.'

'Yes, I'm settled enough. But let's see what there is.'

The first box, the heavy one, contains a treasure of old LPs – the best of James' extensive collection of classical and jazz albums, and some vintage rock & roll. Nancy has sold many of the records but had been unable to part with some of his favourites. I flip through them, wide-eyed.

'Wow, there's some great albums here. Original Elvis, Buddy Holly, Miles Davis, John Coltrane...he had good taste.' I stop, remembering who I am talking about. 'Of course he had good taste.' I turn to look at Nancy and smile at her. She squeezes my shoulder and musters a thin smile in return.

There is nothing here that will help my search, so I pack the records back into their box and open the second one.

'Photograph albums!' Now it's my turn to stand at the doorway to my past, feeling the tug of dread in my belly. On the first page of one of the albums, there I am – little more than a year old – with Martin and my father. We must have been on holiday – Bamburgh perhaps. There are steep sand dunes in the background and I am clutching a plastic bucket in one hand. My father holds my other hand.

On the next page is a photograph of me sitting on my mother's lap, with Martin standing beside us. Martin is smiling. One-year-old me looks as if I am about to cry – my face is wrinkled up and my fists clenched. I gaze at the young woman on whose knee baby-Anita sits. The face and the dark wavy hair are familiar from the photograph on my father's desk, but the expression has changed. This woman – my mother – is smiling, but her eyes look sad.

'I don't think I've ever seen these before.' I begin to turn the pages, studying the pictures of my mother – the woman whose absence has been such a strong presence throughout my life. Again and again, I see a smiling face with sad eyes looking out at me, as if through prison bars. Who was this woman? What was she like?

I trace a finger over the outline of my mother's face. 'She looks so sad. I wonder why?' I turn towards Nancy, as if she might have an answer to this question.

'I don't know, Anita. Your father talked so little about her, about that period of your lives. It was very painful for him to remember those times.' She speaks gently. We are both opening wounds that have been half-buried for years, but never forgotten, and care is called for. Like a heart that is cut open for surgery, perhaps we both need to do this – perhaps it will help to heal the old wounds. But the flesh where the knife cuts feels tender and raw.

I continue to gaze at the photographs, as if I might see right through the grainy black and white images to discover who this woman, my mother, really was. I wonder if Granny Rose was right – that it was my fault that my mother was so sad and that she left us.

'Anita love, why don't you take the photographs? Maybe you and Martin can look through them together sometime. You should have them,' Nancy says at last.

'Yes. Thank you, Nancy. I need some time to go through them, and I'll ask Martin if he wants to see them too. He's due a visit sometime soon.' Sadness pervades the room. I put the photo albums back in the box and close it up again.

The largest of the three boxes sits squarely in the space in front of me. 'Well, if it's here, it has to be in this one.' I peel off the parcel tape that Nancy had put there all those years ago.

'I'm not sure what's in there exactly. I thought I'd gone through all of his papers but maybe I missed something.' Nancy is apologetic. 'I'm sorry. I really ought to know where important documents like birth certificates are.'

In the box is a jumble of books, notebooks, magazines and folders.

'Ah – where to begin?' The familiar feeling of overwhelmment is creeping up again. I sit back on my heels and take a few breaths to curb its advance, then begin to take the books and folders out, one by one, and place them on the floor around me. Nancy, too, remembers to breathe deeply to steady herself. She has learnt to do this at her yoga class. Finally, Nancy and I have found something we share – breathing.

A couple of books about engineering design, an illustrated history of shipbuilding through the ages, a book of Shakespeare's sonnets, a pile of professional journals, some Ordnance Survey maps of Northumberland and Cumbria. I pick out a thick folder that contains my father's old school notebooks and reports, and read – "shows great promise, but must work harder" – "excellent results in all subjects" – "an intelligent and diligent student who could excel in any of his chosen subjects". I feel touched to imagine my father as a young schoolboy, striving and eventually succeeding.

At the bottom of the box is a thick folder of papers – this could be what I am looking for. Opening the folder out on the floor, I read the first paper – a certificate of qualification to work as a draughtsman. One by one, I turn each document over and read its contents out to Nancy – accounts of professional qualifications, prizes, a newspaper article and photograph of the new bridge he had helped design. The remnants of a life.

Eventually I come to a brown envelope with a folded piece of paper inside it. The thick paper is dry and grainy, almost like parchment, and faintly yellow in colour. Two other documents have been slipped inside it and I take them out. I lift back the three folds of the first yellowed paper to reveal a wide page with several columns. Between the red lines, in a carefully executed script, are the details of my father's birth certificate.

I unwrap the second one, the dry paper a faded green colour. It's the marriage certificate of my father and mother – James Michael Rose and Ellen Rushton. The time and place are all there, with the witnesses' signatures to prove that they had indeed become husband and wife on that day in 1948, at the parish church of Alnwick, in Northumberland.

I hold the third of the three documents lightly between my fingers, as if it might crumble into dust through the force of my attention. This must be the one I am looking for. I open it slowly and spread it out on top of the marriage certificate and my father's birth certificate.

'Yes, this is it – my mother's birth certificate! Ellen Rushton – born to Trevor Rushton and Esther Rushton, formerly Hollingsworth, on the seventeenth of April, 1927 – in Belfast, it says. But how can that be?' I'm confused. I turn to Nancy, who is now sitting on the floor beside me. 'These are her adoptive parents, not her birth parents. The man in the office told me that she would have been given a short birth certificate, which wouldn't show any parents' names. It's the adoption certificate that should have the Rushtons' names on it. That doesn't seem to be here.' I search through the remaining papers, but there is no adoption certificate.

'What does this mean?' I look at Nancy again. 'It says the Rushtons are her birth parents. There's no mention anywhere of an adoption.'

'It must mean the adoption was never legally registered. I'm sorry, Anita, but that's what it looks like.' Nancy is trying to stay calm despite the jagged thumping in her chest.

'But can they do that? Can they not register an adoption and just take a child, as if it were their own?' I feel a wave of fury and outrage welling up. 'How could they do that! Is it allowed?'

Nancy reaches out to touch my shoulder. 'Oh Anita, I'm so sorry. I guess people have their reasons for making these arrangements. Of course, they're not supposed to, but sometimes people get around the law.' I can see the look of helplessness in Nancy's eyes, just as I had done on that day, years ago, when the terrible news of Richard's death had pierced through my heart and Nancy had been utterly unable to stop it.

'How could they? I never liked the sound of them. But this! They made a lie of my mother's life.' My father had never had good things to say about Ellen's adoptive parents. He clearly disliked them and had not kept in touch. They had moved to America long before I was born, and if I had ever met them, I didn't remember them. Suddenly I feel impatient to be moving. 'I don't know what to do with this. Shall we leave it for now, Nancy?'

'Yes – let's take a break from it. Put the boxes over here and you can decide later what you'd like to take back with you.'

We re-pack the boxes and stack them in a corner of the room.

'Can I borrow your bike, Nancy? I need to go for a ride.'

'Of course. You know where it is. Will you be back for lunch?'

'I'm not sure – no, I think I'll go to Holkham beach. I can get something to eat on the way.' I feel a growing sense of urgency to be moving. 'I'll be back for supper though.' I am angry, but don't want to take it out on Nancy. It's painful for Nancy to open up her own memories, and I don't want to make it worse for her. 'Thanks for your help, Nancy,' I add, as I leave the room.

I take the bike from the shed and cycle, as if my life depended on it. All the way along the winding coast road I pedal against the westerly wind, until I am spent. Then I wheel the bike into a field. Behind the hedge, hidden from the road, I lie down on my belly on the damp grass and weep.

Seventeen

London – 1981

'Hi folks. Anyone home?' Matt's voice rings out through the cavernous hallway.

'Hi Matt. Just me. I'm upstairs,' I call back from the top of the house. 'I'll be down in a sec.'

As I reach the last flight of stairs, Matt and Jez are squeezing through the front door with overflowing backpacks. With groans and sighs of relief they drop them onto the floor. The journey back from the island has been long and tiring.

I fling my arms around each of them in turn. 'Welcome home! Good to see you both again. How was it?'

'Brilliant! Absolutely wonderful.' Jez hugs me tight and I smell Ambre Solaire, sunshine and salt in her hair.

Linking arms, I lead her into the kitchen. 'Come on, I'll make some coffee. I want to hear all about it.'

'You would love it, Anita. The beaches – long sandy beaches, almost nobody there, except for the people we were hanging out with. And sea all around you – gorgeous turquoise sea, warm too. It's like swimming in a great big bath! And sunshine every day,' Jez gushes. Her deep golden tan is testimony to this. Being tall and slim, Jez always looks good, no matter what she is wearing, but with her gold-brown hair streaked with sun, and a deep ochre coloured dress, she looks radiant. As if she had just stepped out of a fashion magazine photo shoot, not off a plane.

'Where did you stay?'

'We slept on the beach with a crowd of people we met there,' Matt declares. 'Like one big community – French, Germans, some Americans – all sorts.'

'Wow! I didn't know you could do that.' I am impressed.

'There's no-one there to stop you,' Jez says. 'It was fantastic.'

'The only downside was Piraeus – that's the port you sail from. It's hell, but we survived it.' Matt throws his arms out wide to emphasise his point. I've never seen him looking so relaxed. Matt is usually wound up like a tight spring ready to uncoil.

'And what about all of you? Are the others around?' Jez asks.

'Emms is still in Wales with Simon, camping. I think it's quite serious – she's really into him. They'll be back in a couple of days. And Jake's at a festival in Cornwall, or is it Devon this time?'

'And you, Anita? What have you been doing?' she asks.

'Oh…nothing much. I went up to Norfolk for a few days.' Apart from swimming at the women's pond with Julie, and a few bike rides with Jake when he was around, I've spent the last month doing little more than painting, visiting a few galleries, and mooching about the house. 'It's been fantastically uneventful compared to your summer, but that's okay. I needed a bit of quiet time.' I feel as if I have to justify the lack of excitement and adventure that has been my summer holiday.

The truth is, I have felt lonely, quite depressed really, but I don't want Jez and Matt to know this. I feel compelled to hide these feelings, as if there were something shameful about them – as if feeling depressed and lonely as a young woman means there is something odd or terribly wrong with me. But August always grips me like this. The memory of Richard's death still carries a weight that extends right through the month, each year, as if it were happening all over again. The weight of loss, and the loneliness it left in its wake, clings to me each summer, as the limpets cling to the rocks down on St Mary's Island. You can barely prise them off. Julie and Jake did their best but I clung fast to my summer gloom.

The loss of Richard is still with me every day – a constant companion. An unbidden guest at every event. A shadow that follows me through the light of the day and swallows me up into the night. The loss of my father comes up in giant waves, a tsunami of feelings at times when I feel vulnerable and lost. The loss of my mother is something quite different. A deep underground ocean, a foundation to my world, dark and dangerous, vast, endless. It would consume me if I allowed it to. Resisting its pull has taken all my energy since the fruitless visit to Norfolk. Since discovering the empty remnants of my family's past. A past that is not really past, but lives on in me, in my cells, in my blood.

'You must come to Greece with us next year. There's loads of gorgeous men there – Greek god types,' Jez enthuses, drawing me back from the slippery edge of troubled thoughts.

I laugh weakly. 'Maybe I will. But I'm not looking for a Greek god at the moment.'

'You're not still looking for your grandmother, are you?' Matt asks, a hint of incredulity in his voice. He stubbornly refuses to believe that this could be a useful thing for anyone to do. Think about the future, not the past, is his guiding principle.

'Yes I am. I've got the interview with the adoption search person next week.'

'You know Jake still really likes you, don't you?'

'I should hope so! We're best friends,' I exclaim.

'You know what I mean. He really likes you. But he won't wait for ever,' Matt insists.

'Matt, we're just friends. He's not waiting for anything. We agreed it was better like this, and we both have other relationships if we want to.' My irritation is close to the surface and ready to erupt with the slightest provocation.

'Like I said, Anita. But it's your life…' His voice trails off, but the message is clear.

'Come on, Matt. It's up to Anita and Jake what sort of relationship they have,' Jez intervenes, trying to stop an argument from brewing. 'Do you want to see some photos, Anita?'

'Ooh yes, I'd love to.' I'm glad to avoid further confrontation with Matt. I feel like a delicate garment with too narrow seams that could rip open if I move too much, and anger at Matt could just be the trigger for that.

Jez takes out several thick packets with 'Kodacolour' and an image, in deep primary colours, of a bright and smiling family blazed across the front – a perfect family – mother, father, boy and girl. Vivid descriptions of the places they went to and the people they met on their trip accompany each photo. Matt begins to open his mail.

'Oh, yeah! Look at this,' he exclaims, waving one of the letters in the air. 'The Camden Irish Centre wants to buy one of my sculptures. Someone saw it at the exhibition and liked it. They've just been given some money to spend on the centre and it seems they want to give some of it to me!'

'Great! That's brilliant, Matt.' Jez claps her hands. 'D'you know the Irish Centre?'

'Never heard of it. I'll have to check it out.'

'That's fantastic, Matt. So the exhibition is going to bring you fame and fortune after all,' I joke. I still feel bruised by his blunt words, but choose to let them go, and return gladly to the distraction of Jez's photographs.

2

The grey-padded chairs with beech wood arms suggest comfortable formality. On the magnolia walls of the reception area hang a few innocuous paintings of floral arrangements. A cheese plant in one corner breathes a little life into the windowless room. I feel nervous as I wait for my appointment, glad there is nobody else there, waiting, as I am, for information that might point towards a different future – or not, as the case might be. I flick through a magazine about country life, pretending to study the pictures of luscious plants and immaculately designed gardens. There is nothing here to indicate the mission of this place.

After about ten minutes a woman appears in the doorway.

'Hello. You must be Anita Rose.' The statement sounds like a question.

'Yes, I am.' I stand up and briefly shake the woman's outstretched hand.

'I'm Claire Myers. Nice to meet you. Please follow me, Anita.' She leads me down a corridor lit by long strip lights, and into one of the rooms that lead off it. 'I'm sorry I kept you waiting.'

'That's alright.' I feel like a young child under the woman's kindly gaze, and my nervousness is rapidly escalating into anxiety. My palms are damp and I hide them in the sleeves of my sweater in case Claire Myers can see. I imagine she is in her early fifties, with short brown hair showing a dignified sprinkling of grey. She wears a three-quarter length skirt of light grey, fine woollen cloth, and a jacket to match, with a stunningly peach coloured blouse beneath.

'Do take a seat.' I perch on the edge of another grey-padded chair, as if ready to make a quick escape if necessary. Claire sits in an identical chair facing me, placing a notepad on the veneer-covered table beside her. A few more floral arrangements and a poster advertising their services decorate the magnolia walls. The room is empty apart from four chairs and the table. At least there is a window. Intermittent thin strips of a high-rise block of flats stretch between the slanted slats of the blinds. Claire sits back and folds her hands in her lap. I'm sure her penetrating eyes can see right through me, right into my mind that is darting like a swarm of buzzing mosquitoes.

'So, Anita, this interview is an opportunity for you to tell me all you know about the person you wish to trace. I'll see what lines of enquiry might be open, and do some searches for you. I think you've already been informed of some of the obstacles that might come up, but let's first look at what might be possible. I like to start with a positive approach.'

Her relaxed and friendly manner begins to put me at ease. I sit back a little in my chair and rest both hands on the hard wood arms, my fingers gripping slightly for support. I hold my breath.

'I understand you're here to see if you can trace your maternal grandmother. So why don't you begin by telling me what you know about her,' Claire invites.

'Well...my mother died when I was two – a car accident – and my father always told me that her mother – my grandmother – had died when she was born, so she – my mother that is – was adopted – and I grew up thinking I didn't have a grandmother.' I stop to catch my breath. I'm about to hurtle on when Claire reaches over and touches my arm lightly.

'Take a moment, Anita. That's such a lot you've just told me. It all sounds very painful.'

Tears begin to well up at the back of my eyes. There's a dry knot in my throat and my heart is pounding. I grip the smooth, cool arms of the chair more tightly and stare at the dark blue of the carpet to avoid Claire's gaze, fearing I might burst into tears if I let the kind expression in her eyes reach into me. Yet somewhere within I feel something stirring – like a lost part of myself that is longing to allow Claire to see me, to really see my pain. Something inside me is stirring. It feels so small and thin, frail, parched, like a desert creature. I'm sure I can hear it screaming. I feel it rushing up, as if it might leap out and fall right into Claire Myers' lap.

I'm shocked to feel this surge of longing to fold myself into her arms and weep – a woman I have known for barely five minutes – a stranger. A hot flush of embarrassment sweeps over my face and I bring my hands up to hide the blushing. Can Claire read my thoughts I wonder?

'Why don't we pause a moment, Anita. There's plenty of time, so let's take this slowly.' She pours me a glass of water from the jug on the table. I gulp the cool water. The parched creature inside me seems to shudder then scurry back into hiding, like a lizard seeking shade from the midday sun. Claire's calm presence helps to steady me.

'Are you alright now?'

'Yes, thank you.' I feel embarrassed at the wild thoughts that rushed up, unannounced, but I'm beginning to feel safe with Claire and can breathe more easily now. The desire to find my grandmother is burning once again like a fire in my belly. I take a deep breath and continue to tell her what I know about Liza, and the letter to my mother. 'We think it was sent in 1953, which is also the year I was born,' I conclude.

'That's interesting – synchronistic?' reflects Claire, as if speaking to herself.

'You can read the letter if you like.' I take the lilac envelope out of my bag, move quickly through the practised ritual of untying the faded ribbon and taking out the crumpled sheet of paper. I hand it to Claire. Blue ink on white paper. Its simplicity strikes me – a kind of nakedness, an unembellished truth.

Claire reads the letter slowly. As she passes it back to me, I think I see tears brimming in her eyes.

'This is such a sad story. I know this sort of thing happened, but her letter makes it so – so very real, so personal.' Claire seems lost in her own thoughts for a moment. She deals every day with adoption searches, people seeking to trace their unknown families – mothers and children, brothers and sisters. She would be familiar with the many reasons that drive a person to give up a child, but a forced adoption seems the cruellest of all. I can tell that she wants to help me but her expression suggests what I feared – that there is too little to go on. Claire sighs and pulls herself back to the task at hand.

'I must ask you some practical questions, Anita. I think you've already been asked this, but we need to go through all the facts.'

'Yes, that's okay.'

'Do you know if your mother ever tried to find her birth mother?' She crosses her legs and picks up her notepad and pen.

'Not as far as I'm aware.'

'Then this does mean it will be much harder to get a court order to access the records.' She speaks quietly, trying to soften the first blow.

'Yes, I'm aware of that.' I try to ignore the sharp pain that is pricking into my chest, just above my heart.

'Do you have your mother's birth certificate?'

I'm prepared for this, at least, and hand the document to her. This is the final evidence – the telling truth on which the whole charade will hang. I know this. Suddenly I wonder why I am here at all. What's the point? In the end, could there be any outcome other than the one I dread and have so feared facing up to all summer?

'It's not helpful, is it?' I say, still clutching to a thread of hope, despite myself.

'No, I'm afraid not. If there's no indication on her birth certificate of there having been an adoption, it could be very hard to trace her birth mother. It was clearly an unrecorded adoption.'

'You mean an illegal adoption.' The issue of the illegal adoption is like a spark to dry grass, igniting the whole of my being in a flare of anger, like a bush fire out of control in the summer heat.

'Yes, you could call it that.' She holds my gaze firmly, willing me to stay calm. 'It was wrong, but sadly it did happen. There were different standards in those days. Today it wouldn't be allowed.'

We both fall silent. Claire is searching for a thread to follow, a path out of the maze. 'You don't know Liza's surname, do you?'

'No.'

'Or where she lived, anything like that?' Even though she knows the answers already, it's her job to ask.

'The only clue is Belfast — that the letter seems to have been posted from Belfast, so she may have lived there. And, of course, the birth certificate says my mother was born there — though there's no guarantee that isn't also a lie, is there?' The surge of anger begins to intensify. Heat pricks my palms. For a moment I am back in Sybil's living room, the wind licking the flames of the open fire up the chimney and Nancy handing me a lilac envelope, tied with a faded red ribbon. The sweet smell of wood smoke, laced with the scent of old roses, pervades the room.

I pick up the letter and the birth certificate. 'This is all I have,' I say, as if the last remnants of my own life were about to be swept away. Finally tears course down my cheeks as the impossibility of the search looms vast and real. Despair creeps in — a gathering up of hope, only to be casually tossed aside. Claire reaches out and takes my hand. She sits quietly, patiently beside me, until the crying is done and I have wiped my tears away.

'I need some time to think about it — to see if there's a way to pursue this further. Would it be alright if I made photocopies of the letter and birth certificate?'

'Yes, of course, if you think it might help.'

'I'd like to sit with it a while. Something might come up.' So Claire isn't about to give up yet. She will make some inquiries. I sit cradling the wave of despair that has nudged its way into consciousness as Claire leaves the room to photocopy the documents. Beside her competence, I feel small and ineffectual.

'Let's meet again in a couple of weeks,' she says as she hands the letter and certificate back to me. 'I always like to do a follow-up session, even if we can't pursue the search further. To see how you're getting on.'

Once again, I feel touched by her kindness. I swallow hard to hold back the tears that are welling behind my eyes. There is

an endless stream – no, an ocean of salty water – so close to the
surface now that it threatens to unleash an unstoppable flood.
'Thank you. I'd like that. It's just good to know that someone
else is helping me with this, at last,' I manage to reply.

'Of course. That's what I'm here for.' She is smiling warmly
as she holds out her hand to shake mine. 'You can make another
appointment at reception on your way out. And if you need to
get in touch with me before then, you can always call. Here's
my number.' She hands me a small card with her name, title
and phone number on it.

I have found an ally, a companion on a strange and difficult
journey. At least that counts for something.

3

Outside Camden underground station the late afternoon sun is
still shining brightly, a haze of gold now, as the glare is filtered
through the traffic fumes that clog the air. As I've done every
day over the summer months, I glance at the old man sitting
on his upturned box, cushioned by a stack of newspapers. As
he has done every day, he quickly looks away as I turn towards
him, almost in time to appear not to be watching me walk by.
The game has become something of a ritual. I smile to myself.
The regularity of it reassures me – the sense of each knowing
the other is looking, but not looking, amuses me.

It was the strangest thing. A short while after I had first
seen him down on the Embankment, the homeless Irish man
came to inhabit a blocked-up doorway between the entrance
to the station and the Midland Bank. He's always there, all day
and every night. I learnt from Jake that he refuses to sleep in
the men's hostel across the road, despite the staff at Arlington
House offering him a bed on several occasions. He doesn't drink
alcohol, like the other homeless men around the area, and he
never begs. Local café owners bring him food and hot drinks.

He seems content to live this simple existence. In fact, he

appears to choose it. The black woollen coat he has worn all summer is of good quality. Perhaps he was once a respectable, even wealthy, businessman, or lawyer, or professor. I begin to imagine he is a wise man, choosing to live out here on the street to watch over the people of Camden Town, and myself in particular. Am I going mad, I wonder?

It's Tuesday, the first week of the autumn term, and I've struggled to connect with a group of new adult students. They seem to be there only for the conversation. Not one of them really applied themselves to the work, and I feel frustrated. This is not how I want to spend my time. Of course, my real frustration lies with the fact that it has been a difficult two weeks as I waited for the next appointment with Claire, swinging between anger at the lies that were told and despair about the outcome of my quest. In my room I have a small silver key that I know will unlock the door to the truth, but no lock to fit it into. The puzzle seems to be closing in around me. Tomorrow I will see Claire again, but I've failed to renew any trace of hope.

Passing Jo's Café on my way home, I glance in to see him clearing up, preparing to close for the evening. He waves as he sees me. On a whim, I go in and buy the last chicken salad sandwich and a large cup of tea to take away in a white polystyrene cup. My curiosity about the old man living by the station has gotten the better of me. I want to engage him in conversation, find out who he is. Why he chooses to live out there on the street. If he really is a wise man.

Feeling slightly foolish, but also strangely carefree, I re-trace my steps to the station. This time I don't glance then look away but walk directly up to him and hold out the sandwich and tea.

'I thought you might like something to eat,' I offer, feeling a hint of shyness behind the bold gesture of my outstretched hands.

The old man beams back, his gaze strong and direct, the crinkled eyes and toothless grin just as I remember them from the Embankment. His white beard and hair, sprouting out from under the battered black trilby, frame a broad face that is red and creased from squinting all day into the sun.

'I'm Anita.' I don't know what to say next, how to open a conversation with him. But I don't need to – he begins to speak. A jumbled string of words pours out – garbled sounds really – as he continues to beam at me and to nod his head in gratitude for my meagre offering. His words make no sense at all, but he keeps on smiling at me as if we were having a deep and intimate conversation. Maybe he is a little crazy, not quite all there, I think, disappointed. There will be no words of wisdom, no wise teaching about life and matters of the human heart. It's puzzling though, as I remember clearly his words about my reading of the book down on the Embankment – or had I imagined that? Am I the one going crazy? I turn to leave.

'Goodbye then, take care,' I say, and give a little wave, as if he might not understand my words either.

'G'bye. And may the Sacred Heart be with you, now,' he says in his soft Irish accent, as I begin to walk away.

I turn back. Did he really say this? Still the big toothless grin and crinkled eyes are focussed on me, but he says no more. I have no idea which reality to believe, what has really been spoken and what I have only imagined. I hurry away to shore up a fragmenting sense of my own sanity, before I begin to unravel right there in the street.

Wednesday begins fresh and bright, the first signs of autumn in the air, but by mid-morning a dense bank of cloud has descended over the city. As I walk to the station, I feel enclosed by the buildings on each side and the weight of cloud above. In the city it's easy to forget to look up at the spacious sky, even on the clearest day. Then life becomes boxed in and narrow in perspective, without a sense of light and air.

Today I feel this tightness and narrowing of perspective as

I hurry along, my gaze wedded to the dirty pavement. I pray that the meeting with Claire will offer an opening of some sort, a window onto a new view, a lock that will fit the silver key. After the months of waiting, I dread the possibility of coming away with nothing today.

As I walk past the old man, just before entering the station, I don't glance away this time. We are friends now – my offering of food and our 'conversation' has established that – so I look directly at him and nod a greeting. He nods back, the familiar smile brightening up his face for a moment before it settles back into its customary reflection. He seems to be happy. I notice a kind, almost indulgent half-smile, as if he were watching over children playing – a still, benign presence amidst the rush of the morning street.

Sitting on the train as it speeds through the black and noisy tunnel, swaying to its restless rhythm, I close my eyes and focus on my breathing. I want to feel centred, in control of myself, when I meet Claire, able to take in whatever she has to say. I must also be prepared for disappointment. My bag clutched to my chest, I sink into the sensation of breath filling and emptying my body. My mind begins to settle – just enough to notice that there is also a hint of excited anticipation beneath the familiar anxiety. Maybe something good will come out of this meeting after all. My brief connection with the old man at Camden station – I will call him Patrick, a good Irish name – has given me courage. I feel, or rather hope, that our meeting is a good omen, the portent of a sea-change, an opening onto new vistas.

'Good to see you again, Anita. How have you been?' Claire askes, as she places two mugs of coffee on the table and settles into her chair. She wears the same soft grey suit, with the jacket open to show a delicate spring-yellow blouse and a row of small pearls. There is a modest elegance about her.

'It's been quite hard – waiting and not knowing if this will lead anywhere. I can't help fearing it'll be a dead-end.' I'm glad at least that I am able to stay calm as I speak. My fingers trace the arms of the chair. The wood feels smooth, but for the finest of ridges where the grain springs through the varnished surface.

'Of course – that's understandable. This can be a difficult process, and we don't have much to go on.' I want to ask if she has found out anything helpful, but also fear the reply, so I wait to see what she will say. 'I made some enquiries at the General Registrar Office – they hold information about an adopted person's original identity. I'm afraid your mother isn't listed in the register, so that avenue is closed to us.' She waits to see how I will respond before going on.

'I suppose I expected that, but it's good to know for sure,' I say, just managing to hold myself together by tensing my shoulders and stilling my breath.

'If she wasn't legally adopted, we have to imagine why this might be so, and what might have been the circumstances of her birth. There could be other reasons for this, but most likely there was a need for secrecy, which suggests an illegitimate birth – very unacceptable in Ireland in those days.'

'Yes, I imagine that's what happened.'

'I felt the next step would be to look at the institutions in Belfast where unmarried women would go, or be sent, to have their babies. I contacted the Public Record Office in Belfast to find out about these.' Claire pauses.

'Oh, that sounds good. Could they tell you anything?'

'It's a difficult case. If we search in the birth registers for your mother – Ellen, as she's named on her birth certificate – it's sure to tell us that Esther Rushton was her mother. We can ask for this search to be done if you wish, though.' She pauses to see if I will respond. I can't think of anything to say. I know the answer to this line of enquiry, so I bite my lip and look down at the floor.

'And then your grandmother,' Claire continues. 'Elizabeth was a very common name in Northern Ireland at that time, and without her surname they may not be willing to carry out a search. They did say we could submit a request, as we do have a date for your mother's birth, but it's usually against their rules to do this without a full name. And a search of every woman called Elizabeth, or Liza, registering a birth in Northern Ireland at that time might not lead us to your grandmother.' I can feel that Claire is trying not to raise my hopes too high, but I am willing to clutch to the tiniest glimmer of a possibility. Like a spider drifting at the end of the finest of silken threads, an invisible lifeline, until it finds a place to land. And build a web, a home of sorts.

'But there can't have been too many of them. And it would at least give us a list of the places where all the women called Elizabeth had given birth.' It's as if a light had just been switched on inside me. I wonder at how quickly my mood can change. Even my body feels lighter, and all traces of the fear that filled me a moment ago have gone.

'Hmm...I suppose it could. It would limit the possibilities. It's not guaranteed that they will agree to carry out the search, but it does seem our best hope at this point,' Claire says. I am spiralling a strand of hair around my index finger and looking intently at her pad as she writes some notes. She looks up. 'How are you doing, Anita? It must all feel quite daunting.'

'Yes, it does. I'm clutching at straws, I know, but if there's a chance of finding something out, I'd like to try it.' To be truthful, I am feeling excited. Talk of the records office in Belfast and the places where these mothers went to give birth has brought it all a little closer. Liza feels more real, my mother's birth an actual event, located somewhere in time and place.

'Then we'll submit a request – for the Records Office – to carry out a search – for a woman called Elizabeth – also known as Liza – who gave birth on or around April 17th, 1927 – probably in or near to Belfast – possibly at a refuge home for unmarried mothers.' Claire speaks slowly as she writes notes, checking in her file for the date of Ellen's birth. 'Yes?' She looks at me for confirmation.

'Yes. Thank you, Claire.' I smile, a flicker of hope dancing across my heart again. 'Were there a lot of these refuge homes?'

'I've been sent a list of the homes in Belfast. PRONI don't always hold the records of the women who stayed there though. Often they're kept by the institutions that ran them, such as a church or charity. Here, you can take a look if you like.' She hands me a sheet of paper from her file.

'Thank you.' I read down the list. 'The Salvation Army Rescue Home, Belfast Magdalene Home, Edgar Home, the Belfast Workhouse, the Convent of the Sacred Heart.' I pause. My memory is making a connection but it hasn't quite surfaced to consciousness yet. I twirl and tug at the strand of hair, staring at the names, imagining the fates of the women and girls who ended up there.

'If you like, we can fill out the request form together, or you can take it away with you and post it back to me. There'll be a fee to pay but our office can cover that.' I feel relieved that the search hasn't run aground yet. Clearly touched by my story, Claire sincerely hopes for a positive outcome.

'I'd really appreciate it if you would help me. I hate filling out forms!' I declare, and laugh.

'Great. Let's get down to it then,' she says, smiling at me over the rim of her coffee mug.

It's not until I am on the escalator, emerging from the stuffy depths of the underground and anticipating meeting Patrick at the station entrance again, that I remember. The Sacred Heart. 'May the Sacred Heart be with you.' How could I not have remembered this? I thought Liza's letter had been indelibly written into my memory, yet I had forgotten these, her last words. And Patrick – he had used the same phrase at the end of our conversation – or had I imagined that? The Convent of the Sacred Heart – that had to be the one – the place where my mother was born.

I race up the last steps of the escalator, my feet flying over the worn wooden treads. There is Patrick, as always.

'Thank you!' I call as I skip by, flinging my arms open wide and just missing the woman who steps quickly out of my way, no doubt fearing I am one of the homeless insane.

I spin around and head, running, across Camden High Street as the lights turn to red. I want to tell Jake what I have discovered. And Claire too, of course. I will call Claire straight away.

Eighteen

Jake, Matt and I are sitting around the kitchen table, listening to UB40 and the hiss of water simmering in a pan on the stove as we wait for Jez. I like the closing in of autumn evenings – lights on, curtains drawn, turning inwards against the wet and blustery night. I am becoming like my father in his dying months, preferring this time of fading back to the thrusting growth of spring, or the steamy heat of summer months in the exhausted city. I stare through the window, a large black void in the lime green wall, a gaping hole onto the creeping night. As if reading my thoughts, Jake gets up to close the blinds, shutting out the dark. I bring my focus back to the cheerful cluttered kitchen with its green and blue walls and big paper globe ceiling light. It's Jake's turn to cook dinner this evening, and the spicy aroma of vegetable curry has seeped through the whole house.

'It's not like Jez to be so late,' I say. 'Do you know where she might be, Matt?'

'No idea. Probably held up on the tube. The Northern Line's hopeless these days.' He seems not too concerned. 'Last week a train sat in the tunnel for forty-five minutes – they gave no reason for it, as usual.'

'I hope she's alright. Shall we wait?' Jake asks.

'Yes, let's wait for her. I'm sure she won't be long,' I reply.

Jake checks to see if the rice is cooked, turns down the gas and takes two bottles of beer from the fridge. 'Then tell us how your meeting went today, Anita. Did Claire find anything?'

'Well, it took them weeks to carry out the searches, and they came back negative in the end. We're disappointed but not surprised. Still, I think it was worth doing, just to make sure.'

'So, what now?' Jake flicks the caps off the bottles and hands one to Matt.

'Claire wrote directly to the convent where I think Liza might have been, and asked if they have records we can access. The convent said they can't release past records just like that. They were incredibly evasive.'

'What will you do then?' Matt asks, curious about my search, despite himself.

'I'll go to Belfast and visit the convent.' I feel my feet press into the floor and my back grow firm and strong – a new feeling, one I like. 'If they won't show me Liza's records, then I'll ask about Sister Mary. If she's still alive I know she'll help me.'

'Really?' Matt seems impressed at my determination.

'When will you go?' Jake asks, surprised at my newfound resolve.

At that moment we hear the front door open and bang shut. Jez comes into the kitchen.

'My God, what's happened to you?' Matt leaps up and takes hold of Jez's shoulders to steady her. 'Here, sit down, love. What on earth happened?' He gently sits her down and kneels beside her with an arm wrapped protectively around her.

Jez is pale and trembling slightly. A stream of dried blood from a cut on her forehead frames the right side of her face. Her coat sleeve is torn and there is a bloodstain there too. I take her hand, recognising the glazed look of shock in her eyes.

'It's okay, Jez. You're alright now.' I try to reassure her. 'Can you tell us what happened?'

'There was a bomb,' Jez finally utters, her eyes wide and filled with fear.

'Another one!' exclaims Jake.

'You're okay now, sweetie. Are you hurting?' Matt asks.

'Just my head, here, and my arm.' Jez points to the big gash on her forehead and the tear in her coat. 'I'm alright, really. It was just the shock, the noise, glass and metal flying everywhere, black smoke and dust pouring out of the building.' She's staring ahead, as if still witnessing the scene unfolding before her eyes. 'I'd just come out of a shop across the road when it happened. The force of it...someone was badly hurt. I saw him lying there, on the ground, blood everywhere. I think he might have been killed.' At that, she breaks down. Matt and I hold her as she sobs, her body shaking out little ripples of shock. Jake stands anxiously by, not sure what to do.

'It was Oxford Street. The explosion – it ripped through one of the shops. I've never seen anything like it,' Jez continues, once she has recovered a little.

'How did you get home?' Matt asks.

'I walked. I just walked.' She is still dazed and not at all clear about how she got home.

'Have you been walking for a while, Jez? It looks as if this happened a while ago,' I ask.

'I'm not really sure. I don't remember it all. I think I just started walking home.' Jez gestures with her undamaged arm as if to indicate a vague and circuitous route.

'And nobody checked if you were alright?' Matt is readying himself for a rant at the emergency services for not helping the victims properly.

'I wasn't hurt badly, and they had other people to take care of.' She wouldn't want one of Matt's tirades at the government right now. Just his strong presence beside her. I can see how her face begins to soften as he holds her, how he makes her feel safe. I wish I had that in my life. A hint of envy creeps in.

Jake goes into the living room to switch on the television, and returns some minutes later.

'They think it was an IRA bomb, in the Wimpy Bar. An officer was trying to diffuse it when it went off and killed him. That's the second one this month!'

'Why on earth the Wimpy Bar?' I ask.

'They're targeting British interests. The army last time – now business, the economy.' Matt follows the news more closely than the rest of us. 'They want to bring the country down, to make us take their point seriously.'

'What exactly is their point?' Jez asks.

'They don't want us dividing and ruling their country anymore. They want us out, basically, and until the British government starts to listen to them, they'll keep doing this sort of thing. But Maggie Thatcher is only making it worse, refusing point blank to talk with them,' Matt expounds.

'But this is terrible. I can appreciate *why*, but not *how* they're doing it – targeting innocent people like this. There must be another way.' I've been reading up on Northern Ireland's history and feel some sympathy for the people I now think of as my ancestors.

'Not with the Tories in power there won't be. They've been against Home Rule for the Irish for centuries – since their bloody aristocracy first colonised Ireland. The British government holds all the power, so the IRA can only retaliate like this.' He could have gone on, but right now Jez needs him. 'Shall I patch you up, soldier?' he asks, looking at her tenderly.

Jez laughs weakly. 'Thanks, Matt. I must look a mess. Then I think I'll lie down for a bit.'

'Sure. Come on.' Matt takes her arm.

'Do you need help?' I ask, not sure if nursing is one of Matt's many skills.

'No, we'll be fine.'

'We'll save you some supper. You might want it later,' Jake calls, as they head upstairs. He feels responsible for making sure everyone is fed this evening. This, at least, he can do.

Jake closes the kitchen door and turns to me. 'This isn't a good time to be thinking of visiting Belfast, you know. It's dangerous there right now.'

His mane of brown hair looking as if it has just emerged from a spin-dry, his long wiry body, the fine cut of his nose and cheekbones – I am so fond of Jake. I find myself agreeing with him on most subjects, but on this I will have to disagree.

'I know. I'll go when the time feels right,' I say, to diffuse the challenge from Jake, which I fear could weaken my resolve and the tentative thread of boldness that I am clinging to.

2

I decide to write to the convent first. I simply ask if I can pay a visit and speak with someone about a relative who had stayed there some time ago. I don't mention a pregnancy or adoption. Claire has already done this and it clearly put them on the defensive. As she hasn't given names – it's all been anonymous so far – I can write on my own behalf. Sadly, because the adoption search has led nowhere, the meetings with Claire have come to an end.

The response from the convent doesn't arrive until just before Christmas, and when it does, it is suitably non-committal. It would have sent me spinning back into an old cycle of searches that have already proved futile.

December 15th, 1981

Dear Miss Rose

Thank you for your recent inquiry.

We trust you understand that records of past residents of the Refuge Home are strictly confidential. If you wish to make a formal application to access such information, you will first need to send to us documents that prove your relationship to the resident in question.

Once you have done this, we can inform you of the procedures to follow.

Yours sincerely,
Sister Margaret
The Convent of the Sacred Heart

I try not to feel too irritated about the 'Miss'. I write again, asking Sister Margaret if a Sister Mary had lived at the convent around 1927. Receiving no reply, I write a third time. By March I realise there will be no response.

I need to step back for a while, settle into myself, feel where to go next. With Claire's help I have done all I can through the formal channels, so for several weeks I return to painting, absorbing myself in the non-verbal language of image and colour – a space where I can reflect without words.

I am waiting for the right time to go to Belfast. The idea of travelling alone makes me nervous. I would love a companion, but I know this is a journey I must make alone.

Easter passes. The next opportunity will be the summer holiday as I can't afford to take time off from my classes. I'll save my birthday money from Nancy to buy an air ticket.

This idea startles me even more – I have never flown before – but beneath the anxiety a flicker of excitement begins to stir too. I will fly to Belfast this summer, visit Ireland for the first time in my life, and try to find my grandmother.

3

Finally, there are just a few more days to go. The warm July sun is gathering moisture up into the air above London. It's a sultry, humid day. The sky threatens rain, but for now it's still clear enough to make out the London skyline in some detail. Jake and I sit on the wooden bench at the top of Primrose Hill, looking out across the city.

'D'you remember when we first moved here – how we'd sit up here naming all the buildings? The whole of London spread out beneath us,' I muse.

'Yes – Ally Pally over there. St. Paul's, Tower Bridge – and the tower blocks in the East End already looking decrepit.' Jake is chewing on a piece of grass as he surveys the hazy expanse of the city below.

'It seems like a lifetime ago.' I peer out towards a muted green horizon, and for a moment we both fall silent as a multitude of memories jostle to the surface. 'Sometimes I feel as if I could live here forever, but I suppose things will have to change soon.'

'I don't see why. If the council want to move us out, I'm sure we can find another house.' Jake is not prone to making long-term plans. He's quite happy to let life evolve.

'Hmmm. But I've a feeling Emms might move in with Simon. And Jez says she'd quite like to move out of the city – get a house in the country.'

'I can't see Matt wanting to do that.'

'But they might want to get their own home. I know Jez thinks about having a family one day.' I'm feeling troubled by all the uncertainty that has begun to thrust itself into my life. Once again, everything seems about to slip away.

'That would be sad – for us, I mean – but we can always find others to move in with us.' Jake is undefeated by my growing sense of pessimism. I feel the familiar rift that comes between us, between his indefatigable optimism and my sense of pending doom. It's a wall as thin and clear as glass, but it's invisibly there between us, keeping us both a hair's breadth from touching the other.

I cross my arms and settle back against the hard wood of the bench. I don't want to feel this aloneness today. I want to absorb a little of Jake's positive outlook, and anyway, it's too much to think about this right now. There is just one more day of classes before the summer holiday begins, and on Monday I will be flying to Belfast. Excitement and anxiety compete for my attention. I have made all my plans and want to enjoy this moment of idleness with Jake before I set out on my journey.

I had called Martin last night to tell him I was about to leave. He seemed distracted.

'Hi Martin, I'm off to Belfast in a few days, to find Liza. I'm so excited, and nervous too. I'm sure she's alive, I'm sure I can find her,' I had babbled. A long silence. 'Martin, are you there?'

'Yes, I'm here. That's, well, it's great, Anita. I didn't think you'd get this far. Well done.' Martin's voice was hesitant. I know it's not that he's unhappy that I am doing this. Nor is he particularly pleased either. It's just that his life is so full, what with two young children, his bicycle shop business growing rapidly, and the whole of Leticia's large extended family to include. He doesn't really want to have to consider whether he would be pleased or not to find an unknown grandmother. There is just no free space in his busy life for one more dilemma to ponder, one more distant relative to embrace.

'You don't sound too happy about it.' I felt disappointed, even though I could have predicted his lack of enthusiasm.

'It's not that, Anita. It's just that you caught me at a bad moment. Leticia's mum is ill at the moment, so we don't have a baby-sitter and we're having to juggle everything. It's peak holiday season and the bike rental business is really taking off. It's pretty full on right now.' He was apologetic but still distracted, lost in this other world. 'I'm glad for you, really I am. Let me know how you get on.'

'Okay – don't worry about it. I hope it all works out for you,' I had said, feeling deflated but not defeated.

'I hope you find her. Call me when you can.' And he had put the phone down.

I can do this without Martin's support but it would be so much nicer to feel him behind me. He has grown quite distant from me since family life took him over. I feel more than a little jealous – not so much of his family life, as of Leticia. She has taken the place in his heart that I once felt was mine, but I know I have no rightful claim to it. His wife must come first now.

At that moment the afternoon lull is abruptly shattered by a deep rumbling sound. A loud bang booms out from somewhere not far away. It shakes the ground beneath us. The air vibrates and sets my heart leaping into my throat.

'My God, what was that? It felt like an earthquake.' I sit bolt upright and look around to see where the sound came from.

'Look! Over there!' Jake is standing now, pointing in the direction of Regent's Park. Just over the brow of the green hill black smoke is billowing up into an already cloud-laden sky. 'Another bomb?'

I stare at the trail of smoke, trying to comprehend. 'It looks really close – it must be in the park. We should go down and see if we can help.' I jump up and grip hold of Jake's arm, peering through the humid air.

'No, I don't think there'd be any point. By the time we got there the police and ambulances would have arrived – it'll be all cordoned off.' He frowns. 'I don't want to join a bunch of voyeurs gawking at the scene.'

'You're right. But it's awful to just sit here knowing that people might be dying down there. Right at this very moment.' I feel sick. The thought makes me want to cry out.

'I bet it's the IRA again.' Jake takes hold of my arm and turns me to face him. 'Anita, you can't go to Belfast right now. It just won't be safe for you.'

'Jake, they're not after me. I'll be alright. I'll take care,' I argue, but don't feel nearly as assured as I am trying to sound.

'But it's not about taking care. It can happen anywhere, to anyone – to anyone English, that is.' I've rarely seen Jake look so serious – perhaps the time he learnt that his father had been in a car crash and was badly injured, but not since then.

'Jake, I have to go. I have to do this. I'm sure I'll be fine. It's not happening all the time you know, and anyway, there's as much chance of being hit in London as in Belfast. Probably more, in fact. Remember Jez last October. And this.' I wave my free hand in the direction of the park. Jake can't really argue with that.

People have gathered nearby on the top of the hill and are peering through the greenish air, at the cloud of billowing smoke. Some begin to walk briskly in the direction of the scene.

Others are talking in hushed voices – tense, huddled groups. Jake and I return to the bench and sit close, our shoulders leaning in. Is this an obstacle, or an omen, I wonder.

'I hope you're staying in a Protestant area, at least. They won't know if your family were Catholic. They'll just hear your English accent.'

'I'm not a Catholic. My father was an atheist and my mother – wasn't there.' I feel I have to explain something, but am not quite sure what.

'I wonder what they hit?' Jake turns back to the growing pillar of smoke.

'I hope no-one was killed,' I whisper. The anxiety is beginning to take hold now. 'Jake, will you come with me to the airport on Monday?'

'Of course. I can come with you all the way if you want. There's still time to arrange it.' Jake takes my hand and looks intently into my eyes. He brushes the loops of limp curls away from my face. 'I don't know what I'd do if anything happened to you, you know.' He can't quite say all that is in his heart at this moment, but I can read it in his eyes.

'Jake, I love you too. You're my very best friend. But I need to do this alone. I'll be alright, I promise you.' Jake drops his eyes, unsure how much to show me. It's all too puzzling for him, I know – what he feels for me, what I feel for him. Best we stay just friends, as we agreed all that time ago. But this has unsettled both of us and we feel more uncertain than ever, in our different ways. For me, there is a growing panic as I recognise a belief that if I really love someone, if I let them matter too much, they are sure to die. I can't let Jake matter that much. And yet he does.

'Will you call me when you're there – tell me how it's going?'

'Yes, I'll call you. Maybe another time we can go together – have a holiday.'

'Yeah, maybe we can do that.' I can hear from the flatness

in his voice that he's in no mood for planning holidays at this moment. And nor am I.

'Are you sure we shouldn't go down to the park and see what happened?' I ask again. The feeling of helplessness at not being able to stop the tragedy unfolding has become unbearable.

'No. We'd just be in the way. We can find out what happened on the news.' I know he is thinking of his father's accident, how it took ages for help to come, while a crowd gathered and just looked on, not even offering him a blanket or a reassuring word. I squeeze Jake's hand. So much reassurance is needed, by all of us.

We sit for a while longer, watching the dirty smoke disperse and drift high into the gathering clouds.

Part IV

Belfast

Nineteen

Belfast – 1982

As the plane flies over the narrow channel of sea that separates my world from Liza's, Ireland comes into view. It's strange that arriving here should evoke a feeling of coming home. The *idea* of home is one thing – to do with houses and gardens, bricks and stone, family, familiarity. But the *feeling* of home is another – something about the sense of the body in a particular place, the smell of the air and the sounds. The *feeling* of home is about love and friendship – and something mysterious, like the pull of gravity as it attracts feet to earth in an intimate affair of the heart and spirit. I have never really felt at home in the world since my father died. I peer out of the tiny window as the plane begins its descent and the details of the city come into sharper focus.

Up along the wide mouth of the River Lagan the plane sweeps in low, almost skimming the mud banks below. They rise out of the brown water, glistening purple in the morning light, and shallow – as if the land had just taken a deep, slow breath in, then paused. I can almost feel the smooth moistness of the mud, its sinking, sucking pull. As we approach Queen's Island, the two gigantic cranes of the Harland and Wolff shipyards stand like a grand gateway into the city – two angular steel arches that dominate the flatlands of the harbour, announcing Belfast's proud history.

At respectful intervals, the red brick chimneys of old linen mills pierce the low spread of the city, rising steeply out of the edifices of mills and factories – monuments to a grander time.

When looking at maps before coming, I noticed how close Belfast is to Newcastle, my old home city – much closer than London. And yet, by crossing the watery border into Ireland, I feel I am entering a very different world and a different time. This is Liza's world. I step down from the plane onto the tarmac and stand for a moment, on a threshold, breathing in the clear morning air.

I breathe in the familiar smell of the sea, carried on a light breeze. My heart steps up a beat. I feel ready for the challenge ahead.

At the last minute, and on Jake's insistence, I changed my accommodation to a guesthouse we thought would be as 'neutral' as possible. I had wanted to stay near to the convent but Jake's argument about my English accent identifying me had unhinged that decision. So, partly to assuage Jake's anxiety, I chose a guesthouse near the university, to the south side of the city.

The proprietor, Danny MacPherson, is a well-rounded, middle-aged man with red cheeks and stubbly sand-coloured hair. He carries my suitcase up the stairs, tells me to let them know if I need anything, then leaves me to settle in. My room is on the third floor, an attic room with a view over the rooftops to the rim of hills that cradle Belfast.

The room is small but clean and warm, painted white and sparsely furnished – a single bed, narrow wardrobe and bedside cupboard made of chipboard, a table and chair squeezed in by the window. It's functional, no pictures on the walls, nothing extraneous, but it will suit me well enough.

Tomorrow I will visit the convent, but today I want to explore the city. I'm eager to discover Liza's world for myself. I unpack my bag then go down the brown-painted, green-carpeted stairway and out onto a street lined with grand horse-chestnut trees. This must have been an affluent neighbourhood at one time. The houses are imposing, with high-ceilinged, bay-windowed, large front rooms. My attic room would have been in the servants' quarters. Now some of the houses are derelict, empty and crumbling. Others aren't there any more – just gaps in a row of Victorian grandeur, like a mouth with missing teeth. War damage that has never been repaired. Or was it from the Troubles – more recent bombings? Belfast has been battered more than once.

Following the map I have brought with me, I find the Malone Road and begin to walk towards the city centre, past the beautiful brick façade of Queen's University with its elaborate design of towers, turrets and arches. The streets are quiet, almost deserted. None of the bustle of the streets of London. No sidewalk cafes and trendy restaurants, such as you would find in Camden Town or Covent Garden. Life feels restrained, minimal. Everyone seems to retreat indoors as soon as they have done what they have to do. There is little sign of play here, and less of wealth.

As I approach the centre, the increasing presence of soldiers and armoured vehicles on street corners makes it clear why. Graffiti on walls and barricades of sandbags and barbed wire announce that a war-zone is being entered. The ruins of burnt-out buildings, rubble still piled in the streets, leaves no doubt that this is a city at war – a city tearing itself apart.

I feel nervous but not deterred. Ordinary people are walking about, purposefully, minding their own business, and in this moment I feel safe enough. No-one takes any notice of me. Anonymity is a welcome protection.

Drawn to the waterside, I find myself following the course of the river up north toward the docks. Here, the feeling of desolation is greater than the threat of violence. What had been a thriving centre of industry, once housing the world's biggest shipyards, is now a wasteland of car parks and derelict land. Everything is grey, and smells of dust and mouldering sewage. The great arches of Samson and Goliath stand like silent sentries – doomed, like the *Titanic* they helped build, to history.

Living under such a shadow, it must be hard to forget that it was Belfast's expertise in shipbuilding, its greatest pride, that led it to become a target for Hitler's campaign during the Second World War. I imagine how it might have been in its glorious years, in Liza's time – the shipyards throbbing with activity. A large tanker under construction would tower over the docks and the eastern part of the city. Did she live under its shadow? Does she still live here? I wonder if she is nearby, at this very moment. I imagine I can feel her breath on my cheek.

I can almost hear the air reverberating with the clang of metal on metal, and smell coal dust mingling with the salty smell of the sea. It reminds me of the day my father took me around his shipyard back home. I was young, seven perhaps. He was full of pride and humility – proud of his work and of his children, and in that moment also humbled in the presence of both. He held my hand tightly as he paraded Martin and me around the yard. I had loved him fiercely on that day.

The sudden swoop of three black-backed gulls, out on their morning forage, brings me back to the present. Their calls are raucous, beautiful, soaring across the harbour above the sound of human traffic below.

But the decaying waterfront is depressing. I've read that new money is to be invested here, but there are no signs of it yet. It seems that no-one has been motivated to re-build Belfast up till now – but then who would, when the city is so divided? Who would have cared enough, when wave after wave of city dwellers had been forced to leave, to make new lives in the surrounding towns and countryside. Leaving behind a hollow city, against which the intermittent storms of gunfire and bombs fall.

I head back towards the city centre and find McHugh's Bar, reputed to be Belfast's oldest building, and stop for lunch and a rest. I've walked for miles already. The beautiful tiled floors, old beamed walls and ceiling, and cosy, dimly lit nooks to hide away into, make this a welcome haven from the drabness outside. Settling at a table with sandwich and the obligatory Guinness, I listen to the broad and clipped tongues of the locals at the bar. The Belfast accent has little of the soft lilt of Southern Ireland – it's hard-edged, loud. The conversation is cryptic. I'm not meant to understand. I'm an outsider, and not to be included in this world of factions, fear and suspicion.

Curiosity draws me westwards, towards the Falls and Shankill areas of the city. It might not be the wisest thing to do but, having come this far, I want to see for myself the heartlands of this conflict.

At the entrance to the Falls, the first signs are the graffiti and murals that decorate the walls – heroes dressed head to toe in black, guns raised and faces hidden. With the names of the fallen are testimonies to their martyrdom. The side roads are riddled with holes where cobbles have been dug up and used as ammunition in one of many flaming battles.

The so-called Peace Line zig-zags throughout the area. A crude barricade of concrete blocks and razor wire, twelve feet high and uncompromising, it's a chilling monument to a war that reaches right into the homes of the people living here. The design is haphazard, a wall erected swiftly as tensions heighten, cutting a street in half – creating a barrier that slices right through any illusion of community. How could there ever be peace while such a visible sign of hostility scars the neighbourhood? Yet the alternative must surely be worse.

I wonder what it must be like to be a child growing up here – the terror in him as he goes to bed, not knowing if the bombs will come to his street this night. If there will be a knock on his front door, followed by gunshots ringing out in the hallway downstairs. This nightly terror would be the making of the next generation of fighters on both sides of the line.

I'm imagining young Liza here. How would she have survived if this had been her home? I know nothing at all about her.

Not daring to go too deeply into this heartland, I retrace my steps and cross over to the entrance to the Shankill Road. It seems slightly less poor, though the whole area speaks of dire neglect – burnt-out buildings and rubble piled in the streets – the gutted hulks of bombed out vehicles. Across one side road are the wrecked frames of two double-decker buses, angled against each other to form a charred and mangled roadblock. All this is happening today, in a part of my own country, to people just like myself. This is not history, nor a distant land, but the gulf between my familiar world in London and the wreckage of the capital of Northern Ireland feels unbridgeable. Had this been Liza's world? And is she still living here, somewhere amidst the ruin and the waste? If so, it's part of my world too.

I arrive back at the guesthouse late in the afternoon and meet Danny in the hallway.

'Hello. Had a good day.'

I'm not sure if this is a question or a statement, but reply politely, 'Yes, thank you.'

'Ah, good. Are you here to study, then?' His earlier reserve has melted a little.

'No. To search for information about my grandmother, actually.'

'Ah, I see,' though probably he doesn't. Why anyone would come to Belfast at a time like this if they don't have to, Danny would not know. Though the university is still popular with outsiders – students from England, and Scotland too. 'Then you'll be going to PRONI, I guess. That's where they hold all the information.'

'Yes, I'll do that.'

'You need to be a bit careful, you know. Don't be going

into the city centre at night. It's much too dangerous these days. Everyone stays local in the evenings, if they go out at all.'

I'm grateful for this caution, and quite prepared to follow it. 'Is there anywhere local I can get dinner?'

'Ah yes, now – there's Ryan's bar, on the Lisburn Road, that serves food – and a couple of places the other way, near the university. Lots of students go there. You should be okay on your own, I'm sure.'

'Thanks, that sounds good.' After a day of solitary wandering, I feel a sudden urge for companionship, and warm to Danny's openness. 'Have you lived here long, in Belfast?' I ask, to keep the conversation going.

'Me, yes, I was born here. Lived here all my life. Grandparents came over from Scotland long before my father was born, but I'm as Irish as they come.' He laughs, a big, round kind of laugh. Like a barrel of whisky, warm and golden.

'I thought people were leaving Ireland because there was no work, not coming here.' I am aware that my knowledge is scanty, but am keen to understand.

'Well, there was land to be had, if you knew how to work it. The Scots were good farmers, hard-working. The hills of County Antrim were just like home to them, and the powers-that-be gave them the land that was going, when the Irish abandoned it to go off to America and the likes.'

I'm aware that this might be a controversial point, having read about the best land being taken from Catholics and given to Protestant families, how this had deepened the anger and resentment. 'It seems to me that Ireland has many histories, depending from whose perspective it's told,' I say, trying to be diplomatic.

'Ah yes, you're right there. It's a complex mix of loyalties and betrayals, for generations, centuries even. But the Scots could work land that the Irish had left to ruin, that was for sure.'

I suppose that every side in the conflict has an equally firm belief in their own viewpoint. How else is a war maintained?

But I don't want to offend Danny by contradicting him. He seems to be a kindly soul and I have no reason to doubt that his grandparents were hardworking people and good farmers. I change the subject.

'The city feels so empty, even in the daytime. And all the derelict houses – it must be hard to live here.'

'So many people have been driven out by the Troubles, you know. Not safe for their families, and the shipbuilding and other industries gone. There's just no future for the young folk. So they up sticks and go to the towns, or over to England. That doesn't change, at least – the people going off to England. A tragedy, it is.' He pauses a moment and brushes his arm over his forehead, as if suddenly remembering the smudge of soot planted there earlier. 'But we like it here, my wife and me. We'll stay if we can.'

'That's good to hear. I'm sure it'll change one day.'

'Yes, one day. Anyway, I'd better let you get on now. Just watch out after dark, and keep away from the Falls, won't you.' He has, thankfully, assumed from my accent that I am Protestant, though there is really no logic in that.

'I will.'

He scratches his head as if trying to remember something. 'And you should be minding yourself around the university campus too. A woman was shot there a while ago. Political activist she was, mind you,' he adds, as if this fact made her death more acceptable. 'Don't know why the students these days don't just study? Have to get caught up in plots and fighting.' He sighs and shakes his sandy head.

I feel a chill, like the trail of a cold knifepoint, creep up my spine.

'Yes, nowhere's safe,' Danny adds, as if he had read my thoughts. 'Most folk just want life to get back to normal, you know. For all the fighting to stop.'

'I can imagine. Thanks for the advice, Danny. I'll see you in the morning.'

'Oh, I forgot. Sissy told me to ask what you'd like for breakfast,' he calls after me as I head upstairs.

Twenty

It turns out to be a blustery morning, with billowing clouds speeding across the sky. I sit by the window eating porridge and drinking strong black tea. Shadows unfurl over the grey rooftops, streaming after one another like horses in a race.

The maps, guidebooks and schedules that I have armed myself with litter the small table. Most of it will be irrelevant to my search. Though I've spent long hours wondering about it, I still have no idea how to gain access to the convent. I must be careful. A wrong move, another rejected inquiry, and my way might be barred forever.

I will go there today – just to look – and maybe inspiration will strike. I put a map and bus schedule into my bag, along with a notebook and Liza's worn and faded letter.

In the end I decide to walk. It won't take more than an hour. Today I feel like a pilgrim setting out on a sacred journey, and a bus ride is too mundane a way to start.

The route takes me through the botanical gardens, then down to the bank of the Lagan. The tide is flowing out, hurrying by at a dizzying speed. The water is a deep red-brown colour, rich with mud and peat carried down from the hills. The air smells of the high moors after a summer rain. Lazy seagulls ride the tide like small boats swept up in the current and racing back out to sea. Branches of trees, debris, fallen leaves all flow swiftly by, rushing on as if some catastrophe were about to befall any lingering bird, branch or wave.

A red and white lifebelt floats by, midstream, bobbing

reassuringly. As if someone, finding herself adrift in the river, might come across it waiting there to save her.

Over the bridge are streets of old Victorian terraces that have been ripped open, leaving vacant lots and more piles of rubble, now grown into sculptural, shrub-covered mounds. At the end of the road the Black Hills lie silent and morose, their mass silhouetted darkly against the soft grey cloudbank that lies behind them. I feel some comfort at the sight of the hills rising gently up out of the leafy suburbs. They seem always to be there at the end of a road, whichever way I look – guardians of the city.

As I arrive onto the Ormeau Road, near the entrance to the convent, wisps of cloud begin to bleed over the rim of the bowl and roll down into the city, spreading fine, willowy trails through the treetops. It's mid-morning and the wind has dropped. There is a denser quality to the air.

The convent is not what I have been expecting. Set close to the main road, the twin facades of convent and church loom up into the greying sky, imposing in their rectangular solidity. Red Victorian brickwork is offset by grey stone window frames, and the dark blue, almost purple, of the leaded roof tiles adds weight to the buildings' authority. Circular crosses on the gable ends, flanked by two small spires each, remind me of the Celtic cross. The building style is more functional than ornate.

The door to the convent seems decisively shut. The church offers more of an invitation, its heavy wooden door standing slightly open. I enter. The cool, semi-darkness is welcome after the growing humidity of the morning air, and a pew at the back of the church offers an inconspicuous resting place. I sit back and close my eyes for a moment. It's a long time since I've been inside a church – probably Martin's Spanish wedding was the last time, apart from an occasional peep into a village church when I've been out on a bike ride with Jake.

Cool, still air washes over me. The lingering scent of incense, earthy and pungent, envelops me. Streams of coloured light filter through the stained-glass windows that run along the walls of the church, landing in pools on the beautiful mosaic floor. The Tree of Life stretches along the central aisle in muted shades of red, ochre, green and blue-grey tiles. God's home in Belfast has a distinctly Italian flavour. Large paintings of the Crucifixion – the Stages of the Cross – hang between the windows, dark and sombre against the mellow glow that seeps in from outside. The altar glitters with gold.

I can stay here as long as I wish, as if in prayer. No-one will question my presence or my intention. I sigh deeply and try to empty out my chattering mind, but it's hard to shake off the nagging doubts, the questions, the wondering what I am doing here. Am I crazy to come with no plan at all? Around my heart is a faint sensation, a flaking and crumbling, as if an outer layer of plaster were peeling away. I feel raw and exposed.

A woman wearing a dark, knee-length coat and flat shoes comes in and walks directly to a seat on the front pew, as if this were her own personal place in the vastness of this building. I watch the quick movements of her right arm as she makes the sign of the cross. She kneels down and bends her scarf-covered head towards her clasped hands. An old man limps down the aisle a few minutes later, taking his place on the opposite side, at the end of the second row. His clothes look worn and shabby, his thin grey hair a little too long. It hooks over his shirt collar in straggling wisps, like the wisps of grey cloud that are dipping over the rim of the hills. As I watch the old man struggle on to his knees, gripping the pew in front for support with arthritic, claw-like fingers, a feeling of utter weariness and sadness sweeps over me.

For all I know they could be my grandparents, but how would I know. Belfast seems full of people just like them – old, weary, heart-broken, but stoic to the end.

The wave of sorrow that filled the church as the old man entered falls like lead onto my chest, makes me gasp for breath. The sadness is filling me, weighing on me, reminding me of my own sorrows. I mustn't succumb to this feeling. I force myself to stand, my shoulders pushing up against the weight of it. With bowed head I quickly leave the church, its hollow centre no longer a haven of rest but a trap, a swamp, a cave that could swallow me up into its darkness. I have fallen into this place too many times before. With both hands I push the heavy door shut behind me.

Out in the daylight again, I try to steady myself by counting the gravestones that litter the churchyard. Pale sunlight is now streaming across them, each one set at its own tilt, each one grey and lichen-covered. A few have vases of flowers or pot plants next to them, mostly withered and dry now. I begin to walk anti-clockwise around the walls of the church. How solid and substantial they feel. The lives of those who lie buried beneath the grass seem insignificant beside their massive weight – just a passing moment, of little real account in the great and infinite flow of time.

I notice that all the headstones face east, as if the dead are just waiting for the morning sun to rise, when they too will rise again from their dark, mouldy beds. My thoughts travel eastwards to the sprawling rose garden which is the graveyard for Richard's and my father's ashes. I feel a sudden urge to gather those ashes up, hold them one more time in my arms, and scatter them into the wind so that they will be everywhere – blown across oceans and continents – so that I can breathe them in wherever I go.

Feeling slightly giddy, I find a slab of stone that doesn't seem to belong to any of the deceased in particular, and sit down. My thoughts can so easily sweep me into a paralysing world of pain, regret and fear. I'm sliding towards this edge, at the brink of the vortex. 'Don't go there, not now,' a voice inside me seems to be saying.

To stop the momentum, I grip the stone slab and take a few deep breaths. I look up, study the shapes of the leaves of the beech tree that bows gracefully over the dead – the light shining through the almost translucent, delicate green leaves – the fine veins running through them. I breathe in the scent of freshly mown grass and damp earth, and draw my fragile mind back into the moment – the cold stone slab beneath me, the churchyard, the hum of the bees in the honeysuckle along the outer wall.

I have never felt truly safe in the world – certainly not since my father died, and maybe not before that. Always my mind threatened to give way to the pull of the chasm within. In truth, I feel more at home there, in the irresistible, magnetic pull of the darkness, however disabling it is – at least it feels familiar. An underworld of unfathomable, unnamed emotions and strange, disorienting dreams can offer a perverse refuge from the mundane emptiness of everyday life. Bright light unnerves me. It makes the pain too visible. I have grown accustomed to existing at the edge of this shadowy world.

Here, in the graveyard of the church of the Sacred Heart, I feel myself on the very finest of edges – just a hair's breadth between the gloom of the church that is filled with the traces of old sorrow, and the emerald green light of the beech trees that sway and dance above me. I have entered a liminal world, a place between light and shade.

At that moment my attention is caught by a blackbird rustling about in the soil beneath some shrubs, just a few feet away. Its orange beak darts and pierces into the earth until it pulls up a slippery, dancing worm. The doomed creature is quickly swallowed up. The blackbird stops still, as if he has just noticed me. He fixes a bright orange-ringed, unblinking eye on me. The way he looks at me, sideways, yet seeing me directly, is oddly reminiscent of the way Patrick watched me – his head turned so that he was looking straight ahead, yet seeming to see me nonetheless.

The blackbird chirps his melodic song, cocks his sleek head at me, and hops off along the path. He keeps glancing back, as if beckoning me on, so following seems the courteous thing to do. I have no other plan.

The path leads behind the church and past another large and imposing brick and lead-tiled building. This must have been the refuge home itself. This could be the place where Liza stayed, where my mother was born? The very place. The thought makes me falter, catches my breath.

The blackbird trills its tuneful song, urging me to continue. I hurry after it, along the path as it winds through a wooded part of the churchyard, densely planted with tall shrubs and dark yew trees. Their bright red berries look inviting but I know that they are poisonous. I must be near the edge of the churchyard by now, as the path has become narrower, crowded over with nettles, cow parsley, and the branches of un-pruned shrubs. The blackbird is still ahead, up in the branches of a scraggly young ash tree. I catch a glimpse of shiny black wing as it darts through an opening in a hedge. This must be the boundary.

Thick hawthorn bushes block my way, but a narrow gap allows just enough room to squeeze through. Beyond is a narrow path with a low stone wall on each side. The walls are old, like the gravestones, covered with moss and lichen. Tiny rock plants cling to cracks and crevices. On my right the dense shrubbery of the churchyard continues, cool and shady. To the left is a field, empty but for a large oak tree standing majestically at its centre.

I follow the path, wondering if I am trespassing.

After a while it curves sharply to the right and the field comes to an abrupt end where a high brick wall cuts right across it. The wall surrounds an enclosed area. I continue until I find a gate. It's slightly ajar. My heart beats faster – this is clearly private land and I am in Catholic territory. My English accent won't endear me to the locals if I am caught snooping around here.

I peep cautiously through the gate. Beyond is a large walled garden filled with an abundance of vegetables, fruit and flowers, many of which are going to seed as they near the end of their season. A tangle of weeds creates the impression of an abandoned garden, but bright tomatoes and runner beans hold to their branches, affirming that this is still the home of some industrious work.

I step, just a foot or so, inside the half open gate, wondering if I dare go further. The prolific chaos of the planting, along with a certain order of spatial design, intrigues me. The blackbird has disappeared from sight.

The sound of a tight, clipped voice startles me. I hadn't heard her approaching, but she is there, standing right behind me.

'Excuse me! And what might you be doing here, may I ask?' says the voice, clearly female, though with a deep and gravely quality that could almost be mistaken for a man's.

I swing around. There stands the small figure of a nun, dressed head to toe in black but for the white band of her wimple. Her eyes are piercing and accusatory, her lips pinched in distaste.

'I'm very sorry. I was just walking along here and I saw your garden. It's beautiful …' I stop, realising that this woman won't be seduced by flattery.

'This is private land. How did you find your way here?'

'Through the churchyard. I was in the church.'

'I see. You a Catholic, then?'

'Yes,' I lie. At least my grandmother might have been Catholic, so I feel partly justified in this embellishment of the truth.

'You don't sound Catholic, though you look…well, you never know how people look, do you?' the woman says doggedly. I feel she is fishing for something and won't let me go until she finds it.

'I'm English.'

'Obviously.'

'I couldn't just take a quick look round your garden, could I?' I'm feeling unexpectedly bold. 'It looks so lovely.'

'And where are you going, now?' The sister ignores my request for the moment.

'I was just walking – I thought this might be a nicer way to go back than along the road,' which is true in a way. I can't possibly tell her I was following a blackbird.

The woman looks me up and down disapprovingly, then clicks her tongue. 'Oiy, Holy Jesus and Mary.' She sighs and flaps her arms out to her sides. 'Alright then. What's the harm. Follow me,' she clips sharply, as she bustles past me and strides down the central path to the greenhouses. I follow obediently.

'Here, Seamus, this girl wants to look at the garden, now.' She speaks into the moist, warm air of the first greenhouse. 'Keep an eye on her, will you?' Then turning to me adds, 'Just a few minutes, and don't be picking anything, mind you.'

'No, of course not. Thank you,' I gush, surprised at this small success, though with no clear idea of what I'm doing here. Except, of course, that I am now in the walled garden of the convent, and a step nearer to Liza's life.

Seamus emerges out of the leafy world of the greenhouse as the sister walks briskly back down the path. She collects a large bunch of flowers that lie, already picked, by the gate, before disappearing out of view.

Again, I am startled. The old man that I saw in the church just a short while ago is walking towards me, wiping his hands on a soil-soaked cloth. His limp is distinctive, as are the wisps of thin grey hair that trickle over the threadbare collar of his shirt. He stoops over like a question mark. So that he can look straight at me, he tips his head forward and upwards, and peers at me from under heavy eyebrows. Pale and paper-thin lids blink over dark brown eyes.

He looks as surprised as I am. With spirals of red hair flowing out from a knot on the top of my head, a pair of faded blue jeans, orange sneakers and a bright crimson top, I must be either a shock to eyes accustomed to seeing only the dark habits of the nuns day after day, or a delightful kaleidoscope of colour.

Seamus, it turns out, is employed as head gardener, since there are not so many young nuns at the convent these days.

His grey flannel trousers, held up by braces, testify to this honourable position, marked as they are from top to bottom with smudges of well rubbed in soil and grass stains. The shirt, probably once white, is now an over-washed grey, worn and torn in places.

The weight of sadness that clung to him in the church feels lighter out here, in the garden, where he is clearly in his element.

'What you be doing here, then?' he asks. The question seems genuine, a little polite. I feel compelled to tell Seamus the truth, though not immediately.

'I was just walking from the church, along the walled path, when I came across your garden – the gate was open. I was just taking a look when the sister came by.'

'Sister Bridget? Don't mind her. She's a prickly one, but she doesn't mean bad,' he reassures me. 'Here, I'll show you around. Nothing much else to do.' I glance at the beds of weeds, the broad beans beginning to turn black, hanging heavy on their stalks and begging to be freed, the glossy tufts of spinach gone to seed. I accept his invitation gladly.

As he leads me through the neatly planted but excessively overgrown rows of vegetables, Seamus talks constantly. I'm not sure if he is actually talking to me, or just continuing a life-long monologue to himself, which I have become privy to for this brief moment. It soon becomes clear that I don't need to respond in any way, but nevertheless I listen with rapt attention to his story.

'Never thought I'd be here this long. Just came to help them out in the war years, when the sisters were all busy with the wounded and the homeless, you know. No-one left to take care of the garden. What a mess it was when I came – so much to do. The girls were still here then, and they did their bit, but none of them had any idea how to keep a garden, really. And they didn't stay that long. Except the long-timers who still live over the way. Sad that, the ones who had nowhere else to go.'

We arrive at the flowerbeds, which take up almost half of the walled garden. There are flowers of all colours and varieties, liberally interspersed with wild flowers as Seamus calls them, or weeds as they are to Sister Bridget. Wave after wave of colour – soft pastel pinks, blues and lilacs – shocking red and hot orange – pure white, delicate lemon and magnolia in all shades fill the densely planted beds. The air is heavy with their scent.

'Anyway, they needed someone to look after it proper-like. And it was good for me – kept my mind off things – my wife, my little boy. Lost them in the blitz, you know. Who'd have thought that – no-one saw that coming. Still can't quite believe it. My little Sean – who'd have thought it. Just two years old he was. And Connie, pretty little thing.' Seamus is telling me his life story – the one important story that he has to tell – in a flat and monotonous voice that could have been very hard to listen to, but his words have captured my full attention. Here is a man with a loss that cuts deep into his soul, and I feel a thread of kinship with him.

'I'm so sorry,' I half-whisper.

'Not your fault,' Seamus says pragmatically, and continues with his monologue as he limps slowly between the flowerbeds. 'Always thought I'd leave one day, get a job in the shipyards again, maybe even marry again. Or go away to America like lots of them did. Plenty of jobs over there, they said. But I didn't. I stayed here. They kept telling me they needed me here, I couldn't leave them. So that's what I did. I stayed here.'

We've reached the end of the central path and Seamus stops by the wall. It's lined with fruit trees, carefully tended and laden with ripening plums, apples and peaches. He turns to look at me as if he has just noticed I am here, then reaches up and plucks a peach from the nearest tree. 'Here, have one of these – nice they are. My speciality, these. No-one round here grows peaches like I do.'

'Thank you. And thank you for telling me your story. It's very sad.'

'Ah yes, a sad story, but that's how life is here in Ireland. Maybe it's better in England – you're from over the water, yes?' He can turn his attention to me now that he has unburdened himself of his own troubles, for now at least.

'It's different.' I'm unsure how to respond with as much candour as he has shown, yet not take away from Seamus's moment. 'People have their problems. Some have sad lives, some are luckier, but everyone has worries I think.'

'And what brings you to these parts?' he finally asks, as we begin to walk slowly around the outer wall of the garden.

I want to tell him exactly why I have come, what I am seeking here. Seamus's story has brought us together. We have become like friends in this short while and his honesty and his suffering have touched me.

'I'm looking for my grandmother. I think she stayed here for a while, when she was young.'

'Ah, in trouble was she?' he asks knowingly. 'Most of the girls came here in trouble, or to stop them getting into trouble if they were thought to be up to it – you know what I mean, now?'

'Yes, I know what you mean. I think it's possible my mother was born here, but I'm not sure. In 1927. This is what I want to find out. You won't tell anyone, will you?' I am suddenly nervous that I might have said too much.

Seamus nods. 'I understand – have to be careful with these things.' Then he stops walking and ponders a moment. 'A tricky one this – there was always so much secrecy about.'

'Did you work here when the refuge home was still running?'

'Oh yes, I did that – only closed a few years ago. Saw lots of them come and go, I did. Sad cases, some of them, but bright young things mostly. And then there's the old ones who still live here, over in the houses. Nowhere else to go I guess, or too afraid to leave. Like me, I suppose. Much the same as me.' Seamus trails off into thought. I imagine there are more stories to be told, but Seamus has said enough about himself for now.

'So how are we going to find out about this grandmother of yours, now, I wonder?' Seamus muses. I note the 'we' with some surprise.

'Do you think you can help me?'

'Maybe I can. I know the ways of this place.' He smiles wryly and winks. 'And I know which of the sisters you can trust with a secret. That goes a long way, to be sure.'

'Thank you, Seamus!' I'm overjoyed, but restrain myself from throwing my arms about his neck – I don't know him that well yet, and besides, he looks so frail and brittle I fear his bones might crumble in my hands if I touch him too roughly. 'Then maybe you can help me to find a Sister Mary, who was my grandmother's friend.'

'Holy Jesus! If there aren't a dozen Sister Marys for every lost girl who came through those doors, then I'll be damned.' Seamus holds his arms up to heaven and laughs, a thin, tinny laugh – I guess he doesn't laugh much these days, and the sound comes out tight and strained. His vocal cords just aren't accustomed to the movement. 'But never mind. I have an idea. The Mother Superior is called Mary – we can start there.'

I love the way Seamus says 'we' – how he has taken on my cause and is clearly animated by the challenge. I listen carefully as he explains what we will do.

Although it's only a short way from the garden, it takes us a while to reach the convent. Seamus limps slowly, and I follow with a basket of runner beans and tomatoes over my arm. We arrive at the back door – the kitchen door. Seamus enters and beckons for me to follow.

'The cook's a good soul. She'll help,' he whispers.

The cook is a short, plump woman with a broad and flushed face, and podgy hands that are, at this moment, deftly kneading dough, patting and pummelling and slapping in quick succession. I keep close behind Seamus, conscious of my unusual appearance in this black and white world of the good sisters. I wish I could fade into the background but instead here I stand, like a ray of fire in the dim and sweltering kitchen.

'Well, Seamus, and what have you brought us today?' asks the cook as we walk in, peering at me and the basket of vegetables with equal interest.

'Ah, Sister, good day to you. I've brought a young friend along. Anita – this is Sister Frances.' Then without waiting for further questions he goes right to the point. 'Anita here has a message from an old friend of Sister Mary. Wants to give it to her personal-like.'

'Ah, does she now,' says Frances, letting the dough rest on the floury table for a moment, and turning her attention to me. 'So you want to see the Mother Superior?'

'Yes, I do. I've travelled from London with some news for her.'

'Hmm. Well, if it's important perhaps she'll see you. She's very busy you know – doesn't usually see unexpected visitors, not without prior arrangement.' Sister Frances cocks her head on one side and studies the mound of soft bread dough for a moment. 'Alright, just for you Seamus, being as you're a good friend and all that. I'll see what I can do.' Then turning to me she asks, 'Can you come back tomorrow morning, then?'

'Yes, I can.'

'Good. I'll do my best to fix up an appointment for you.' Then as an afterthought she adds, 'And I suggest you wear something a little more – em – appropriate, if you don't mind me saying so.'

My face flushes, pink as my shirt. I feel self-conscious in the presence of this down-to-earth and kindly woman of middle age – humbled by the sister who makes bread and prays and feeds her community day after day, year after year. It's with a mixture of some respect and also a little pity that I imagine the lives of the nuns who live within these walls.

'Of course,' I reply quickly. 'And thank you for your help.'

'Can't promise anything, mind you, but I'll see what can be done.' She is curious to ask what the important news is, coming from London and all, but she knows her place. Instead, she beams at me and hands me a currant biscuit from a cooling tray on the bench behind her. 'Here, for your journey home.'

'Nothing like a mystery,' I hear her mutter to herself as I am leaving, 'even if you can never solve it.'

Twenty-one

I perch on the edge of an ornately carved wooden chair. Sunlight spills from the large skylight windows that dome over each end of the long corridor. The perfect geometric design of the tiled floor glistens in the light, and the smell of polish sharpens the air. I feel as insubstantial as a young bird waiting to be plucked from its nest by a bird of prey. The image of the white dove – a sacrifice, an offering to the prowling cat – flashes into my mind. It seems wrong to be sitting here in this holy place, waiting to see one of God's handmaidens, when I have committed such an act. I feel tainted. Old shame is rising through the rubble of memory.

Seamus's plan had sounded straightforward, but now that I am here, I know I will have to put on an act, pretend not to know something that I do know. That makes me nervous. There's a lot at stake, a lot resting on this meeting. After seeking and hoping for so long, finally I am close to the truth, but the plan could so easily go wrong. Seamus feels confident though, so I take a deep breath, try to relax my hunched-up shoulders, compel my fidgeting hands to rest quietly on the arms of the chair, and resolve to trust him. I will walk into the room expecting to see Sister Mary, my grandmother's friend.

Remembering my college drama class, I try out the 'acting as if' exercise while I wait to be called – simple in theory, but I had never been successful in the past. This time is no exception. I close my eyes, imagine the woman I want to see standing in front of me, try to generate all the associated feelings of a long-wished for meeting finally fulfilled, and fail utterly.

I open my eyes again and look around. The corridor is empty, the sun still shining, the neatly tiled floor still polished to a bright sheen. I can't sit still. Feeling as if I am tied up and trapped, I want to burst out, fling my arms wide and shout. Anything. Just to hear my voice, a voice, a sound, in the holy silence of this place. Are they all sleeping?

My nervousness is escalating into acute anxiety when, thankfully, the door opens and a young novice appears, all fresh faced and shining.

'Mother Superior will see you now.' She holds the door open for me.

I fumble and drop my bag as I stand up, then hurry through the door as if it might close and the magic world disappear for ever if I'm not quick enough. The young woman closes the door behind me, leaving me alone in a large, wood-panelled room with the Mother of the convent. I stand with my back to the door and stare at the woman in front of me who leans over her desk, sorting through a pile of papers. Finally, she looks up at me.

'Come in. Please take a seat,' commands the tall presence, gesturing to a chair in front of the large mahogany desk. The voice that speaks to me sounds distant and hollow. The Mother Superior sits down in her own place and stares back at me without a trace of emotion on her face. She's an imposing figure. She must be close to six feet tall, with a sharply hooked nose, highly defined cheekbones and piercing grey eyes. She sits upright with her hands resting on the table in front of her, a picture of discipline and strength. If she is curious about the news I bring, she doesn't show it.

Suddenly I feel inexplicably, guiltily terrified. Something is stirring in me, like the hint of a memory, a feeling of déjà vu, yet I know I have never been in a place like this before. The floor begins to tilt and the walls are pressing in on me.

As I step forward a wave of dizziness washes over me. The strength drains from my legs and I feel faint. A rush of nausea halts my steps – the walk to the chair feels like a vast gulf as the room begins to spin. Reaching a hand out, I stumble the last few steps and grip the chair to steady myself. The floor surges up to meet me, like the swell of a rough sea.

'Are you alright?' she asks, slightly alarmed as I almost fall onto her hard wood floor.

'Sorry – I don't know what happened. I just felt faint for a moment.' I carefully lower myself onto the chair. 'I'm alright now, I think.'

'Here, have a drink.' She pours a glass of water then waits patiently until I'm ready. 'I understand you have some news for me.'

Clarity is called for with this no-nonsense woman. How different she is from the image I have created of Liza's friend. I focus my mind and declare my intention. 'My grandmother stayed here for a while, many years ago. She had a friend called Sister Mary who I want to contact. I thought maybe it was you who was my grandmother's friend, but now I'm not so sure.' As the words tumble out, I feel foolish. The ploy sounds thin, not very plausible. But at least I'm here, in the inner sanctum of the convent, and I will find out what I can.

'I see.' The Mother Superior studies me over the arch of her nose, showing no sign of surprise, or irritation, or curiosity. 'It seems unlikely. When was your grandmother *staying here*?' She emphasises the words. Clearly she understands the nature of my grandmother's visit.

'Around 1927. I'm not sure for how long though.'

She lets out a sharp sound that's half laugh, half exasperation. 'Then I'm quite sure I'm not the one who was your grandmother's friend. I was barely born at that time!'

'Yes, I can see. I'm very sorry to have troubled you.' I feign disappointment for a moment. 'But I wonder if you would be able to help me find her? Perhaps you know where she might be now?' I add, as if as an afterthought. Maybe I'm not doing too badly at the acting.

I can see that she would have liked to end the interview at this point, but something makes her re-consider. Perhaps she can, after all, empathise with my dilemma, even find it in herself to help me. It would only cost her a few minutes of her valuable time.

'Oh, alright then. 1927 you say?' She moves over to the bookshelves on the far wall, walking so serenely she could have been gliding on ice, with head held high and shoulders pulled stiffly back. She studies a row of books, leather-bound ledgers that hold the convent records, and pulls one out. For some long minutes she methodically turns pages. I watch as she draws a long bony finger down each page.

Finally, she comes back to the desk with the book in hand. 'There seem to have been three Sisters with the name of Mary living here at that time.' She peers at me again, in the way that makes me feel like prey in the sight of a soaring eagle. Inside, my heart flutters. I peer back into the Mother Superior's eagle eyes and will her to go on.

She continues. 'One went to work in Africa many years ago and there's no record of whether she is still there, or still alive. Those records will be elsewhere.' The words land in me, flat and heavy. 'Another died of consumption, in 1944. The war took its toll on the health of the Sisters, you know.' For a moment she softens, remembering the sacrifice of those who have gone before her. I briefly glimpse the heart of this stony creature – the compassion that surely led her into this life of service. My own heart is wavering. Could this be the Mary I am looking for?

'The third one, bless her soul, is still with us. She's very frail now – in both body and mind.'

'Is she still here, in the convent?' A vestige of hope is returning.

The Mother continues to read for a moment. I watch as her

eyes scan down a few lines, then she closes the book decisively. 'That is as much as I can tell you, I'm afraid.'

'Do you think I can visit her, the last one?'

'I don't think that would be possible. I'm sorry.' She returns to the wall of books and replaces the ledger. Without turning to face me, she declares in a voice empty of emotion, 'I am sorry I cannot help you with your request, Miss...?'

'Rose – Anita Rose.'

'I wish you a good day, Miss Rose.'

I feel so close to finding the lock that my silver key will open – this just *has* to be the Mary I am seeking. But this remote and eagle-eyed guardian of secrets is refusing to help me. I know she knows something more, but she is going to make sure it stays secret. Her bluntness has jarred me. I feel shaken. Without saying a word, I fold my hands together and nod towards her back. If I spoke, I would cry out. I might lash out. I could grab the book and run. I want to pick up the mahogany chair I've been sitting on and break it against the unyielding floor. I need her to know she has just broken my weary heart all over again.

Instead, I turn and leave the room.

Twenty-two

The next morning, I return to the gravestone where I had sat just two days before – the stones facing east, the dead as if waiting to rise again with the sun. I feel devastated at my failure, but I cannot leave this place until I find out where Mary is. I have to find her. The Mother's sudden change of heart made it clear that there is something she doesn't want me to know. I must find out what it is.

Patiently I wait – for an idea, inspiration, a new plan – but nothing comes. I am sinking, so low I will soon meet the bones of the ancestors in their graves. But not my own ancestors. I fear that Liza has just slipped out of my reach, for good.

I sit until dusk begins to fall, then return to the guesthouse and go to bed. My sleep is heavy and without dreams. The morning brings aching limbs and a weariness of heart, but no more hope.

In the night there's been fighting in the Falls area again, Danny tells me. Someone was shot and his son, a fourteen-year-old boy, badly wounded. Catholics. The Prods came to their house in the night. There'll be more trouble after this. Danny doesn't comment on the rights and wrongs of it – just gives me the bare facts.

I can only imagine the terror of that family as their house was burst into by armed men in the middle of the night. There would have been nowhere to flee to, no time for thought of escape.

I need to walk, and I need to hear a familiar voice. Head hunkered down, I hurry the three blocks to the nearest phone box. Tension in the streets is palpable today. I see people armoured into their own worlds, collars up and mouths firmly shut, as they make their way to work.

'Jake, I'm glad you're in.' I'm relieved it's Jake who picks up the phone.

'Hi there. How's it going?' His voice as cheerful as ever. Some normality in a world of hostility and strangers.

'Not so good.' I tell him about my meeting and the feeling of hopelessness it has left me with.

'So what are you going to do now?'

'I really don't know. Do you have any ideas?'

'You could sneak back in and steal the book. You know where it is.' It's typical of Jake to suggest a mad idea like that – but for a moment I can imagine doing it. The idea of avenging the eagle-eyed one makes me laugh. 'Perhaps I will! Maybe when they're all at prayer. I'll have to watch to see what their schedule is.'

'Exactly – you're really thinking like a spy now.' We flesh out the plan together and laugh at the ludicrous scenario we are creating – me creeping into the convent at midnight, hiding behind holy statues to dodge the praying nuns as they file past on their way to chapel. To steal a dusty old ledger from the Mother Superior's office.

'Oh Jake, I can't really do that. I'll end up in jail!' I finally come back to earth. 'Seriously, do you have any ideas?'

'Maybe you could go back and ask for another interview with the Holy Madame. Try to persuade, or bribe or barter with her.'

'I did think of trying to get another appointment, but honestly, if you'd seen her – I know there's no point in trying to change her mind.'

'Is there anything you could blackmail her with?'

'Probably, but I haven't found out what it is yet.' We both laugh again. That's exactly the problem – something untoward has happened and she doesn't want me to know about it.

'What about the old guy – the gardener, or the cook – could they not help you again?'

'I could ask them, but I don't want to get them into trouble. I think it's too risky for them. There was some trouble last night and everyone's edgy this morning.'

'What kind of trouble?'

'A shooting. Someone was killed – in the Falls area. It's nowhere near where I'm staying though,' I add quickly, realising the conclusions he'll be jumping to.

'Jesus, Nita, you've got to come home! It's not safe for you to be there.'

This time I think he might be right. At this very moment I long to be in the safety of my blue room up in the attic, with my friends around me and the dull routine of classes to go to. I feel homesick.

'Maybe I should.'

'You can change your ticket. Just go to the airport, or call them up.'

'But I'll feel terrible if I haven't done everything I can here – I know I will.'

'But at least you'll be alive!' I hear the urgency in his voice, and somehow it challenges me to keep going, contrary to what he intended.

'Jake, I'll be okay. Really, I will. D'you remember how you kept telling me to be patient, not to give up? Well, I have to try everything I possibly can. I'm sure there'll be a way. I just have to find it.'

I can understand Jake's feelings, but it always seems worse to witness someone else's perceived or imagined danger from afar, than to be in the midst of your own. At least you can look around and take action. I want to try again.

And so, I return to the churchyard and settle myself on the cold slab of stone, my place of reflection, and begin circling the Mother Superior's words in my mind.

'The third one, bless her soul, is still with us.' If indeed she is the 'third one', Liza's friend Mary is still alive, but what exactly does 'still with us' mean? Simply that she's still alive? Or that she is still in the convent?

'She's very frail now – in both body and mind.' Frail in body – if she's ill, she might be in a hospital or care home. And mind – could she be mentally ill?

Seamus kept talking about the ones who didn't leave – the ones who had nowhere else to go. Like himself. The girls who were left behind. Is Mary with these left-over girls, and living near the convent? It's a thread to follow, at least.

I untangle my knotted limbs and stretch to wake up my body. A chill has settled in the air this morning. The houses where the 'old girls' live are round the back of the convent. I'll knock on every door. Or wait until someone comes out, and ask if they know Sister Mary.

People are clearly nervous because of the shooting, hurrying in and out of the church without stopping to gossip, as they might have done on another day. Two women emerging from the entrance look at me with suspicion as I walk past. I quicken my pace, attempting to look purposeful. Behind the church and past the large three-storied building which looks like a factory, with its steeply sloping leaded roof and tiny attic windows. I'm sure this must have been the refuge home, and the laundry – there was always a laundry. The place where the girls lived and worked.

Further on is a long single-storey building that stands back a little, in its own gardens. It's new, built of brown coloured brick with clean, sharp angles. The utilitarian, white-painted window frames are all uniformly hung with net curtains. Attached to the roof are TV aerials instead of chimney stacks. This must be the home of the ones who never moved on, who life has passed by.

A man approaches me and asks for directions to someone's house – his aunt he says. I reply that I don't know. The man seems to retract into himself on hearing my voice – my accent is betraying me. He asks what I am doing here. I reply that I'm also looking for a relative who lives here. He clearly doesn't believe me. A few moments later I see him knock on the door of a large house at the end of the cul-de-sac – the curator's house, or the rectory perhaps. Another man, dressed all in black, comes out and marches straight towards me. He says I should leave at once, or he will have to call the police.

It's shocking to be thought of as a criminal, or a terrorist – I'm not sure which it is, but most likely the latter. I cannot contain myself. I begin running. Through the churchyard, into the woods, and out onto the path to the walled garden. I have to see Seamus after all.

He behaves strangely, not looking at me directly, speaking in short, curt monosyllables. He doesn't seem interested in how the meeting went. I understand. He doesn't feel safe speaking with an Englishwoman today. I feel bad for trying to involve him again, and realise I will have to do without any more help from him or Sister Frances.

Hopelessness sets in – deeply and truly entrenched this time. I should change my flight and return home as quickly as possible. What on earth am I doing here, searching for an elderly nun I have never met before when the city is in the midst of a bloody war?

But instead of returning to the guest house I find I am re-tracing my steps, as if an invisible hand is guiding me back. I stop at the entrance to the church and go inside, this time to pray. I sit at the back again, breathing in the cool pungent air, my head bowed in a gesture of defeat that might resemble one of reverence and devotion. Thinking this is the end, and that I'm saying goodbye to Belfast and my hope of ever finding Liza, I feel the grief well up and tears trickle down my cheeks.

What happens next may be complete imagining. Another moment of madness. I think of Patrick and all the non-meetings and non-conversations we had – conversations that seemed to say so much despite the lack of words. I imagine a voice is telling me not to give up. Saying there is a way. I sit very still and I wait – I am not sure for what, but I am being compelled to wait and to listen. The church seems to be filling with light, a warm glow that pierces through the darkly coloured windows. I remember my painting – down at the bottom, the light coming through out of the darkness above. This is the moment it was pointing to.

A feeling of conviction worms its way into my thoughts – a conviction that Mary is nearby, in the convent or in the houses at the back. I decide to go there again, despite being warned off. No blackbird this time, but a stray cat leads me back to the homes of the old girls – a row of doors, each one painted blue. I walk slowly along the row. Only one has a small wooden cross nailed to it.

I knock.

After a few moments the door opens with a tentative squeak. A small elderly lady, dressed in nun's robes and a cream-coloured cardigan, with her long hair let loose around her shoulders like a fuzzy white halo, peers out through the narrow crack of the doorway. There is a delicacy about her, a transparent, ethereal quality. The bones of her face and hands are slender and frail – they remind me of my father's, when he was preparing to die.

'Sister Mary?'

The old woman brings her fingers to her mouth and gasps. 'Liza!' Her faded green eyes open wide, startled. Then she slams the door shut.

I step back, also shocked by this momentary contact. My heart is throbbing against my breastbone, pumping the blood into my throat so that I feel it pulsing, pressing, and I want to cry out, to wail, to drop to my knees and howl like a wounded animal. I have crossed the threshold, stepped into Liza's world, and a storm of grief is gripping my throat.

I clutch my fingers together and don't know what to do. I wait.

After some minutes the door cracks open again. I look into

her eyes, misted over like a window streaked with rain. I step a little closer.

'Liza, you've come back, please God?'

'No, I'm not Liza. I'm her granddaughter, Anita. I've come from London to see you. I had hoped so much to find you – and here you are.' Tears well up in my eyes and I find myself reaching out to Mary as if she were, indeed, my own long-lost friend.

'Oh my goodness, Holy Mary! Liza's granddaughter! I can't believe it – after all this time.' The words tumble out and the hint of a smile softens her face, lighting up the soft green eyes for a moment. And then, as if in a dream, as if we are both sleepwalking towards each other, she steps into my open arms. We cling to each other, briefly, a tight knot of longing and despair momentarily finding a purpose. Each afraid the other might vanish back into the world of dreams at any moment.

'Come in dear, come in,' says Mary, as we disentangle from our fleeting embrace. 'Sit down. Here.' She directs me to a solitary high-backed chair by the electric fire, and pulls up another chair from beside the table for herself. She makes me feel like royalty, with my red hair tied back, and my long, pale blue cheesecloth dress as demure as they come. I allow myself a moment to indulge in the kindness of my grandmother's special friend.

'Extraordinary!' exclaims Mary, as she gazes at me. 'You look just like her. The hair, the eyes, and I can see her fiery spirit too – though a little sad, I think.'

I feel suddenly awkward. I shift and fold my arms. I thought I hid my feelings well, but this woman who I have known for just a few moments is looking right into my soul and seeing me – with the clarity of starlight piercing through a black sky. I don't know how to respond, but Mary continues.

'She was a pretty young thing, your grandmother. Full of life, a bright spark, and kind too...' Mary's eyes mist over again. I wonder if she will cry, but instead she smiles and looks at me sweetly. 'You can be proud of her. She was a good young woman, despite all her troubles.'

'She trusted you. She said you might be able to help me – or at least, my mother. But it's me who has come. My mother is dead.' I stop with the blunt weight of those words.

'You shouldn't have to carry the burden of the past so heavily. I see you still carry it. Poor girl. What you have had to go through – what she had to go through. And your mother too. Oh dear, you've got me weeping now.' Tears spill over and course down the lines that wrinkle the thin skin of her face. I imagine the cracks of a dry riverbed finally filled with water as the rain falls.

'I hope my coming here isn't too upsetting for you.' I feel concerned that I have burst into Mary's fragile world, knowing nothing about her or how she manages to hold her aging self together. My presence here could be tearing down the only fortress she has left, for all I know.

Mary shakes her head and leans over to grasp my hand. 'It's alright, dear. An old lady has a right to cry now and then.' Again, the sweet smile softens her face, and I feel relief.

'I have to know what happened to Liza – and to find out if she's still alive. I have a letter from her – she said you could help ...' My voice trails off. Now it's my turn to let old tears spill over, but my sadness is tinged with joy at finding Mary alive. I taste the salty water on my lips. I want to ask her if Liza is alive too.

Mary reaches for my hand again. 'Of course I'll help you.'

'Is she still alive? Is Liza alive?' A note of desperation has crept into my voice.

'I'm not sure if she is. Maybe she is.' Mary looks at me and all I can feel is my heart's beating. There is nothing else. All my hopes are tied up in this moment. 'I have something for you. When Liza went away, she gave it to me, with the letter. She wanted me to give it to your mother if I could. Sadly I never did find her, but I see the letter found you, eventually. I'm so glad. The circle can begin to close now – the broken line can heal.' She sighs and pauses, as if talking so much has strained her frail body and she must stop to catch her breath. 'I've been holding the threads all these years and I need to let them go before I pass on. So I'm very glad you found me.'

She squeezes my hand then goes to a cupboard in the corner of the sparsely furnished room. She knows just where to look, even though it's many years since she placed it there. Mary takes out a book and hands it to me.

'This belongs to you.' There's a note of reverence in her voice. I see relief on her face as she passes on her charge at last.

The book has a beautifully embroidered cover, worn and faded with age by now, and a tiny silver lock that has kept it closed to prying eyes.

I gasp and look up at Mary. 'I have the key!' I take the purse out of my pocket, and the key out of the purse. It matches the lock perfectly.

I feel Mary's fingers, as light and fine as gossamer, resting over my own. 'This is for you to do alone. It's your story. I'm only a witness to it. Take the diary Anita, read it if you can. Then please come back to see me before you leave Belfast.'

I appreciate her wise words. I do need to do this alone, and am grateful for her understanding. I put the key back into the purse, and the diary into my bag. I want to run back to my room and open it right away, but I also feel called to stay a moment longer with Mary. She sees my hesitation.

'Tell me about yourself, Anita. There's a story in you too – something that led you here to look for your grandmother, I know. I see it in your eyes.'

I feel grateful for the invitation. Now I'm ready for Mary to see me, and I know that few words will say much to this perceptive woman. I speak briefly about my mother and father, Martin and Nancy. I pause. After dreaming for so long about Liza's story, wondering about it, imagining into it, I no longer know how to tell my own. 'I fell in love with a young man called Richard. He died when I was seventeen.'

'Ah – I see. I see it all there, the shadows in your pretty blue eyes, just like Liza's. As if she still lives in you, her story living on in yours.' She is looking intently at me, inviting me to continue.

'My father died of cancer nearly six months after this.' And that's it. That's my story. It sounds sparse as I lay it out like this for Mary, the parched, bare bones of my story. But I know she is feeling every breath, hearing every cry.

'You've had a hard journey too. I see why it's so important for you to know about your grandmother,' she says, after a long silence. 'But a story doesn't end – it goes on and on. Tell me what you are doing now, your life in London.' She smiles at me as she stands up, and moves towards the stove where an old soot-blackened kettle is quietly simmering.

'Alright.' I sigh, glad for now to return to the present and things that are easier to speak about.

Mary makes tea while I entertain her with stories of my life as an artist in London. Then she admits that, since coming to live over here and giving up her duties in the convent, she has finally been able to indulge her own secret passion.

As we chat – just like old friends united after a long absence, as if the years and the generations made no difference – she shows me her sketches and watercolours – of the gardens, the convent, its residents. Among them is a painting of a young girl with long red hair and bright blue eyes, holding a baby in her arms.

2

'Martin, hi, is that you? The line's very bad.'

'Yes, it's me. Hi Anita. How's it going? I've been hoping you'd call. I wanted to apologise for being so unhelpful earlier – it's just that ...'

'I know, Martin, you've been busy, but it's okay now, really it is.'

'So what's the news?'

'I've found her! I've found her, Martin – at least I've found Mary and she showed me a picture of Liza with our mother, and she gave me her diary. And I'm going to read it now and then maybe I will be able to find her...' I stop, breathless.

'Wow, that's amazing. I really didn't think you'd manage it. Sorry I couldn't help, but it's great that you've found Mary – and Liza's diary – incredible! We'll know what happened to her then...' I'm glad to hear Martin say 'we', glad he is finally showing some enthusiasm for this search.

'Our grandmother, Martin! Just think of that!'

'Yes – it's hard to know quite what to think, but it's amazing, really – I don't know what to say.'

'Listen, I'm going to run out of money soon. I'll call you again if I find Liza. If I don't, I'll call you when I get back to London.'

'And then come and visit me in Spain, Anita. Have a holiday. It's ages since you've been here.'

'Will do. Must go now...' The pips interrupt and we are cut off. I hang up the phone, feeling cleansed out, as if I've been washed through with fresh rainwater. Martin's reluctance has weighed heavily on me. Now I feel his support, and it fills me with strength.

Part V

The Wounding Past

Twenty-three

Belfast – 1982

I close the door behind me and pull the chair close to the window. A streak of afternoon sunlight angles across the table. I look out over the rooftops of Belfast, my breath light, my heart pulsing in my ears. Liza's diary lies on my lap, a testament in faded gold and burgundy. It smells dusty. Faint traces of dry wood and lavender. The years of silence seem to weigh heavily, and the intricately embroidered silk cover is worn and stained with age.

I take the purse from my pocket and the small silver key from the purse. Finally I can unlock my grandmother's secret.

The key turns reluctantly in the rusted lock, stiff from lack of use. The lock that has kept Liza's story hidden all these years. I am sure to be the only person to have read the diary, besides Liza herself. It was meant to be my own mother sitting here, but the reality of life is never as it was meant to be in the world of hopes and dreams. At last, acceptance of this stark truth has begun to creep into my heart – like a quiet stream, like a soft breeze with a sharp chill at its core.

I open the book. On the first page the words 'My Diary' are printed in large and flourishing letters, with sweeping tails to the ys. The blue ink has turned greenish with age, the paper stiff and grey.

"

March 16th, 1926

*Today we had a visitor, Mrs Mallone, the lady from the big
house at the other side of our village. My mam invited her
in to talk about some sewing she wants done. She has been
travelling all round the world with her husband, she told us.
They are very rich. They went to the Far East, she said —
India, China, Tibet. I didn't know where these places were,
but she described her round journey and now I have a sense
of them being somehow underneath us, beneath the earth
where Ireland is. It was odd seeing such a grand lady sitting
by our fire drinking tea with my mam, telling us all about
her travels. She's very nice, Mrs Mallone, not at all like some
of the rich ladies who come here with their sewing to be done,
full of airs and graces, and treating Mam like a servant.*

*Anyway, she gave me a present — a diary — so I can write
about all the exciting and wonderful, and also sad things that
will happen to me in my life as I grow up, she said. It has a
lock and a little silver key so that nobody but me can read it.
It will be my book of secrets.*

*Mrs Mallone also brought some designs that she wants us
to embroider for her. She says they're sacred symbols from
the Far East. Some seem familiar to me, like our own Celtic
designs. My mam is going to let me embroider some of Mrs
Mallone's cushions, as I've now learnt to do this quite well.
'A good Catholic woman can always make a living if she
knows the needlecrafts', my mam is always telling me. I'm
sure she's right about that, as she does quite well herself.*

*I'm very happy to have a diary. It's the first thing I've
ever had that is really mine. I share my clothes, my bed,
my schoolbooks — everything — with my sisters. It feels very
special to have a place to write down my secret thoughts, a
place that is all my own.*

March 19th

*The first thing I have to write about is an unhappy one.
That makes me sad, but my life has many unhappy days
like this one.*

*The day began as usual, with my pa having us all pray
together before he went out to work on the farm and we were
sent off to school. He makes lots of money but it doesn't seem
to make him happy. He's always angry when he comes home.
And he's very strict with us. We have to pray every morning
and night, go to church all day Sunday, and never speak in
front of him, unless we're spoken to. He frightens us children.*

*When he came home this evening the little ones were
playing in the kitchen, making lots of noise, our mam
clattering about with pots and pans, and there was no end
to the chaos everywhere. He just flew into a rage, started
shouting at my mam and all of us. The twins began crying,
which just made him madder. He yelled at Mam to stop their
noise, but she couldn't. She dropped the pot of potato stew
and it went flying over the fireplace. Then he threw a jug
at the wall and it broke into a shower of little pieces — little
shiny pieces of white china skittering over the floor in a pool
of dark water.*

*By this time Mam was scared. She was cowering in a
corner, crying for him not to hit her, or any of us children.
This made him even more angry and he flared up like a fire
and lashed out at her. He hit her hard, across the face, and
her face swelled up all purple and blue, like a damson.*

*I don't know why he got so angry. We children hid out of
his way in case he had a go at us too. Sometimes I see him
beating my mam till she's all bruised and bleeding.*

*I don't know what she's done to deserve this, but I know
that every year she goes on retreat — to seek forgiveness, she
says. She wears sackcloth and sleeps on a bed of ashes, and
has to hit herself with a long whip — as penance, to purify all*

her sins, she says. She comes back weeping and bleeding, and takes to her bed for a week. Then I have to nurse her better, and look after my brothers and sisters too – all six of them. I'm tired of doing this but I have to do it anyway.

I don't know what her sins are – I thought she was a good and God-fearing Catholic so I don't know why she has to be punished like this. It doesn't seem right to me. But she never stands up to my pa, or anyone else for that matter. I wish she would. I wish she would shout back at him and stop him from hitting her. I think she's very weak. I know I shouldn't criticise my parents, but I can't see what is right in all of this. Sometimes I hate living here. I wish I could run away, but I don't know where else to go. Certainly not to Uncle Brendan's! We always have to be on the look out for Pa. Tonight all the little ones are quiet – they know not to anger him more when he's in this kind of mood.

March 24th

Things are very tense between Mam and Pa at the moment, so I spend as much time as I can outside. I love to walk over the fields, hide in the woods, swim in the river in summer. I feel happy when I am outside in the green world. I wish I could live there forever.

Today, instead of going straight home from school, I went up into the heart of the woods, as I often do, to my secret den. It's a special place – no-one else knows about it, no-one else ever goes there. The ground rises steeply to form a ring of earth around a hollow. It's just big enough for one, or maybe two people to lie down in. Tree roots burrow into the ring of earth, and their tall trunks tower over the den. It's completely hidden by a green canopy of leaves in summer. I feel as if I'm high up in a nest with the birds and squirrels.

Here I feel at peace, and safe from all the anger and fear at home. Today I read some poems from the book we're studying

*at school – W B Yeats – romantic he is, our teacher says –
and imagined I was far, far away.*

April 2nd

*The spring rains are falling today, hard and fast, so I had to
come straight home. I've been embroidering Mrs Mallone's
designs from the Far East. I especially like one of them. It's
a continuous line that weaves in and out to make a never-
ending path, like a maze, a place that you can't get into and
can't get out of, or a secret place, like my den.*

   *She said it's called the Knot of Eternity. This makes me
think of everything, the past and the future, all gathered up
and woven together, and nothing is lost or forgotten or out
of place, just all tied up together forever. I feel peaceful when
I'm working on it. Even though Liam is crying and the
twins are fighting and Sheena keeps annoying me with silly
questions. I don't listen to them anymore – they don't make
sense – 'why, why, why?' 'Why did God make Catholics
and Protestants?' 'Which one is right?' Anyway, she should
be asking Pa if she wants to know about what's right and
wrong. He's the only one who is allowed to pass judgement
on that in this house. Apart from Uncle Brendan of course,
but when he's not here, Pa is there in his place.*

April 10th

*I hate Sundays more than every other day. I can't go to the
woods, or do my embroidery, or read a book. We have to wear
our best clothes all day, sit up straight, be very quiet and read
the Bible when Uncle Brendan is here, which is most of the
day except when we are all in church. We have to call him
Padre even though he's really our uncle because he's also the
priest. And he is Pa's big brother who was like a father to
him after their own father was shot dead by the Prods, a long*

time ago. Padre tells us this story often, but Pa doesn't like to speak about it so much.

Today he told us that our grandfather was a brave man and he died for us, so we should be grateful and always respect the Catholic Church. I didn't see the reason in that. My pa just scowled and looked glum.

'Did he die for us like Jesus Christ died for us?' I asked, before I could stop myself. My pa looked about to slap me but stopped himself because Padre was there and you can't go slapping people in front of the priest, even if he is just your big brother.

The good thing about Sundays is that Pa is also on his best behaviour and never once has he shouted at us or hit my ma when Padre is here. I don't know if he's frightened of him, or trying to impress him like Sheena is with the teacher at our school, but it gives us all a rest when he's quiet like this for Uncle Brendan Padre. I think my pa is confused about all of this. Me, I'm just glad he didn't slap me because it's Sunday.

I think my pa believes that the Padre really does have God on his side, speaking in his ear and guiding him, as he tells us. I'm not so sure about this myself. For me, God is on the side of the likes of the romantic poets, and me too, I hope.

April 26th

Today, April 26th, 1926 – a very special day!! A day to remember, forever and ever.

Today I met a young man! I met him by chance, on this bright spring afternoon.

As I often do, I went to my secret den after school and was lying there, happy and at peace with the world. I stayed as long as I dared, with the fresh green leaves dancing above my head, and sunlight trickling through the branches of the great oak and beech trees. The birds were singing and squirrels scurried up and down the tree trunks. Here I can dream, and imagine that life will be sweet one day.

When I thought it was getting late, I jumped up and began running home, as I always do. My mam would be waiting for me – if Pa arrived home early and found me missing all hell would be let loose. I flew down the path that leads through the woods to the open field, and then on towards our village.

At first I didn't see him as I got close to the gate at the edge of the woods. I was startled when he stepped out and offered a hand to help me over the stile. We stood there, each staring at the other. His dark brown eyes seemed to reach right down into me – I could feel a gentle tug there, as if his eyes had cast a fine thread and hooked my heart. It flapped and fluttered like a fish caught on a line.

I don't know if it was seconds or minutes, or even hours, that we stood there, his hand held out towards mine, our eyes fastened together. My mind had flipped over and disappeared down a crack – I was emptied right out as his gaze flowed through and through me.

Eventually he smiled, his face softening like butter on warm toast.

'Hello. I'm Arthur. I'm sorry if I startled you. I saw you running...'

'I'm Liza. Hello,' I said, feeling suddenly shy, and I felt my own face melt and smile back at him. And that was how it all began.

We talked a little – I can't remember quite what we said, but I remember his warm smile and his voice that sounded like a song. We agreed to meet again, there by the gate, on Thursday afternoon.

April 28th

This afternoon, when I had finished school and Arthur's work was done, we met again, just as we had planned. He was waiting for me by the gate. He looked so handsome, standing there in the dappled shade of the trees, his face as brown and smooth as a sweet chestnut and his dark wavy hair blowing in the breeze. I love how it falls into a soft curl across the left side of his brow, how he tosses his head to the side to flick it away from his eye, then looks at me with his head at a tilt. I love the broad sweep of his cheekbones, curving out towards the tips of his ears, and his strong jaw, the weight of it, the sheer determination of it.

I remember the sweet scent of wet grass and I swear I could smell the fresh green of the beech leaves unfurling from their winter buds.

We walked through the woods, and we talked. I felt such happiness as I have never known before. We talked about our lives, our pain and joy, and all we dreamed of for our futures.

He's seventeen, just a year older than me, and he's a Protestant. This isn't a problem for us, but it would be for everyone else if they knew. There's terrible tension round here between the Prods and Catholics. Most of the Prods I know seem like good people, just like us as far as I can tell. But my pa says we should never forget what they have done to our people — it goes back generations, it's our history, he says. He gets angry whenever their name comes up — begins to shout and threaten them, as if they were there in the very room with us. He reminds us that they killed his father, then he becomes silent and disappears inside himself, like a snail shrinking into its shell. I guess he's sad about his father dying. I suppose I might be too, if he died, though I think I would be relieved as well.

Arthur lives in the next village and works on a farm there. He's tall, brown-haired, with deep brown eyes. He's strong, and so handsome.

I think I'm in love. This must be love — I have never felt so happy in all my life. If I died tomorrow, I would die happy because now I know what it is to be in love.

I look up from the diary. Two collared doves have perched on the rooftop opposite my room and are cooing loudly. The clock in the hallway chimes the hour, then the quiet of late afternoon spreads out again, like a soft blanket over the city streets. I can hear the beating of my own heart, and feel the ripples of my own first love reflected there. But how harsh my grandmother's life had been. Between the lines of Liza's simple account, I glimpse a story of terrible hardship, suffering and fear, made bearable only by young love and the hope of escape from her father's violent home.

Liza feels close, her presence, her passionate spirit becoming real to me. I feel torn between the excitement of finding her, through her words, and shock at the discovery of such violence in her father, my great grandfather – an angry man full of bitterness and hate. For a moment I wonder how my life might have been if I had tied myself to Eddie. I am sure violence is in him too. Inwardly I shudder – with fear, and also with relief to have escaped my great grandmother's fate.

Anticipation is tinged with trepidation as I continue to read.

May 8th

Now I have a very big secret to keep. We can't let anyone know about our love, so we meet up on the wild moors or deep in the woods where no-one will see us. Arthur knows all the land, the farms, exactly where people go and where they don't go. Yesterday I took him to my den. He's the only person who knows about it, but I know I can trust him with this, my other secret.

Today, for the first time, he held my hand. We were running down the hill towards the stream, laughing. He was chasing me and I stumbled. He caught my hand and we kept on running. It felt the most natural thing in the world to do, to run down the hill, hand in hand with the wind flying in our faces.

May 12th

*I feel as if I'm in heaven! I can't imagine ever being happier
than I feel today.*

*Today Arthur kissed me for the first time. It was on
the wooden footbridge that crosses the river, just where it
flows along the edge of the woods. The river was full after
yesterday's heavy rain, and the dark water was rushing below
us. We were hidden from view by the tall trees. Half way
across he stopped and turned to face me. He touched my cheek
lightly and drew my face close to his. Our lips met. We kissed
tenderly. I felt a world of promises in that first kiss – worlds
to be discovered, dreams to be unwrapped – with care, with
delight, and sometimes recklessness. My body tingled and
came alive. I felt beautiful in a way I have never felt before.*

I no longer feel like a child – I am a young woman now.

Liza could have been writing about my own first love. My
memory returns to Richard, to our first kiss – the moment
on the steps down to the beach when he turned and reached
towards me. My heart splits open again, and the tears well up
in my eyes. In Liza's words I find myself, as if we are the same,
my grandmother and me. We were both young, just sixteen,
when we first found love. Fresh, open, full of hope for a bright
future. But we were both naïve too. Life would not fulfil our
hopes and dreams as we had believed it would.

I come to an entry that rekindles my own sense of loss, and
of regret, as I read of Liza travelling where I had not quite
dared to go.

July 31st

*It's mid-summer and the dizzying heat makes the air heavy
with rain. It was the rain that led us to lie together today, for
the very first time.*

*A thunderstorm had driven us to shelter in the disused barn
that sits on the far side of the hill. We lay on a pile of hay –
still sweet smelling despite having been left there years ago
– listening to the rain clattering on the tile roof. Now and
then a roll of thunder, retreating into the distance, rumbled
through the steady rhythm of the rain. I could hear Arthur's
breath, soft beneath the splatter of rain and the thunder, and
my own breath, rising and falling in rhythm with his. It just
happened. It felt so natural. Our bodies came together, our
arms and legs wrapped around, his chest pressing into mine,
my soft belly against his. We kissed and the breath seemed to
flow from my heart into his, and from his back to mine, then
down deep into the throbbing, aching place. His hands moved
over the curves of my back, beneath my dress, down over my
thighs. My fingers gripped and pressed into his firm body. We
flowed into each other. When he came inside me there was
first a sharp pain, but he was gentle with me when the pain
came, and soon the rhythm of our bodies flowing together
took me over. I melted in waves – soft, expanding, melting
waves. I dissolved out through my fingers and toes and my
breath. There was such pleasure as I have never felt before.
Like being in heaven, to be sure.*

Afterwards we both laughed and laughed with joy.

*I feel like a real grown woman, and a beautiful woman,
now. Arthur makes me feel beautiful inside. Nobody ever
made me feel like this before.*

October 4th

*After that first time I told him we must take care but I fear we
weren't careful enough. I am now quite sure I am with child.
I've not bled for two months and I feel sick every morning. I
often feel tired, and my breasts have begun to swell up and feel
tender. I remember it was like this for my mam each time she
was carrying one of the little ones. I feel very afraid.*

Today I told Arthur that I'm sure I am carrying his baby. He was so sweet and kind. No-one has ever been so kind to me as he is. He hugged me and kissed me. He said we would marry and live together in a small cottage near the farm where he works. He would work hard and I could earn money taking in sewing for the rich ladies.

I feel happy, and scared, and so confused with all these different emotions. I don't know what to do. I must try to hide the baby until Arthur has sorted everything out and we can marry and move into our own home.

But it feels so wrong to pretend this isn't happening. I feel full of joy and life, and I want to shout out over the hills and tell everyone that I am to have a baby, and that Arthur loves me and we are to be married!

December 20th

Now I'm in real trouble. My mam has finally noticed. She doesn't know what to do either. She daren't say anything to Pa for fear of what he might do, but of course he will have to know in the end. I hope I can move into the cottage with Arthur soon, so my father won't be able to control my life anymore, so I'll be free. Arthur is working harder than ever to earn enough money for the two of us and our baby.

As afternoon light fades to dusk, I read on, pausing now and then to look out over the city. The rooftops turn from grey to black and shadows deepen. The first evening star appears between the scudding clouds.

In places the entries are incomplete or written in fragments – words, phrases, an unfinished sentence. Where Liza's voice is silent, I piece the threads together as best I can.

Twenty-four

Ballycraig – 1926

It was a Saturday morning when it all came out. A bitter cold day with a northwest wind whipping through the crack beneath the door.

'What be with you, Liza? You've been standing there all morning with that cloth in your hand, looking like a fool. As if there were time to be wasted round here, by Jesus. Stop your dreaming, girl, and get that cleaning finished before your father comes back,' her mam admonished.

Liza had been gazing out of the window, thinking of her baby and the cottage she and Arthur would rent. Snow covered the distant bare hills and the creatures of the land had turned to sleep for the winter months. She absentmindedly rubbed a hand over her belly as she turned back to the fireplace and the stack of pots waiting to be scrubbed.

Her mam noticed her daughter's dreamy expression and the tender way she touched her belly. It was a gesture she would recognise. She had, after all, enjoyed being pregnant those first three times. After that, having babies had become a chore, another burden to bear. Liza's mam tried to brush the thought aside, but it stuck to her like a leech. She was staring at Liza. Her daughter, pregnant? Surely it could not be. She could not bear such a calamity to befall her own family. She had seen it happen to others – the whole damn shame of it.

'Liza, what's that you're carrying? It's not fat from the meat you get round here, to be sure. What's with you, girl? Answer me!' she demanded.

Liza hung her head. She couldn't hide it any longer. The baby was growing more visible every day. She rested both hands on her round belly and muttered, as if to herself, 'I'm going to have a baby.'

'You're going to have a baby! A baby! Liza, how could you? How could you do this to me, and to your father? Shame on you, girl. God's shame on you, you wicked girl.' Her mam sat down heavily and dropped her head right into her hands. 'Oh God, what did I do to deserve this? As if my life were not hard enough. As if I have not always done right by you – and you repay me with this.'

Her mam's mind was filled with a continuous complaint, an angry litany – about her children, her husband, the neighbours, the weather, all the work she had to do. Mostly it took the form of a silent stream of annoyance that tormented her inwardly. Sometimes, as it was about to do now, it poured out as an audible torrent towards those around her. She would have gone on like this, but for the sound of the gate closing in the yard.

'Your father! By Jesus – don't say anything to him. Hide yourself, girl.' Her mam took the wet cloth out of Liza's hand and pushed her towards the stairs. 'I'll talk to you later. Go up to your room now.'

Liza shared a room with her three younger sisters, but thankfully they were out helping their father on the farm as it was Saturday. He believed that all of his children – boys and girls, young and older – should share in the work, so every Saturday morning they were sent out to the yard or the barns or fields – wherever they could be made use of. Only on Saturday afternoons were they free to run out and play.

Liza sat alone on a corner of the mattress that the four

girls shared and listened to her parents arguing downstairs. Outside the sky was grey, heavy with the snow that would soon fall. Inside, the walls of the room were plastered white, the floorboards darkly stained and polished smooth by the many stockinged feet that had run back and forth, around the horsehair mattress that sat squarely against one wall. She couldn't wait to get away from this place – to move into her own home with Arthur. There would be flowers on the table and coloured rugs on the floors, and warm woollen blankets and plates with all her favourite trees painted on them.

Eventually she would have to face her father's wrath, but she hoped that by then she and Arthur would be ready to start their new life together.

She heard her father leave the house again, slamming the door behind him. A while later her mam's footsteps sounded on the stairs. The latch on Liza's bedroom door clicked open and her mam came in, carrying a bundle of old clothes. The stuffy smell of mothballs and camphor wafted in with her.

'Here, try these on.' She threw the clothes at the floor and stood over them, hands on hips, waiting.

'What are these for?' asked Liza, as she held up a long linen smock and an old jacket several sizes too big for her.

'To cover you up, of course,' replied her mam scornfully. 'This will hide you for a while, till we think what to do. How far gone are you?'

'I'm not sure exactly. About five months I think.'

'Jesus and Mary! Five months! There's no getting rid of it then.' Her mam threw her hands up into the air as if berating God himself.

'Getting rid of it? I wouldn't do that. I want the baby. We're in love – we're going to get married.' The thought of getting rid of her baby had never crossed her mind, and it shocked her.

'Married! Don't be such a fool, Liza. What do you want with being married, at your age? A fine lot it's brought me, to be sure.' She furrowed her brow and tightened her lips. She might have said more on the subject, but instead returned her attention to her wayward daughter. 'Who is the evil wretch anyway?'

'His name's Arthur. He works on Taggart's farm and he wants to marry me, so he does.' Liza felt fiercely protective of Arthur and their baby. 'And he's not evil. He's Christian, like us.'

'Catholic?' asked her mother.

'He's Protestant, but that doesn't mean he's bad – he's just as good a Christian as any Catholic I know,' she defended.

'How dare you say such a thing against the good Catholic people! We'll have to see what your father thinks about you cavorting with a Protestant cowhand, by Jesus. He'll put an end to your cheek, to be sure,' said her mam, furious beyond belief.

'Please don't tell him, not yet. I'll work something out,' begged Liza. Anticipation of the full weight of her father's anger filled her with terror.

'Well, put these on for now,' her mam spluttered, as she nudged the over-sized clothes towards Liza with her foot. 'I don't know what you think you can work out though. You've worked yourself out good and proper now, as far as I can see. Please God, after all I've done for you, this is how you repay me.'

Liza heard her mam's complaint continue on as she stomped down the wooden stairs. She held the baggy smock up against her blossoming belly and breasts, and smiled secretly to herself. Despite it all, carrying Arthur's child inside her gave her strength and joy.

When she told Arthur that her mam had found out, he promised to double his efforts, to work extra hard. Very soon he would have enough money saved to rent the cottage, he told her. He worked long hours over the next few weeks, so they could only meet on Saturday afternoons when Liza's work at home was done. Her father must not suspect anything out of the ordinary.

Whilst she waited, Liza began to embroider a cushion for her baby to sleep on. She chose a piece of fine blue linen, the colour of the sky on a bright summer's day, and began to stitch Mrs Mallone's design into it. In silver, gold and green threads she wove the sacred symbol, called the Knot of Eternity, into the blue cloth. She created a beautiful gift to welcome her baby into the world.

For several weeks Liza and her mother upheld the lie. Her sister Sheena had guessed it too, watching Liza dress and undress for bed. In the end it was Sheena who let the secret out. She hadn't meant to – she just wasn't thinking. Liza had always been the wild one, hard to tame in her mam's eyes. Sheena was different, absent-minded, a little slow – something not quite right about her, their mam thought. Because of it, she had to be indulged in a way the others weren't.

It was over supper one evening, when the family were gathered and the meat stew had been served.

'You know my friend, Brigid – her mam had another baby last week. It's her eighth. She says it'll be her last though,' said Sheena, after their father had said grace.

'Oh, that's nice for her,' said their mam through pursed lips, hoping Sheena's chatter wouldn't annoy father.

'They're going to call it Connor. Nice name for a boy I think,' said Sheena. 'What will you call yours, Liza?' She glanced innocently at her older sister. Liza gulped and nearly choked on a mouthful of stew. Their mam quickly cleared her throat and clattered the ladle in the pot as she lifted it back onto the stove. But too late. Father glowered, first at Sheena, then Liza, then their mother. He looked at each of them, in turn, one more time. Everyone fell silent, even the little ones, who recognised a scene brewing even though they had no idea what it might be about.

'Eliza?' he said, looking at her beneath lowered brows. He had the menacing air of an animal about to pounce – muscles clenched, power restrained, eyes glinting and fixed. Her heart beat faster. Now was the moment to escape, to run – but where? She couldn't run to Arthur's – it was too far on a dark night, and her father would catch her before she was even out of the door. She was frozen to the spot. Her legs went weak and her stomach churned over. It was like falling into a peat bog, being sucked deeper and deeper and being unable to pull herself out. She wanted to scream 'Help!' but her voice stuck in her throat and she couldn't even whisper, 'Yes, Father,' as she had been taught to do when addressed by him. Reluctantly she lifted her eyes to meet his. The pupils were red – she could have sworn it.

'So what do you have to tell me, girl? What is this about?' he said in a low and steady voice, carefully preserving energy for the attack.

'What, Father?'

'What do you have to tell me?' He began to raise his voice. 'Stand up, girl. Turn around.' He surveyed her full belly. 'I see. And for how long have you been keeping this shame a secret?'

'I'm pregnant by about six months now, Father.' She tried to make it sound quite normal and matter-of-fact. What else could she do?

'And who else knew about this?' He turned to look at his wife, who had turned as white as the snow covering the crests of the hills, and looked about to faint. 'So you knew too! And what kind of a fool did you think you would make of me, hiding this from me? Have you no shame either, woman? What kind of a bed of sin has this house become?' His wife, Liza's mother, was trembling now, her body already curling into the habitual shape of one who had been beaten to the ground many times.

'I'll deal with you later, woman. Take the children upstairs now. I need to have words with my eldest daughter – shame on our house.'

She hurriedly shooed the little ones upstairs and followed them, only faintly relieved at this short reprieve.

'So, Eliza, what do you have to say for yourself? How do you intend to account for your sinful condition?' He clearly enjoyed drawing out the inevitable punishment. The lingering threat only added to Liza's fear, which of course was the intention.

'I'm...I'm sorry, Father. I fell in love with a young man. He's a good man. He'll marry me, he will. He'll make an honest wife of me – we won't bring shame on you. Please give us a chance to show you.' Liza was retreating from him as she spoke. She stood up tall but inside she felt as if she were crouching on her knees, praying like she'd never prayed before in church.

'You have already brought shame on me, on my family. The whole county will be talking about us – my good name, that I've worked so hard to make, ruined – ruined by a girl, a slut, a whore. You're no child of mine. This is not what I brought you up to be!' His attitude suddenly changed, as if another being had taken possession of him and he no longer seemed to see Liza. He spoke as if to some other version of himself that flickered in a distorted nightmare scene before him. His jaw was clenched like steel and his eyes stared into the night as his rage finally reached breaking point. He grabbed her arm and struck her across the side of the head. Liza fell against the wall. He continued to grip her arm tightly and slapped her face, hard, with the back of his hand. Her lip split open and began to bleed.

'Please, Father, please,' was all she could utter before he hit her again, sending her flying into the table and crashing to the floor with a shower of broken crockery and hot stew.

'Stand up and take your punishment like the good Catholic I brought you up to be. No child of mine goes grovelling in the dirt when punishment is due. Stand up, girl!' he shouted. His face was ugly with rage, his fists white at the knuckles. He punched her in the chest as she struggled to her feet. Liza collapsed again, grasping for breath. There was blood in her mouth, blood running down her face. A searing pain ran through her chest and down her right arm. She couldn't move.

Her father kicked her in the back where she lay, before grabbing his hat and coat and storming out of the house.

For the rest of the evening the children stayed quietly upstairs while their mam dressed Liza's wounds and put her to bed. No-one spoke of what had just taken place. Each nursed a terror that their turn would come soon.

Their mam knew that it would be her turn next. And so it was. He returned several hours later, smelling of whisky and unsteady on his feet, but not too much so. The little ones were wide-awake but quiet in their beds. They held their breath. Sheena was scratching plaster off the wall with her fingernails. There was a large patch of bare stonework by her sleeping place where she had scratched rivulets of plaster away during many a fearful night. It helped to calm her.

Liza listened to the dull thuds of her father's fists landing on hardened flesh. She could hear her mam's pitiful pleas. He said not a word as he did his business with her.

Then he left the house and all they could hear from the kitchen was their mother sobbing quietly. Father didn't return for nearly a week.

Twenty-five

Belfast – 1981

I place my breakfast tray on the small table by the window and pour some tea. I don't feel like eating but Sissy has brought a plate of soda bread and scrambled eggs up to my room. I'll try to eat at least a little of it. She has been kind to me and I don't want her to think I am ungrateful.

My sleep was restless, disturbed by dreams. Once again, I am walking across the marshes in the mist, trying to reach Richard's grave. The marsh keeps expanding, the beach retreating further out of reach, and I feel such desolation, anxiety growing out of a sense of utter aloneness. Out of the mist the vision of the grandmothers appears. This time, the one at the front of the line is stepping towards me. Now I can see her clearly. She has long curls of red hair, just like my own, and her blue eyes are darkened hollows. Tears stream down her face as she reaches out to me. Then they dissolve back into the mist and I am left alone.

I open Liza's diary as I sip the strong black tea. The entries become increasingly erratic, confused, often scribbled in haste and unfinished. I read between the lines to try to grasp the story. As I read, my heart is breaking. I am shocked to know there has been such cruelty in my own family.

January 24th, 1927

Today my pa returned home from wherever he has been – no one dared to ask. He said it was all sorted out. I am to be sent away to the Convent of the Sacred Heart in Belfast city to give birth to my baby in secret.

My parents are so angry and ashamed of me that they don't want anything to do with me and my baby at all. It's hard to believe, but that is the truth.

I am to be punished for loving Arthur, as if love were a sin that God could not forgive. Arthur is to be punished too. He will be sent away – to Australia my pa said. Pa has forbidden me to leave the house, so I can't even say goodbye to my sweetheart. Of course, Pa knows we would run away together if we could. I so wish we had run away before Pa came back. I didn't know it would come to this. But we have nowhere to go – Arthur hasn't earned enough money for the cottage yet, although he worked so very hard.

Already I miss him dreadfully – he's the sweetest person I have ever known. How could God punish our love? Now I am angry with God, as well as my pa, and the anger is eating away at my heart.

Through almost a full turn of the seasons Arthur and I met, whenever we could. We lay in the grass beneath the grand swaying branches of the trees, watching the change from spring to summer, then to autumn. We saw the leaves unfurl, dance with the sunlight, then put on their colourful coats for a while, before falling to the ground in heaps of rustling brown.

Now it's all taken away. He is gone and I may never see him again. My life is over. I will never find love and happiness like this again.

I used to be called Liza but they have taken my name away too. Here in the Refuge Home they make all the girls change their name. They say it will help us to put our sinful pasts behind us – make a new start with a good Christian name.

Here I'm called Elizabeth. I was christened Eliza but no-one ever called me that – except my pa when he was very angry. My mam wanted to call me Eliza after a character in a book she had read – in the days when she read books, before all the babies came along one after the other. My pa said it would give me ideas above myself and I should have a proper Irish name, but in the end he said that John the Baptiste's mother was called Elizabeth, so he guessed it would be alright after all if I was Eliza. That's what my mam used to tell me. In those days my mam could get her way with him – but not anymore.

So now I am to be Elizabeth. I prefer Liza. Sister Mary calls me Liza. She is very kind to me. She is not much older than I am but her life is so very different from mine.

Sister Mary follows three rules – one, be kind to fellow beings who are suffering – two, be devoted to God – three, be obedient to the Church. Despite my sins, she likes me. She says my spirit is free and that is something beautiful which I should never change. She calls me a child of nature and says it's not really my fault that I got into trouble with Arthur. Mary says that we are alike. We were both looking for love. She found God and I found Arthur. I feel she understands me.

Today she sneaked a red apple into my pocket as I was finishing the laundry.

They took my clothes too, so I have to wear this dreadful grey gown and monstrous cap that hides all of my hair. I wonder if Arthur would still love me if he saw me now, looking so bedraggled and ugly? I've grown pale and thin, apart from my big belly, which grows rounder every day. I love to touch it, to stroke it. I like to sing to my baby. If it's a girl I'll call her Eleanor. If it's a boy, he will be Arthur, after his handsome pa.

All day we have to work or pray. The only time I have to myself is at bedtime. This evening I buried under my blanket and ate the apple from Sister Mary before writing in my diary. Thank goodness I have this at least — otherwise I think I might go quite mad in here. Despite Mary's kindness I feel very alone.

Now I must sleep. I feel so tired.

February 21st

Another long day in the laundry room. There is an endless amount of washing to do and I'm very tired now. This work is so hard and so very boring. I long to be running in the fields or hiding in my den with Arthur. I miss him so much.

March 7th

I'm getting very big now — my belly is round and smooth like a great big onion. I tried to hide it at first — to hide you, my little one — to pretend it wasn't happening, hoping somehow it would go away — you would go away. But I was also thrilled to be carrying you. I wanted you so much, even while I feared what would happen when they found out. I'm sorry if I could not welcome you, my little one, with the whole of my heart — sorry if I wished you away at times — but I was so frightened about what would happen to me. I still am frightened. But I am happy that you will soon be with me. We will make a good life together, somehow.

April 6th

Today it's Easter Friday and we didn't have to do laundry. I'm glad. The washing room is hot and steamy and noisy, and the work hard. I fainted yesterday and they let me lie down for a while, but then I had to go back to scrubbing and wringing. They say that hard work will turn us from our sinful ways and make good women out of us. And they say that prayer will turn us towards God and the good Christian life. So today we spent all day in the chapel, praying for our fallen souls and listening to sermons. My knees are sore from so much kneeling. I think the life of the Sisters is hard too – they have to do this all the time – though some are so unkind to us that I don't feel sorry for them at all.

April 26th

It was very hot in the laundry rooms today. I felt weak and could barely climb up the stairs after working all day. Catherine and Celia helped me back to the dormitory. They thought I must be ready to have my baby. Catherine is pregnant too, but she has a while to wait for hers. I like her. She is older than me and lived on her own in the city before she came here. Mary said she is one of the 'fallen women', but I think she is very nice. She showed me how to tie up my hair so I can still look elegant beneath this dreadful cap I have to wear.

Tonight I have some pain in my belly, so I think they are right – you will come soon, my little baby. I feel afraid. I wish my mam were here. I wonder if she will come when you are born. And I so wish Arthur was here. I wouldn't feel so afraid if he were with me.

But soon you will be with me, my little one. Then all will be well.

Twenty-six

Belfast – 1927

It was nearly midnight when the pains began to come fast and fierce. Liza cried out like a creature from the wilds – an unearthly sound rending the cloistered silence, echoing through the convent halls and waking all the girls. Each one crouched in her bed fearing the moment when her own time would come.

'Shh, shh. There, there,' cooed Sister Mary. Liza gripped her hand so tightly that Mary's fingers turned purple. Sister Agnes bustled about with towels and hot water, wiping Liza's brow, checking her belly, the size of the dilation. Liza moaned and thrashed. Outside, rain tap-tapped against the windowpanes.

'I can't do it. I can't, I can't,' she wailed between contractions.

'Of course you can. Be brave, Liza,' encouraged Mary.

'Just one more push now. The baby's nearly here – I can see its head begin to crown, to be sure I can,' cried Sister Agnes excitedly. Both women had assisted at many births, but each time it was a wonder, a holy terrifying wonder. The doctor hovered in the background, ready to step in if needed.

Finally, at about seven in the morning, the baby came. Liza lay back in the bed, completely spent. Through a haze of exhaustion and swirling hormones she heard her baby's first cry. It sounded far away, but when they brought her and laid her – wiped clean and wrapped in a white towel – in Liza's arms, that cry was the most pressing, the most engaging sound she had ever heard. It opened her heart and a flood of emotions poured out. Liza cried for joy, out of relief, in love for her little baby daughter.

'Oh, she's so beautiful! Look, Sister Mary, look at her little fingers, how they curl round mine. Isn't she perfect ? – my sweet little girl.' Liza gazed into her baby's eyes and those deep and soulful eyes gazed back, as if searching. And when they had found what they were seeking, they closed contentedly. Liza continued to gaze at her baby, stroking her velvet soft skin as she wriggled and snuffled and made little sucking noises.

'You can feed her if she's ready.' Mary spoke softly, not wanting to intrude on this special moment. She knew that a mother and baby need time to get to know each other, to fall in love with each other. Though she would never have children of her own, she gave generously of herself to those who did.

Liza took the baby to her breast – awkwardly at first, but they soon found the way to connect. Their eyes locked, each finding herself in the steady gaze of the other. She felt a wave of feeling that swept from her baby's eyes, through her heart and down deep inside her belly, like a figure-of-eight of energy swooping down and curving back up again. It reminded her of the first time Arthur had looked into her eyes. It was like the feeling she had when they made love. Arthur was here with them too – his love, his warm brown eyes, reflected in his baby daughter's gaze.

'I'm going to call her Eleanor,' she whispered to Mary after a while, as the baby drifted into sleep.

'Eleanor. That's a beautiful name. Look, she's sleeping now. Shall I put her in the crib while you get some rest yourself?'

'Yes, thank you. Please will you lie her on this cushion.' Liza pointed to the blue cushion that lay beside the bed. 'I embroidered it myself, especially for her. I want her to always have something of me near her when she sleeps. I hope it will be a comfort to her.'

'That's lovely, Liza. I'll do that.' She took Eleanor from Liza's arms and settled her in the crib, on the soft blue cushion that had been embroidered by her mother. Soon both were sleeping soundly. Sister Mary tiptoed out of the room.

When Liza woke, she still felt dazed from exhaustion and the rush of emotions that had been flooding through her since the contractions began. She lay for a moment, enjoying the soft and tender feeling in her heart, aware of the shadow of pain that still scarred below her belly. Her whole being had been prized open and love had flowed in. She had been told not to move too much.

Liza turned to look at Eleanor in her crib. It was like a primitive magnetism, the pull to orient towards her baby. But Eleanor wasn't there.

She hauled herself up in the bed and peered over the edge of the crib. No baby lay tucked up into its corners. The blue embroidered cushion had gone too. Where was she? A wave of fear ran through Liza's body. Her heart began to pound in her chest and press up against her throat.

'Sister Mary!' she called, but she hadn't the strength to make herself heard. She began to panic as a feeling of dread swept through her.

Liza pulled herself out of the bed and walked shakily towards the door, a hand trailing along the wall for support. She had to find her baby. Nothing else in the world mattered in this moment. Every sinew of her being strained towards Eleanor, wherever she might be.

From the doorway she looked down the long corridor. Sunlight filtered through the high windows that ran along one side, casting a pattern of gold and shadows across the polished floor. There was nobody in sight. She tried calling again for Sister Mary. This time she heard a bustling down at the other end of the hallway and two nuns appeared. One was Mary. Liza didn't recognise the Mother Superior until she was close.

'Elizabeth, my dear, you shouldn't be getting out of bed yet. You need to rest. Come on now, let us help you back,' said Mother Teresa, not without kindness.

'Where's my baby? Is she alright?' asked Liza, as the Mother ushered her back into the medical room.

'Your baby is fine,' declared Mother Teresa. Mary looked pale and said nothing. They helped Liza back into the bed.

'Then where is she? I want to see her. She'll need feeding by now. She needs to be with me.' The panic was rising in Liza's chest so that her breath came sharp and quick.

'Your baby is in safe hands.' Mother Teresa cleared her throat, wondering where to begin. 'Your parents, your father that is, thought it best that your baby be given to a married couple who can look after her well and give her a good life. There is an acquaintance of his whose wife was unable to have a baby of her own. They longed for a child, and your father thought this arrangement would suit everyone well. It was his wish that the baby be handed over to them without fuss, as soon after the birth as possible. This was his decision. I'm sorry, Elizabeth, but we had to follow his wishes.'

'No, No! He can't! He can't do this. The baby is mine, not his. Bring her back. She's mine,' cried Liza. Sister Mary's eyes brimmed over with tears.

'Elizabeth, there's nothing we can do now. Your father made his decision and Mr Rushton has taken the baby away. I'm sorry,' said Mother Teresa, wringing her hands.

Liza felt the air tighten around her like a web of fine metal thread. She wanted to scream, to unleash the cry of pain that leapt up from her belly – the animal cry that had come so readily during the long hours of labour – but the sound caught in her throat. A wave of nausea washed over her. Reaching out, she grasped hold of Mary's hand.

'Help me, please help me,' she whispered.

Sister Mary knelt down beside Liza, her cheek damp with tears. 'Holy Mary, please help us,' she whispered back.

★

When Liza woke from the sleeping potion she had been given, she felt drowsy and confused. It took some moments to remember what had happened, where she was. She had given birth to a baby girl, then they had taken her away. It seemed like a dream. She doubted if it had happened at all, then the terrible truth began to cascade, fully and incontrovertibly, into consciousness. It came thundering down like a storm over the hills.

'Oh God. My baby girl,' she gasped, as the truth landed, flat and heavy as lead, in the garden of her heart. She clutched her face in her hands and began rocking, forwards and back, forwards and back. Salty water seeped between her fingers and over the backs of her hands.

Her face hurt where her fingers clutched and pinched, but she felt only the searing pain that had ripped her heart in two. With Eleanor gone, she would never feel whole again.

'I'm sorry, there was nothing I could do. We would have had it different if we could,' said Mary, as she sat by Liza's bed the next morning.

Early light rippled through the frosted glass of the small window. The room was white and clean, and smelt of disinfectant. There was a table with a white cloth covering it, and a locked cupboard containing medicines, towels and other necessities. The shelves by the small window were empty but for a blue and gold-painted statue of the Virgin Mary, here to watch over the sick and the fallen. Liza stared vacantly at the statue.

'Mother Teresa didn't want it this way either. Usually they give the babies to the orphanage, so the mothers can still see them if they wish to. But your father was adamant.'

'Did he come here, my pa? Did my mam come?' asked Liza.

'No. He sent Mr Rushton instead. He arrived soon after

Eleanor was born.' Mary seemed ashamed to speak these words, but she continued nevertheless. 'He brought a letter written by your father, with his instructions for Mother Teresa. She told me they are wealthy and they live in England. He comes here on business from time to time. That's how your father knows him.'

'My God! England! We've got to get Eleanor back. I'll never find her if he takes her to England.' It was worse than she had even imagined. The wave of nausea rose up again. Liza had been unable to eat since discovering Eleanor was missing, and was still weak and exhausted, but she struggled to get out of bed. 'Sister Mary, you've got to help me get her back before they leave.' She began tugging at Mary's arm in desperation.

'I don't know how we can do that. He left no address, nothing. Mother Teresa says your father wants nobody to know about this. He made up a story about you going to work at a house in another county, so no-one at home will know about your baby. That's how he wants it to be. I'm so sorry, Liza,' said Mary, her eyes full with the sorrow of it all.

'Is he really that ashamed of me?' Liza was aghast.

'He wrote in his letter that it would be in the baby's interest to have a good home with good Catholic parents who would look after her properly, give her good chances in life,' said Mary, knowing very well that Liza would be the best parent of all for Eleanor, but feeling that she deserved to know the truth.

'But how can it be good to take a baby away from her mother? He doesn't trust me to look after her, but I could. He thinks I'm bad and he wants to punish me.' Liza paused for a moment. 'He doesn't want to see me again, does he?'

'He said nothing about seeing you again, Liza.'

'And my mam?'

'There was no word from your mother.'

'She won't come for me, I know she won't − not if my pa doesn't allow it.' The stark truth of her situation was becoming clear. As far as her father was concerned, she didn't exist anymore. And her baby had never existed at all. She was nothing. He had cut her loose, without an anchor or a sail, a small boat tossing helplessly on a black sea.

Her heart sank more deeply than it had ever sunk before. Not even on the night that he had beaten her till she bled had she felt this wretched. All that was precious to her had been torn away, and those who had once given her security had abandoned her to whatever bleak fate lay ahead. She lay back down on the bed.

'I am nothing, then. I have no mother, no father, and no child. My sweet Arthur has been sent away. What will become of me, Mary?' Sister Mary had no answers. Her heart was full of tears.

Liza closed her eyes. For the moment she had no strength left to fight her fate. She was sinking into a hell so deep she feared she might never return. She could do nothing but submit to its ruthless pull.

For nearly two weeks Liza's spirit hovered between the worlds, as fever deranged her mind and ravaged her body. Sister Mary sat by her bedside, day after day, wiping the sweat from her face and dabbing cool water on her lips. When Liza settled, Mary prayed. When she fretted and tossed, Mary was there, holding her hand and talking to her, pleading with her to hold on, to return to life.

Liza travelled through strange worlds, dark worlds. As the dreams took hold of her, she called out – a frightened cry, a jumbled message, words that made no sense to Mary. Liza had gone far away and Mary feared greatly for her.

On the twelfth day, Liza finally opened her eyes and saw Sister Mary sitting in a chair by the white wall, praying. Her eyes were closed and she whispered Hail Marys as she passed the beads of her rosary between her fingers. She had long and slender fingers – graceful, thought Liza. She might have been a painter, or a musician, had she not chosen the religious life. Maybe she was an angel.

Liza watched Mary, absorbed in her prayers, allowing time for the fragments of her mind to coalesce again. She was still here in the room where she had given birth to a beautiful baby girl, then lost her. Liza closed her eyes and fell into a fitful sleep.

When she woke again Mary was there, looking into her eyes. Liza saw the concern on her face, and reached out a hand to touch her friend's graceful fingers.

'Thank you for staying with me,' she whispered. 'I saw an angel in my dreams – I think it must have been you.'

'Oh Liza, I was so worried about you. You've been very ill.' She lightly dropped a kiss onto Liza's forehead. 'Don't try to talk. You must rest and get well now. I'll get you a warm drink and something to eat.' She slipped out and returned a short while later with a bowl of soup and some warm milk with honey.

Mary had made it her mission to help Liza. In the days and weeks to come she would assist her recovery in every way she could.

2

As Liza's strength returned, a fury began to grow in her. It filled her with a bold courage. As soon as she was well enough to leave her sick bed, she went down to Mother Teresa's room, usually out of bounds to the girls unless they were summoned. But this was a special matter.

She knocked loudly on the big wooden door. The sound echoed down the empty corridor.

'Come in,' came the Mother Superior's voice from inside the room. She looked surprised as Liza appeared in the doorway, the ragged spirals of her long red hair framing a face that was thin and pale. Liza's blue eyes, like two big pools of dark water, stared at her from across the room.

'Elizabeth, how are you now?' she enquired, not happy with

the unsolicited visit but, aware of Liza's fragile state of mind, she didn't turn her away. 'Come in and take a seat.'

'No thank you.' Liza entered the room but stayed standing. She was determined not to be manipulated by a pretence of kindness.

'Then what is it you want, dear? I do hope you are fully recovered from your illness.' Mother Teresa was silently praying that a scene was not about to erupt. She prayed in vain.

'I want my baby Eleanor back,' declared Liza, feeling strong, recklessly strong in the face of the one who now held the power over her fate. Liza had not yet realised this fact. She thought she still had her freedom, at least. 'It's not right to give her away. I'm her mother and I want to look after her myself.'

'I'm very sorry, Elizabeth, but you're just a child yourself, just seventeen years old if I'm not mistaken, and you have no means of looking after a baby. Your father and mother decided it was for the best that your baby be adopted. I can assure you she will be very well taken care of by her new family.' Mother Teresa's voice was firm and steady. She instinctively stood up behind her desk to meet Liza eye to eye.

'Her new family! I'm her only family. These people are strangers – they don't know her as I do. You can't do this to us!' cried Liza, rapidly losing control of herself in the face of the Mother's remote and expressionless gaze.

'Elizabeth, it is your father's will, and I do believe it is also God's will that your child has the best possible chance of a good Christian life. You have sinned in a way that is unacceptable in the eyes of both God and your father, and you must accept the consequences. You cannot be given the divine responsibility of raising a child in this world with such a burden of sin on your soul. We are going to take care of you here. We will help you to atone for your sin and become a good Catholic again. I don't mean to be harsh, Elizabeth, but in the end you will see that it's for the best,' she said, calmly, persuasively, and with a smile that aspired to benevolence. Inside, her heart was in turmoil, but she would not let Liza see this.

'No, no, NO! I want my baby back. I will not let you do this to us. Just tell me where these people are. My father need never know that you told me. Please, just tell me where they have taken her.' Liza could not contain her tears any longer. She broke down sobbing, clenching her hands and stamping a small foot on the bare floorboards. The hollow wood of the floor was unyielding – it seemed to mock her futile attempt at assertion.

The more Mother Teresa spoke in her calm and sanctimonious voice, the more Liza spiralled into the heart of her rage and despair. Mother Teresa, feeling she had the upper hand for a moment, decided she had heard enough. She needed to take control of the situation.

'Elizabeth, that is enough. You do not address the Mother Superior in this way. Please go back to the dormitory immediately,' she commanded, not exactly stamping her own foot, but stamping her authority into Liza's wayward consciousness nevertheless. 'We can speak later, discuss your future plans if you like.' She rang a bell that sat on her desk, then turned away from Liza to study the contents of a bookshelf on the far wall. Her heart still raced, but she held herself motionless, giving nothing of her heart away to Liza.

After a moment Sister Agnes appeared at the door.

'Sister Agnes, please take Elizabeth back to her room,' she said, without turning to face either of them. 'Make sure that she resumes work and normal routines as soon as she is able to. Thank you.'

'Yes, Mother Teresa.' Sister Agnes ushered Liza quickly out of the room and back up the narrow winding stairs that led to the girls' attic dormitory, cramped and stuffy, dark beneath oak beams and the sparse row of tiny latched windows that were grained over with years of soot-drenched rain.

There was kindness that was sweet and gentle, like Sister Mary's, thought Liza. It invited life to unfold, like the spring sunlight inviting all the buds to open, each in their own unique way.

Then there was kindness like Mother Teresa's, which seemed devoid of heart but full of sense. It stemmed from reason alone, claiming to be for the ultimate good but having no eye or ear for the ordinary truth of a situation.

Or maybe such kindness sprang from opportunity. Liza had learnt from Mary that her father and Mr Rushton had paid the convent handsomely for their 'arrangement'.

And then there was something else. It made no pretence at kindness. It was dishonest but pretended to be virtuous. It was cruel but paraded as divine righteousness. Liza's father was only concerned with the appearance of things. Her belly, round and fertile, had been nothing more than sinfulness and shame to him. He couldn't see the life that was growing in there. How things appeared to others seemed of more importance than the life-blood of his own family. He had sacrificed his daughter and granddaughter out of a fear of how others would judge him – in particular, how Uncle Brendan Padre might judge him. He seemed to fear his older brother as if God Himself did, indeed, reside within him – Uncle Padre, God the Father, all the same. Liza saw her father clearly for the first time in her life – a weak and frightened, and very confused man. But it was too late.

She sat cross-legged on her bed and scratched at the skin on her arm. She was at fault. She had not seen this coming, not protected Eleanor, not been strong enough to keep her or to get her back. The self-criticisms came like knives at first, then like a swamp that began to suck her down. She was guilty, she had failed, she was useless and had no future ahead of her. If he knew what had happened, even Arthur would hate her for losing their precious baby. She scratched and picked at her arm until it bled. This, at least, was a pain she could bear to feel.

★

When Liza was well enough, she returned to work in the laundry. All of the girls had to earn their keep whilst their souls were being cleansed of sin.

It was two in the afternoon and she had hidden herself in the drying room, behind the clean white sheets and the tablecloths from the hotels that employed their services. She crouched in a corner on the bare stone floor, hugging her knees to her chest. In here at least it was warm and she could rest. She felt so tired and weary. Even breathing required great effort. Her chest collapsed with each exhalation and she barely had the energy to take in the next lungful of air. She was drowning in this lifeless place. The endless drudgery of the work, the thick stone walls of the convent, the placid smiles of the sisters all around her – it was stifling her, squeezing every last ounce of spirit from her bones. She felt sure she would die if she could not escape from this place, but she had nowhere else to go.

Without Eleanor and Arthur, life had lost all meaning. She had lost a piece of her own soul and she had no idea how to find it again. Liza huddled in the darkness behind the rows of white sheets and silently wept.

Only at suppertime, when each girl was seated in her allotted place at the long table in the dining hall, was Liza's absence noticed. Mother Teresa ordered a search of the building. Naturally it was Mary who found her. She knew where Liza went when she needed to be alone. But there was no avoiding the consequence of a transgression of the rules – even Mary could not protect her from this. She was taken by two of the older nuns to Mother Teresa's room once supper was over.

'Elizabeth, I know you have been through a difficult time, but you have to put all of this behind you and move on now. You have been caught disobeying rules too many times of late, and you will be severely punished if you don't do better. I cannot be making excuses for you any longer. My patience with your misdemeanours is running short.' The Mother

Superior was determined to assert her authority from the beginning this time.

Liza was silent. She looked down at the floor, picking a scab on her left arm and pushing the toes of one foot along a crack in the floorboards. The room smelt of old books. A clock on the desk ticked loudly. The warm glow of the table lamp cast shadows along the folds of the oxblood red curtains that hung over the windows. The windows were tall and leaded. The curtains came right down to the floor, Liza noted.

'What do you have to say for yourself, Elizabeth?' snapped Mother Teresa, impatient with the girl's silence.

Liza glowered at her through tightened eyelids. 'Give me back my baby,' she demanded, only just holding back the anger that was always close to the surface these days. She looked like a wild animal, a mother lion with her long red tresses, ready to pounce.

'You know that there is nothing at all I can do. The matter is closed. You must try to accept it and move on, Elizabeth. It's time to be thinking of your future, unless you want to stay here forever.' Mother Teresa was barely containing her own irritation. After all, none of this had been of her making. She was only the executioner of the father's wishes, and she had begun to find the whole situation extremely tiresome.

'I can't move on without Eleanor. She's a part of me. There's nowhere for me to move on to without her. Bring her back!' Liza's voice began to rise and tremble. Her hands were shaking. Suddenly she sprang towards the neatly arranged, large mahogany desk in front of her and swept a pile of papers onto the floor, then grabbed hold of a book and was about to hurl it across the room. Mother Teresa grasped her arm and quickly snatched the book from her hand.

Liza pulled her arm free and stepped back. Her right hand returned to picking the scab on her left arm. A drop of bright red blood sprang out and trickled down her forearm.

'Elizabeth! Stop doing that. You're hurting yourself, you foolish girl.'

Liza dropped down to the floor, with her elbows pressed hard against her knees and a handful of unkempt hair clutched tightly in each fist. She started to rock, backwards and forwards, singing in a high, shrill voice, 'My baby lies over the ocean, my baby lies over the sea.' She kept singing the words, like a chant, like the prayer of the hopeless, the song of a soul deranged, until Mother Teresa couldn't bear the piercing sound a moment longer. She stepped over, grabbed Liza's forearms, pulled her onto her feet and slapped her face.

'Stop that, Elizabeth!' she commanded, struggling to keep her own anger at bay now. She took the bell from her desk and rang it loudly. Within moments the two sisters were at the door again.

'Take her down to the Penance Room, and make sure she isn't let out until I say so.'

The sisters led Liza away, still chanting her song – 'Bring back, oh bring back, oh bring back my baby to me, to me,' she wailed, as they dragged her down the long corridor and out of Mother Teresa's hearing.

The Mother Superior sat down wearily behind her desk. The girl was feeble-minded, quite deficient, clearly. Something would have to be done about her.

Liza found herself alone in a small cell with walls that were completely bare, but for a crucifix hanging above a hard and narrow bed. On the bed were two grey blankets and a thin pillow. There was a small wooden table and chair, a washstand with a white metal bowl and matching water jug and, high up in the wall, a tiny window that looked out onto a small patch of sky. The stone floor was grey. Apart from this the room was white and empty.

She stood in the centre of her cell, looking up at the blue square of sky, as one of the sisters turned a key in the lock. She was a prisoner.

Liza felt confused. She couldn't remember exactly what had happened in Mother Teresa's room. She had felt angry, that was for sure. And she had felt the trickle of blood running down her arm. Words had been spoken but she couldn't recall them clearly. She turned slowly around, making a complete circle until she came to face the window again. High up in the sky a bird flew by just at that moment. Free. But she was down here, lost and bound.

Moving stiffly, as if her whole body were in pain, Liza laid herself down on the punishing bed. She lay there and stared up at the ceiling. A brave spider had found its way into the cell and was creeping hesitantly across the whitewashed expanse. It would find no life to feed on here.

Liza lay as still as stone, until they came to fetch her.

It happened in the early morning when the girls were working in the laundry and the sisters were at prayers in the chapel. Mother Teresa wanted it done when no-one was there to witness. She would simply tell the other girls that Elizabeth had moved on.

A small black motor vehicle turned up at the side entrance, far away from the door to the laundry rooms at the other end of the building. Four men dressed in white coats climbed out and were directed to the Penance Room. It took only two of them to strap Liza into a white coat with long cords, which they tied about her in a way that wrapped her arms around her chest. She had not slept all night, and was too weak and confused to fight. It felt almost comforting to have her arms wrapped tightly around her body like this – almost safe.

They led her away.

Twenty-seven

Belfast – 1981

I need fresh air. My anger is rising as I read Liza's story. Her pain has lodged deeply into my veins like shrapnel. Adrenalin pricks my muscles. I must get out. I need to move, walk somewhere, anywhere, or I might go quite mad too.

I lock the diary and place it under my pillow, put the key back into the silk purse and into my pocket, then take my jacket and head down the stairs to the street. It all feels so present, as if it were still happening now. I wish I could have been there to protect young Liza.

I'm remembering my own time of terrible loss, when my world collapsed, without warning, and I was left adrift – Richard, then my father, and my mother long before that. But I've not suffered such cruelty as Liza had to endure. Fate was cruel, but there was support and love around me. Liza had no-one to turn to – even Mary, her one true friend, had no real power to help her.

I walk briskly in the direction of the city centre, hardly noticing the streets I had been so curious to explore just a few days ago, oblivious to the people passing by.

An odd thought springs into my mind: 'Did you know that the eggs in a woman's ovaries are already formed when she's in her own mother's womb?' Emms had asked me once. She loved to read about all kinds of strange and fascinating things. 'That means we were there already, in our grandmother's body, before our mother was even born. Isn't that amazing!'

So I was there, the very beginnings of me, when Liza was going through all of this. This story was truly the beginning of my life too. I carry all of this history in me. A lineage of loss and exile, of lies and betrayal, guilt and shame, a curse passed down through the generations. I wonder how far back it reaches, how far into the distant past. The grandmothers of my dream seem to hover around me, gathering, crowding in on me, clamouring to be set free. I walk faster to escape the suffocating feeling.

I find myself in Donegall Square and jump onto a bus that is pulled up outside City Hall, without thought for where it might be going. I need to get out of this troubled city, to breathe clean air again. The small lives of those caught up in the Troubles are big with pain and the very air feels polluted by it all. The war between Protestants and Catholics is not only out there on the streets – it was waged in the heart of Liza's father, and so many people just like him. I feel fury at what he did to Liza, and to my mother. Now it has come to me to seek redemption for their broken lives – our broken lives, for this is my inheritance.

The bus crawls out through the suburbs, north towards Whitehead. Once the rows of fishermen's cottages end and there is open road ahead, I get off the bus and begin to walk. Dark clouds are sweeping in over the estuary now, gathering over the water and spilling down onto the city. Already black streaks of rain are falling over the shadowy banks on the far side of the Lough.

I make my way down to the beach. The tide is low, leaving an expanse of grey silt and mudflats below the seawall. My feet slither over broad bands of kelp that form brown heaps along the high-water line, and crunch into mounds of empty mussel shells. I weave between shallow pools left by the tide, and barnacle-encrusted rocks. After a while I give up trying to keep my feet dry and splash through the cold seawater.

A cormorant comes to rest on a stone pillar that juts out of the water – the last remnant of an old jetty. It spreads its wings proudly before hunkering down to face the storm. On the beach, the broken wheel of a child's bicycle lies tangled in a length of old rope. The familiar smells of salt and seaweed fill the brooding air. The cranes of Belfast docks pierce the gloom behind me as I walk. Ahead, the Carrickfergus chimneys belch out dark smoke, to be quickly swallowed up into the rolling clouds.

A wind begins to whip up, scattering the sandpipers to seek cover, and then the rains arrive – a spattering at first, soon growing into a torrent. Within minutes I'm drenched to the skin, my denim jacket giving no protection from the North Atlantic storm that has swept in around the headland. I keep walking into the face of the wind, my shoulders hunched around my ears, hands clenched in my pockets and my head bowed. I see only the wet ground beneath my feet. The silt opens into small pools, sucking each step in for a moment, then releasing my foot with a squelch. The rain drives harder and I walk faster until my breath, too, comes fast and hard.

Then I am running. Leaping over pools. I slip on wet stones, stamp into the muddy ground. A scream is surging into my throat. The scream I held back at Richard's funeral. That I had been so scared of that night on the beach. When I fell asleep on damp rocks. Under the searching beam of light, circling round and round.

Now it comes, forces its way out. A long piercing cry, pulled out of me, my guts spilling up. I open my arms and reach my face up to the descending skies. The cry I have carried inside me all these years now sears through me. Liza's pain comes pouring out with my own grief. Her fury fills mine with a terrifying force. I am howling like a wild beast, raging for both of us.

I squat down in the mud and pull handfuls of wet hair into my hands as I rock, forward and back, forward and back, sobbing and calling out to the tumbling dark skies. I call out my pain and my anguish – until I am emptied out. Cleansed. It is done. My voice has been released, and Liza's too.

As if in response to my cry, there is a distant flash then a roll of thunder from beyond the low horizon. As if we have been heard, Liza's story no longer a secret hidden shamefully from the world. My own pain has finally found its voice. And we have been witnessed by the hollow wind and the darkening rain.

The tide is creeping in. As I stand again, I am ankle deep in water and my clothes are soaked through. The mudflats have disappeared from sight, giving way to the dark motion of a restless sea churning around me. I feel a fire burning up from my belly to my heart and, in this moment, I know I love her – Liza, my Irish grandmother – fiercely.

Twenty-eight

I arrive back from the beach and creep in without being seen. After a long soak in a hot bath, I sleep deeply, waking to the chorus of morning gulls. There's a freshness in the air after yesterday's storm, a hint that autumn will come again – even though it is still early August.

Suspecting that Liza's troubles have barely begun, I pick up the diary with a growing sense of dread. I can hardly bear to read more, but I must. I need to know.

There is a gap of many years between the last entry and the next. Once the diary resumes, she leaves only hints and ragged traces of a story, and I must imagine into the horror of Liza's life during those intervening years.

October 4th, 1938

Last week a miracle happened! Mrs Mallone, the very same one who gave me the diary all those years ago, visited the asylum. She met with some of us women in the day room. She said she had been before but I don't remember. They must think I'm getting better. Only the ones who are well enough are allowed to meet important visitors.

I learnt that Mrs Mallone is one of the patrons of the asylum and visits us from time to time. She brought some books for us to read.

I'm happy that she remembered me. She was very sad to see me locked up in here, and said she would try to help me. When she asked what I needed, I told her I wanted to write again. I left my diary behind when I came here, and could she visit Sister Mary at the convent to see if Mary knew where it was.

The nurse, who was sitting there with us, said this was a good sign, and I should be encouraged to write if it helped me.

Mrs Mallone did just that, and Mary told her it would be in the office. Mrs Mallone gives money to the convent as well as the asylum, so they had to give it to her when she asked.

The thing is, I've had the key with me all this time. I always carried it with me, so nobody could open my diary.

And now I have my book of secrets with me again.

October 17th

It made me so sad to read about the past. I cried a lot. In here they give me drugs and they tried to burn out my memory with electricity. My memories are cloudy. My old life feels so far away, as if it had happened to someone else. I only remember being locked up on the ward, and sometimes in a windowless room on my own. I remember the cries of people at night, and their long grey faces, still and silent in the day — like ghosts, each one sitting for hours on the edge of their bed, motionless. Then one would start screaming and all the others would join in — screaming and banging and making the most awful row you could ever imagine. These were my memories.

But after reading my diary I have begun to remember my old life.

*A window has opened
and I glimpse blue sky again,
after years in the dark.
I feel pain in my heart again,
where I felt only a leaden weight for so long.
And I feel breath in my lungs again
where there was only dust before.
How strange to rejoice in feeling the pain*

Ah – I've just written a poem! Not a very good one, but still, it gives me some comfort to write down my thoughts like this. Like W B Yeats. Maybe I am still romantic, after all.

October 29th

Now I feel mad with anger. There are rats running around in my belly, gnawing away at my insides. And a swarm of bees buzzing in my head. I can't think straight.

As I began to remember my old life, and all that had happened to me, I got more and more angry. I threw a chair against the window in the day room one morning and it broke the glass. So they locked me in the room all on my own again, for three whole days and nights. They call it the isolation room, but I'm never alone in there – there's always the rats and the bees swarming about. There's no peace in there. Peace is in the woods, in the den, in the arms of a handsome young man called Arthur. I can barely remember what he looked like now. He had dark wavy hair and eyebrows that crinkled up into a funny zigzag line when he was concentrating, or feeling something deeply. They crinkled when he kissed me – now I remember that.

I had a baby girl, and they took her away from me. And look at me now. I'm a wretched, ugly woman full of

*angry rats and bees buzzing in my head. I'm not mad –
I'm just very angry.*

*I had a baby girl
So beautiful and sweet
But now I'm full of angry rats
That eat
My heart away*

*This is all making me so tired. They gave me a
strong drug after the chair episode and it made me feel
so wretched and lifeless. Then the buzzing and gnawing
began again. And now I'm just weary. I must sleep.*

December 13th

*They told me that if I'm good, I can walk in the garden.
But if I'm bad, I'll be locked in the room again. If
I'm very bad, I might be sent for more electric-shock
treatment – that's what they call it – electric-shock. But
it's not really a shock. A shock is when you find that one
of the other patients has stolen your slippers, or when one
of them starts shouting in the middle of the night and
wakes you up.*

*This is more like an assault, a violent attack. Your
whole being is under attack, as if they're trying to kill
you but don't get it quite right, so you just hang there
in an agony of pain, thrashing about, all helpless and
out of control. You feel like a fly caught in a spider's web,
your limbs all stuck to the threads that won't let you go,
and the threads pierce right through you and hurt you as
you struggle to get free. It's like being impaled from your
fingers to your toes, and your head to your feet. It should
be called electric-hell treatment. If they want to send
someone to hell, this is how to do it.*

I don't want to walk round the garden like a woman sleep-walking. I want to run across the fields with the young man called Arthur holding my hand, and the wind flying in my face.

Today the rats went away. Instead I feel something like a glowing fire in my belly. This is new. I like it. I feel a bit wild, like a mountain river.

Wild, like a mountain river
Strong as an old oak tree
Hot as the midday sun
Fierce as a raging sea.
Soon, soon I will be free

January 3rd

I feel as if I'm waking up from a long sleep. I won't let them put me to sleep anymore. I'm not mad. It's just that being in here for so long makes me feel mad. Being with the crazy folk, I go crazy like them. I want to get out but the gates are locked and the walls are too high to climb.

I long to be free, I do. All my life I've been longing for freedom. For a brief moment I felt free – when I was with Arthur, in the woods, walking over the fields and moors, throwing stones from the bridge into the river and making wishes. Then, I wished to be with him forever. Now, if I could throw a stone into the river and make a wish, I'd wish to see Arthur and my baby Eleanor again – even just once, to know they are both well.

Eleanor will be growing up though, not a baby anymore. She'll be eleven years old by now I reckon, and she won't know me at all. I think she wouldn't want to know me, if she could see what has become of me, her mother. That makes me sad, but I hope she's happy and being looked after well, wherever she is.

Another miracle has happened! When Mrs Mallone met Sister Mary at the convent and told her that I was here, Sister Mary decided she must visit me too. She asked to be put in service at the asylum, and they have sent her here for six months. She's to help Sister Brigid who tries to turn our wretched minds towards God.

There's not much hope of that happening – except for the fellow they call Saint Patrick who is always preaching to the walls, as if they could hear him at all. He thinks he's Jesus, so he must have a direct line to God anyway. He's really mad. Most of the others are just very unhappy, or angry, or frightened, in my view. There's one old woman who sits on her bed pulling out handfuls of hair, wailing in such a pitiful little voice, like a child. She sounds very sad to me.

And there's Alma who does these crazy dances, jerking her body about and spinning. I think she just feels trapped here, like me. She'd probably be fine if they let her run about in the fields. I told her we could escape together, go and live in the woods and be free. I imagined her spinning and me running in the sunlight. But she got scared when I said that, started snivelling and crying, so I didn't ask her again.

I wonder what they think about me. I wonder if they saw me doing something odd in those times that I don't remember. I don't know – I have scars all the way up my arms, from my wrists right up to my shoulders, so something must have happened.

Anyway, I'm so happy today. Mary has arrived, and this morning we had a chance to walk around the garden together. I don't have much to tell her about my life these last years. They are lost years to me. I've just been existing here, not living at all. But Mary was kind, as she always was to me, and wanted to hear about everything I was thinking and feeling. I told her that I want to escape this place. 'We'll see,' was all she said. I know I have to convince Mary that I'm well enough to live in the world outside – then I believe she'll help me, if she can.

April 23rd

It's good having Sister Mary here. We walk in the garden and talk every day, whether there is sun or wind or rain. I'm becoming more well each day because of this precious time I spend with her. Sometimes we even laugh together. I can't think what there is to laugh about but her bright presence lightens my heart, and we manage to make a joke of the strange life that's going on here at the asylum.

She told them that I am well enough now to work in the laundry and, as I've done laundry work at the convent, I'm qualified well enough for it. Here it's a privilege to get off the wards and into the laundry room, not a chore as it was in the refuge home.

I feel so lucky, so blessed to have two good friends – Sister Mary and Mrs Mallone. Some of the poor wretches here have nobody at all. I see them, day after day, sitting on their beds like grey, empty shells. I think I was like that too for a long time, but I don't remember those times very well. Just the feeling of a heavy mist swirling all around me, and the sense of a thread that I was trying to catch hold of – but the thread kept fraying, unravelling and drifting back into the mist. It was like being lost in a dream that I couldn't find a way out of.

I walk through mist
with a weight in my heart
trying to catch hold

of a thread of meaning
a lifeline, something
that will anchor me to life
but there is only death all around me.
The thread drifts out of reach
and dissolves
back into the mist

May 16th

Spring is blossoming all around and I feel new life
growing inside me too. All of the leaves and flowers have
burst out of their winter buds. I feel just like them. I
need to burst out of this stifling world. Outside it might
be hard and frightening, but in here it's a living death.
I'd rather be free and face the dangers than slowly waste
away, year after year, in this prison. But the doctors say I
can't leave, I'm not well enough.

Sister Mary said she'd help me to escape though! She
knows I'll be alright outside in the world. She says my
spirit is as strong as ever. It's just been clouded over for a
long while, but she sees it begin to shine again.

Now I remember the time when I was ill and I saw
her praying for me. I thought she was an angel. That's
what I call her now – my Angel Mary.
I feel so lucky.

August 4th

I am so excited and nervous and afraid all at once.
Tonight I am to flee this prison, for good. Mary and I
have planned it all. If I'm caught, I will be in terrible
trouble, and so will she. They'll probably lock me
up again in the room, and give me a big electric-hell
treatment. Then I'd be lost forever, I know – I saw it

happen to a young man who tried to escape once, and now he's like a ghost, all collapsed into himself and barely able to move at all. Just slumped in a chair all day long, doing nothing, saying nothing. Not even crying or shouting, like the rest of us. So it's very important that I don't get caught.

The plan is that I'll pretend to be ill. I'll eat some rowanberries from a tree in the garden that will make me a little sick — but not too ill, of course. Mary is on sick room duty tonight. Hopefully I'll be the only one there.

When everyone is asleep, at two o'clock in the morning, she will take me down to the back door of the house, out through the big kitchen. She'll unlock the iron gate at the bottom of the garden before she goes to bed. No-one will know. Then she'll let me out by the kitchen door and I'll be free — once I have got through the gate, I'll be free.

It's a simple plan. I'm going to pick the berries now, and prepare the things I will take with me. Then all I can do is pray that we don't get caught.

Twenty-nine

Belfast – 1939 and 1981

The iron gate closed behind her with a hollow thud. She held her breath, listening – for a door opening, a shout, an alarm being raised. There was no sound but the wind whipping through the tall spruce trees that lined the wall. She was safe, for now at least.

Liza stood outside the gate and looked out over the hills, breathing in the crisp, clear air. She was free. After twelve interminable, empty years, she now stood at the edge of the world with a whole new life before her. She hardly dared believe it. She wanted to clutch tight to the moment for fear it would slip back into the misty world of dreams. But it didn't. Her feet were standing firmly on the green grass and the cold night air filled her lungs.

A full moon cast its silvery light over the field that stretched down to the bank of the stream. So many times she had looked out on this field, through the misted windows, between the iron bars, longing to run across it. Right down to the stream and up over the wide hills beyond, lying in silent folds all along the ancient skyline. But tonight it would not be safe to run in the moonlight. If someone saw her, she would surely be caught and taken back to the old prison world.

Turning to her right, she headed down towards the edge

of the wood. The shadow of the trees would hide her well enough. She clutched her small bundle of possessions – tied up in a thin grey blanket – to her chest as she ran. The thick woollen coat she had picked up by the back door was much too big and flapped about her ankles.

Along the path that ran by the wood, across the stream, down a farm track, then – finally sure that she was out of sight of the old manor house that was the asylum – she struck out over the open moor – running, running, clutching her bundle of possessions. The moon shone, the clean wind blew, her red hair streamed out behind her like a flame. She ran until the clouds covered the moon and the faintest hint of dawn began to show.

By the time the morning bell rang and they realised she had gone, she would be far away.

The sun had risen high above the horizon by the time she stopped. Light flooded the hills and the clouds, which had threatened rain during the night, were now dispersing, leaving the sky swept clean and fresh. In the distance Liza could see the outskirts of the city – the buildings all crowded together, chimneys already billowing out their morning load of sooty smoke. But first she must eat and rest.

She found a ruined sheep-pen tucked into a sheltered spot on the hillside. The walls of the pen were covered with lichen, the stones crumbling and tumbling in, but it gave her some shelter. She could hide here for a while.

Sitting on a large slab of stone, she laid down her bundle, untying the corners of the thin grey blanket and spreading it out on the rough grass before her. Proudly she placed her possessions in a row, feeling like a worldly woman with all these things that were her own – a hairbrush with a plain wooden handle, a small cake of soap, a book, a green ribbon for her hair, a pair of socks, a blue woollen cardigan, a spare set of undergarments, and the wedge of bread and cheese that Sister Mary had given her.

They both knew the danger Mary had put herself in by helping Liza escape, but she was a kind soul, a good friend for whom nothing was more important than helping someone in need.

Liza ate half the bread and cheese, wrapped up the rest for later, then curled up inside the stone pen and slept. She slept until the sun came around to the other side of the hill. Unfolding her aching body from its tight resting place, she stretched and brushed the tangles from her hair. Today there was a new feeling of strength in her limbs. Her body was remembering how it used to feel, in her old life, when she ran over the fields and the moors. As if gathering her old self up after years of neglect, she stood tall and looked out over the land.

Ahead lay her future – she would follow the sheep trails that criss-crossed the hill, then walk along the riverbank until she came to the road. And on, down into the city. Today, finally, her life could begin.

By the time she reached the city, evening was creeping in, stealthily, though there was yet light enough to see her way. The streets were still bustling with life – people hurrying to and fro, finishing their business for the day.

Everything looked different from the way she remembered it, from the way it had been on those rare visits with her father when she was no more than ten years old. Now, the wide streets were clean, the shops full of glittering lights and shiny new things to buy. A few people still wore the long woollen skirts and headscarves, the baggy trousers and flat caps that she was accustomed to from village life, but others were smart, clean, proud-looking. Women with swishing skirts up nearly to their knees, and tiny hats perched upon sleek hair-dos, strutted on heels as high as could be. Men with tailored suits and slick brimmed hats strode along the pavements as if they owned them.

Horses pulling carts and fancy carriages had been pushed aside by the new-fangled cars with engines, chugging and honking their way along the street. Belching out smoke and fumes as they rolled by, they created an uproar that assaulted Liza's senses. Dogs barked and chased these new masters of the road, like messengers of a passing age whose job it was to berate the upstarts for their hubris.

In the wide streets of the city centre, the tramcars that she remembered from her childhood had been replaced by the strangest of vehicles. Metal rods poked from their roofs and hooked them up to wires that ran above the roads. The windows were covered over with glass and the weary passengers stared out vacantly.

Life swept about her, rushing in all directions. People shouted and argued, cars and trolley buses clattered by, children ran, calling out to each other and laughing.

Liza had become accustomed to the stillness and the drugged silence of a world with few words. She stood in the middle of a cobbled street, like a weather vein spun this way and that by the clamour and motion around her, not knowing which way to go.

No-one seemed to notice the woman in the long grey coat and old, mud-soaked shoes, her bedraggled red curls streaming down her back and a small, ragged bundle of possessions clasped to her chest. As if she were invisible – as if she had been gone so long that she could no longer be seen – life passed her by. Even though she stood in their midst, seeking with her eyes for contact, not a soul acknowledged her presence.

Liza felt utterly alone. More alone than she had ever felt before, here on this crowded street. A small boy ran into her from behind. He ran on without saying sorry, as she stumbled and almost dropped her precious bundle.

The slow pace of the big house and its tranquil garden had offered a backdrop of timelessness to her days and nights. The old mansion that had been her home for so many years seemed to exist in eternity. Now, the light was beginning to fade. She was thrust into time, and time would soon run out. She must find a place to sleep before the city nightlife awoke. She had heard about the fate of women who walked the streets after dark, and this fear drove her on.

With no one direction presenting itself as more promising than another, she turned left at a crossroad and began to search for a room for the night.

The street lamps were being lit now, one by one. Ahead was an inn, lights glowing from narrow windows and a crowd of men outside talking, laughing in loud gruff voices. There would be rooms here but she feared to walk past the men and into the inn. She walked on.

Meandering lanes eventually led to a building with a sign that advertised rooms for rent. It was a seedy alley that she found herself down, but she was tired and wanted to hide away from this strange and threatening world. She longed to lose herself in sleep.

Liza knocked timidly on the door. It was opened by a matronly woman with big hips and round rosy cheeks. A button of a chin protruded beneath a small rose-bud mouth – both looked oddly out of place in the otherwise largeness of the woman. Damp trails of greying hair straggled across her brow from beneath a green and blue headscarf. An apron, stained with food and coal-dust, covered a long black dress that suggested she might be a widow.

'Yes?' Her voice bellowed above the rumble of the street.

'Do you have a room please?'

'How many nights?' asked the woman, eyeing her warily.

'I'm not sure. A few nights, two weeks, until I find a permanent place to stay.'

'Show me your money. Two nights up-front, then payment weekly, in advance, if you want to stay longer.'

Liza laid down her bundle on the doorstep, untied it and took out her purse. Sister Mary had given her just enough money to pay for a room and one good meal a day for the first two weeks. By then, she must have found work to pay her own way. Mary had given her every penny she could scrape together. Liza prayed that Mary was not in trouble for helping her escape.

She offered the woman a few coins.

'Alright then, that will do for two nights. Then we'll see.' She picked out two large coins. 'No men in the rooms, mind, and no funny business. Or you're out right away, now. Understood?'

'Yes, ma'am. Thank you. You don't have to worry about me.' Liza had never had anyone to worry about her before and she was not about to be starting with it now. She gathered up her belongings and followed the woman along a dingy hallway, up a creaking staircase, and into her room. Her room. For the first time in her whole life she had a room that was all her own.

2

August 15th, 1939

I've decided to stay here for a while. I feel safe enough and it's quiet most of the time. In the morning and evening, when people are going to work or coming back home, the motor cars rattle past, hooting their horns at each other. But then it all settles down and I can hear the gulls flying in from the sea again. This area is called The Markets and many Catholic people live here.

My room is simple, but it's clean. There's a very narrow bed along one wall. Mrs MacGuire, the landlady, is just making sure — she is very strict about there being no men in the women's rooms. 'It's not that sort of house,' she told me on my first morning here. Along the opposite wall is a cupboard with drawers for me to put my belongings in. They don't even fill one drawer, but maybe in time I'll get more things to fill them with. I feel excited when I think of that – of the things I might buy in the city when I am earning my own money. There's a lamp on top of the cupboard and I'm sitting on a rickety wooden chair in the corner, between the cupboard and the window, with a wooden table to write on.

On the other side of the window there's another small table with a bowl and jug of water for washing myself. And under the bed is a tin pot. The lavatory is down two floors, in the back yard, so I can use this if I want to go in the middle of the night. I've never had such a thing before. It's painted white, with pink roses on one side.

From the window I can see down to the street below and out across the rooftops to the hills beyond the city. It's nice to be up here in the attic, to have a view of everything.

August 22nd

Mrs MacGuire seemed very unfriendly at first but she's not so bad really. Her husband was killed a few years ago. He was in the IRA she told me, and it was the English who got him. Since I told her I come from a Catholic family she has been much nicer to me. I don't feel like a Catholic anymore – after all I've been through it's hard to believe that there is a God in Heaven, but I don't tell Mrs MacGuire that. I will go with her to church on Sunday, since she asked me.

I have to find work here in Belfast, so all these last days I've been walking the streets of the city till my feet are sore, knocking on the doors of all the big houses. Most of them are quite unkind and turn me away but one

house has given me some mending to do – to try me out,
the lady said. Another asked me to come on Mondays to
help with the laundry, as their usual woman is sick at the
moment.

I hope there will be more work soon. I don't ever want
to end up in the workhouse – that would be just as bad
as where I've come from. And I can't go to another refuge
home in case they tell the convent or the asylum, and
send me back there. I have nowhere else to go, so I must
work to keep myself now.

I am sure I can pay my own way. I have to.

Now, as it's Saturday, I will go for a walk down to the
docks and sit by the water to watch the boats coming in
and out. I wonder if this is where they sent Arthur away
to Australia. I wonder if I will ever see him again.

September 3rd

A terrible thing happened today. Mrs MacGuire told me
she heard about it on the wireless. It seems we are now
at war with Germany. That's another country in Europe,
quite far away from here, but we are all in the war
together, she said.

It's not our bloody war, she said. It's the English
people's war. But they'll drag us all into it, like before.
All the young men and the lads, hardly out of school,
they'll all have to go and fight abroad somewhere.
Terrible it is. There'll be more trouble here in these parts
because of this. More fighting, more bloodshed, to be sure,
if they expect the Catholic lads to fight in their bloody
war. That's what she said.

I didn't know what to say. Mrs MacGuire's sons
might have to go and fight, and she didn't want to lose
them as well as her husband, bless his Catholic soul.

Then she told me there would be jobs in the mills and

factories for the women, what with all the men away at war. I could get work there if I wanted.

They call it helping the war effort, she told me, but for the women it's really about escaping the drudgery of housework all day long. It happened in the last great war and it will happen in this one too.

Once again, I didn't know what to say, so I just said, Thank you for telling me, Mrs MacGuire. I hope your sons will be safe.

I feel afraid. I had enough of fighting all around me when I lived at home with my mam and pa. Now I just want to live in peace and earn an honest living, but I can't change the things that other people do so I will have to do my best with the situation.

October 15th

Mrs MacGuire was right. The war has started and all the young men are leaving the factories and mills to go and fight in the army. When they asked the women to come and apply for their jobs, I went right down there and took my place in the queue.

When it came to my turn and they asked my name, I didn't know what to say. I don't want them knowing who I am in case they send me back to the asylum. I said I was Tara – it was the first name that came into my head – and I made up a family name. I don't want ever to use my father's name again so I said I was Tara McCormac.

They didn't ask any questions – just wrote it down and signed me up for a job in the linen mill. So at work I'm Tara McCormac and at home I'm Liza. Now I have to remember which name to use when.

Some of the women were sent to the munitions factory to make weapons. We make cloth that will be made into uniforms for the soldiers, and another special *material made out of the flax. They will make this into parachutes. Who would have thought that? Anyway, I'm glad I'm in the mill and not munitions. I don't want to be responsible for people getting killed.*

We work ten hours a day at the mill, and Saturday mornings too. And I still do sewing in the evenings, when I can get it. On Sunday I go to church with Mrs MacGuire, to pray for our boys in the army, which all leaves me very little time to myself. But that's alright. I am earning enough money to pay my rent and buy the things I need, so I feel proud of myself, though it's a strange life to be getting used to.

November 22nd

Sometimes, when I'm standing there at the big looms, watching the threads of linen be whisked through the machine, I wonder if the flax that makes this cloth came from my father's farm. I wonder what he would think if he could see me now. I wonder if he's still alive at all.

And then I start to wonder about my brothers, because they most likely have been sent to fight in the English army's war too. All three of them would be just the right age for joining the army. Even Liam – he must be seventeen by now. Is that old enough to go abroad to fight in a big war? I think it is. So now I'm worried for my brothers and must pray even harder, even though I don't believe in God anymore.

Arthur was seventeen when I first met him. How sweet life seemed then, compared to now, at least.

January 18th

Mrs MacGuire told me they decided not to force the young Catholic men into the army because many

Catholics are angry about fighting in the English war, and it would just make things worse here. But still many of them go. It's strange being in two wars at once – the big war with Germany – the whole world is fighting in that and we're supposed to be on the side of the English. And this other war where the Catholics here in Northern Ireland are fighting the English and the Protestants. It's hard to know what's what anymore. All I know about England is that Eleanor is over there. I hope she's safe from this war.

The good thing about the big war is that there are more jobs for the women, and we are all growing our own food now. Every Saturday afternoon I go with Mrs MacGuire to our allotment on the edge of the city. We are growing carrots, potatoes, onions and cabbage. I love to dig my hands into the wet soil and plant the seeds, or pull out the grass and weeds, even though it's so very cold. There I feel close to my old den in the woods, with the smells of earth and grass and fresh air all around me.

The bad thing about the war is that it's not safe to walk about in the evenings, as I used to, because all the lights are out as soon as dusk settles in. I miss that. But I'm usually too tired to walk these days, after standing all day at the loom.

February 3rd

I've made some new friends at the mill. Not really good friends like Mary was, but they're nice enough – normal, not mad like the ones in the asylum. We talk and laugh together in our lunch break, and it helps the day go by. Last Sunday, after church, we walked out along the Malone Road to have tea and scones at the Dub Tea Rooms. I felt like a smart city woman then, drinking

I flick through the rest of the diary. Liza had begun to leave long gaps – empty pages with just an occasional entry – as if she intended to come back later and fill in the days and weeks and months that had passed. The entries are brief, sometimes just a few lines, or a poem.

She seemed so young and naïve, having lost such a big part of her life, her growing up time, during the years in the asylum. But I sense her catching up as the war takes its toll. She would have been twenty-nine years old when the war started – the same age as I am now.

I can imagine Liza working hard, with no real pleasure or distraction to soften the harshness of wartime life in the city. Mrs MacGuire seemed to be an anchor for her but there was no mention of a man in her life, except for the brief entry about Barry. Was Liza too afraid to risk the fragile independence she had forged for herself? Or did she feel that she was 'damaged goods', as the expression went? In those days twenty-nine was considered very old for a woman to be still single. Yet the war was changing all that, with so many young men being killed and many women left alone, like Liza.

I come to the late spring of 1941.

June 7th

Now I cannot remember home
without seeing fire
raining out of the sky
like a wild and untameable storm.

Where was God that night
when we stood in the streets,
smoke and flames whipped around us,
and the faces of the dead
staring up at the terrible deed?

Our city is a shell now,
charred and splintered
shards pierce up into the dark sky.
Burnt bodies have littered the way.

Where were our fathers
when our world fell at our feet
and we were left orphans —
every one of us —
without a bed to sleep in?

Life has run dry here
and we have no voice
to cry out
against the deepening night.

June 23rd

Such a terrible thing, I cannot find words dark enough
to describe it. We had not expected this. Nobody thought
Hitler's planes would fly this far, Ireland being right at
the very edge of Europe as it is, but they did. Nobody

*was prepared for it. And now the city we knew has gone.
Half of it has been destroyed completely.*

*So many dead. Many more have lost their homes.
I went down to St George's Market to buy bread and
cheese, as I always do, but the whole grand arcade with
its glass and metal arches glinting in the sunlight – like
a cathedral it is to us ordinary folk – instead of bread
and cheese and butter, it was full of bodies, all laid out
waiting for their families to claim them. Hundreds of
them, lying in rows under white linen sheets. It was
terrible. The stench of the dead was terrible.*

July 18th

*People have fled to the country and the towns outside
Belfast. I stayed because I didn't know where else to go.
This is my home now. But Mrs MacGuire's house was
burnt down.*

*At night everyone walks out of the city to sleep in the
fields and up on the hillsides. Here it's dark and there are
no houses to be bombed. Everyone is the same now. We're
all without a safe bed to sleep in. We're all afraid.*

*The government have to feed us because we have
no home and no jobs – the factories and shipyards
were bombed too. So at least I don't have to go to the
workhouse – we're all the same now. We all have nothing
left. Except that I was able to bring my diary with me. I
had packed it into my bag that day, with my sandwiches,
meaning to write in it during my lunch-break. My whole
life is in here, the treasures and the pity of it all, and I
couldn't bear to part with it.*

*Sleeping at night under the trees and bushes on the
hillside, babies crying, their mothers crying or scolding,
the children shouting out in their sleep – it's then that
I try to remember my old home, the fields and the hills*

that I loved. I remember my secret den in the woods and imagine I'm lying there, safe beneath the dancing leaves of the big oak trees. And then I can fall asleep.

August 11th, 1942

It's taken a long time for life to get back to normal but it seems the German's have lost interest in Belfast, having nearly wiped us off the face of the earth anyway. Slowly people come back to the city. The docks and the factories and some of the houses are being rebuilt, but it all takes time. I live in a small room in a house with twelve people who I don't really know. But we accept each other because we are all the same. No-one in our house worries whether you are a Protestant or a Catholic anymore – we just try to get along. Anyway, I could never hate a Protestant because Arthur was one of them.

I don't know what happened to Mrs MacGuire. I think she left Belfast after her house was blown to pieces. We were both lucky we were out at the time, walking home from the late shift at the mill as we were.

Now I work in munitions. I don't like it – I don't want more people to be killed. But we have to do it.

Even though it's very hard, still I would rather be here than in the asylum. I feel normal here. I feel like everyone else. I have a life of my own at least.

My mind stretches back to Uncle Bert's stories. It feels odd to be reading about the same war, but from the other direction, as it were. Liza's story unravels forward in time from a distant and very different past. Uncle Bert's war unravels back in time from a present that I am part of.

Like two pieces of a broken thread, Liza's story and mine meet in the war. I find, in this unlikely tapestry, a proof that my grandmother existed in a time and place that is connected to my own. She is part of my own world. The war, a violent bridge that links us together.

My mother and father lived through the same war in Newcastle, were part of Bert's stories, even as Liza survived its devastation in Belfast. Their worlds were not so far apart after all. Through Liza's story and Uncle Bert's, the threads of our lives are connecting.

I imagine these threads being tied across time. Not a smooth joining, or a seamless graft, but a crude and rough knot. Yet it gives me a sense of something solid, something of substance growing at the core of my being – an intimation of my own roots, my history, finally finding ground. It's a new, an unfamiliar feeling.

I remember a line from one of Liza's poems – 'Strong as an old oak tree'. For the first time in my life, I can imagine feeling like this too. The broken line begins to mend.

I continue reading. Then, after a gap of several empty pages, I come to the last few entries in Liza's diary.

April 12th, 1947

The war is over and they are rebuilding the city. But how do you rebuild a person's life, let alone a whole country's? I feel so weary from it all.

When the men came back most of the women lost their jobs, went back to the housework. I was lucky. I got a job back in the mill. I work on the Damask now. I am told this is a privilege, I should be grateful and not complain if the work is hard. The massive looms, with the rows of punched cards clanking down the pretty designs – it's deafening. You can't think with all that noise going on.

At least I never had to go to the workhouse, which I'm proud about, but I wonder more and more – now that the war is over and there is time to wonder about such things — I wonder what is the point of all this.

And I wonder why I survived when so many died. Children with their whole lives ahead of them — mothers who needed to be there looking after the little ones. Why was my wretched life saved when theirs were cut off like that? There is no justice, no fairness in it all.

I have a nice little place to live now, with two rooms all to myself and an old couple downstairs who are kind enough to me. But all I do is work.

I want to taste the fresh air blowing over the hills, and walk in the fields again.

November 3rd

The heart gathers burdens as it journeys through a life,
some from deep in the past, secrets of the ancestors,
their untended wounds.
A lineage of grief rolls on into the future,
pulling lives apart and scattering dreams.
We are helpless in the grip of our wounding past.

December 26th, 1948

It's time for me to go home now, but I want to see Sister Mary again before I leave. I want to give her a letter for you, my daughter, Eleanor. Perhaps one day she can find out where you are and send my letter to you. Dear Eleanor — where are you now?

I went to mass on Christmas Eve at the big church next to the Convent of the Sacred Heart. I knew the Sisters would be there on Christmas Eve.

I sat near the back and hid my face beneath a wide-brimmed hat so that nobody would recognise me. There was Mary, looking as sweet and kind as ever, but much older, her face lined and a little sad, I thought. The war has aged all of us. She was with all the Sisters, up at the front of the church, and I couldn't find a way to talk to her. I felt disappointed that I couldn't speak with Mary but also glad to see that she had survived the war.

She didn't see me, right at the back of the crowd of people. I was about to leave when I heard a voice calling my name – my own name – Liza.
It was Mrs Mallone.

'Liza dear, how lovely to see you again,' she said to me. 'How are you?'

I told her I was well enough, and that I had come here hoping to see Sister Mary. I had a message to give her. Mrs Mallone said she would arrange a meeting for us, and she did just that. So next Tuesday I am to see my dear friend Mary one more time, before I leave.

I will give her a letter for you, my Eleanor, and also my diary. I want her to keep it in case she ever finds you. I want her to give you my diary, if she can, so you will know your mother's story.

I was nervous being in the church next to the convent again. I am still afraid that someone will recognise me and take me back to the home, or to the asylum. After all these years and all that has happened, I still fear that. So I must go away from here.

Now I will lock my diary for the very last time and put the key into the envelope with the letter. I feel I am putting my whole past behind me as I let go of my diary.

But one thing I know. I will leave with dignity this time, with my head held high.

Eliza O'Neal

I close the diary and let it drop onto my lap. The shadows of evening are falling along the walls of my room and clouds over the sea are tinged with red. My heart feels heavy with the grief, with the sorrow of it all.

In the distance I hear a ship's foghorn as it approaches the harbour at dusk. As a child I was afraid of this mournful sound, booming through the night from far out at sea, but when my father told me that the foghorn saved people's lives, I came to love its melancholy calling out over the night sea.

Now, the familiar sound gives me some comfort.

There is so much to digest in Liza's story, and so much to read between the lines, between the sparse entries of the last years. But I feel that I know my grandmother, at last. I feel proud of her. I clutch the diary to my chest and gaze out of the window of my room, here up on the top floor of an anonymous guesthouse in the still splintered heart of Belfast.

I pick up a pencil and the small sketchpad that I brought with me, and begin to let the pencil trace over the page. My hand is led by the feelings in my heart. Again, the twisting thread of the Knot of Eternity begins to appear, then the looping through it of the Celtic knot. As I weave these familiar patterns together, they become a vessel to hold the memories and the pain of Liza's life. I draw for Liza, and pour her sorrow into it.

I begin to bring colour to the picture – soft pastels, with strong streaks of red for Liza's fiery spirit, and purple-black for all the loss in her life, and in my own. I can feel how alike our lives had been, despite being so profoundly different. I begin to understand something Mary said to me – how I have carried the burden of the past through my own life. Liza and I are tied together through a shared suffering and neither of us will be free, truly healed of our loss and pain, until the other is.

A beautiful picture begins to emerge that contains both Liza's beautiful spirit and her broken heart. I will give it to her if we ever meet.

Now that I have read the diary, I need to see Mary again. The last part of the story is missing. What did Liza mean by 'going home' and 'leaving'? Was she returning to God – going home to Heaven? Did she want to die? She felt her life was without meaning – that was clear.

Or did home mean the place where she had grown up?

Tomorrow I will visit Mary again. I still nurture a hope that I will find Liza alive. Whoever Liza is, whatever she has become through the years of her difficult life, I need to see her – for myself, for Liza, and for my own mother, Eleanor.

Thirty

Belfast – 1981

We sit in silence as the small clock on the dresser quietly ticks the minutes away. It takes me back to my childhood home. How fiercely Granny's three clocks competed, but there was no race to be won so they went on endlessly – tic, tic, tac-tic, tic-a, tic, tac. Mary's clock has a gentler pace that seems to say 'all things will pass – even this will end one day.'

A pair of deep red velvet curtains frames the one small window of Mary's living room. The faint trickle of afternoon light that finds its way in, through the net curtain, lies in a narrow strip, still and burnished, across the dark wood of the floor.

There is so much I want to ask but words feel hopelessly inadequate. Instead, the eloquence of silence presents itself, and we allow it to envelop us awhile.

Mary is glad there is now another who can bear witness to Liza's story. It's been a heavy load for her to carry alone.

My heart overflows with gratitude, sorrow, anger, relief, and in the whole world only Mary understands this symphony of feelings.

There is so much to say and yet there is nothing that needs to be said. We both know. Held by Mary's quiet presence, the warmth of companionship and a secret shared, I taste a feeling of safety that has eluded me for much of my life. The minutes tick by as I settle into this precious moment with Mary – Mary who, undoubtedly, Liza owed her life and her freedom to.

'Thank you, Mary,' I say at last.

She simply nods. Then she stands and goes slowly to the cupboard where she keeps her paintings. I notice a slight flicker of pain crease her face as she lifts herself out of the chair, a barely perceptible limp and a forward stoop as she walks. I'm aware of Mary's frailty. Perhaps she's not well but she would never show it, never complain of it to me.

'I'd like you to have this, Anita.' She hands me a sheet of thick rough paper – the painting of Liza and baby Eleanor. Now it's my turn to simply nod. Of course I should have the only picture there is, ever will be, of my mother and my grandmother.

'There's something I need to ask you,' I say, as Mary settles stiffly back into her chair. 'Were you found out? Did you get into trouble for helping her escape? I know Liza would hate to think you had suffered because of her.'

'Don't be worrying yourself about that, now. I'm fine,' Mary replies quickly.

'But what happened? Did they suspect you? Were you punished?' I wonder about her status, living next to but not within the convent walls as she does – wearing a nun's habit but letting her hair flow free. There is also something about guilt, blame and punishment that I'm trying to work out for myself. The question of whether I had caused Richard's death has crystallised over the years – without me noticing the slow, solidifying process – into a definite and pervasive sense of guilt. It has layered over the older and more nebulous sense of blame for my mother's death, which Granny Rose had subtly instilled in me.

As if reading my deeper thoughts, ignoring the question I had asked, Mary replies, 'There is no blame. Things happen in life, sometimes mistakes are made, misunderstandings, accidents happen – we're human beings, Anita, imperfect beings just doing the best we can. The mysterious ways of life and death are beyond our control. I don't regret anything. Neither should you. I'm glad for everything I've done in my life. If others didn't like what I chose to do, I can accept that. We all bear the consequences of our choices and our actions, but we don't need to carry guilt for them if we have love in our hearts. You are not guilty, Anita. Nor was Liza.' She winks slyly at me and laughs. 'That's what growing up has taught me. I think I've grown up at last!'

In that moment I see, within this frail old woman with the halo of white hair and a graceful stoop to her shoulders, the young woman she once was. The bright and kind spirit who was Liza's closest friend, her saviour, shines through her translucent form. I see the young woman with the slender hands of a painter and a deep and boundless longing to experience love and devotion. Though her body is ageing, her spirit seems young and strong. And I think perhaps that is how growing old is meant to be.

'What about God? Have your experiences of life changed your faith, your devotion in any way?' I ask.

Mary taps her chest softly with her fingers and a light, sweet laugh trips out. 'In here.' She smiles. 'Always in here. There's no use looking anywhere else – not in the church, not in the prayer books, not up to heaven.' I understand. This is what Richard and I were grappling to name that evening, sitting on the floor at the bottom of the stairs. The day we had rowed out too far.

'How can I ever thank you. I know you've done nothing but good in your life. I wish I could do just a fraction of that.' I feel humbled in Mary's presence.

'It's not about what you do, Anita, it's about who you are. Now you just go along being yourself, and you'll be fine. But that's been hard for you, I know, because you've had to carry this burden from your past – your mother's and your grandmother's pain, as well as your own. You need to lay their past to rest now, so that you can find out who you are. Create your own path through life. And then you'll know exactly what to do.' She is looking earnestly at me now.

'Yes, you're right. I can feel how their loss and their pain have been living on in me. As if the suffering, the unhealed wounds of their lives has been shaping my own, causing things to go wrong – the same loss, the same broken dreams. I need to free myself – I know you're right, Mary.' I look at the painting of Liza and Eleanor. 'I need to see Liza, if she's still alive. Do you know where she is, Mary?' Finally, the urgent question, the one I hardly dare ask for fear the answer will be no.

'I don't know if she's still alive. I haven't heard from her for many years now. We're all getting old and we don't travel anymore – I mean Mrs Mallone and me, as well as Liza. But I know that she went back home to her village – back in 1948, after she came to see me with the letter and her diary. That's the last time I saw her.' Mary falls silent.

'How was she then? How did she seem to you?'

'Weary, sad – she seemed lost. She wanted to go back home, back to her village – she had an idea about going back to the beginning, as if she could magically start over again. Belfast had worn her down – the war and all. And you know, she never completely recovered from the asylum, though she was strong – strong enough to make her way, that is.'

Mary stops, glances at me then down at the brown and red patterned rug that covers the floor between our feet – hers resting side by side and daintily squeezed into blue slippers with a posy of red flowers embroidered across the toes, mine half-naked in a pair of strappy sandals. 'I don't know, Anita. I prayed that it would work out for her. She deserved a rest, some peace. I suggested she go to Mrs Mallone's house first. She would tell her what was what in the village – Liza's parents, I mean. She was very afraid of meeting her parents.' She pauses for a long while, chasing her memories back through the years.

'I saw Mrs Mallone now and then,' she continues, 'until she

became too unwell to travel to the city anymore. It was she who eventually found out where your mother was living. She was such a help to everyone – a great lady. She knew people, those in power, and through her contacts she found out your mother's address. That's how I was able to send the letter to Eleanor.'

The pieces are now falling into place.

'It took her a while to find out, but she managed,' adds Mary, as if she feels the need to apologise for the delay.

'It's alright. I appreciate how hard it must have been to trace someone in those days – especially with the country still recovering from the war. It's hard enough now!' I study the patterns of light that dance across the floor, as the leaves of a tree outside set them shimmering. 'I have a lot to thank Mrs Mallone for too. She lived in Liza's village, didn't she?'

'Yes, in the big manor house. If she's alive, I'm sure she'll still be there, but she was older than Liza and me. She may not be with us anymore.'

'I understand. Did you hear anything more from her about Liza?'

'Well, she told me that Liza's mother had died not long after Liza had been sent away. Consumption, they said, but I think she died of a broken heart. No mother can bear losing a child, whatever the circumstances, and Liza's mother wasn't a strong woman – not in the way that Liza was.'

'Yes, I gathered that from the diary. And what about her father?'

'He survived almost to the end of the war. In the end it was some disease of the liver that got him – just a few months before the war ended.'

'Ah yes, I gather he liked to drink. Maybe that was what got his liver – that would be suitable justice.' I notice a hint of pleasure, like the sweet taste of revenge, as I say this.

'I know he did terrible things, damaged people's lives, but he was suffering too,' Mary replies. Like Emms, she tries to see all sides of a situation.

'But as you said, he has to accept the consequences of his actions, like all of us. He wasn't the victim. Even if he had suffered in his life, he was still responsible for what he did to Liza – and to my mother.' My anger is rising – a kind of fiery righteous anger that gives me strength – not the futile rage I am so used to, that storms right through me and uproots me, leaves me feeling wretched and helpless. This anger feels clear and wholesome.

'You're right, Anita. But fury like he had doesn't come from nowhere. I think he carried a sickness that went back for many generations. He was angry about all the Catholic people had suffered – how they had been betrayed and oppressed – for centuries. Liza told me how he would sometimes talk about it when he'd been drinking, getting more and more angry as he told the old stories of his people, and his own family troubles. He was just a young boy when his own father was killed. He was brought up by his older brother, who later became a priest. I think he loved and feared his brother in equal measure, and he was confused about what was right and wrong in the eyes of God.' Mary paused for a moment, wondering how to go on.

'There is something else I think you should know, Anita. Mrs Mallone told me about this – I'm not sure if Liza ever knew. He had got Liza's mother pregnant before they were married…'

'What! Then how could he treat Liza like that?'

'I imagine he felt a lot of shame, being brought up by a priest of a brother. And maybe regret too. They got married and Liza was their first child.' Mary pauses, takes a deep breath. 'The brother was somehow mixed up in it all – he was a young priest at the time, just beginning his ministry, and I can imagine it was shameful for him that his brother got a young girl pregnant like that. Perhaps it would spoil his prospects.'

'Oh my God. So Liza's father was punishing himself. That was it – he was punishing her for his own sins – as he saw it, as his brother saw it.'

'He carried the weight of his own ancestors' suffering, like you have done. But you can stop this terrible cycle of pain, Anita. You have the freedom to change it.' Mary looks at me with a soft and misty look in her eyes. It belies the power of her words.

'I will. If I can do it, I will. Now I have the feeling that if I can heal this pain inside me, I will be doing it for all my grandmothers.' I'm remembering the dream that has haunted my nights since Nancy discovered Liza's letter.

'And for those who may come after you, too. That is most important.'

'Of course.' I ponder this for a while. I know I can't have children of my own unless I can mend the brokenness inside of me. I can't bring a child into a life that is so fragmented, just to fill it with yet more pain.

'The lineage that is passed down from mother to daughter is so powerful, and it has been deeply wounded for so long. It needs to be healed and strengthened. Our poor suffering world needs this.' Mary's attention is now stretching away from me, as if she were communing with an unseen presence far away.

I feel challenged by her words, and inspired. I hear them as a gentle call to battle, but a battle of the inner sort that means laying my own demons to rest.

'I need to see Liza. I must go to the village. If she's still there, I will find her.' The last step of my journey is in sight.

2

I call Nancy on my way back to the guest house. I hadn't known that I needed to speak with her until I am walking past the phone box. Its bright red and dirty glass door beckons me. The metal and paper smell of its inside has a familiarity that is reassuring – my connection to home during this stay in Belfast – and here I am again, with an unexpected longing to hear Nancy's voice. Despite all our struggles, she is the one who has come closest to being a mother to me. Now, as I face the possibility of meeting my own grandmother, I have the sense that things will change between us, and I have a need to say goodbye to an old way of being with Nancy.

'Anita, I am so glad to hear from you! Martin told me you had found Mary – do you have any more news?' She sounds genuinely eager to know.

'Yes. I can hardly believe it. I'm going to Liza's village tomorrow. I'm sure she's there – if she's still alive, that is.' My words tumble out in a hurry. I only have two coins for the phone.

'That's great news! At least you will know – at least you will have done everything you could to find her. Well done, Anita, for getting this far.' There's none of the old wariness in Nancy's voice and I'm surprised at her enthusiasm. Something has changed in her too.

'Thanks, Nancy. I just wanted to let you know. Think of me tomorrow!'

'I will. Shall I tell Martin?'

'No. I'll call him after I've been to the village. I want to tell him myself.'

'Of course…' At that moment the pips interrupt us, and the line goes dead.

'Damn,' I curse out loud. I have no more change and I haven't given Nancy the number. Still, I'm glad to have heard her voice. I feel her beside me, at long last.

Part VI

Home

Thirty-one

Ballycraig – 1981

'Phah. That won't be doing it,' she mutters under her breath as she pokes her nose over the rim of the steaming pot. The cat, twining itself around her ankles, mews. 'And what do you have to say about it, Hector?'

'Mi-aow,' comes the reply.

'Hmmph. A touch more gentian root, I'd be guessing. Definitely no more corn poppy,' she says to Hector, as she sniffs the brew that's bubbling away over the open fire. An iron stand that Liam built for her years ago supports the rod that suspends the pot. It's a complicated and precarious contraption but it's served her purpose for many a year, and Liza is not about to change it now.

'If that doesn't cure old Gerry's ticker, it'll shut it down right dead, it will,' she laughs.

'Miaaaaaow,' objects Hector. He is a large cat with long black and white fur that gives him a regal air. And he knows it too – makes out like he's boss in the small household.

'Sorry, Hector – I didn't mean it. Gerry'll be fine. This be the best cure there is for hearts that have gotten all full of anger like his. You'll see – he'll be sweet as pie, back to his old self again, after this.' Liza drops another handful of herbs into the pot, gives it a stir, then puts the lid on to let the brew simmer.

'Come on now, Kitty, move over and let an old lady sit down.' She nudges a sleepy-looking ginger tabby off her chair by the window and drops down heavily onto the warm seat. All that walking through the woods and fields to collect the valerian root and poppy has made her legs ache. She puts her feet up on a stool and notices the scratches that crisscross her shins – like a game of noughts and crosses. It was Liam's boy that taught her how to play that game. Her skin is so toughened up by now she hadn't even noticed the brambles tearing at her legs.

She sits back and closes her eyes. Kitty hops back up onto her lap and Hector slinks around the chair legs, before settling on the windowsill to gaze out onto the garden. Liza's herb garden is overflowing with aromatic scents and buzzing insects come to taste the last fruits of summer, before she chops it all back to dry in the shed.

The shed was another matter. Liam had been happy to build the house for her – a wooden hut it was really, but to Liza it was like a mansion. He let her have it built right there by the path up into the woods, so she could be near to the den. Of course, he didn't know about the den, but he didn't mind her living at the edge of the farm, on the very rim of the village. It was better that way. Neither of them wanted the village folk to be asking after her too much. In the end they came to think she must be the other one – Sheena. Folks were mighty confused but they let her be, didn't bother her too much. And once they found out she was good with the herbs, they came when they were sick. Other than that, they mostly left her well alone.

But the shed. She had to beg and plead to get the shed. 'Why do you want a shed when you've got everything you need in the house?' Liam had asked her. As if he didn't have enough work to do, and little enough money coming in these days. But Liza, his big sister, who had been like a mam to him when he was very little – he had to do it for her in the end.

She wakes with a start as Hector mews loudly and thumps

to the floor. Kitty leaps off her lap to follow him to the door. Liza looks out of the window to see what the disturbance is.

Her heart stops for one long, tremulous moment. The breath struggles to squeeze its way into her lungs. She falters as she tries to pull herself onto her feet, and sits back down again with a bump, gripping the wooden arms of the chair. She waits for her breath to catch up with her, then tries again.

Because it's the safest place to be when she feels unsure, she backs up towards the fire. She stands there with Gerry's angina potion hissing sweetly in the pot behind her. The warmth of the fire creeps through her skin and into her blood. She begins to sweat. Wringing her hands together like a wet cloth, she tries not to cry out. 'On my good soul, it can't be!' She hears her voice, as if it comes from far away. Not her own voice at all.

There's a timid knock on the door, then another. Liza stands still, holding her breath, wringing her hands, not knowing what to do. There is a third knock. The door isn't locked – it won't lock. The wood has warped so that the door and the frame no longer match and it stands just ever so slightly open. The wind comes through the gap, shrill and harsh in the winter months. Liza doesn't know what to do.

The door opens, just halfway and very slowly.

'Eleanor!'

Thirty-two

If there had been a quicker way to Ballycraig I might have taken it, but now I'm glad not to have missed this circuitous route. After three bus rides, a long wait at a small hamlet with nothing more than a row of cottages and a small church, and endless time to absorb the rolling green hillsides that pass by, I'm finally approaching the village. The slow journey has offered a welcome transition from the harshness of Belfast and its conflicts.

We swerve round a sharp bend and there is the sign for Ballycraig, just before the bus lurches over a small hump-backed bridge. I have arrived.

As the old red bus clatters to a stop, two young children jump up and run to the exit, their shrill cries piercing the soporific afternoon air. An old man who has been sleeping at the back is startled awake. With a jerk of his head and a sharp spluttering, neighing sound, he looks around to see what the commotion is. The children's mother follows them down the aisle and pauses to exchange a few words with the driver.

'Thanking you, Arthur,' she says to the man at the wheel. 'No rain tomorrow then, I be thinking.' She's nodding towards the clear sky beyond the grimy grey windscreen of the bus.

'Didn't I tell you so?' the man replies. 'I be guessing the harvest will go ahead then. Tell old Mac I'll be down there later, just as soon as I get this old clanger back to its shed.'

My breath catches. Arthur – it couldn't possibly be? No, probably not. I look at the man. It's hard to tell his age but he's probably not very much over forty. No, he is definitely not my grandfather!

I thank Arthur and step down. It's good to stretch out after the last long leg of the journey. The bus had meandered this way and that, stopping at every village, farm and crossroad within the county. It rattled and rolled, chugged laboriously up gentle slopes and careered down into the green valleys on the other side, as if brakes had not been discovered around these parts yet. I feel stiff and a little tired.

This seems to be the main street of the village. A row of cottages on each side stretch a short way then come to an abrupt end. Three of the cottages are fronted with shop windows, one displaying bread, another meat, the third fruit and vegetables. There is a general store with a large Walls ice cream sign by the door, and a tiny shop front filled to the brim with wool, rolls of coloured cloth, bed linen, tablecloths, underwear, shirts, dresses – in fact every kind of garment you might possibly need for village life must be crammed into that tiny space.

I walk the length of the street and back again. It doesn't take long. At one end is the pub. There are several lanes, mostly mud and gravel tracks, partly grassed over, going off the main street. Once the rumble of the bus fades, the afternoon air is still and quiet. Even the birds are sleeping. The air smells of newly mown grass and the lingering fumes from the bus. A boy races by on an old bike with a clanking chain, sending a shower of pebbles clattering across the road and briefly cutting through the afternoon lull.

All I have is Mrs Mallone's address, and the information that Liza's family own, or did own, a flax farm. I decide to ask at the pub where Houghton Manor is.

There is the now familiar moment of silence as I enter and heads turn towards me. Unlike in Belfast, where suspicion, sometimes outright hostility, seemed to greet me when I entered a pub or café, here the welcome is more of surprise and curiosity. Not many strangers pass through here.

'Half a Guinness, please.' I try not to sound too English, as if that were possible. Apart from the proprietor, there are just three other men at the bar, each staring at me with expressions that give nothing away.

'Here you go, then,' the barman says, as he finishes pouring the Guinness to perfection. He is a thickset man with a shiny bald head and long beard that give the odd impression of an upside-down face. He looks friendly enough. Once the shock of seeing a stranger in his pub has subsided, he might be open to conversation.

'Thank you.' I seat myself at the bar.

'And where be you from – what brings you to these parts?' he asks, his curiosity overcoming his reticence to welcome an English woman into his pub.

'I'm from London.' I decide to explain, so as to quickly circumvent the painful divide that gouges through every aspect of life in Northern Ireland. 'My grandmother grew up here and I've come to see if I can find out about her.'

'Aha, one of those that got away.' He half chides, half smirks, rubbing his voluminous chin then scratching the top of his over-large belly as he speaks. 'Most of them packed up and left sooner or later. If it wasn't the famine, it was the lack of work, or the war, or some such thing. All the young folk been an' gone overseas, looking for better times, since ever history can remember. They had to, most of them. No prospects for the lads that didn't have their daddy's land to inherit, you know. And with all the young men leaving, the lasses had to go too, sooner or later.'

'I know. Terrible it was,' I affirm.

'Aye, terrible it all was,' he echoes. 'The lucky ones shipped off to America – could get rich there. But the rest, they went to London or Liverpool or some slum where there was nothing to do but navvying and drinking.' He puts his glass down on the bar with a thud and leans towards me. I can smell the alcohol on his breath. He is more than a little drunk, despite the early hour. 'Pretty Irish girl like you, what you doing living over there?' I'm not sure if he is trying to make a pass at me, or criticising me for living with the enemy.

'I grew up there. But I wanted to come back here, just to see where my grandmother came from.' I feel it's time to be making a move. 'There's a woman I'd like to talk to who knew my grandmother – she lives at Houghton Manor. Do you know where the manor is?'

He pulls back a little, as if the name itself draws a certain respect. 'Ah, the Manor. They're good enough folk there. I guess they'll help you, to be sure.' He scratches the back of his shiny bald head and gazes up at the beamed ceiling, as if seeking directions there. 'Best way is go back down the road to the baker's, take the lane off the right there, and walk – about half a mile I'd say – till you get to a crossroad. Go right again. It brings you all the way round the back of the village, behind us here, but it's the best way to go if you don't want to be getting lost. You go through some woods then you'll find the manor after the ford and up the hill a short way. Can't miss it – there's a big gate with the name on it.'

'Thanks. That doesn't sound too hard to find.' I quickly empty my glass and leave.

The man who opens the big oak door looks as if he has been there since the famine itself. His face is wizened and pink as a new-born baby's. Whispers of white hair shoot out from behind each ear, looking for all the world like cobwebs that have hung there for years. The black suit, too, looks as if it's been hanging from his shoulders for decades, never quite finding the coat hanger at the end of each day. It's creased and threadbare, yet the signs of elegant formality are still there.

The Mallones' butler leads me into a drawing room to the side of the spacious, marble-floored entrance hall. Furniture that had once been chosen for exquisite design and craftsmanship now lies about the room, scattered and dusty, in no particular order that I can discern. The casualness of it offends my sense of aesthetic. I have an urge to re-arrange the room back into the elegance it no doubt once possessed.

Mrs Mallone's fascination with the Orient is evident. Hand-painted Japanese screens, a carved rosewood table and matching chest from India, bronze statues of Buddhas and gods of the Hindu pantheon meet my gaze at every turn. There are colourful thangkas on the walls and expensive-looking Chinese vases balanced precariously on small rickety tables.

'Sadly, the lady of the house passed away, not long ago now,' says Mrs Mallone's faithful servant. His hands tremble, ever so slightly – a constant small dance that seems to be all that keeps him going. Parkinsons, I think, and wish there was something I could do to help him find rest from this constant faltering motion.

'I'm sorry to hear that. I understand she was a very kind person, that she helped many people during her life,' I reply, reflecting Barnes' politeness of speech.

'Oh yes, she did that – helped many people, did m'lady.' His stiff formality is beginning to soften a little. There's a touch of sadness in his voice, on his crinkled baby face. He must have loved her. I gaze through the streams of dust that dance in the sunlight – two broad yellow beams that have found their way through tall Georgian windows into this still, forgotten room. The dry air smells of dust.

My eyes come to rest on an elegant chaise longue covered in subtly textured pale green damask. Three cushions lie propped against its hard back. I can hardly believe what I am seeing. They have the very same design on them as the cushion that now sits in a dusty corner of my own room in Primrose Hill. Liza had most likely embroidered these too. The Knot of Eternity – here it is, in this hot and stuffy room in a small village in Northern Ireland. I can feel Liza's hand at work. I feel her close. I have entered her world and my mind begins to spin with excitement and something that tastes like fear. Suddenly I am confronted with the very real possibility that I might be about to meet her, to actually see her, face to face, in the flesh. My own grandmother. How will it be to meet her, what will she be like, what will she think of me turning up in her life unannounced? Will she like me at all? I have hardly even considered these questions during all the years of longing and searching.

Barnes is telling me about Mrs Mallone's good works. I bring my attention back to him, to his trembling hand as it gestures in the thick air, to his voice softening like honey in the late afternoon sunlight.

'She helped my own grandmother too – in fact she helped to save her life. I can't thank her now, but I can thank you instead.' Barnes beams at this, and his face flushes even pinker. 'I've come here to try to find her – my grandmother I mean. I wonder if you might know of her, or her family.'

'Maybe, maybe. I've lived here most of my long life. I sure as Jesus know most of the folk that's been here since that time.' Now he is settling back into his natural Irish voice.

'Her name was Liza O'Neal. She was born in 1910. Her father had a farm and grew flax, and she had three brothers and three sisters.'

'Ah, yes, yes – old O'Neal's farm. He was the only flax grower in this village at that time. I know the family you mean. The eldest girl went off to work in County Clare when she was quite young. Pretty one she was. The other was a bit simple, not fully there, you know, but a good, kind soul.' Barnes furrows his brow as he struggles to remember.

My heart is beating fiercely against its bony cage. 'That's them! That's Liza! I know that's her. Please Barnes, tell me what else you know about them.'

'I know as one of the boys went off to America to make his fortune. Another one, poor lad, was killed in the war – he didn't have to go, but he went fighting the Germans for Mr

Churchill. A big scandal it was here – sending the Irish boys off to the war to help the English. People were angry, indeed they were, and quite rightly so, to my mind. Left just the youngest one, Liam they called him, if I remember rightly. The girls – two of them married I guess – not seen them for a long time. The other, the simple one, she stayed on with her brother – I think she did.'

'So are they still here – Liam and Sheena?' I ask, barely able to contain my excitement.

'Farm went to Liam, being as he was the only son left. I guess he's still there, growing the flax or whatever they grow there now.' Barnes is holding his left hand with his right to try to steady it. My own excitement is increasing his agitation. 'Not sure 'bout the girl. Maybe she's still there, maybe she's not.'

'Oh, I can hardly believe it. Can you tell me where the farm is – and then I'll leave you in peace. You must have things to be getting on with.' Every cell in my body is jumping now. I'm ready to run all the way to the farm.

'Aye, I can tell you. It's on t'other side of the village, near the big woods. Here, follow me, and I'll show you the path that leads up over there.' Barnes leads me out and slowly around to the side of the big house. Grand lawns spread out, neatly mowed, but the wall of shrubs that runs around the edge of the garden is dishevelled, rampant with years of untamed growth. Barnes points across the grass to an opening.

'See that path over there – it runs right down to the village. Then you cross over the main street and take the lane that goes up next the butcher's shop. It weaves around by the river then past the edge of the woods. Eventually it takes you all the way to the O'Neal farm.' His quivering hand points to a narrow opening between two overgrown rhododendron bushes. 'Stay on the path and you can't miss it.'

Thirty-three

Liam doesn't know what to make of me at all. He stares and stares as if he has seen a ghost. His face turns white, his hands clenching and unclenching by his stocky sides. Words begin burbling out of him – a long string of words, hardly making any sense.

'Jesus and Mary, it's a ghost come back to haunt my mam and pa – just like when Liza herself came back – like she'd risen from her grave and come back to get her revenge on the living – except that Mam and Pa weren't living anymore – so she had come the wrong way and should go right back to where she'd been.' He stops and gapes, his mouth wide open. If his thinning hair could stand on its ends, it would. His pace slows a little. 'I hadn't seen her in so many years, you see. I thought she'd passed over too. But there she was, standing at my door looking old and worn out with life.'

'Liza?' I ask. 'She came back then?'

He doesn't seem to hear me, carries on speaking as if to himself. 'And now this one. Just like my Liza, when I was a young lad and she was my beautiful big sister. The red hair that burned like autumn, her blue eyes, the whole damn sweetness of her.' Liam begins to cry, smears a dirty fist over his face and apologises. Now he looks at me keenly, asks who I am, what I want here. I tell him.

He takes me to the path and sends me on my way.

★

It isn't far. An old picket fence and a gate that wobbles on its hinges mark the border of Liza's home. The garden is a profusion of herbs. A wash of scents – sage, thyme, mint, rosemary – drift over the path as I walk past them, each in turn casting its dizzying spell.

A movement at the small window to the left of the door catches my attention – the swish of a cat's tail, a shadow moving through the gloom inside. Spiders have spun a veil of silvery webs over the corners of the window, adding to the sense of darkness beyond the glass.

The house is little more than a wooden cabin with a tin roof and smoking chimneystack. The front of the single floored dwelling has a door in the centre, with one window to each side of it – so simple. The door hangs very slightly ajar. Liza must be home.

I hesitate, gather myself, and tap softly on the door. The wood had once been painted green, but now the paint has peeled back to leave a pale, weathered grey. I stare at the door, almost closed, open just a crack. A strong and pungent smell of herbs – nothing I can recognise this time – escapes through the gap. I hear the mewing of a cat, like a baby's cry, behind the door.

I knock again. Nothing. And once more, a little louder.

Tentatively I push the door – it creaks as it swings open. I stand in the doorway facing a small figure, barely visible in the dimness of the room as my eyes adjust to the twilight.

An old woman stands by the fire, holding her hands out in front of her as if she has just dropped something. Her eyes, as blue as sapphires, are open wide. Long strands of silvery curls flow down over her shoulders. Across her shins and bare feet I notice bright red scratches, and a dark bruise on her left ankle.

'Eleanor! Oh, Jesus and Mary, my baby, my Eleanor! Is it you? Have you come back?' The words just come tumbling

333

out of her as if they'd been waiting right there on her tongue all these years.

'Not Eleanor – I'm Anita. I'm your granddaughter.'

Liza spreads her palms open, her heart springing out to her fingertips, as she drops to the floor. I step forward and kneel down in front of her on the dry wood boards, clutching my hands together. As if in prayer. Water hisses in the pot over the fire. The pungent scent of hedgerow herbs. I gaze into her eyes, a film of water misting over the deep blue.

I see myself reflected there, in Liza's eyes. I am home, at last.

Prologue to *angel wing*

I had left the fire burning so that she would feel warm and cosy in my kitchen, curled up on the mattress that Liam had brought over from the house. From my bed in the other room, I could hear the soft low breath of sleep, like the snuffling sleep of a child, and my heart was so full and open I could have died right then and been happy.

Anita had arrived that afternoon, walked into my small hut by the woods, on the edge of our family's farm that my little brother Liam now cares for, and the world changed about me forever. There she stood in the doorway with the sunlight streaming in behind her and setting her red hair aglow. The granddaughter I had never met, had not even known had come into this world. She had searched for me and found me, come all the way from London to my home in Ireland to mend the broken line.

Eleanor, my darling daughter, taken from me at birth – she had been waiting all these years for this meeting, suspended in the moment of her dying, calling out to me and I to her over the years and over the sea that kept us apart. Calling out my name. And I heard her, finally I heard her. She was on her way to find me and I was here waiting all along. Now, Anita's arrival has closed the gap so that her mother's voice can reach me and I can know her at last.

It was on the very first night Anita slept in my hut that I began to hear Eleanor's voice, so clear and strong as if she were right here with us. Hanging in the space between our lives, just waiting for the moment when the frayed threads of my life and Anita's came together. She told me everything. As she was dying, she told me all about her life. The words that follow are her words. I wrote them down faithfully, just as they came to me. At first in bursts and fragments, but then the story stretched out from the past and met me here, in my home in Ireland where it all began. Now I see the pattern that has run through our lives. Now we can, all three, begin to heal the wound and free ourselves.

Tomorrow I will go with my granddaughter, Anita, into the woods and say goodbye to Eleanor. We will build a fire and have a proper funeral, with a poem and a song to let her spirit fly away on.

Acknowledgments

A big thank you to ~

~ Kevan Manwaring, for inspiring me to begin and offering helpful comments on an early draft of the novel

~ Liz McCormick, dear friend and fellow writer, who has been there at every step of the way, supporting and giving feedback at each stage. Thank you, Liz, for encouraging me to devote more time to writing and for keeping me going through it all

~ Friend and colleague Roz Carroll, who has given so generously of her time to read and read again, always offering insightful comments and ideas with great warmth and enthusiasm

~ My writing group, Chris, Pam, Nairne, Frances and Jan, for their companionship, inspiration and lots of fun along the way

~ Ashley Stokes and Anna South for their in-depth reading and reviews of the manuscript at various stages of development

~ Joan Davis for her lively perspective on the novel, a welcome view from Ireland

~ Wilma Miller for her generosity in opening her home to me and answering my endless questions about Northern Ireland and its people

~ Holt Library, Norfolk, for providing the resources to research into Northern Ireland's history and politics, record-keeping, adoption and ancestry searches

~ The Linen Hall Library, Belfast, for making available its rich collection of books and photographic records of the city's social history, culture and much more

~ And all my friends, family and colleagues whose on-going support has sustained me throughout the writing of this novel

About the author

Linda Hartley studied dance and creative writing at Dartington College of Arts, UK, then went on to train as a somatic movement therapist and psychotherapist. She has worked in these fields for many years as a therapist and teacher, developing professional training programmes in Germany, the UK, Lithuania and Russia. She has offered workshops and retreats that explore the relationship between movement, image and words, and currently leads retreats in the Discipline of Authentic Movement in her Norfolk studio. Writing has always woven through her practice.

the broken line is her first novel, and *angel wing* is its prequel.

Linda lives in England, near the North Norfolk coast.
www.lindahartley.co.uk

www.ingramcontent.com/pod-product-compliance
Lightning Source LLC
Chambersburg PA
CBHW061116100726

47911CB00013B/559